MONDAI NAI

MONDAI NAI

by

KING HURLEY

PAANDAA
ENTERTAINMENT

Boulder, Colorado

ISBN Number 10: 0-9774188-5-5
ISBN Number 13: 978-0-9774188-5-5

Library of Congress Control Number: 2006909078

First Edition: March, 2007

Cover and interior design by NZ Graphics, www.nzgraphics.com

Printed in the United States of America

Published by Paandaa Entertainment, Boulder, Colorado

Visit our Web site at: www.paandaa.com

"By three methods we may learn wisdom;
First by reflection, which is the noblest;
Second, by imitation, which is easiest;
and Third by experience, which is bittersweet."
~ Confucius

This book is dedicated to
the three most powerful words on the planet Earth,
"I love you."

1

Farewell America

"Above a hollow rock
An ivy hangs.
One small temple."
~ Shiki Masaoka

What was the saying? "When opportunity knocks . . ."

That, I supposed, explained my eagerness to spend the last semester of my Master's program in rural Japan.

It was completely out of character for me, but I had acted on impulse and signed up for the trip. It was a good thing I did. Had I thought it out, fear probably would have won the day and I would have stayed the course at Thunderbird University in Arizona.

However, once the ink was dry on my application, I found a few good reasons to explain my impromptu behavior. First, I now had six uninterrupted months to fully explore life without boundaries, to go full throttle into a foreign land without anyone looking over my shoulder. Second, I would never find a more unique and fascinating country to challenge my own belief systems, to push my "personal envelope" into areas I had never explored. And third, if I did it right, I would come away from the experience with a deeper understanding of what was most important in life. What I could not possibly know was that the journey would also be filled with imminent disaster.

Had I a crystal ball, I would have seen that I was destined to evolve more in the coming months than in all my previous years. I would be stronger, yet more humble; more enlightened, yet more aware of my limitations; more vulnerable, yet more in tune with the sanctity of life.

But I was not the lucky owner of a crystal ball on that Saturday, the 31st of December, 1983. I was, however, a tangle of emotions as I boarded the plane that would transport me to the island of Honshu and the metropolitan madness of Tokyo. I had checked two bags I hardly remembered packing, another uncharacteristic act for a guy obsessed with organization and detail. My mom had assured me I had everything a young man would need, given my destination. I carried my precious backpack onto the plane, stored it in the overhead, and dropped unceremoniously into my window seat.

The previous night's "sayonara" party had been a huge mistake. I was as hung-over as a man could be. Jay Edington, my closest friend and an All-American linebacker with a big heart, had plied me with a drink he'd concocted called a Flatliner, a powerful elixir of vodka, espresso, Bailey's, and some Norwegian chocolate liquor. Then the old cake-in-the-face joke he'd played on me when I was sufficiently drunk had left me with an aching nose.

On top of the major headache and throbbing nose, I was also the owner of a lingering heartache. A month ago, Karen and I had officially and irrevocably severed our relationship after three genuinely spectacular years. A fine farewell! All I had in honor of our time together was the letter she had given me as she boarded her plane to Europe and the marketing internship that was awaiting her in Bonn. She had softly and sweetly asked me to not open her letter until I was on my flight to Japan. Four weeks of anticipation.

I took the letter from my shirt pocket and stared at the words written in Karen's careful script across the envelope. *Kai: my lover, friend, and personal massage therapist. Good luck.*

That was me: Kai Waters—lover, friend, and personal massage thera-pist. This last one made me smile. How often had a shoulder rub or foot massage evolved into a long night of outrageous lovemaking? That, I would definitely miss. But the comment also made me think. There had to have been more to our relationship than that after three years, didn't there? I hadn't just thought of Karen as a gorgeous University of Iowa cheerleader who could drink most guys under the table and make love with the energy of a long-distance runner. Or had I?

She was also extremely smart, creative, and funny, three traits I admired. Good, I thought, tangible qualities. That's more like it. I had always found her Performing Arts major exciting as hell, even if it did strike me as a tough way into the working world. What I liked best about her, though, was how a small town girl from Lake Oshkosh, Wisconsin had managed to matriculate to a huge Midwestern campus and had never lost her small town charm, that streak of innocence I could feel every time I put my arms around her.

Now it was officially over. She might just as well have written, *"Former lover, former friend, and former massage therapist."*

I had no clue what an amazing woman Karen truly was or that I was walking away from an extremely special relationship. I believed I would be just fine with our separation. But sitting here today, a so-called free man, I found myself wondering about the dynamics of the relationship's demise. Why had we decided to part ways? Was it foolishness, fate, fear, insecurity, flight of fancy? And what was that dull ache I felt in my stom-ach? Was it the fear of being alone? Was it the realization that I would soon be living in a foreign country with no one to lean on? Or was it the fact that I was facing six months of discovery that would almost certainly include emotions I had never before touched in my young life? Maybe it was some subconscious fear of missing out on once-in-a-lifetime experiences like this one had I stayed in our relationship.

As I pushed back my headrest, I felt my 6'2" frame unfold and my thoughts begin to race to the faces of the people I would be meeting and the challenges I would be facing as a foreigner in a land not known to embrace anyone of anything other than Japanese blood. I decided, there and then, to take this as the ultimate challenge. I would be the exception. I would put a new face on the term "foreigner." Good, I thought, a show of confidence. Keep it up, Kai. You're going to need it.

It was hot and stuffy in the plane, and seats all around me were filling fast. So far, the one next to me was unoccupied, and I could only hope it stayed that way. I could spread out, stretch my legs, and enjoy some privacy. Not a chance, I thought, watching the steady stream of people come my way. It was inevitable. The question was which fellow traveler would it be? Please God, not the overweight businessman with his wrinkled suit and exhausted expression from what looked like too many late-night meetings and sleep deprivation! And not the guy with the mirrored sunglasses and the gold jewelry draped around his neck! You wouldn't do that to me. Not for a twelve-hour flight to Tokyo.

Oh! Now here was a definite possibility. She was around my age, Asian, and very enticing. She appeared to have a serious side if her expression was any indication, but I could handle serious for a few hours. She was waiting patiently while an older couple wrestled their bags into the overhead bin, and I studied her the way a man in a fantasy does the girl of his dreams. She was wearing a baggy Harvard sweatshirt, a pair of faded blue jeans, a weathered Boston Red Sox baseball cap, and looked like a fashion model who had chosen her outfit from the bins at the Salvation Army.

"There's an empty seat right here," I wanted to shout. Instead, I used every ounce of mental telepathy I possessed to convey the message, and damned if it didn't work. She stopped at my row and looked down on me.

"May I join?" she said as if she had her choice of assigned seats. Stunning.

"I was hoping you might," I managed to say. "Need some help with your bags?"

"I think I can manage," she said, easily tossing her one suitcase into the overhead and showing off the lean, hard body of a kung fu fighter. Then she dropped into her seat, and her smile lit up the plane like a roman candle.

"My name's Liliko," she said in English touched with a sensual Oriental accent. I was staring. When I caught myself, she laughed. "Now you're supposed to say, 'And I am . . .'"

I shook my head and laughed. "I guess I am, aren't I?" I held out my hand. "I'm Kai Waters."

"World traveler." She took my hand.

"Not exactly. Exchange student," I said because nothing else was generating from my hung-over brain cells.

"Really? Where at?" It seemed to me that she held my hand a second or two longer than simple common courtesy called for, but then my imagination was the only thing working on all cylinders at the moment.

"I've got three days to explore Tokyo before heading to the Japanese Institute of International Studies. Near Mount Fuji."

"I most impressed, Kai-san," she said playfully.

"How about you?"

"I am taking my Harvard diploma and returning home. My father was not too keen on me coming to America in the first place, and now I am expected to repay his generosity by putting a year or two into his business."

"America's loss," I said.

Her eyes narrowed. "Did I detect a compliment?"

"I'm just picturing the string of broken hearts you must be leaving behind," I said. "You're extremely beautiful."

"Well, we will see what you think of me after 12 hours of listening to me rant and rave." She was laughing again, and I heard a touch of flirtation in her voice. "So you decided to study in Japan. Why?"

"Because the situation has all the makings of a cultural bonanza, Liliko, and I intend to make the most of it."

To that end, as I told her, I was going into the semester with a minimum class load. My base of operations would be a tiny town situated at the foot of Mount Fuji called Fujinomiya, a sixty-mile trek from Tokyo. My fellow students would be a select mix of foreign exchange students, thrown together with 50 Japanese businessmen who, I assumed, would be as eager to learn from us as we were from them. The picture was solidly painted in my mind. This was my first time overseas, and I was determined to enjoy every facet of the Japanese experience. I was ready and willing to expose myself to the unique and special intricacies of a way of life founded upon 5,000 years of island evolution and life principles honed by the ancient Samurai.

"Who wouldn't be excited?"

Liliko listened to me with a warm smile on her face. "You may be surprised at what you find."

"You sound like my parents," I told her.

Thankfully, Mom and Dad had thrown their support—if somewhat reluctantly—behind my decision to study in Japan. They had warned me against unachievable expectations, but they also knew their son. I only knew one way to approach life: take the bull by the horns and ride it for all it was worth. So far, that philosophy had produced a minimum of scars over my twenty-three years. True, all my experience had been in safe havens created by educational institutions that had very little to do with the real world. I had gotten my undergraduate degree at the University of Iowa and was pursuing my graduate degree in International Marketing at Thunderbird University. These were great places to learn about business, but I was smart enough not to equate the insular bastions of higher education with the realities of everyday living.

"And before college?" Liliko asked.

"I was raised in the suburbs of Chicago and lived in a house full of love, athletics, academia and laughter. It was an enviable upbringing."

Liliko and I talked until the plane was airborne. Then she put on her headphones and reclined her seat. I opened Karen's letter. It was less than a page long and written in her neat, polished hand. The letter opened with the words *Hard to believe we're going our separate ways, isn't it?* It ended with a friendly admonishment typical of Karen: *Don't grow up too much while you're in Japan.*

Karen and I had a running joke about the disparity in our maturity levels. In fact, I was always rather amazed that she and I had ever connected. She was a year older and decades more sophisticated than me. It was true we had plenty in common, but there were also notable differences. We were both ambitious and positive, tackling our studies with a vengeance. She was as sexually aggressive as I and just as eager to satisfy me as I was her. I enjoyed chiding her about her quest for spirituality and I hadn't yet risen to her level of philosophical seriousness. She saw us as a serious couple; I fell in love with her the moment we met. Karen was surprised and a little hurt when I committed to the semester in Japan. I think she was also relieved. Three days later she announced her intention to intern in Europe. Without really saying so, we had turned the page on our relationship.

I did read one part of her letter a second and third time, because it said so much about Karen. *You should enjoy these six months, Kai. You'll be a different man when you come back. And Europe is exactly what the doctor ordered for me.*

I read those words one last time and felt a seed of anxiety cracking open in my stomach. I was on my own. The lifeline back to a world where predictability was the rule of thumb was gone. I folded the paper, put it back into the envelope, and tucked it into my shirt pocket.

Next to me, Liliko was breathing softly, and I stared at her profile for a minute.

Then I reclined my seat and closed my eyes. An image of my parents filled my head. Both had lived through World War II. Both had been huddled next to their radios, like most Americans, when news of Pearl Harbor echoed across the airwaves on December 7, 1941. They had lived with the vivid and almost incomprehensible scenes of that unprovoked attack and shared a nationwide enmity toward the Japanese. Dad had been drafted into the Army as a 19-year-old kid with no idea where the island of

Okinawa lay in the deep and foreign waters of the west Pacific Ocean, and yet the battle over that seemingly insignificant piece of ground would become one of the hardest fought and costliest in the war against Japan. Dad was one of the many thousands of casualties and had earned a Purple Heart for his efforts.

Forty years later, he still viewed what was now one of our staunchest allies with caution; so did Mom. When they said, "Be careful" to me that morning at O'Hare Airport, they were, of course, talking like all parents would about the hazards of travel and the pitfalls of the unknown, but also with just a hint of that 40-year-old history.

That was my last thought before falling into a fitful sleep, crowded with dreams of family and friends and punctuated by the recurring image of a placid lake and impenetrable forests in front of the most formidable snow-capped mountain I had ever seen. Nearly two hours later, I awoke with an unquenchable thirst and a dull headache. I retrieved my back-pack and reached into the side pocket for a bottle of water, two aspirin, and the *Backpacker's Guide to Japan's Island Wonders*. There was the image from my dream staring back at me from the guide's cover: a lake as vividly blue as God had ever envisioned, forests of pine sculpted like watchful sentinels, and Mount Fuji, both the highest point in Japan and the mountain serving as sentinel to my final destination.

"Wait until you see it," Liliko said from the seat next to me. She gestured at the photo. "It is astounding."

"I can't wait," I told her.

"So what do you have planned for your three days in Tokyo?" she asked with a curious gleam in her eye.

I decided to be bold. "I'm hoping to find a beautiful young woman to give me the full tour. After all, what better way to see the city than through the eyes of a native?"

"This must be your lucky day, Kai-san," she said. "You found her."

"Seriously?"

She nodded. "And I say we begin the tour right now." She leaned closer and lowered her voice. The subtle hint of her perfume mingled with the sweetness of her breath when she whispered, "Have you ever heard of the mile-high club?"

It took me a second for the meaning of her words to sink in, but by then she was already unbuckling her seat belt. "Meet me in back in fifteen seconds."

I felt a rush of blood coursing through my veins, and my mouth was suddenly dry. I counted to ten, unbuckled my seat belt, and stepped into the aisle. I feigned a casual stroll as I made my way toward the restrooms in the back of the plane, hoping I hadn't misinterpreted her invitation. The one on my left opened suddenly, and Liliko pulled me inside. She had no sooner locked the door than we were kissing furiously and pulling off our clothes. Was this actually happening? In the back of an airplane thirty thousand feet above ground? I guess it was. Liliko leaned back against the mirror, and I entered her. A moment before we both reached orgasm, her shirt fell away from her shoulders. In the mirror, I found myself staring at a tattoo that covered half her back: it was the image of a Bengal tiger underscored by a circular Yin and Yang sign and ringed in flames.

I ran my hands over the tattoo, drew her near, and felt her shudder. I exploded inside her at the same moment. No protection, no second thoughts, no nothing. How stupid could I be?

"Wow!" I whispered.

"Wow is right," she said with a raspy giggle. We held each other until our hearts slowed and our breathing returned to normal.

"So that's the Mile-High Club," I said, feeling the weakness in my knees. "Everyone should join."

I assumed every eye was watching us as we made our way back to our seats, but I didn't care. I had just experienced the most exotic sex of my life, and I didn't give a damn who knew it.

The rest of the flight was like a dream, two secret lovers enjoying the lingering magic of their intimacy. Just before we arrived, I opened my pack and took out a notebook containing four pages of key Japanese

words and phrases that formed the backbone of my fledgling Japanese.
Three or four of those phrases were dedicated to getting me from Narita
International Airport to my hotel in downtown Tokyo, and Liliko helped
me practice.

"Good afternoon." *Konnichiwa.*

"Taxi, please. Hilton Hotel." *Hilton Hoteru o kudasai.*

"I'm a dumb American. Can you help me?" *Watakashi wa America-jin
de totemo wakarimasen.*

"I like that one," she teased.

"Well, I figure everyone needs a self-effacing line or two to make the
natives smile."

I had put two years into the study of Japanese during my Master's program. I was consistent in my approach, if not wildly dedicated. There were
other interests that earned the wilder side of my dedication, several of
those being social in nature. My consistent approach left me competent in
the language, but a far cry from fluent. Fluency, among other things, was
at the heart of my quest here in Japan. What better way to achieve that
than to be dropped into the Japanese countryside in the company of classmates and roommates whose first language was Japanese? My language
skills would soar. I would reach fluency almost by default.

I was two days away from learning just how wrong this assumption—
and so many others I had made—would be.

"I cannot be seen getting off the plane with you, Kai. I am sorry,"
Liliko said suddenly.

"Why not?"

"Because I would have to explain it to my family, and I do not want to
have to do that. Can you understand?"

It wasn't exactly a question, but I nodded anyway. "What about our
tour?"

She smiled. "I would not miss it for anything. I will pick you up at
your hotel on Tuesday, at noon. I will show you a side of Tokyo the
tourists never see."

Gaijin Mistakes

"A crane
Shading in the evening twilight
Trailing its smoke-like wings."
~ Kakio Tomizawa

A s we began our approach, the city of Tokyo filled my window with a shock of steel and glass. A skyline as brash and crowded as Manhattan rose from the sea, hailing visitors to a nation fueled by industrial might and propelled by the financial juggernaut it had become over the past three decades. I had studied hundreds of photographs of the city, but I was still unprepared for the sight.

The airplane banked and I caught sight of the city's downtown corridor. The Shinjuku business district and a wall of 50-story buildings held my eye. I knew the names of some of the international giants that occupied the buildings, but it was the men and women working there I found myself trying to picture. They, more than anything, would distinguish Tokyo from its counterparts in the West, cities like Chicago, New York, and Los Angeles. I wondered what made the people in those offices tick. I wondered what motivated them, what frightened them, and what made them laugh. I wondered how different their young men would be from the guys I hung around with back home. I wanted them to be different and I suppose I expected them to be. I wondered about the women; they couldn't all be as extraordinary as Liliko. How would they see a *gaijin* from another part of the world? I had not come to Japan for romance but, like most guys, I also held the fantasy of the beautiful Asian girl and the debonair American who sweeps her off her feet. I caught Liliko's eye and thought, so far so good, Kai-san.

The plane veered away from the coast, and I had a moment to gaze down on the rugged terrain beyond the city. From the air, it was easy to see that the island of Honshu had risen from the sea a million years ago in what had to have been a violent display of volcanic activity. The result was a tight pattern of narrow valleys and steep, heavily wooded hills. The prevailing color was green, but in more spectacular shades than even the most imaginative painter could conceive: the haunting, rich olive of towering firs; the sprightly grass-green of rice paddies; and the vacillating, mysterious verdure of pines in silhouette against the bottle green of the sea. I could see that these steep, arborous hills had saved the majority of Japan from cultivation and guaranteed its rugged beauty.

The aerial view also explained why the Japanese people had been forced by nature to shoehorn themselves into the valleys and to maximize as much of the country's itinerant coast as humanly possible. They had adapted. I could also see that as the population had swelled, the bulldozers and road graders had swept inland. Acres of bamboo, firs, and pines had been sacrificed in the process.

"My father calls it the price of progress, and maybe he is right," Liliko said thoughtfully. "But I still think it is sad."

The loudspeaker crackled overhead, and the pilot informed us that we would be on the ground at Narita International Airport in twenty minutes. I could feel a flutter in my stomach that was part exhilaration, part nervous energy. I couldn't wait to get my feet on the ground.

I walked off the plane thirty seconds after Liliko. If the two men who met her in the concourse were family, their greetings lacked even a hint of warmth. No smiles, no glee, no joyous embraces. In fact, the set of their shoulders and the deliberate way they studied the concourse made me think they were bodyguards, and their black suits were a dead giveaway.

The one with the closely shaved head relieved Liliko of her suitcase. The one with the flowing black hair put a protective hand on her arm, and they moved with hurried steps down the concourse. The crowd swept them up, and I decided it was none of my business; for all I knew her father could be the CEO of Sony or the Deputy Prime Minister.

I turned my attention to the airport and the mass of people flooding the terminal. The headaches of deplaning, I realized, were the same ones travelers could expect at LAX or O'Hare. The first hint of a land 6,000 miles from home was the smell: not distasteful, just different. It struck me the moment I entered the terminal, an olfactory assault that hinted of soy sauce and fish, wall-to-wall people, and traces of an industrial energy that ran 24-hours-a-day, part pollution and part overload.

There was also something about the picture that seemed to lack color. I found my eyes recording a world of blacks, whites, and grays. I saw it in the décor, where purpose and function seemed a higher priority than style. I even saw it in the artwork—such as it was—leaving me with the impression that it had been designed less to catch the eye than to exalt an orderly, fabricated landscape. I also saw it in the people, who struck me at first glance as wearing cookie-cutter expressions and uninspiring clothing. It was not until I looked closer that I saw the intensity of the expressions, the alertness in their eyes, and a quiet, biting humor held closely in check.

I found nothing out of place: not the furnishings, not the flow of traffic, and not the positioning of the airport employees. I found nothing too loud: not the terminal announcements, not the canned Muzak, and certainly not the shuffling of feet or the greetings of family and friends, which struck me as more scripted than spontaneous. The lighting, like almost everything else, was subtle and unobtrusive. If there was an inkling of radical thinking to be had, I saw it in the teenaged boys with the loud shirts, faded jeans, and sideburns and the girls with the rising hemlines and dangling earrings.

Of course, I was a *gaijin* observing a new world with *gaijin* eyes.

Everyone had told me to expect the usual delays at customs, but the only break in an otherwise orderly flow came from the agent who did a double take at the wound on my nose. I wanted to say, "Don't blame me, officer. It was an uninspired practical joke at the hands of half-drunk American scoundrels." But by that time, I was hauling my luggage toward the currency exchange counter. My teachers had called Japan a cash culture. Their warning was clear: I should not count on my credit card to get me out of a tight spot. It seemed to imply that the Kai Waters they knew was destined to get himself into a tight spot somewhere along the line. With this in mind, I converted a $100 traveler's check into what was roughly 25,000 yen. This was a serious step, a signal that turning back was not an option.

I went outside. It was winter in Japan and chilly, but after what I had left in Chicago, it felt like the first day of autumn. I carried my suitcases and overstuffed backpack to the taxi stand and employed a well-practiced *"Tokyo Hilton Hoteru o kudasai"* to make my intentions known. But because my faith was clearly lacking in this first of many forays into the Japanese language, I showed the taxi driver a photograph of the Hilton Hotel and pointed to what I assumed was the address. He may have nodded, but he didn't bother to respond verbally. Smart man. The upside was that he didn't break out laughing.

Just as I was about to hop into the backseat, I glimpsed Liliko and her two escorts climbing into a glistening black limousine. Well, I had to hand it to her. The girl travels in style, I thought with a smile. Good for her. Maybe she'd bring the limo along for our tour tomorrow. Right, Kai. Fat chance.

As it turned out, my own taxi was a lot closer to a limo than a cab, at least by American standards. First and foremost, it was immaculate both inside and out; secondly, the seat covers were white lace instead of cracked plastic. Hard to miss.

I settled back in my seat, watched my driver exit the airport and almost laughed out loud. You did it, Kai. You're here, I said to myself. Tokyo was a forty-mile drive from the airport. Up ahead, I watched the bright lights of the world's fifth largest city dusting the horizon. There were 10 million city dwellers in Tokyo alone and another 120 million filling every nook and cranny of livable space on an island the size of California. I had done my research. The country was 99.9% Japanese—with a few Koreans, Chinese, and Brazilians sprinkled in—and from everything I had read, the natives did not look favorably upon immigration. Good thing I wasn't planning to overstay my welcome. I could, however, expect to stand out.

The organized sprawl that characterized the city's outer reaches said something about Tokyo's orderly population boom because it was marked by mammoth apartment buildings in perfect harmony with a spate of oversized billboards touting Japan's industrial giants. I used every name to test my knowledge of the country, from Sony and Panasonic to Mitsubishi and Suzuki. The Japanese were an exporting machine, no doubt about it, and cars and electronics headed the list. How often these days did we see *Made in Japan* imprinted on everything from coffee mugs to calculators? In return, Japan only imported what they couldn't make: coal and grain, bananas and beef, textiles and fuel oil.

My Dad's generation made fun of it. In their eyes, *Made in Japan* meant *made cheap.* My generation was beginning to understand that *Made in Japan* was synonymous with *made pretty damn well.* The Japanese had risen from the ashes of World War II, intent on conquering the world with their industry and innovation. How, I wasn't sure. That was why I was here. I had heard rumors of their intense dedication and unrivaled work ethic. I wanted to see it in action.

I wondered how the proliferation of the "love hotels" I began to see as we entered the city fit into that equation. They were easy to spot, shaped like castles, sailing ships, and riverboats. I wondered if I would have occasion to visit one of them. I had come to Japan with a credo: Keep an open mind. If keeping an open mind led to a visit to a sex hotel, well . . .

One of the more peculiar facets of the trip from the airport was the incessant ringing coming from inside the taxi. Eventually, I realized its source as the dashboard and, after the third or fourth time, I came to the conclusion that some type of sensory device was informing my driver every time he exceeded the speed limit. And every time, he dutifully slowed down, his expression neither annoyed nor disturbed. He accepted the control function as just another fact of life in a society predicated on order. No wonder most Japanese took the train.

We left the expressway for Nanko Road and the heart of downtown. The sun was setting as we found my hotel. The Hilton was probably the newest building in a neighborhood of office towers, apartment houses, and government buildings constructed with an eye on maximizing space, first and foremost, followed by a nod to aesthetic design, if there was anything left over. Tokyo was, I imagined, either a very frustrating place to be an architect or a very challenging one.

When I arrived at the Hilton, I was greeted by no less than twenty genuinely enthusiastic hotel employees on my way from the entrance to the reservation desk and up the elevator to my room on the 4th Floor. Tipping them all was not within my meager budget, and the bellman that helped me with my bags refused my offer with a wave of his hand and a polite bow. I was already learning.

When he was gone, I surveyed the room. The word "small" applied to every stick of furniture, including a bed the size of a baby's crib. Well, Toto, we're definitely not in Kansas anymore, I thought. Get used to it.

I knew this was going to be a tall order, however, as soon as I stepped into the bathroom. There was no toilet. Instead, there was a ceramic hole set in the floor in one corner. It's hard to relax with a magazine or the sports page when you are squatting over a hole the size of a dinner plate. As I assumed the position and felt the burning sensation in my legs, I wondered how in the world I was going to accurately gauge my aim. Somehow I managed to hit the mark and in a strange way felt proud of my illustrious achievement.

The sun had now set and the night lights of downtown Tokyo were glimmering outside my hotel window. It was a spectacular sight, but I was too tired to enjoy it at the moment. I closed the curtains and pulled off my pants and shirt. I didn't bother unpacking anything other than my sundry bag and just barely managed to get my teeth brushed before curling up on my miniature bed. As uncomfortable as it was, I was instantly and soundly asleep.

I awoke with a start at 5:00 a.m. Tokyo time and spent ten full seconds wondering where in the hell I was. I was stiff and groggy and disappointed my bed hadn't grown even a centimeter during the night. "You're in Japan, hotshot," I mumbled. "Get up. It's already mid-afternoon back home."

I stumbled into the bathroom and turned on the shower. I had every intention of spending the next thirty minutes under a hot spray, a ritual I had mastered back in the college dorm. Then I stepped in and discovered a showerhead that only came to the middle of my chest and water pressure that made the plumbing back home seem like paradise. No matter. I was in Japan and the streets of Tokyo were calling me. I wasn't going to waste the morning complaining. I threw on a pair of Levis, an Iowa Hawkeye sweatshirt, and a jacket. I filled my pockets with traveler's checks and Japanese yen and headed for the elevator.

I was just in time to see the sun cresting above the horizon, far out over the Pacific Ocean. As the first golden rays filtered between the city's precipitous walls of steel and concrete, I felt a swelling in my chest and realized I was smiling. My objective for the next three days was to touch, smell, taste, and enjoy every sensory experience that Tokyo offered before catching the scheduled bus to Fujinomiya. I started walking. My feet carried me along the streets in search of the historic Asakusa District. I tried not to be too obvious about the street map I had purchased.

I didn't know what Liliko had planned for our tour the next day, but I assumed it would be less cultural and more social than a trip to the Asakusa District.

In the beginning, I found it interesting that there was nothing terribly oriental about the thoroughfares of modern Tokyo. Except for the Chinese and Japanese ideograms staring down from hotel and office marquees and those painted across the entryways of restaurants and shops, I could have been in any Western city of size. The differences came slowly, maybe because the streets were only beginning to come alive. I watched as the hotel and restaurant cleaning crews along Shizuoka Dori dumped copious amounts of cans and bottles collected from the previous night's business, in preparation for the morning trash pick up. Sake, beer, whiskey, wine; I was amazed at the consumption a Monday night had produced. It brought to mind a warning proffered by one of my advisors about the Japanese "need" for the release of alcohol. He didn't explain. He said I would find out soon enough.

On Ainu Dori, I peered into the windows of a half dozen restaurants and discovered a new art form. Entrees of the day were displayed in perfectly replicated plastic forms and each piece of fruit or vegetable, cut of beef, or slice of fish was painted with remarkable realism. They were presented on place settings of spotless porcelain alongside wine-filled crystal goblets. The effect was so astoundingly real that it made my mouth water and I realized how little I had eaten over the last 24 hours.

By 7:30, the sidewalks were roiling with humanity, and I watched the working world overtake the peaceful early morning hiatus. It was like standing in the middle of a lazy river when a dam breaks. People of every ilk and purpose flooded the streets. It did not necessarily strike me as a happy crowd, but it was a determined one. A swell of sound filled my ears: percussive footsteps, backfiring buses, perfectly tuned cars, and hushed voices speaking rapid fire Japanese. My expectations of Tokyo at the heart of rush hour were wholeheartedly met.

I saw the first Shinto shrine on the outskirts of Asakusa. It was a simple building with sloping, concave roofs. The wooden poles that rose in a V-shape from the roof formed a support for rounded crossbeams that were typical of Shinto construction and probably represented something of significance. Unfortunately, I knew almost nothing about the Shinto way. That it coexisted with the practice of Buddhism was apparent by the appearance of a Buddhist temple, rising in the shape of a multi-roofed pagoda on the same block.

Across the street, an elegant garden commemorated the bombing of Tokyo in 1945 and the 100,000 people killed during that one, devastating 24-hour-period. According to a placard in front of the garden, bombers dropped flammable oil that consumed the district and brought chaos to innocent civilians. I stood on the banks of the Sumida River and found it hard to believe the area had been covered with charred bodies 40 years earlier. There was no sign of the destruction. The Japanese had persevered, probably, I thought, beyond the expectations of everyone but themselves. And now look at them! They had found a new way to make their mark on the world, through commerce, culture and a way of life that many in the West found irresistible.

I reversed my course and started back. I took the long way, wandering into and out of the residential quarters' narrow lanes. The pace of life switched gears here. I smelled the fresh fragrance of soy sauce and steaming noodles emanating from a noodle seller trundling his cart down a dimly lit alley. When he reached his destination, he came to a halt and played a few notes on a wooden flute. Shopkeepers in cotton kimonos were standing outside their shops, gossiping and giggling, probably wondering what the *gaijin* was doing in their neighborhood. I heard the sweet sound of people in clogs click-clacking to and from a public bath along Kengyu Dori, clutching towels and soap, and decided it was time to fulfill one of the many things on my to-be-experienced-in-Tokyo list: the ancient ritual of the bathhouse.

I didn't get far.

I had not taken two steps when I saw the owner's jaw drop at the sight of a blonde, blue-eyed foreigner walking through his door. After a moment of paralysis, he called out to his wife in the back office and she came scurrying. She managed a short, polite bow and, in her best, if broken, English said, "So sorry, but this a private bath."

I nodded. I may even have smiled. *"Hai,"* I said, understanding now that I had invaded a neighborhood bathhouse, probably patronized by the same people every day. The last thing they needed was a *gaijin* disrupting their routine.

As I stepped back outside, I felt a momentary jolt of disappointment, if not out-and-out rejection, but I was not about to be deterred. If the locals would not have me, then maybe the hotel bathhouse would. I was, after all, a paying customer and in the words of the Hilton's concierge, an "honored guest." The wind had picked up since my early morning excursion and I decided to take my chances with Tokyo's legendary public transportation. I walked back to Edo Dori and caught the first southbound bus I saw, somehow managing to board, hand over my money, and find a seat without causing an international incident. Finding my stop, I realized, was another matter.

The bus was packed, but a wide-eyed *gaijin* was of little consequence here. Good, I thought. I could handle a couple of minutes of anonymity. The bus followed the river for two miles and stopped at every intersection. I tried to make sense of the street signs using my trusty road map, but on instinct decided to jump off when I saw the river making an abrupt bend to the southeast. When my feet were safely on ground, I tapped into my ever-evolving intuition as a world traveler and determined I had overshot my mark by two blocks. I considered this a major victory.

Ten minutes later, I walked through the doors of the Tokyo Hilton Hotel. With the help of an exceedingly polite woman at the main desk, I managed to convey my desire to visit the hotel's bathhouse and was directed to a stairway leading to the basement.

I was met at the bathhouse entrance by a girl with the delicate features of a high school sophomore, give or take a year. Our communication was halting at best and punctuated by hand signals and polite bows. My impression was that she had few blue-eyed, pale-faced men wanting to use the bathhouse, despite a high number of foreign guests at the hotel. Apparently, though, there were no rules forbidding it. She laid one small and one large towel in my hands, and then directed me toward the men's locker room.

The first thing that caught my attention was the complete lack of, or apparent need for, security. It may have been called a locker room, but there were no locks on any of the doors. The patrons had stored their belongings in cubbies, trusting they would be there upon their return. I spent thirty seconds convincing myself that theft was not the problem here that it was in Chicago. In the States, we hoped for the best. Here, someone walking off with my backpack was apparently not a consideration. It just didn't happen. In fact, I was probably the most unsavory person in the entire place. Okay then.

I stripped off my clothes and stored them and my pack, with as much faith as I could muster, in one of the lockers. I was stark naked and feeling a little more comfortable with my public nudity when a prune-faced woman walked in with a vacuum cleaner in her hand. She strolled up to me as if I had recently been transported down to earth from another planet and positioned her tiny body with unabashed curiosity directly in front of me. She stared at my "unit" as if the sight of a white man's private parts was a completely new experience for her. The equivocal look on her face suggested an internal debate over the ancient question of whether or not white men were truly more "hung" than their Asian counterparts. As for me, I was momentarily paralyzed and too tongue-tied to ask how the debate was going. It did not occur to me for the better part of ten seconds to wrap myself in a towel. Gratefully, I was rescued when the receptionist hurried in and shooed the old woman away.

"So sorry," she said, backpedaling and bowing in the same motion.

We each managed weak smiles. I grabbed my towels. The locker area opened onto a room that vaguely reminded me of the communal shower at the gym back home. Waist high water spigots were positioned along the walls. Dangling from the spigots were small plastic buckets and bars of soap. On the floor in front of the spigots were stools no taller than six inches and clearly designed for human beings a lot more diminutive than me.

Beyond the showers was an enclosed area dominated by a steaming hot tub the size of a small swimming pool and crowded with men, all naked and all Japanese. While they may have thought their inquisitive glances were discreet, it was obvious that I was a spectacle worthy of some attention.

My study of Japanese traditions having skirted the issue of bathhouse protocol, I was not at all sure where to go next. Looking at the inviting steam rising from the surface of the tub, I started in that direction. It was a bad move. Before I had taken more than two steps, another young, pretty, and very frustrated attendant waylaid me.

"You must clean first before entering," she said, using halting and unpracticed English to chastise me. She did not add, "You uncultured American slob," but her expression said it all.

I relied on my limited Japanese to apologize. "*Yurushite kudasai,*" I said. *Forgive me.* I bowed slightly and allowed her to lead me back to the shower room. She sat me down on one of the tiny stools, took a wiry brush from the buckets, and lathered it with soap. Then she scrubbed my back with enough force to set my skin afire. I could not decide whether to laugh or cry, but I was smart enough to observe several other Japanese bathers using their small towels to clean themselves and I did the same. The bucket was used for rinsing—another keen observation on my part— and I poured the water over my head and back, much as they did.

This done, I assumed that now I was fit for the steaming bath, but as I approached the steaming tub, the looks on the faces of the Japanese businessman that were submerged in the bath's mysterious depths seemed to say *This tub is for Japanese only.* I did not know if I was reading their expressions correctly or not, but I felt an outcast, a true *gaijin.* It was a unique feeling for me and surprisingly uncomfortable.

I quietly walked past the tub and headed into the massage room. Interestingly, I could feel immediate embarrassment mirrored in the eyes of the massage therapists, and I would have done anything to relieve them of this feeling. Unfortunately, I was at a loss. How do you fix what you do not understand?

I was politely guided to the most distant table, and I found it amusing to see the therapists arguing over who was to be relegated to this ugly intruder. Seniority apparently ruled and the youngest of the group, a woman in her early 50s, shuffled my way. The massage that followed was somewhere between excruciating and surreal. For her size, she was a surprisingly strong and powerful woman, with an aggressive bent. She began by using her hands and fists to pummel me into submission. Then she stood on my back and, as diminutive as she was, proceeded to beat me like I had never been beaten in my life. An hour later, I felt as if someone had taken a baseball bat to my entire body.

I could hardly move. As I heaved myself onto my bed, I realized I had almost no memory of getting dressed again or of making my way back to my room. I also had no idea how many poor Japanese people I had left confused, befuddled, or embarrassed in my wake, but it occurred to me that I had gotten off to one helluva rocky start for a guy convinced of his own survival skills. On the other hand, I decided, how much worse could it get?

I awoke at 1:30 in the afternoon with a dreariness brought on by jet lag, half starved and surprisingly eager for another round of Japanese indoctrination. After the beating I had endured, I expected to feel like the worst part of a head-on collision, but I didn't. I was sore but energized. I could not explain it. It must have been those Japanese feet. Was it possible the woman was not trying to kill me after all? Maybe I would pay her a return visit the following day and find out for sure.

I migrated to the bathroom, splashed water on my face, glanced at my reflection in the mirror, and gave myself an encouraging if not wholly convincing smile.

"Sushi," I said. "What else!"

I ventured out again five minutes later. The Tokyo streets overflowed with humanity and I merged with the masses as if I had done so a hundred times before. The wind had turned a sheen of light rain into an icy mist. While the change in weather didn't do much for the mood of my

Japanese brethren, I was delighted. Here, after all, was another facet of life in Japan and I wanted to experience it all. That was the great thing about being young: one minute you felt foolish and out of place and the next you felt bulletproof.

There were a dozen restaurants within a block of the hotel, but I was looking for something casual. Nothing struck my eye until I spotted a hole in the wall on Kanda Dori called Shohuju's. I had always equated busy with good when it came to restaurants and Shohuju's was overrun with customers. To my eyes, they all looked relatively content. Why not, I thought.

A set of glass doors slid open automatically in front of me and I stepped in. A crowd of businessmen sat at lunch and every eye turned in unison at the sight of the youthful American who was apparently unable to figure out why the doors would not close behind him. A stinging wind raced into the room. If ever looks could kill, this was probably it. An instant later, the proprietor's wife came running over. She was uttering a string of words I could not interpret, which was probably a good thing, and ushered me off the mat that regulated the door. She sat me at a table in the corner, far from harm's way.

I smiled sheepishly. "*Arigato,*" I said as politely as possible. "*Domo arigato.*"

This caused her to bow slightly in return. "*Douitashi mashite,*" she intoned in Japanese. *You are welcome.* Hallelujah, I thought. Bona fide communication. I was elated.

Relying on hand signals, pictures, and two or three well chosen words, I managed to indicate my desire for sushi. A few minutes later, I was rewarded with a beautifully arranged assortment of eel, scallops, halibut, and raw shrimp. I didn't recognize the green, flower-shaped dollop sitting on top of the halibut as wasabi. Without thinking, I gobbled the entire piece in one bite. The wasabi hit my throat like a jalapeno doused in hot mustard and I was suddenly choking, coughing, and once again drawing the unwanted attention of an entire restaurant. The proprietor's wife again came to my rescue, thrusting a glass of water into my hands and nodding her head as if I might not understand that the next step was to drink it. I took her suggestion to heart and chugged the entire glass. The business-men got a nice chuckle out of it, so I guess there was an upside. The down-side was another massive failure in my quest for quiet assimilation into Japanese culture. I was humbled, yes, but ready to give up? Not me.

———

3

A Walk on the Wild Side

"Spring departs
Birds cry
Fishes' eyes are filled with tears."
~ Basho Matsuo

I attributed a mid-afternoon sinking spell to the 12 hours I had spent in an airplane the previous day and decided a short nap was well-deserved. I curled up on my bed and was instantly asleep. In the hazy dream that followed, I was suddenly on the steep slopes of Mt. Fuji scrambling toward the summit and the shadowy figure of a woman I took to be Liliko. Her imploring wave and the echo of her voice beckoned me on.

My legs were heavy and my lungs burned, and a piercing scream paralyzed me in mid-stride. I saw the dragon's shadow seconds before his huge, scaly body crested above the mountain's snowy peak. With wings no less wide than a commercial jet's, he swooped toward me, belching fire and screeching. But the sound that shook me awake was not the dragon's scream; it was the broken English of two cleaning ladies who had apparently entered my room after I failed to answer their knock.

They were small and pruned faced, like a pair of forgotten walnuts, and they were clearly more embarrassed than I was. "So sorry to interrupt," the bolder of the two said. "Would you like us to turn down your bed, Mr. Waters-san?"

I smiled and shook my head. "Maybe later. *Arigato*," I said, realizing I would probably have slept away the entire night had they not come to my rescue. That was not my intention. Tokyo's world famous nightlife was calling to me, and I wasn't about to let a little jet lag get between me and a night on the town. I threw on a blue Polo shirt, a pair of faded Levi's, and my cowboy boots. If I was going out, I might as well flaunt the fact that a big, young American had come to town and was ready for Tokyo's finest.

I checked my wallet; I had 25,000 yen and $200 worth of traveler's checks. I had been thoroughly prepped by friends and counselors on the cost of living in Tokyo. The operative word was expensive, or "damn expensive," as Jay Edington put it. He also said, "They don't call it the city of $10 cups of coffee and $200 taxi rides for nothing. The good news is that there are more places to get drunk in Tokyo than in the entire state of Illinois."

I headed for the elevator with a plan of action nicely mapped out in my mind. I would stay as far away as possible from the jazz clubs with the $70 covers and the "hostess" clubs that would deplete my entire stash before the girls and the drinks even arrived. I could handle a $6.00 beer and an $8.00 shot, but not more than one or two.

I crossed the lobby to the front door and ventured onto the street. A flash of neon lights illuminated corridors of tall buildings and reminded me that Tokyo's nightlife didn't operate on a schedule like we did in the States. There was no last call, no mandatory closing time, and no shortage of people willing to stay out all night.

"Avoid any club with an English-speaking doorman," a well-traveled cousin had warned me. "It's a guaranteed tourist trap. Go where the Japanese go, the "shot clubs" and the discos. And you only need to know two names: Shinjuku and Kabukicho. Ask any cabbie."

And that was what I did. "Ah," my taxi driver said in English so broken that I had to lean forward to understand him. "Shopping, drinking, or dancing?"

"Start with a drink. Maybe some dancing later," I said.

"Ah-so." He grinned a conspiratorial grin which I had no chance of interpreting. It was probably my cowboy boots, I decided.

Shinjuku Station was less than ten minutes away and streams of screaming neon and a riot of high-pitched shrieking—a meld of cars, trains, and wall-to-wall people—brought me to the edge of my seat. He pulled up next to a sign that read *Central East Exit.*

He pointed and said, "Shinjuku Station, Piss Alley, Eastmouth, and Kabukicho. You walk now. It's all here."

When they said two million people passed through Shinjuku Station every day, I believed them. It was a tidal wave of humanity that pushed me toward the East Exit and canyons of stone and glass towers ringed with halos of light. Even the most vivid imagination would have had trouble describing the turmoil. It had to be seen. Every avenue was packed with bars and adult shops, pachinko parlors and nightclubs. I saw a sea of young Japanese partiers mixed with a small sprinkling of foreigners and the expressions on their faces ranged from totally confused to awestruck. Mine probably showed a little bit of both. Every nightclub had a doorman checking IDs. Every bar had a bouncer patrolling the entrance. Every adult shop had a barker enticing passersby with their wares. Every parlor had a pitchman doing the same. I wasn't encouraged to hear most of them speaking broken English; I was looking for an area of town catering more to locals and kept walking.

I crossed the tracks into Shomben Yokocho, or what my cabbie called Piss Alley. This was getting closer. An assemblage of ramshackle huts was sprinkled among a sprawling collection of shops, restaurants, and bars that looked like they belonged in a place called Piss Alley.

High end shopping set Shinjuku Eastmouth off from the cultural cornucopia of Piss Alley, and I could see someone dropping a fortune here in an afternoon. But at this time of night, the flood of people seemed drawn like a magnet toward Kabukicho, part red light district, part sex carnival, and awash in neon lights that burnt a swath of yellow, orange, red, and green for blocks.

I saw swarms of men in three piece business suits that looked as if they had just gotten off work and were desperate for some form of escape—a woman, drugs, whiskey, or something far more bizarre—before heading for home. I stared openly at men in shiny sharkskin suits who looked as if they never went home. I heard the laughter of youthful revelers hopping from one club to the next, the night young and full of unexpected opportunity. I saw a small group of foreigners and wondered what they were searching for here in a world where the enterprise of choice seemed to be sex. Every block seethed with a plethora of hostess clubs, strip shows, pornographic theaters, and pornographic emporiums. I saw signs for peep shows, pantyless tea rooms, and "nude shows in private rooms." Barkers shouted from the doors of massage parlors and saunas. I walked past one bar after another that promised the most beautiful naked women, the most erotic sideshows, and sights worthy of the wildest imagination. I was beginning to believe them.

I followed a dozen Japanese college kids into a disco and found myself forking over a 2,500 yen cover. Ten bucks, I thought. I could afford that, couldn't I? I stepped inside, and my world began to spin in the wake of glaring strobe lights, flashing spots, and six-foot-high speakers filling every nook and cranny with the pounding sound of Michael Jackson's *Thriller*.

The dance floor was girdled with floor-to-ceiling mirrors and a hundred Japanese kids obsessed with their own reflections and dancing as if every other person was a pariah to be avoided. I ordered a whiskey and water and cringed when the bartender said, "Twenty-five hundred yen." Another ten bucks! Damn.

Well, you've come this far, I thought. You might as well find someone to dance with. Easier said than done, I found, as one Japanese woman after another looked at me as if the plague had just swept into the room. Must be those cowboy boots again, I decided. At least they were polite about telling me to take a hike.

I listened to the Bee Gees sing "You Should Be Dancin'," and the irony of the lyrics was enough to make me realize that a disco in the middle of Tokyo's red light district was a good place to end my evening excursion. I chalked up the twenty dollars I had spent as an investment in my ongoing cultural enlightenment and returned to the streets of Kabukicho.

I was still in the mood for a beer, but I decided I could get that at the hotel bar. I retraced my steps to Shinjuku Station and joined the exodus of people and cars traveling down Koshu-dori. The brisk night air felt good on my skin, and I started walking. I hadn't gone two blocks before the Hilton appeared on the horizon. Another six blocks, and I was home.

A doorman, a concierge, a bellhop, and a woman whose title eluded me all nodded polite greetings, and I responded with the requisite, "*Konbanwa.*" Good evening.

A six-foot-long clipper ship, designed down to the last masthead, main sail, and bowline, festooned the entrance to the hotel bar, and the mariner theme carried over into the bar itself, all emblazoned with dark woods and brass fittings. Every table was occupied and most of the bar stools. The clientele was nearly all Japanese businessmen in the company of women who were almost certainly not their wives; either that or their wives were all young, alluring, and churning with sexual energy.

I found an empty stool, caught the bartender's eye, and called, "*Kirin biru, kudasai.*"

Beer and glass arrived less than sixty seconds later; I initialed the tab with my room number. I hadn't taken two sips before a woman sat down at the stool next to me.

She said, "May I join you?" as if I might actually have a choice in the matter. The look in her eye told me rejection was not something she often had to endure. On the other hand, who in the world would say no to a woman as beautiful and exotic as this one? From her mahogany skin, coal black hair, and gimlet eyes, she was flawless.

Her body beneath a sheer silk shift took the imagination to places most men only visit in their most erotic fantasies. Mine was working overtime even before I said, "Sure," and nodded rather lamely toward the stool.

"I am Kona." She offered me her hand. A blue and red tattoo, looking like the vines of ancient ivy, climbed up her arm, disappeared inside her dress, and emerged again like tendrils of lace embracing her neck.

"My name's Kai." I could smell her perfume, but it was more like the fragrance of a tropical flower rising from the forest. Intoxicating. "Would you like a drink?"

"Oh, yes. Thank you." With her accent, I could hardly understand a word she said and found myself leaning her way.

"Kona. That's a pretty name," I said.

"So is Kai." I hadn't thought of my name as pretty before, but it sounded just fine coming from her.

"You are a rich American." This sounded like a phrase she had been well prepped to say.

"American, yes. Rich, no. Sorry," I said, but I could see by the look on her face that she didn't believe me. Rich American was not two words; it was one.

I realized the bartender had served her a goblet of champagne neither she nor I had ordered. Well, maybe this wasn't her first time, I thought with a touch of cynicism. It didn't matter. When she touched her glass to mine and held me with those eyes, I felt a rush of blood to the secret parts of my body. Why fight it?

"So you're a champagne drinker," I said clumsily.

"I love those tiny bubbles," she confessed. "And it makes me just a little crazy. So be careful."

One beer and a half glass of champagne, and we were already flirting. What next? I wondered.

"Where are you from? Tokyo?" I asked.

"Oh, no. Not Japan." She shook her head as if righting this gross misrepresentation was important to her. "Pahang."

"Pahang?" The name was not familiar to me. "Where's that? In Thailand?"

"Malaysia." She sipped her champagne seductively and then bowed her head demurely. I didn't know which gesture to believe. "My village is called Karak," she said. Now I heard a touch of guilt. "In the Pahang Province. Across the mountains from Kuala Lumpur."

"A long way from home," I said, wondering how a village girl from Malaysia ended up in downtown Tokyo plying Japanese businessmen and wayward American students for drinks and who-knew-what-else.

"It is no longer home. I can never go back," she said without emotion.

"Sorry," I said.

She shook her head as if the time for regrets had long passed, smiled as if only this moment had any meaning, and ran her fingers over the back of my hand. Her fingers seductively traveled up my arm, along my shoulder, and down my chest.

"You find me attractive?" she asked.

This, I could tell, was not the first time she had asked someone this question, and the tilt of her head assured me she had never been disappointed with the answer.

"Stunning," I said, and it was true even if I knew I was following the script exactly as she had written it; or someone had written it for her.

"Are there women like me in America?"

Let's see? Stunning, bewitching, exotic, and seething with sexuality. Nope, not many. "No," I said.

"And you are not like the men who . . ." She hesitated. Was this part of the script? I had to wonder. She looked at me beneath hooded eyes, took my hand, and pressed her lips against the back. "Wouldn't you like to invite me to your room for another drink, Kai? The view must be beautiful."

I didn't answer because refusing her seemed almost sacrilegious, a gesture so uncommonly unthinkable that it would be taken for a terrible insult. It was not intended to be an insult. And it was not some idealistic aversion against sex for money. At least I didn't think it was. This was an amazingly beautiful woman. I could imagine exploring her body and finding it irresistible. Then why was I resisting? I didn't know for certain, but Kona was way ahead of me.

"Or we could have another drink here, and you could tell me all about America," she said. There was neither anger nor disappointment in her voice; I heard something, but I wasn't sure what. Maybe she was implementing Plan B: taking me for another drink before finding more receptive prey.

"Sure," I said, but the drinks were already there. The bartender had even poured my beer for me. Nice guy. I laid $25.00 on the bar and said, "Thanks. That'll be all. Keep the change."

I didn't start to feel woozy until my beer was half gone. I saw spots thirty seconds later, and my foot slipped off the barstool. "Damn."

"Are you alright, baby?" Kona asked, her voice sounding far more concerned than our 40-minute acquaintance probably warranted.

"I think I'd better go up to my room. It's been a long day." I listened to my voice and realized I was slurring my words.

"Come on, baby. Give me your hand." She put her arm around my waist and kissed my cheek. Nice, I thought, and wondered if my legs would hold me. Two beers and a watered down whiskey? Come on, Kai. Pull yourself together.

"Thanks," I said as she steered me toward the door.

The trip from the bar to the elevators felt like a stroll through quicksand. I didn't remember the doors opening or closing, but we were suddenly being carried upward. I felt sick. Not in the elevator, Kai. Show some style, will you?

"Come on, baby," Kona said. "Time for bed."

"Sixth floor," I said, but we were already stumbling down the hall.

"I know," she assured me. "Room 620."

I felt her hand searching my pockets and tried to stop her. "It's okay, Kai. I need your room key."

"Oh, yeah. Sorry." I could hardly talk.

She propped me up and keyed the door. It swung open. My next semi-conscious thought was the odd sensation of falling face first on my bed. A woman's face flashed before my eyes an instant before I lost consciousness, but it was not Kona's, it was Liliko's face.

I didn't feel Kona remove my boots or peel off my jeans, but both were on the floor at the foot of the bed when I came to eight hours later. I felt like a man recovering from a bout of paralysis. My joints hurt more than my muscles, and my head didn't so much throb as buzz.

I groaned, but it was more because I was dazed than hung over. "What the fuck?"

I rolled off the bed and had the presence of mind to see that I was alone. Thirst and dehydration drove me toward the bathroom. I turned on the water in the sink, cupped my hand, and drank. I traded my hand for a glass and drank some more. I splashed water on my face and couldn't bear to look at my reflection. Relying completely on a very limited supply of motor skills, I climbed under the inadequate spray of the shower. It was here that my first coherent thoughts began to coalesce. Kona. The bar. A couple beers. Falling off my barstool. What would the boys back in Chicago think?

"Oh, shit!" It suddenly hit me. Sweet little Kona had drugged me.

I jumped out of the shower and ran soaking wet into my room. I checked the pockets of my jeans, but my wallet wasn't there. Neither was my passport. The wallet I found on the floor next to my suitcase. A hundred and fifty dollars and two hundred-dollar-travelers checks were missing.

"Kona, you little bitch!"

I felt the blood rushing into my head and my fists balling up at my side. My first impulse was to punch something, anything. I settled for a litany of self-deprecating swear words. When I was done, I told myself to find the passport. I searched the room from top to bottom, knowing long before I had finished that she had taken that, too.

4

Yakuza

"A snake slipped away.
Only her eyes, having looked at me,
Remain in grass."
～ Kyoshi Takahama

I returned to the shower and stood under a cold spray for five minutes, composing myself, and running down the list of problems the woman named Kona had caused me. Money would have been a bigger issue had she found the rest of my traveler's checks. In that respect, I counted myself as fortunate. I would have to contact American Express to see how quick they would be in replacing checks stolen by a Malaysian hooker. The cash, all 20,000 yen of it, was history; not exactly pocket change for an exchange student on a shoestring budget. I could always hit up my dad if things got tight, but I had never done that in the past, and it wasn't likely I would start now.

My passport was another matter. I could not imagine spending eight hours at the American Embassy explaining my dilemma, but my options were limited. I needed a passport; I was a foreigner in a foreign country, and my Illinois driver's license would only get me so far.

So much for my personal tour, care of the most beautiful woman I was likely to meet in the next six months. Unfortunately, I had no way of contacting Liliko, which meant I would have to wait until she arrived and explain how stupid I had been. Maybe she would feel so incredibly sorry for me that she would offer to wait in line with me at the American

Embassy, offering solace and comfort for the awful reception I had received in her country. Sure thing, Kai. Count on it.

I dressed much as I had the previous night, less the cowboy boots. I went downstairs and reported the theft to the Hilton's Chief of Security. He and I talked with the day manager of the bar, and both promised to put the word out with their respective staffs.

"I would not hold my breath, if I were you, however," the manager said. "This Kona does not sound like one of our regular girls. They know better than to bite the hand that feeds them, if you get my drift."

"Then who was she? She said she was from Malaysia. Some village across the mountains from Kuala Lumpur," I said.

The two men looked at each other; I had obviously struck a cord. "Consider yourself lucky, kid," the security man said eventually. "But next time you have the urge to pay for it, stick with the local crop, if you want my advice."

I began to say, "But I didn't . . ." before coming to the stark realization that I was wasting my breath.

"We'll keep our eyes open," the manager said, and earned a sober nod from the Chief of Security. Security, my ass, I thought.

I hardly noticed the limousine parked out front of the hotel because the woman standing next to the door looked as if she had stepped out of a fashion magazine. Today, Liliko's torn jeans and Harvard sweatshirt had been replaced by a cashmere sweater and conservative black slacks. She looked ten years older, but no less sensational.

"Are you ready to play tourist?" she called to me. Her escorts wore the same black suits and watchful expressions as they had at the airport. If they were excited to see Liliko's American companion, I had to wonder what they looked like in the throes of a bad mood. Up close, they looked nothing short of dangerous.

"I've been looking forward to it since we said goodbye at the airport, but unfortunately, I have a problem with my passport."

Liliko didn't look disappointed; she looked concerned. "Come. Get inside. Tell me what happened." She saw me gazing at her escorts and laughed. She made a magnanimous gesture from one man to the next. "This is the Lone Ranger and his faithful companion, Tonto. Oh, wait. Or is it the other way around? I cannot remember. But my father will not let me go to the bathroom without them, much less a tour of the city."

The Lone Ranger and Tonto didn't seem to understand a word she said, but it was hard to miss her mocking tone. When we were safely inside and ensconced in black leather, the doors locked around us, and we set out. "First stop, Harajuku," Liliko said.

Then she grasped my hand the way a concerned lover might and turned her keen gaze my way. "So what is this about your passport?"

"It's embarrassing." I took a deep breath and forged ahead, sparing her none of the details: the bar, Kona, the proposition, the drugs, the theft, even my conversation with the Hilton Security Chief this morning. "Like I said, embarrassing."

Liliko was pragmatic. "A woman like that does not expect to be rejected, Kai-san."

"What can I say? She wasn't my type," I said with a well-intended touch of sarcasm.

Liliko smiled when she heard this. "Does that mean you prefer baggy sweatshirts and crooked baseball caps?"

"That and the kind of class and style it takes to wear baggy sweatshirts and crooked baseball caps," I told her.

The lines of Liliko's face twisted downward, and her gaze took her beyond the window of the car to the crowded sidewalks. "You said she mentioned Malaysia," she said without looking back. "Did she say where?"

"Yeah, she did. She said she was from Pahang Province. From a village east of Kuala Lumpur. I think she called it Karak."

"Karak." Liliko repeated the name, unconsciously correcting my pronunciation, but also hinting unintentionally of something beyond her familiarity with the name. What, I couldn't tell. Then she twisted away from the window, faced me again, and held my eye. "You also said she wore a tattoo. Can you describe it?"

I nodded. "It was like the vines of a plant climbing up her arm and lacing around her neck. It was blue with small red flowers. Why? What does that have to do with it?"

"Not everyone in Tokyo wears a tattoo, Kai-san. In fact, it is frowned upon in some circles. Actually, it is frowned upon in most circles." Liliko leaned forward and knocked on the glass that separated us from her escorts.

The center panel slid open, and Tonto, the one with the flowing black mane, peeked back at her. He bowed his head deferentially and said, "*Hai?*"

Liliko spoke to him in curt, rapid Japanese that I could not possibly follow, except for the emphasis that she placed on his real name: Muira-san. Muira, a.k.a. Tonto, responded with a series of grave nods and closed the panel again.

"He will make a call or two about your passport. Do not worry," was all Liliko said about their conversation. "And since we have the car for the entire day, we should enjoy the tour."

"*Arigato, Liliko-san.*" I was dying to ask her who Tonto was calling, but I didn't want to insult her. She was my host. She was offering to help when it would have been just as easy to drop me off at the American Embassy and wash her hands of the problem.

"*Douitashi mashite, Kai-san.*" She laid a hand on mine as we drove. We took the winding road around Harajuki Park, but there was no mention of leaving the car for a stroll through the gardens.

We crept along Takeshita-dori and in and among side roads lined with noodle stands and yakitori vendors. Record stores blasting the sound of a new wave of Japanese electronica disco music sprang up next to boutiques and costume shops. Liliko and I made fun of trendy teenagers weighted down with shopping bags and thirty-something women trying to look like trendy teenagers and failing miserably.

We wound our way through a sprawling garden anxious for a change in the seasons and under stone bridges that looked as if they had been carved from solid earth; Liliko didn't bother with their history, and I didn't ask.

Then, suddenly, she sat forward and nearly shouted. "Ah. The Sumida River. We should eat. Are you hungry?"

"Starving," I answered, but by then she was already banging on the privacy panel. When it opened, she pointed to the cruise boat docked by the river and rattled off an excited request that brought a scowl to Tonto's face. This was clearly not on the itinerary.

They pulled over reluctantly, and Liliko and I jumped out. She held my hand as we jogged toward the boat. We were the last ones aboard before the vessel nudged away from the dock and headed for the slow moving current at the center of the river. The boat turned out to be a floating diner with tables for two or four and striped tablecloths. Very quaint.

It was late afternoon, but we ordered rice balls, raw shrimp, vegetable tempura, and cold sake. "Late lunch," Liliko called it.

The limo, I noticed, matched our progress from the frontage road that curled along the shore. Nothing subtle about it. We were 40 minutes into our river ride and halfway through our meal when Liliko's pager buzzed. "We should get off at the next stop," she said after glancing at the number.

The privacy panel was already opened when Liliko and I settled back in the limo's leather seats.

"We found her," Tonto said calmly in heavily accented English, and then finished the sentence with rapid fire Japanese that I had no idea how to comprehend.

Liliko nodded, equally as calm. "Good."

When the panel was secure again, she translated the rest of Tonto's comments. "We found her. The girl. And your passport."

"You're kidding?" I realized I was more shocked than elated. And this time I couldn't resist asking, "How?"

"My father knows some people," was how she responded. And then, as if filling in all the missing pieces in this rather nebulous explanation, added, "He is very resourceful."

I could tell by the way the Lone Ranger was driving that our tour was officially a thing of the past. We headed west and then north through a sea of tenement houses built with only one architectural aim in mind: maximizing every square inch of physical space both up, out, and sideways. I couldn't imagine that rectangular structures had ever been erected with such efficiency. But unlike the areas in Chicago and New York where similarly constructed buildings sprang up, these were not slum neighborhoods populated by people who didn't give a damn about aesthetics. These were well-tended middle class neighborhoods populated by men and women—many single, but many not—who hoped very soon to be more than middle class.

The roads were spotless. The buildings glistened as much as apartment houses could. I saw men in overcoats and women in heels. I could feel their energy as much as I could sense their purposefulness.

Eventually, a sign written in Chinese characters hailed the onset of a commercial area called Ginza. An amalgamation of office towers, apartment houses, and retail shops gave the area a feeling of age and maturity I hadn't felt in Roppongi or Shinjuku. Liliko spent most of the journey on the limousine's phone talking in animated Japanese.

She hung up in time to say, "We are here."

"Here? Where?" I replied because the limo was still winding its way through crowded side streets.

"Ginza is an entertainment district that most tourists do not get a chance to see. And it is too bad. This is where the best jazz is played. It is where the best Japanese restaurants are," Liliko said and then, with a touch of cynicism, added, "Sorry, no McDonalds, Kai-san."

"I'm crushed," I said.

The neon lights were already starting to flicker as the setting sun eclipsed the horizon and hailed the onset of another Tokyo night. On one corner, two restaurants were already teeming with customers flanked by a dance club that wouldn't be full for another two or three hours. Halfway down the block, a shot-bar welcomed a group of businessmen who would probably spend most of the evening in the hostess club next door.

Across the street, a barker stood outside a porn theater while two young women adorned the window of a massage parlor. The next block was much the same, right down to the crowded sidewalks, the din of urban clamor, and the light show.

"So why are we here?" I decided to ask straight out. "Is this where your father found Kona?"

"She would not have entered Ginza on her own," Liliko assured me.

We rounded the corner onto Odakyu-dori. The narrow block, with old apartment houses forming canyon walls on either side of us, had a claustrophobic feel to it. Ground level, I saw a gallery, a French restaurant, a Turkish bath, and two massage parlors. Only in Tokyo, I was beginning to think.

The limo drew to a halt in a no parking zone outside a restaurant that I might have taken for unoccupied had there not been four men in pinstripe suits huddled at the entrance. Smoke spiraled from their cigarettes, and peels of laughter cracked the air even as they waved off two European-looking kids and stepped aside for two Japanese men dressed in dark suits with flowing hair and dark glasses.

One of the doormen acknowledged the limo's presence with the kind of nod that made me think we were expected, but he made no move to approach us.

I was just about to reach for the door handle when the privacy panel opened, and Tonto peeked back. He said, "I am coming back. He needs to know."

"Hai," Liliko replied. And then to me, she said, "Muiru-san is going to join us for a moment. Then we will go in."

"Okay. Great." I felt a tendril of unease creeping up my spine. I nodded toward the restaurant. "What's this place?"

"My father's club," was how she replied.

"Your father is in the restaurant business?"

"He is in many businesses, Kai. Be patient."

The back door opened and closed, and Tonto filled the cross-facing seat opposite us. He talked, and Liliko interpreted.

"If you want your passport back," she said, "You should know that it was not stolen by a common streetwalker."

"She certainly wasn't common, on that we agree," I said.

To Tonto, she said in Japanese, "Show him," and I actually understood her.

"Show me what?"

Tonto peeled off his jacket and then unbuttoned his shirt. He stripped it off. Every inch of his torso, arms, shoulders, and back were covered in brightly colored and remarkably detailed tattoos. A mural of turbulent seascapes, flying fish, and clawed eagles covered his chest and stomach. As he turned, showing me his back, the tattoo morphed into a sweep of mountains and fire breathing dragons.

"His legs are the same," Liliko told me.

"We are yakuza," Tonto said proudly.

I was still staring. "Yakuza? What is that?"

"In America, you would call it the Mafia," Liliko said simply. Then she said the word in precise syllables. "Ya-ku-za. Each sound represents a number: 8, 9, and 3. Together they equal 20. Twenty is the losing hand in Oicho-kabu, a card game much like your Blackjack."

"The losing hand? Why the losing hand?"

"*Yakuza* is derived from the phrase 'without worth in society.'" Liliko explained. "In the past, the *yakuza* were gamblers and street peddlers, renegades and roving bandits. Then they began serving the Shoguns, mostly in seeing that their will was done, by whatever means. Later, the *yakuza* began to control things like construction work and the docks, just like your mafia did in the early 20th century. Then came gambling, liquor, entertainment, and . . . and other things."

I knew my mouth was open and on the verge of saying something, but the words hadn't formulated yet. "Drugs," I finally managed to say. "And prostitution. Like Kona."

"In some cases. Depending on the clan."

"And your father . . .?"

"Yes. He is *yakuza*," Liliko answered. "He is the *Oyabun* of the Yamaguchi clan."

"*Oyabun?*"

"Father. He is also the *Kumicho*. Boss. Capo. As my grandfather was before him," she said rather casually. "His followers are called *kobun*. Which means 'child.' My father runs the clan and provides protection. They . . ." She looked at Tonto and the Lone Ranger as examples. "They are his legions. A *kobun* must be willing to give their life to protect the *oyabun*."

"The knife," Tonto said. He raised his left hand, and I noticed the severed pinky finger for the first time. He said, "*Yubitsome.*"

Liliko explained. "In the old days, a gambler who welched on a debt forfeited his little finger. Now, a disobedient *kobun* atones for his wrongdoing by presenting his oyabun with a gift."

"His finger?" I was shocked. "Jesus."

"He would give up much more than his finger for his clan, Kai-san," Liliko assured me. "They value nothing more than loyalty."

"And you? Your tattoo? Does that mean . . .?"

"I am my father's daughter. Nothing more. There are no women in the yakuza. At least, not officially."

"And Kona? Where does she fit into this?"

"She is the property of the Taoko clan." When Liliko said the word *Taoko*, Tonto clenched his teeth and then spit out the open window.

"Oh. The competition. I get it," I said.

Liliko shook her head. "No, the Tokyo clans are not at war. The Taoko clan's members are freelancers from Osaka. They bring women here from Thailand and Malaysia, promising them jobs, and then turning them into prostitutes. Kona is one of them. But the Toyko Hilton is Yamaguchi territory, and she was there without my father's permission. Now . . . well, we will see."

"Enough. We must go," Tonto said.

He buttoned his shirt, fixed his tie, and replaced his jacket. Then he knocked on the privacy panel and opened the door. The Lone Ranger met us on the walk, and we started toward the restaurant.

Our escorts nodded to the men at the entrance the way colleagues do, but Liliko ignored them. I was a head taller than even the tallest of them, but they didn't seem intimidated by my size. I also nodded, but it was the kind of gesture that said, *Yeah, I know I'm in your territory, and it's the last place on earth I want to be, believe me. I just came for my passport.*

Inside, a wide, brightly lit room rang with the incessant *whir* and *clang* of a busy Pachinko parlor and reminded me of a crowded casino floor in Vegas.

"Pachinko is our obsession," Liliko explained. A pachinko looked liked a slot machine that delivered tiny chrome balls through a vertical maze, part pinball machine, part one-armed bandit. The chatter of hundreds and hundreds of moving pachinko balls and the animated men and women playing them flooded the room and mixed with the soothing sounds of a talented jazz pianist who deserved a more respectful venue.

"Popular," I said.

"It creates a huge amount of cash flow and entertains our patrons," Liliko assured me.

For every man dressed in black, there was another strutting across the floor in pinstripes or sharkskin. They emerged from smoke-filled parlors where poker and *oicho-kabu* were the games of choice, and back rooms where drinking was the sole source of entertainment. And for every man, there was a woman making him feel important or desirable or both. They reminded me of well-placed flower arrangements, dressed in period pieces that brought to mind the Roaring Twenties, French *haut monde*, or the pomp of the current jet set crowd. Whatever the heart desired.

"We call them comfort women," Liliko explained. "They get paid to look good and listen as if the man footing the bill was the greatest orator on the planet."

It was not surprising that every eye in the club discreetly took note of my presence, the blue-eyed *gaijin*, and walking at the side of the *Oyabun's* daughter would probably keep them talking for most of the night.

Two men dressed head-to-foot in sharkskin were posted like sentries at the foot of a wide staircase, and their dour eyes watched us trundling in their direction. The pair inclined their heads to the Lone Ranger and Tonto as if they were longtime friends and then parted ways for Liliko and me. Our escorts followed, but now they kept a respectable distance.

"I will introduce you," Liliko said to me in a low voice. "Do not be surprised at what you see, Kai-san. Remember, *yakuza* has its own rules. And one of those rules has been violated. Justice in their eyes might not look like justice in yours."

That had an ominous sound to it that I tried not to think about as we moved from the head of the stairs into an open area that was part boardroom, part nightclub. Seven or eight tables were clustered beneath a string of elaborate chandeliers that sent a yellow glow over a gathering of eight men, all but one standing and very serious, and one woman, on her knees in the middle of what could have been a small dance floor. It was Kona. Even in this light, I could see how the seductive beauty she had so easily captured my imagination with last night had been replaced with a drawn and pasty pallor and tear-streaked mascara. Her hair had been cut and lay in a heap on the floor. Oh, my God! Was this really the same woman?

But it wasn't Kona who dominated every ounce of energy in the room; it was the man seated at a round table next to the room's cherry wood bar. He stood as we approached, taller and more angular than any of the others and elegant in a silk jacket the color of alabaster. Salt and pepper hair framed exaggerated cheekbones and eyes that were like impenetrable masks.

"My daughter," he called.

"Father." She bowed respectfully.

"Is this your friend?"

She nodded and said, "May I present Kai Waters from the United States. My father, *Oyabun* Ter Yamaguchi." And then she gestured to the man at the *Oyabun*'s right hand. "And this is my uncle, Kohji Yamaguchi. He is my father's senior advisor. His saiko komon."

"It's nice to meet you." I bowed deeply to both men.

"Is this the woman?" the *Oyabun* asked brusquely, his English rough but easily understood.

I looked down at Kona, heard a low, plaintive groan, and saw blood dripping from her bandaged left hand and pooling on the floor. *Yubitsume*, I thought. Oh, no! And then I saw the severed little finger lying on a bloodstained cloth at the center of the round table. Next to it sat my passport, two $100 traveler's checks, and a fan of paper bills that was almost certainly the 20,000 yen she had stolen from my wallet.

"Is this the woman?" he asked again.

I dragged my eyes away from the finger and the blood and forced myself to respond "*Hai . . .* yes."

"Very well." He trained his eyes on a man standing very much alone in the corner. I could see by his rumpled suit, bound hands, and haggard face that he was not part of the Yamaguchi clan. "Taoko."

"She is banished," the man whispered.

Liliko interpreted for my benefit. "That is Sakae Taoko, head of the Taoko clan and keeper of the woman who drugged you last night and stole from you."

I wanted to say, "I'm not sure the punishment fits the crime," but I was smart enough to understand that sarcasm had no place in this setting.

"My father wants you to understand that the woman forfeits her finger not for stealing from you," Liliko explained, "but for trespassing on Yamaguchi territory."

Oh! That makes much more sense, I thought in amazement. "I see."

She said, "The police would have dealt with her much more harshly, Kai-san. I assure you."

I finally swallowed my fear and said, "And her hair? Why cut her hair?"

"She cut her own hair," the *kumicho* of the Yamaguchi clan said. "Signifying her banishment and her exile."

I watched the tears roll down Kona's face. Behind the tears lay a confluence of emotions that surely included anger and resentment, but I also sensed fear. Banished, she was now completely alone, and I didn't imagine anyone in this room planned on helping her relocate back to her native Malaysia.

I looked at Taoko. "Why didn't you take his finger instead?" I asked.

"Kai!" Liliko said sharply.

This time her father interceded and said, "A fair question. But his punishment, I assure you, Mr. Waters, will be more far reaching."

He did not elaborate because, at that exact moment, Kona sprang from her knees with surprising agility, a wounded animal prepared to attack. I saw the knife materialize from under her shirt. It was shaped like a stiletto and glistened even as she raised it over her head, roared with anger, and dove toward *Oyabun* Yamaguchi. I heard Liliko scream and the *saiko komon* gasp.

I acted purely on instinct, springing forward and grabbing Kona's wrist a split second before the tip of the knife could pierce the *kumicho's* heart.

Kona's raging cry echoed in my ear as we tumbled to the floor. The blade impaled the bicep of my left arm, and something warm spilled over my skin. When it scored the humerus bone, I felt as if I had been shot and lost consciousness.

The last thing I heard was Liliko calling my name.

I was out for nearly nine hours and most of those were spent wandering through melting landscapes with rose-colored rivers and burning jungles populated by Minotaur and Harpies. I should have been at a Grateful Dead concert instead of in a drug-induced state.

My leg hurt worse than my shoulder when I came to, but all I could see were the wide, serene eyes of Liliko as she peered down at me from the side of the bed. That alone was worth the heroics.

"Hey," she whispered, and her scent transported me for a brief instance back to my induction into the Mile-High Club. "You are awake."

"How long have I been out?"

"All night. How do you feel?"

"Like I have been hit by a truck. But all I remember is Kona trying to stab your father."

I tried to lift my head off the pillow. The opulence of the room looked like something out of Hearst's Castle. "Where am I?"

"Your hotel. The Presidential Suite. At my father's request," she said.

"Tell him thank you."

"It is I who should be saying thank you," a voice said from the foot of the bed.

"Mr. Yamaguchi," I said. "How are you?"

He and Liliko's uncle stepped up to the side of the bed, and it was the *saiko komon* who said, "A man who saves the life of a *yakuza shatei*—a younger brother—wins the respect and protection of the entire clan. A man who saves the life of a *wakashu* or a *shataigashira*—a lieutenant or a street boss—is forever in the clan's debt."

"But a man who saves the life of the *kumicho*," *Oyabun* Yamaguchi said, "that man becomes part of the clan, honored, respected, and a party to all its privileges." He switched to Japanese and said, "You honored me, and now I honor you."

Liliko began to interpret. "He said, 'You honored me . . .'"

But she saw me nodding and allowed me to finish his words. "'And now I honor you.'"

Oyabun Yamaguchi invited his daughter to lift the sheet from my throbbing right leg, and when she did, I found myself staring open-mouthed at a tattoo that had been carved into the entire length of my leg as I lay sleeping. I was too shocked for words. I should have been impressed with the intricacy of the design: the Bengal tiger emerging from the heart of a black and gold yin-and-yang sign looked almost alive, and the Japanese *hiragana* that ran beneath it must have been the mark of the Yamaguchi clan.

"You are now an honored member of the yakuza," Liliko's father announced, and I could see them all awaiting my response.

My initial reaction was to scream, "Get that thing off my leg," but that passed quickly when I recognized the gravity of this honor.

Then something compelled me to extend my hand to the clan's

Oyabun and *Kumicho*. When he took it in his firm, sure grip, I said, "I'm honored, *Oyabun* Yamaguchi. *Arigato.*"

Here I was thanking a man for tattooing my leg totally and completely without my consent and expecting me to be thrilled with my honorary induction into the Japanese underworld. It was odd that the depth of his courtesy and honest gratitude made it acceptable. When I saw the warmth in Liliko's smile, I even felt slightly proud of this remarkable piece of art that someone had drawn on my skin in less than eight hours. "It's really amazing, isn't it?" I said to her.

"Almost as nice as mine," she teased, her words evoking our secret time together and making me wonder if it would ever happen again. All I could do was smile.

Then I looked at her father and his senior advisor. "I'll wear it proudly," I said, thinking: Wait until the gang back home sees this; I'll never be able to go to the swimming pool again.

The bedroom door swung open just then, and a man dressed in a three-piece suit marched in with a female assistant at his side.

"Ah, Doctor," *Kumicho* Yamaguchi said. "Let me introduce you to Mr. Kai Waters. Kai, this is Dr. Hideki Iwakabe, your surgeon and savior, and my good friend."

"And how is our patient?" the doctor asked me in perfect English.

"Good. Thanks to you," I said. "*Arigato.*"

"All in a day's work."

Perfect English and a bag full of clichés, I thought. "How bad was it?"

"It could have been far worse. Thank goodness the knife missed your artery. It was a clean wound and should heal quickly. Loss of blood was our biggest concern, but fortunately Miss Liliko acted quickly and did, if I may say so, an expert job of wrapping your wound." He gave the shoulder a satisfactory nod. "We will change the dressing before you leave for the countryside and pay you a visit in a week or so."

He turned my shoulder over to his assistant and then focused on my tattoo. "A work of art," he said and sprayed the whole of my thigh with an aerosol mist that killed the pain in a matter of seconds.

He left the spray, seven days worth of antibiotics, and a bottle of painkillers. Then he gave me my marching orders. "Spray the leg no more than three times a day and follow the instructions on the bottles," he said. "An infection is the last thing you need."

When my shoulder had been dressed anew, the doctor and his nurse took their leave.

"A warning to be heeded," the clan's senior advisor said to me as his boss and daughter prepared to leave. "The girl disappeared last night."

"Who did? Kona?"

"She eluded her escorts. She had the look of revenge in her eyes, as you saw for yourself," he said. "We will find her in due course, I am certain of that. But until we do, be wary on your travels."

Terrific, I thought. That's just what I need. "Thanks for the warning."

"My men will see you to the bus station when the time comes," Oyabun Yamaguchi said to me. He offered me a deep bow, and I did my best to return it. "You are family. Stay well."

"Stay well, Oyabun," I replied. "Arigato."

Liliko was the last to leave. She perched on the side of my bed. I could see in her eyes that we were not to see each other again.

"Kai-san. You are family now," she said. "Which means . . ."

"Liliko." I took her hands in mine. "I know what it means. I don't like it, but I understand."

"I will not forget you."

"I will not forget you." Truer words, I thought, had never been spoken. "Stay well."

5

Journey to Fujinomiya

"The wind from Mount Fuji,
It called me from afar.
Here, a souvenir from Edo."
~ Basho Matsuo

A s I stood outside the Hilton Hotel, backpack slung over my good shoulder and suitcases at my feet, I asked myself if I had ever spent a more disastrous three days. Edo, as Tokyo was called in the days of Shoguns and Samurai, had thoroughly humbled this upstart graduate student. I doubted any one foreigner had ever fumbled his way through as many cultural mishaps as I had, but I also had to credit myself for at least stepping up to the plate and taking everything the Edoka could throw at me. It was a small consolation.

I had stepped off the plane with two years of what I called intense Japanese language training only to discover that my verbal skills would just about qualify me for the first grade. My listening skills may have been even more inept; I had to admit that the subtleties of Japanese speech left me floundering. I wondered whether that was a comment on my study habits or a black mark on the American educational process. It was probably some of both, I decided. Worse yet were my bumbling ways and behavioral miscues. Inexcusable. Why? Not because it didn't happen to travelers worldwide. It did. But I wasn't a tourist. I was a student and, as a student, I had failed in my research.

I gave myself a "C" only because my intentions were good and because I didn't lack for effort. But a "C" wouldn't do once I reached the Japan Institute of International Studies in Fujinomiya. According to my itinerary, I would be meeting seven other graduate students at the station—three American, two Canadian, and two French—and I spent a quick moment wondering if Tokyo had left them as perplexed and puzzled as it had me.

It was a safe bet, I decided, that none of the seven would arrive on campus as an honorary member of the Japanese *yakuza*. I doubted seriously that any of them could match the tattoo I now carried as a permanent memento on my right thigh. They probably hadn't been drugged, robbed, and humiliated by a woman who was now roaming around Tokyo without her little finger and most of her hair missing, a woman now banished from the clan that had turned her from a village girl in Malaysia to a street walker selling herself to affluent Japanese businessmen.

The Yamaguchi clan's senior advisor had suggested strongly that I keep a sharp eye out for Kona, as if she might be lurking in a doorway ready to pounce on me and recover her honor. I wasn't worried. If I felt anything for her, it was pity. What was she supposed to do now? The minute a potential employer caught sight of her missing finger, they would know she had been branded and banished by the *yakuza*, and they would no more hire her than fly to the moon.

The limousine driven by the Lone Ranger pulled up in front of me, and Tonto jumped out. He wasn't happy when I told him I planned on walking the five blocks to the bus station. I was determined to navigate those blocks without the aid of my street map, a last ditch effort to salvage a shred of dignity. I told myself to put the past three days into a compartment in the back of my mind labeled To Be Examined Later. You have six months to right the ship, I thought. Go out and do it.

Tonto stored my suitcases in the back of the limo, said a word or two to the Lone Ranger, and fell in directly behind me. We didn't talk. We walked. Tonto was exactly one step behind me. As the blocks fell away, a sense of anticipation gathered in the pit of my stomach. Nervous? Yes. Excited? Absolutely.

The stab wound on my left shoulder ached by the time we rounded the corner onto Imagu-dori, and I wished now that I had taken another pain pill before checking out of my hotel. The bus station stretched from one end of the block to the other, a hub of transportation that was no less busy than the trains or the subway. There was another prevailing feature that struck my fancy: a total lack of chaos. I loved that about the Japanese, more than likely because attention to detail was one of my own obsessions.

Finding the right bus was easier than it might have been because a huge placard was taped to the side of one bus proclaiming in red, white, and blue: *Students of Japan Institute of International Studies—Welcome to Japan.* I caught sight of four other *gaijins* huddled in front of the vehicle's luggage bay and realized this was the largest gathering of non-Asians I had seen in the last 72 hours.

The limo pulled up at the corner. Tonto gathered up my suitcases. He set out in the direction of the bus. I glanced into the front seat of the limo and said, *"Arigato,"* to the Lone Ranger. "If we meet again, it'll be too soon," I thought. But for some reason, I didn't feel I had seen the last of my dedicated escorts.

I hadn't taken three steps before colliding head-on with a woman who seemed as absorbed with her surroundings as I was. She was navigating a cart topped with five suitcases, bursting at the seams. I was busy trying to put names to the group standing next to the bus. It was a disaster waiting to happen. She gasped and I laughed.

"My fault," I said, reaching out to steady her rather precarious load. "Are you alright?"

Now she laughed, and when she did, the radiance in her smile was like a rush of fresh air. "I'm fine. Clumsy."

I looked at her luggage cart. "But well prepared," I teased.

"I know what you're thinking: enough for a lifetime." Long, dark curls framed an oval face and eyes the color of emeralds. She was captivating. She also wore a wedding ring and I had wondered how a woman her age could manage six months away from her husband. "Are you one of the grad students headed for Fujinomiya?"

"I am. I'm Kai Waters."

"Sandy Hall. I'm from San Francisco."

"A California girl." I held out my hand. "Chicago, by way of the University of Iowa."

"A Hawkeye. I'll try not to hold that against you."

There was that smile again. Wait until our Japanese cohorts get a look at this girl, I thought. They will not be able to contain themselves. Maybe that explained the wedding ring. I said, "I'll give you a hand."

"Thanks. You're a lifesaver."

By the time Sandy Hall and I had worked our way through the crowd to our bus, Tonto had stored my suitcases in the luggage bin. He gave me a discreet nod and started back toward the limo. I returned his nod with a slight nod and gave thanks for the chance to be just a student again.

The group of four I had seen moments ago at the luggage bay had dwindled to two, a guy and a girl. He smiled, but it was the kind of high-minded smile that inevitably led to sarcasm. His first words confirmed my suspicions.

"Ah, stragglers! Must be American," he said to us with a well-qualified hint of mockery and a distinctively French accent. "Late and over-packed. How predictable."

"Is that your way of saying hello?" Sandy asked, before I could tell the guy to go to hell. "We may have to work on your manners."

"Don't mind him," his companion said with far less attitude but a similar accent. "I'm Mavis Jourdan. He's Pierre Trepanier. He has a superiority complex that's not to be taken too seriously."

"Unless you'd like to learn how the world turns in three easy lessons." Pierre grinned.

My, my, my! An elitist with a fuck you attitude, I thought. Pierre had the lofty air of one to whom things always come easily: girls, money, and position. Manners, as Sandy noted, obviously had not been part of the package. I asked myself if it was possible to hate someone after only thirty seconds. I guess so, I thought.

I offered Pierre a dismissive glance and took hold of Mavis's outstretched hand. "Nice to meet you, Mavis," I said. "I'm Kai Waters, from Chicago, Illinois."

"So that's where that twang comes from," she teased.

If Mavis was French, she was also blessed with a healthy dose of Asian blood. Her Eurasian features were drop-dead gorgeous. Her skin was porcelain and her dark eyes were tinged with golden flecks. If first impressions meant anything, she was as unpretentious as Pierre was insufferable. Before the insufferable one could get in another word, I stowed my gear and climbed aboard.

The blonde sitting in the first seat was petite and brimming with southern hospitality. "Hello. I'm Darlene Tucker." If I had to guess, her accent was either Texan or Louisianan and very easy on the ears.

"Kai Waters." Sandy, Mavis, and Darlene. Three very different women in a span of ten minutes. This was getting better all the time. "Where are you from, Darlene?"

"Texas, silly. Where else? Dallas, Texas." Spoken with pride.

"That was going to be my first guess," I said and took the seat opposite her. "Your first time in Japan?"

"Japan, yes; Asia, no. I've been to Malaysia and Thailand a couple of times and most the rest of the world at least once. Guess that's how you get to be fluent in five languages. I'm going for my sixth here."

"A world traveler. I'm impressed."

"It's no big deal, really," she said, though everything about her said it was. "I'm an ice skater, semi-pro. It's like having a free ticket to see the world. And my parents love to travel, so it's great. This is my first time abroad without them. Don't know how that's going to be."

An ice skater, a linguist, and a Texan to boot. I studied Darlene's Cardin outfit and Louis Vuitton luggage, estimating that the two together carried a value just slightly less than my parents' house back in Deerfield.

My first impression of Darlene may have included words like loud, brash and presumptuous, but, for all that, she still struck me as an interesting study. I told myself not to judge too quickly. In fact, compared to Pierre, the fucking Frenchman, she was a walking, talking treasure.

"I think I'll introduce myself to our friends in the back," I said, gesturing to the couple in the rear of the bus.

"They're Canadian," Darlene said, as if I should prepare myself for a mild disappointment.

It took less than two minutes to realize how wrong Darlene was about the pair. Michael Frenette, an Ontario native, was a tall, strapping guy with an equine face, a toothy smile, and Dumbo ears. His handshake won me over first thing. "Judge a man by the grit in his grip," my dad liked to say, "and you'll rarely judge him poorly." The quiet confidence in his deep-set eyes added to his appeal. He called himself "an aspiring diplomat" and plainly had the wry sense of humor to sustain him in that field. He ended every other sentence with the Canadian version of "Ay," as in, "Where you from, Kai? Ay?"

The other Canadian was stunningly beautiful and introduced herself with a warm smile that could heat up the coldest Canadian winter night. She shook my hand with a deep sensuality as her fingers curled around mine and said, "I am Sherri Samstone, a Canadian Viking looking for my next adventure and new lands to conquer!"

At first, I wondered whether Michael and Sherri were a couple, the way she smiled every time an "Ay" came out of his mouth. But I soon realized that she was from Quebec and because there was no resemblance between her near-Midwestern accent and Michael's Ontario plunk, she was simply enjoying the sound.

Sherri was a Scandinavian beauty. She had little-girl features, an innocent smile, and flyaway blonde hair that was closer to white than gold.

"A throwback to a Norwegian heritage that my family can trace back to the Vikings," she said, with considerable pride. Despite Sherri's little-girl allure, there was a seductive air to her, and the red bra peeking through her sheer blouse made an unmistakable statement. At least it made an unmistakable statement in the eyes of Kai Waters and his 23-year-old hormones.

"I think we're in for a good six months," I said, making certain I included Michael in this far-reaching pronouncement.

"As long as school doesn't get in the way," Sherri said with a laugh.

"Can't let that happen," I said.

I saw our driver board the bus and heard the door swing shut. The engine rumbled to life. It must be 9:30, I thought. It had to be. We were in Japan, and our itinerary called for a 9:30 a.m. departure. I glanced at my watch. Yep, 9:30 exactly! I was already taking the precision and punctuality of the Japanese for granted, but not without considerable admiration.

Something compelled me to glance toward the street again; the limo hadn't budged. "I'm fine, boys," I wanted to shout. "You can go back to doing whatever it is you did before I saved the life of your boss." Teach me to be heroic, I thought.

I settled into the seat in front of Sherri and Michael and was pleased when Sandy Hall joined us.

"We're still one short," she said as the bus began to inch forward.

"No, we're not," Michael replied. He pointed out the window.

A last minute arrival—not surprisingly, the fourth American—was racing alongside the moving bus and calling out to our driver, "Got room for one more?"

He was laughing and seemed unembarrassed about putting our departure a full thirty seconds behind schedule. The driver glanced at his side mirror and brought the bus to a halt. The front door slid open. The straggler clamored aboard, a little winded, but full of enthusiasm.

"*Arigato. Omatase,*" he said. *Thank you for waiting.* It may have been the most common of phrases, but it demonstrated a fluency in Japanese far superior to mine in terms of pronunciation and diction.

He carried himself like an athlete. Striding toward the back of the bus with his bags in tow, he said, "Hello," to Darlene, held Mavis's eye just a split second longer than casual contact dictated, and ignored the look of disgust that Pierre projected his way.

"Hi. I'm Mitch Palmer," the new arrival said, glancing from Sandy to me and dropping into the row ahead of us. "Sorry I'm late. Buses don't run on time in San Diego and I was hoping the same could be said for Tokyo. I should've known better."

"San Diego. So that explains your tan," Sandy said with a quick smile. "We don't see enough of the sun in San Francisco to look like that."

"Looking like that," I thought, probably also referred to Mitch's model good looks and an easy smile that suggested he knew as much. He had a healthy ego, but not a fucking-Frenchman attitude. This was the kind of ego I could live with.

"Actually, the tan has more to do with volleyball," Mitch admitted. "I've been on the pro circuit for two years."

"So why in the world would you be taking six months off from that to take graduate courses in the Japanese countryside?" Sherri couldn't help asking. I was curious, myself, now that I thought about it.

"Because pro volleyball might get you a nice tan, but it doesn't go very far toward paying the bills," Mitch explained.

"That's the perpetual dilemma," I heard Michael Frenette say from the seat behind me. "I say we find out how the Japanese handle it. Ay?"

"Ay!" Sherri and I said at the exact same moment, and even Michael burst out laughing.

I was impressed with how easily the five of us had bridged the gap between total strangers and comrades in arms. It reminded me of how reliant we were on the spoken word. Without words, we were left with intuition and observation, and the western mind was not nearly as adept at those skills as we were with our limited vocabularies.

I had come to Japan intent on mastering a new spoken language. But, as our bus pulled out of the station, fought through one lane after another of crowded traffic, and inched toward the expressway, it occurred to me that I should broaden my goals to include communication on several levels. If I could learn to observe without preconceived expectations and if I could learn to reach out with more subtle tools than the spoken word—tools of the heart and soul, for example—there just might be layers of growth here in Japan well beyond those definable by the classroom. Was it a lofty goal? Perhaps. Was it one worth reaching for? Why in the world not?

We were told to expect a three-hour journey to Fujinomiya and the campus that lay at the foot of Mount Fuji, and the better part of those hours would clearly be spent winding our way through Tokyo's concrete jungle. True to form, traffic dictated a snail's pace that allowed me another view of the city. Gray skies and black thunderheads painted the concrete and glass with hues even more subdued than the previous three days. The city was a churning machine pushed on by mass transit. Masses of humanity fell away, minute by minute, mile after mile, until the palette of rural Japan turned the urban gray and black into blues and greens. There was a palpable lifting of urban weight as we penetrated rural Japan. High rises and factories, warehouses and tenements all abdicated to rice paddies, sugar beet fields, and poultry farms. It was a progression that gave me new perspective on Japan and a sense of communion I would never have anticipated, as if things here were not so different from home. Working the land was as universal as the need for sustenance.

I glanced out the back window of the bus on two occasions, but my good friends Tonto and the Lone Ranger were nowhere to be seen. Apparently, we were beyond the borders of the Yamaguchi clan's influence. I was on my own. Good, I thought.

We entered Kanagawa Prefecture south and west of Tokyo and were confronted with rugged, deeply cleft hills, patches of fir and pine, and a sense of rural calm.

Mavis left her seat at the front of the bus. A woman of poise and culture, I imagined she needed a break from the likes of her French companion. She made her way down the aisle toward an obviously superior crowd at the rear of the bus. Extending her hand to Mitch, she introduced herself and held his gaze well beyond that expected of two graduate students compelled only by learning. I may have been a naïve Midwesterner with minimal life experience, but even I could see the instantaneous chemistry. Well, I thought, good for them.

"Mavis is a European name, isn't it?" Mitch asked. "But you obviously have roots elsewhere, as well. Not to be too forward."

"He means your Asian heritage, I think," Sandy teased.

"He means he can't help staring, but that it's your fault for looking as good as you do," Sherri said, picking up where Sandy left off. "And he'll probably let go of your hand about the time we get to Fujinomiya."

"Oh, yeah. Sorry," Mitch said, releasing Mavis's hand and grinning sheepishly. He and I shared a look of complete understanding. "But Sherri is right. I was staring, and it is all your fault."

Sherri caught Mavis's eye. "I think that was a compliment."

Mavis rescued him. "My mother is Chinese. She's from Yichang, on the banks of the Yangtze River. Unfortunately, I don't know much about it. We've never had the chance to visit. But I'd like to someday."

"You'll love it," Mitch said. "I've been there, and it's beautiful."

"You've been to China?" Mavis could not believe her ears. I think we were all a little shocked. "How? Why?"

"I was raised in the Methodist church. I traveled with my parents to the Hunan province as part of their missionary work. Changsha, the capital, is only a hundred miles from the Yangtze. I was eighteen when I went back as a missionary myself, and we used the river to travel into the countryside."

If Mavis and Mitch had demonstrated a physical attraction for one another, this revelation cemented a connection that struck me as having long-term potential. When Mavis asked, "What was it like?" Mitch couldn't have refused her in a million years.

He began with his first impressions of China as a boy, then launched into a series of colorful vignettes that were more than just entertaining. With each story, it became ever more obvious just how dedicated Mitch had been to his missionary work and how close he had become to the Chinese people. I listened with one ear while absorbing the passing beauty of our host nation.

Our journey was exactly an hour and a half old when our bus driver left the highway for a rest stop that was clearly noted on our itinerary. No improvisation here, I thought. 11:00 a.m., Expressway Rest Stop # 26. Ten minutes. It was right there in black and white.

All eight of us stepped off the bus and I had the utmost faith that our ten minutes began at that exact moment. I looked for the usual designations for restrooms separated by gender, but found nothing of the kind. Heedless to the ramifications of this obvious oversight, I walked into a cavernous room lined with ceramic holes exactly like the one I had left behind at the Tokyo Hilton. There were no private stalls, no privacy walls, and no accommodation for gender, age, or modesty. Men, women, and children, old and young, were attending to their business without concern or embarrassment. Drop your drawers, pee, wipe, and go about your travels. The only embarrassed guy in the place was *moi*. And *moi* decided he could wait until he got to his dormitory in Fujinomiya.

We set out again at 11:10 precisely.

Rural Japan spread through narrow valleys, over stark terrain, and through dense forests, everything a nature lover could want. Looming on the horizon and filling the front window of our bus stood the snow-capped cone of Mount Fuji. It was impressive, and growing ever more impressive the closer we got.

The road followed a rolling stream, past a lake of brilliant blues that reminded me of home. I had been too consumed with simply surviving the Tokyo experience to feel homesick, but this wasn't longing I was feeling; it was the pleasant warmth of knowing that home was a mooring I could always attach to when a bout of homesickness struck.

Beyond the lake, rice paddies cut in perfect geometric shapes surrounded a village nestled at the base of low rising hills. A man guiding his ox and plow through the fields stopped and studied our passing. Maybe we were a sight rare enough to warrant a short break. Two women with bamboo bonnets looked up from their work. One of them graced us with a wide smile and waved. We all waved in return.

Our bus swept past stone farmhouses and a sight uncommon to our trip thus far: dairy cows. Now I did feel right at home. A stone bridge with three rounded arches, probably older than any bridge in America, spanned a river running high on its banks.

Thatched roofed houses with square gardens and stone retaining walls signaled our entrance into Fujinomiya. The town was not as small as I had imagined it. A pagoda with three perfectly symmetrical roofs rose above the town square, a ringed corona marking its highest point, typical of Buddhist architecture. The Shinto shrine was more difficult to spot with its simple one-story construction and cradled roofline. Like the steepled churches of small towns across America, there was an energy marking both the temple and the shrine that struck me as central to the simplicity of life the town projected. I wondered if it was true or just my fanciful side hoping it was true.

A sign of the times, however, was the Toyota plant south of the town and across the river. It struck me that this factory was probably as central to the life of Fujinomiya's people as the temple or the shrine, and maybe more so. Who knew how many of the townspeople they employed?

A road took us past hillsides dedicated to rice paddies waiting for spring to arrive and into the mountains, carving a nomadic path through a magnificent pine forest that looked as if it had been tended by a team of constant gardeners. We burst through the trees into a tastefully landscaped clearing so close to Mount Fuji that it looked as if you could walk out the door and make snowballs on its summit.

The campus of the Japan Institute of International Studies, JIIS, sat at the back of the clearing. It was comprised of simple rectangular buildings that could have been lifted from any liberal arts college built in the 1950s. The rectangles were two stories high with narrow balconies fronting the dormitories and small square windows peeking out from the classrooms.

Bridging these was a low-lying building I guessed to be the dining hall.

As the bus pulled into the parking lot, I was amazed by how small the entire facility was. I was also struck by how serene it seemed to be, surrounded on three sides by spectacular pines and sentineled by the ancient mountain, towering in the background. The serenity, however, was shaken at its core the minute we came to a halt at the entrance. A rousing cheer rose up from a group of fifty or so Japanese men, some in suits, some bundled in heavy jackets, but all seemingly pleased by our arrival. I took in their faces and estimated the range of their ages to be between twenty-two and thirty. At first glance, it was a good mix.

I saw four or five women, but they all seemed part of a separate group, probably faculty and administration. I did some quick addition: fifty plus guys and maybe ten women. Interesting. Maybe, I thought, the town of Fujinomiya would be swarming with available girls. Forty years ago, these people were our mortal enemies. Today we were wayfarers traveling a similar path toward . . . toward what? Understanding, I supposed. In any case, here was my new home for six months. And here were the people who would populate my world.

I was excited and I was sure a certain amount of my enthusiasm resulted from the genuine elation our arrival was generating. Sure, it was probably due in part to the curiosity factor, but my curiosity was piqued, as well. Let the games begin.

The school's Dean, Dr. Masami, was the first to greet us as we disembarked. A spry, gray-headed gnome of a man, his stature was diminutive even among Japanese.

"Welcome! Welcome to the Japan Institute of International Studies," he said in broken English. And then he tried it in French for the sake of Mavis and Pierre. She giggled. The Frenchman rolled his eyes. Then the Dean said, "We are honored," in Japanese.

I was all smiles as the staff introduced themselves. Two, a man and a woman, spoke English as if they had lived in the States their entire lives.

"I am Neko Katayama," the woman said in English so flawless it sounded almost musical.

I'm sure I must have looked a bit like a 14-year-old with his mouth hanging open, but everything about Neko Katayama was flawless, from the waves of silky black hair that tumbled down her back to the magnificent curves that came to life beneath her tailored business suit. I took her hand. Her grip was warm and self-assured.

"Welcome Waters-san."

"Thank you. Neko-chun? Is that correct?"

"Katayama Sensei will do fine," she said, meaning Professor Katayama. "See you in language studies class."

"I'll be ready," I assured her. And indeed I would.

The student administrator pinned a nametag on my chest and called out my name to my classmates. "Waters-san."

Five men, presumably my roommates, descended on me. A round of handshaking and backslapping eased whatever anxiety may have been lingering, and I felt a sense of camaraderie I wasn't absolutely certain I would find. Every new situation had elements of uncertainty to it. I knew that. Even the most confident person could not predict the ebb and flow of events yet to come, and every person added to or subtracted from the human equation tipped the scale of those events in one way or another. That was life. That was the fodder of adventure. Five roommates who had almost nothing in common with an American from Illinois drew me further into the adventure.

So far, so good, I thought.

———

Mount Fuji Football

"What luck!
The southern valley
Makes snow fragrant."
~ Basho Matsuo

My new roommates led me away from the bus with my suitcases in tow. Thank goodness. One suitcase I could have handled, but I knew my left arm was not quite up to the task of heavy lifting yet.

The dorm was a two story, flat-roofed affair beyond a stretch of green grass. It was neatly appointed with raised gardens and concrete walks. Neat was the operative word.

I tried to get their names straight. Yasuhiko Takeda struck me as the oldest of the group, probably because he took the conversational lead and made two of his brethren carry my bags.

I felt pretty sure I would remember Karushi Suzuki's name because of the motorcycles bearing the same name and because of the perpetual cigarette in his mouth. Suzuki did not offer his assistance and chuckled when Takeda suggested it. So much for seniority.

Masato Kudoh was built like a middle linebacker, a short middle linebacker, and had the smile of a mischievous alley cat. I liked him immediately.

The tiny man who led the way into the dorm introduced himself as Tatsuo Ikeda. If I had been forced to guess Ikeda's age, I would have said sixteen and not a day more.

Last was Homare Moto. There was about him an unmistakable energy, or at least his electric smile conveyed a sense of excitement that
appeared just a little forced, as if he genuinely desired me to feel wanted.
Moto opened the door to our sparsely furnished dorm room and said in
his best English, "Home sweet home. Welcome, Waters-san."

My roommates, I noticed, had wasted no time decorating the walls of
our common area with posters of naked Japanese women. Okay, then, I
thought. They're human. Excellent.

"Come," Moto said, leading me down a narrow hall with three bed-
rooms the size of walk-in closets on each side of the hall. In the first, I
caught a glimpse of one small cot, one four-drawer dresser, and several
unopened suitcases. My host pushed open the door of Room #4 and a
piece of Japanese trivia popped into my mind. The number four represented death in Japan and was a number to be avoided at all cost. No
wonder there was only one cot in this room and a small closet. And no
wonder it was I, the American *gaijin*, who was being asked to live with
5,000 years of superstition and mythology.

Moto entered only long enough to drop my suitcases on the cot and
then waited for me in the hall. I took a paper bag from my backpack and
stopped at the door. I pointed to the room number. "Four," I said in
Japanese. "Bad luck."

"No, no," Moto assured me. His electric smile now had a nervous
twitch to it. "Only a Japanese wives' tale."

I nodded. Sure thing. "Very good," I said without much conviction but
sensing a sincerity in Moto that made his disclaimer less disturbing. I gave
him a friendly pat on the back and then pointed to the door at the end of
the hall. "Bathroom?"

"Ah, yes. Bathroom," he responded in English.

I used a nod and a wave of the hand to indicate my rather urgent need
for a pit stop and then closed the bathroom door behind me. Hallelujah!
The bathroom may not have been built for 6'2" Americans, but it was
equipped with two bona fide American toilets. Maybe the Japanese were

evolving or maybe they were realizing how spoiled we Americans were. Either way, I was ecstatic. A shower stall and a Japanese-style soaking tub were fast making this my favorite room in the dorm.

When my business was finished, I rejoined my roommates in the common area. A flood of Japanese conversation came to a sudden halt, and they all switched to broken, determined English.

"Why don't we speak Japanese," I suggested, my first attempt at convincing them that my priority was mastering their language, not teaching them English, heaven forbid. "Please, Japanese."

Kudoh, the middle linebacker, shook his head as if to say that the use of Japanese was neither necessary nor polite. "We learn English. English will make our companies proud, very proud."

Yeah, well, learning Japanese will make my parents proud, I wanted to say, and a little less demonstrative about the coin these six months are costing. In Japanese, I said, *"Nantokashimasu,"* or something approximating *we'll figure it out.*

When they laughed at this, I wondered how close I had come to making my point. Instead of worrying about it, I joined them at the rectangular table that I imagined was to be the site of many gatherings. With the young ladies on the wall looking down on us, I opened the paper bag in my hand, extracted five individually wrapped packages, and passed them out. This, I had learned, was a Japanese tradition. A gift for the host—in this case, five hosts—was a matter of honor and respect. Even Suzuki put down his cigarette long enough to rip open the package, a ritual they all clearly relished. I had collected some of Motown's most memorable songs and recorded them on cassette tapes: Sam Cooke, the Temptations, Smoky Robinson, Marvin Gaye.

"Motown. Rhythm and blues," I said in English. In Japanese, I said, *"Kayoukyoku."* Dance music.

"Ah! Rock 'n Roll," Ikeda said. He jumped up and headed for his bedroom. "Elvis."

I shook my head. "Not Elvis. But good," I called.

I listened to myself talking and realized I sounded like a cartoon. Talk in whole sentences, I told myself. A few mistakes won't hurt.

Ikeda returned with a bulky black boom box, perched it on the edge of an empty bookcase, and plugged it in. I waited to see how they would react to Wilson Pickett singing "In the Midnight Hour" and was not disappointed. Kudoh clamored to his feet and began a series of gyrations that might have resembled dancing in a colony of giants. Ikeda knew the song by heart even if he did not understand the words. Takeda, a string bean who towered over his comrades and was still three inches shorter than me, pushed his wire-rimmed glasses up his nose and drummed the tabletop. Moto took in the scene with wide eyes and a look of bemusement. Suzuki smiled out the side of his mouth and smoked.

I caught his eye. I tried to say, "Are you with the Suzuki Company? The one that makes the motorcycles?"

"Oh, big time Suzuki, big time," Takeda teased. He went on to explain that Kazushi Suzuki was the eldest son and heir apparent to the company of the same name and a dominant player in the Japanese car and motorcycle industry. "Famous playboy, our Suzuki-san is, famous playboy."

Suzuki did not protest Takeda's claim nor was he embarrassed by it. He had the looks and he obviously had the money.

"Did you see his sports car in the parking lot?" Moto teased. "Super fine sports car, one of a kind."

"I will take you for a ride sometime," Suzuki said in lazy, broken English.

I said, "*Arigato,*" and then asked if his company had sent him here to study or if it had been his choice. The question elicited a sneer.

"A waste of time. Six months of partying," he said.

"Suzuki-san is not much interested in the U.S. He does not think you have much to teach us," Takeda said. "Not me. I work for Mitsubishi. I want to know everything about your country and its consumers. Who they are, what they buy, everything."

That was a tall order for a sheltered Midwesterner, but I found

Takeda's thirst for knowledge similar to my own and saw a chance for a reciprocal relationship. "I'll do my best," I said, and then looked Ikeda's way. "And you, Ikeda-san? Are you a student of international business, as well?"

"International politics," he corrected. "My father is Shadeki Ikeda. He is the ranking member of the House of Councilors from the Kochi Prefecture. I graduated from Tokyo University a year early and now I am a year into graduate school."

I was impressed. I wanted to say, "How in the hell old are you?" but I didn't.

"You will teach me about Western democracy, yes?" Ikeda said. "And all about Elvis."

I didn't tell Ikeda that I preferred the Beatles to Elvis, but I felt comfortable discussing politics. And now that I thought about it, I looked forward to it. Who better to learn from than the progeny of a big-wig politician?

"Excellent," I said, and Ikeda replied with a grateful bow.

Then he said, "If you want an insider's look at industrial Japan, Waters-san, better to talk to Kudoh-san than our man from Suzuki. He is an engineer at Toyota and a little more interested in the Japan-America dynamic. No offense to our famous playboy," he said with a grin.

Suzuki blew smoke toward the ceiling and laughed. "My recommendation exactly."

"Toyota," I said with an admiring tone to the barrel-chested Kudoh. He looked like a bear completely at ease with himself and his place in the world. I wondered how true that impression was. His easy smile was a much needed counterpart to Takeda's emotionless face and Suzuki's cool aloofness. It occurred to me how much more advanced these gentlemen were in the ways of the business world than I was at this point in my life. What a boon it would be to my learning curve if I could just figure out how to tap into their experience. In Kudoh's case, I chose an end-around approach that might tap into his apparent interest in bodybuilding.

I raised my right arm as if I was pressing a barbell and said, "Do they have a gym or a weight room here on campus by any chance?"

Kudoh flashed a delighted smile when the gist of my question became clear to him. He imitated my bench press and said, "A weightlifter. Very good! We can lift together. Maybe tomorrow. You and me."

This was almost too good to be true, having a workout partner in the same dorm room. Sure, I would have to adjust my routine to accommodate my damaged left arm, but I wasn't going to let myself go into physical remission just because of a little stab wound.

I nodded and said, "*Ashita! Yoidesu-ne!*" *Tomorrow. Very good!*

Then I let my smile take me to the last member of our household and clearly the most enigmatic of the five, simply because reading Moto was a challenge. My expectations for a good relationship were high, however, simply because of the positive energy he exuded.

"*Dochira Kara, Moto-san?*" I asked, remembering at least one complete sentence in the native language. *Where are you from, Moto?*

"Ah!" he replied as if I had actually made my point. He switched to English and effectively killed my momentum. "My hometown is Kyoto."

"In southern Japan, your nation's first capital," I said. Now you're just showing off, I thought lamely.

"Home of the Sony Corporation. My employer."

"The company's rising star," Kudoh said with a wink. "Big time marketing executive."

"No, no," Moto said as if he had been insulted. "I have much to learn, much to learn."

"Me, too," I said. Interestingly, Kudoh and Moto conveyed warmth that the other three seemed unwilling or were uninterested in projecting. I knew from all I had read about Japan that it was a big step for her people to accept a foreigner as anything more than a useful object. True friendship might be a lofty goal to pursue with these two, but I could already see us developing as positive and even productive roommates.

The best I could hope for from Suzuki was probably indifference, though he might loosen up after a few beers. That I could see happening. Ikeda, on the other hand, seemed to study me as if I were a lab rat. Okay, I could handle that. I might use him in a similar fashion. Takeda seemed to view me the way a student looked at a final exam: I was a necessary evil. His company had sent him here to extract what he could from the setting, and I was part of the setting. That was fine, too. If I left Japan with a couple of lasting relationships and a different view of the world, I would consider the semester a success. I would be a better man for it. In return, I would give the best of myself to these five guys as well as any other student who happened to cross my path, with the possible exception of the Frenchman. After all, I was a guest here. I would honor my hosts with an honest effort and an open invitation to camaraderie, if not outright friendship. That was a game plan with which I could live.

Each of my roommates then presented me with a gift, which was a tradition of their role as my hosts and was done without regard for their acceptance or rejection of my stay here. It was a matter of honor and superstition, and the Japanese did not overlook tradition.

First, Ikeda placed a small clay cat in front of me. It appeared to be waving its paw at me. "It is meant to symbolize a warm welcome," he explained. Ironically, the cat was also smiling, but it was a dilatory smile that suggested something like, "Yeah, but just don't overstay your welcome, Waters-san." Okay, I got the message.

Moto presented me with a set of porcelain chopsticks with black and red inlay. They were beautiful. "To help you practice," he said, and I took him to mean, "To practice eating with a little more dignity than you Americans tend to display."

I offered him a small bow. "*Arigato*, Moto-san."

The robe that Takeda passed on with a deep bow was made of an ornately decorated silk, sewn in remarkable detail with the design of a crane on a bamboo branch. I held it up in front of me. We all burst out laughing with the realization that it might actually fit an American 5th Grader but not a second year graduate student reared on a good old-fashioned meat-and-potato diet.

The beer mug that Kudoh thrust into my hand was an inexpensive white clay, decorated with a dragon that looked as if Happy Hour could not get here fast enough. It was the size that impressed me. I could picture two cans of Budweiser just filling it to the brim.

"Happy Hour," I said in English. They didn't get it, so I tried it in Japanese. I must have come close because they all nodded as if there would be many such occasions.

No doubt they were all most excited about the porn magazines that Suzuki spread across the table in front of me. I gave the pages an obligatory scan and was fascinated to see that any and all traces of pubic hair had been magically removed during the printing process, as if a team of diligent Japanese had erased the hair by hand. Most interesting. Not that the editing did anything to dampen our rather salacious enjoyment of the models gracing the pages.

It was a good start for six guys grappling with a new setting, new roommates, and issues with language, tradition, and acceptance. A good start indeed.

I shook their hands, bowed clumsily, and gathered up my gifts. I returned to the room I would be calling home for the next six months. Looking around this tiny space with a miniature bed, one window and a closet the size of a phone booth, I realized that any apprehension or fear I might have been harboring had been bested by my adventurous spirit and a swell of pure excitement. I had cleared the first hurdle. The size of the bed and the starkness of the walls did not matter in the least. I was here to finish my Master's studies and I had no doubts about achieving that goal. But I realized I was also here to learn more about myself. Who was this man I had become and who would he be tomorrow? What did I really want out of life, beyond a career? The security blanket of family, friends, and a house I could always retreat to were gone. So were the boundaries. What I had going for me were the life skills I had developed within the confines of those boundaries and with the support of that security blanket. It was time to shed my skin and grow into the next version of myself.

When the gear from my suitcases had been stowed in the closet, I opened my backpack and found a place for the very few personal items I would keep on the nightstand next to my bed or on the narrow shelves under the window: a copy of Lao Tzu's *Tao Te Ching*, my journal, a couple of magazines, my address book, and the clay cat Ikeda had just given me.

I tossed my backpack on the bed and walked across the room to the window. Outside, huge snowflakes had begun to fall and a misty veil was moving down the slopes of Mount Fuji. A thick, wet blanket of snow was already coloring the campus grounds in hues of white and silver. The snow was like a magnet. People were already gathering. I saw Sandy and Sherri in their winter coats, catching snowflakes with their tongues. I saw Mitch and his roommates burst through the dormitory door with a loud whoop and a football. Where had that come from? Outstanding, I thought.

I turned away from the window and dug a pair of faded jeans, a sweatshirt, and a jacket from my suitcase. I laced up my tennis shoes, felt a sharp stab of pain travel up my left arm, and headed toward the door.

"Football," I called to my roommates. "Football, Kudoh-san. We need a middle linebacker. Football, Moto-san."

Kudoh came blasting out of his room dressed in a soccer jersey and jeans. He tossed me a floppy straw hat and shouted, "Football, Waters-san," and something that sounded like, "You big time American footballer."

Well, not quite. But I was ready and willing to act like one.

By the time we were outside, the snow was floating from the sky in flakes the size of cotton balls, perfect for snowballs and snowmen. The temperature was mild, compared to Chicago, and energizing. Within minutes, the athletic field adjacent to the campus was alive with people, laughter, and a palpable sense of camaraderie.

Mitch and his roommates challenged us to a friendly game of touch football, and we accepted. My roommates may never have played a lick of football, American style, but that did not do a thing to dampen their spirits. We carved out a couple of loosely defined boundaries, and I used hand signals and bad Japanese to explain the general concept of the game. A team cheer erupted spontaneously and came out sounding like a mix between "Banzai" and "Kick ass."

Since I was the experienced, knowledgeable American, I appointed Moto our quarterback and Kudoh our designated power fullback. Ikeda, Suzuki, and Takeda lined up next to me. I showed them the rudimentary techniques of blocking, which they immediately forgot. I centered the ball to Moto, thankful my right arm still functioned. Moto in turn handed it to Kudoh. Kudoh took the ball in two hands, made an about-face, and dashed toward our own goal line.

I wanted to shout, "Wrong way," but I was laughing too hard and Kudoh was too excited. Why spoil a good thing?

The day could hardly have gotten off to a better start. We were covered from head to foot in mud and snow. There was no shortage of laughter and the cheers of several enthusiastic female fans rewarded our efforts. What more could we ask for? On top of everything else, the entire affair was conducted under the glorious visage of one of the world's most spectacular mountains.

There was something revealing about the football game that struck me only after it was done. I could see my Japanese counterparts embracing the game much as I did, as a means of escape and a vehicle of laughter, almost as a place to lose one's self. Because they didn't know the rules of the game or care about the intricacies, they were not compelled to be overly competitive. They didn't seek a leadership role. They were not concerned about mistakes. No one was watching their performance. I knew enough about Japanese culture to recognize that performance, particularly in the workplace, was not easily put aside. This was not Tokyo, Kyoto, or Osaka where every word and every decision was scrutinized, analyzed, and judged. This was a winter wonderland and they were like children on vacation. I was curious what tomorrow and the start of classes would bring.

When the first hints of evening cast dark shadows over the campus grounds and the snow turned from white to gray, the game was called.

We slapped each other on the back and returned to our dorm rooms. It was dinnertime.

We quickly realized that the ideal situation was not six guys and one shower, but only Suzuki seemed to find the arrangement untenable. He used the English word "crazy" a lot, although I was not convinced he knew just how versatile the word really was.

Crazy or not, we were all dressed and headed for the dining hall at precisely 6:00 p.m. I was almost too hungry to introduce the term "famished" into my roommates' vocabulary, but I said it anyway. "I'm famished, Moto-san."

"Famished?"

I thought of the Japanese words for "hungry" and "very" and ended up putting the words in the wrong order. *"Suitemasu totemo onaka."* Moto grinned. He corrected me. *"Totemo onaka suitemasu."*

I just nodded, wrapped an arm around his shoulder, and said, "Right, famished."

Austere would not have adequately described the dining hall. Spartan, maybe. Stark, plain, sparse. It was a room with tables, chairs, and no frills. Dorm Six had its own designated table and Kai Waters had his own designated chair. Improvisation? Not on your life.

I thought about this. We lived with many distractions back home and in cities as bustling and chaotic as Tokyo, my Japanese colleagues also lived with many distractions. Maybe the dining hall was the perfect place to really focus on the people around you and the blessings at hand. Maybe it was one place to put aside the stress and anxiety of the world. And maybe I was thinking too much, not an uncommon problem for me.

I let my eyes wander. If the hall was simple and plain, it did not lack for energy or enthusiasm. While Mitch, Michael, Pierre, and I had separate tables and our assorted roommates to keep us on our toes, the girls shared one table. Their escort was a petite, animated woman in her late 20s, by my estimate. The dynamics were no mystery. Fifty Japanese men and five diverse and attractive females! To say the girls were hot commodities would have been a monumental understatement. The men were riveted by them. Not surprisingly, the girls did not seem to object to the attention. Peels of laughter rolled from them as they examined the prospects at each table. Their escort must have had a few intimate details about some of the men because it sounded like a slumber party, given the giggles and the amused expressions.

I also heard tales of our Mount Fuji football extravaganza making the rounds throughout the hall. Word had it that the extremely gifted team from Dorm Six, led by the talented quarterback Moto-san, had over-whelmed the team led by the American volleyball player, Mitch Palmer. The final tally, 12 to 6, did not seem to matter. We were the champions of the world, at least for this day. "Wait until the girls' table hears that," I told my roommates with a wink.

Four Japanese ladies, as stern as they were tiny, acted as both chefs and servers. I could hardly contain my anticipation for our inaugural meal. This had less to do with culinary expectations than it did the fact that I was weak with hunger.

Whatever culinary expectations I did have were utterly dashed the minute my tray was set in front of me. A piece of dried and dusty fish that someone had forgotten to behead reminded me of an alewife on the beaches of Lake Michigan after a long summer; not an appetizing sight. A small clay bowl had been filled with grayish beans that, according to Kudoh, had been buried underground for a full year and allowed to cure, ferment, or stagnate; I wasn't sure which.

"A Japanese delicacy," he said with relish.

A Japanese delicacy that smells like a pigsty, I wanted to say but didn't. I watched my roommates as they devoured the beans. I felt nauseous. Not in a million years, I thought, and pushed the bowl aside.

That left me with one option: a large bowl of steaming white rice. I did not examine it too closely on the offhand chance I might find something as objectionable as a year spent fermenting underground. I dug in, holding the bowl in one hand the way Ikeda and Moto were doing and shoveled it in my mouth using my chopsticks. Never had a bowl of rice tasted so good. I savored the flavor simply because I had the feeling rice was going to be my food of choice for the next 180 days. That, I thought, was a lot of rice.

When dinner was over, the six of us headed back to our room. Classes commenced the following morning and the weight of that reality settled on us the way any pending venture might. On the bright side, Kudoh was not quite ready to relinquish celebrating the afternoon's championship and he slipped a cassette tape in his boom box. Suddenly, Aretha Franklin was belting out her classic version of "Respect." I hoped Kudoh was a better student and weightlifter than he was a dancer, but I had to give him kudos for effort and energy.

When Aretha was done, we all settled around the table in the common area. Ikeda brewed tea and Suzuki cracked a beer. The conversation turned to work because the six months spent here at the JIIS campus were, I discovered, a direct extension of their jobs, the stature of their companies, their performance, and, most of all, "face."

"We were chosen by our companies to represent them," Moto explained. I heard a sense of pride in his voice, to be sure, but also a hint of dread. "We are the face of the company here at the Institute and how well we do here will echo throughout the company. At least it will at Sony. Failure is not an option, no more than it is in the office."

"You must have been chosen for a reason," I said, and found myself looking from Moto to Takeda.

He bowed his head. "There are many at Mitsubishi with far more talent than I," he said with considerable modesty.

I wanted to say, "Then why didn't your company send one of them?" but I didn't. I told myself to button my lip and listen for once. I glanced at Kudoh.

"I am a hard worker, but not much else. I will try not to dishonor my company," he chimed in. "Look at me. Do I look like Toyota's top engineer to you? Perhaps they are hoping that six months here will hone my skills and help me lose twenty pounds."

Suzuki laughed through a cloud of smoke. He was not laughing at Kudoh, but at a thought or a concept that made him both sad and rebellious at the same time. He gazed at his four Japanese compatriots, half in exasperation and half in rebuke. Then he filled his lungs with smoke and set his dark eyes on me. He set both rebuke and exasperation aside.

"In our country, Waters-san, a direct request is considered vulgar. Self-praise is, well . . ." He searched for a word, and Takeda helped him.

"Unmannerly."

"Yes, self-praise is considered unmannerly," Suzuki continued. "A host will apologize for the poor state of his hospitality even when his hospitality is lavish to a fault. I see it in my father all the time. I have heard him denigrate his house and his gardens. I have heard him call his car shabby and unpresentable and my own mother old and uncultured. Of course, he means none of it. He is just following convention. It is the Japanese way."

"You will hear the head of a corporation or a respected doctor apologize for his bad behavior," Takeda said sheepishly, "when his behavior could not have been more refined or acceptable. That is our way."

"In Japan, Waters-san, we admire modesty. We find humility virtuous. Boasting is most distasteful, most distasteful. Well, not for me necessarily, but for most," Suzuki said, and they all found a reason to laugh. I was glad because the tension in the room was high. Still, I wanted to hear more and Suzuki accommodated me. He said, "Do not let that fool you. All Japanese are not modest and many have discovered subtle ways of boasting. But that is the exception, not the rule."

"It is probably true that Americans and Japanese work more than any other people in the world," Ikeda said in a most studious fashion. "But our work ethic is more extreme. It is a throwback to a longstanding patriarchal legacy of loyalty between the samurai and the feudal lord who was both his employer and his master. It is crazy to think that we are still influenced by a system that goes back to the 1600s, but it is true."

"The Samurai were given a privileged position in the clans of their lords and masters," Kudoh said, "but they paid for it by committing themselves to the strict code of conduct and honor of the Bushido."

"Ah, yes, the code of the Bushido," Suzuki said sarcastically, and I could see the others blanch at his tone. "Loyalty, obedience, and honor."

"All of which the Samurai valued above life itself," Kudoh said with significant pride.

"And much of that code lives on today," Moto said to me. "It is different in some respects, but much the same in others."

"We here in Japan have created a culture of shame," Ikeda said without the emotion I expected.

"Well, across the ocean, we've created a culture of guilt, so don't feel bad," I replied, my attempt at levity far less successful than I had hoped. I glanced from one roommate to the next and saw that Moto carried this burden of shame perhaps with even greater gravity than his peers, or at least it appeared to weigh heavier on him. "My apologies. I didn't mean to make light of the situation."

"There is a term here in Japan. *Karoshi*. In America, you call it the disease of stress," Moto said. "*Karoshi* kills ten thousand men every year in Japan, probably more. It is a national epidemic. There is no other way to look at it."

I shook my head, hoping that I had heard him wrong. "Ten thousand?"

"Work obsession is a virtue, Waters-san," Kudoh said.

"And weariness is a sign of weakness," Moto added, and I could see no sign of disagreement among the others.

"Instead of doing anything about it, like taking a day off to spend with the family or cutting back our hours, we get an occasional massage. Oh, and we drink of course," Takeda said.

"Ah, yes. The best way out of a tough jam that I know of," Suzuki said, hoisting his beer. His toast may have been laced with cynicism, but I also heard a hefty dose of pride, as well. "Business samurai!"

"Business samurai!" Kudoh called, pumping his fist.

"In a culture of guilt, Waters-san," Takeda said when the cheers died down, "you live in fear of what your own conscience will tell you. It is that inner voice. Maybe it comes from your Christian upbringing or your parents. Not us. We live in fear of bringing shame on ourselves or our families, even our country. And every day we fear bringing shame on the companies we represent."

"A loss of face," I ventured.

They all nodded as if I had spoken the magic words.

"Even more so than in America, we live in fear of what others think of us," Moto said. "Our careers are dependent upon conforming to a path long ago laid out for us."

"A very narrow path," Kudoh said.

"A very stupid path," Suzuki retorted.

He drank and they all ignored him. I wondered for a moment if he was really the rebel he portrayed himself to be. All the outward appearances were there. I still could not help wondering if the heir apparent to such a huge enterprise as Suzuki might not have some demons lurking inside. First impressions were a tricky business and not always as accurate as they were purported to be. I decided to give Suzuki-san the benefit of the doubt. After all, I had six months to get to know him better. I also reminded myself that this was Japan and I might not know any more in six months than I did at this moment.

"As bad as losing face is, Waters-san, it is even worse to cause another to lose face," Kudoh said.

"Indeed, yes," Ikeda said. "We do not ask if someone has had a good sales month or why their marketing plan did not work as planned, never in public. We never ask someone in public how his or her business trip went or whether a meeting was successful. Why? Because if it went poorly, they will be humiliated. If it went well, then it might bring humiliation to someone whose meeting proved less successful. Do you understand?"

"We have a saying, Waters-san," Moto told me. "The eagle never shows his talons for fear of making the rabbit feel small."

"I like that," I said. "In America, the only way to get ahead, it seems, is to show your talons."

I took Moto's saying to bed with me, along with other bits and pieces of one of the most remarkable conversations I'd ever had. I tried to narrow it down to one cohesive thought, knowing if I didn't, I would never go to sleep. My motivation toward academic achievement at JIIS was relatively straightforward: I seemed to have been born with a burning desire to succeed at anything I laid my hands on or put my mind to. I got a thrill out of learning. It was apparently more complicated for my roommates. Their companies had handpicked them. Performance was not enough. Excellence was the barometer for success, and the step below excellence was deemed a failure. That, I thought, was a tough formula to live by.

I took two pain pills, my antibiotics, and numbed the tingling on my right thigh with the aerosol spray Dr. Iwakabe had given me for the tattoo. Then I propped myself up in bed using a paper-thin pillow and reached for my journal. I turned to a blank page and wrote: *It's been four nights since I arrived in the Land of the Rising Sun and I am probably already a different person.* Oddly, it seemed longer than four nights. Japan had been all consuming. Time and distance had been veiled in something I could not exactly identify. Maybe it was a protective device against homesickness because I certainly didn't feel homesick. Maybe it was a quantum leap into the future with fewer connections to the past than I imagined. I probably should have been scared by such a thought, but I wasn't.

I wrote about my many misadventures in Tokyo. I was surprised at the detail I went into about my encounter with Liliko's father and the clan that he ruled. I was also surprised at my ambivalence about the tattoo now emblazoned on my thigh. One part of me was slightly embarrassed. How was I supposed to explain it to anyone who mattered? Another part of me seemed to see long-term significance in it, as if the tattoo was a symbol of the man I was becoming.

I left it at that, and then went on to describe the seven foreign students who had joined me at the Institute, penning a two-line description of each of my roommates. It was not the most evocative writing I had ever done but I blamed it on fatigue. The next entry would say more, I was sure.

I did one last thing before calling it a day. I listened to a side of one of my Japanese language tapes, or listened, at least, until my eyelids began to close.

I realized how grateful I was for the mental and physical fatigue of a very full day because sleep would have been otherwise impossible given the size of my bed. Hail the Asian physique: powerful, compact, and *short*.

My dreams were some of the most vivid of my life, and they all revolved around food. The cheeseburgers were as juicy and irresistible as the ones served at Harry's Diner on Main Street in Deerfield. The popcorn smelled exactly like that which permeated the air of Mickey's Pub on a Friday night in Iowa City.

When I awoke, I was curled in a fetal position. One hundred and eighty more nights like that and I would probably go home a hunchback.

I sat on the edge of the bed and reviewed my class schedule. It had been designed for maximum free time. I had entered the semester needing only six credits to graduate, and the idea was to enjoy the entire experience in Japan rather than squander six months with my nose buried in a book. Mondays and Wednesdays I would spend the two hours from 8 to 10 honing my language skills. This meant four hours a week gazing at Ms. Neko Katayama. That I could do without the slightest problem. From 10 to Noon, Mondays and Wednesdays, I would be taking a class titled Japanese Culture—A World View with Professor Narita. Thursdays had been reserved for an 8 to 12 session with Dr. Adrian Barrett, the only non-Japanese professor on campus. Rumor had it that Dr. Barrett was taking a six-month sabbatical from Stanford to share his experience and expertise in organizational behavior with this select student population. He had the kind of background you rarely saw and always hoped for. I couldn't wait.

7

The Fish

"I caught a petal from a cherry tree.
Opening my fist
I find nothing there."
～ Kyoshi Takahama

The fish stared back at me from my breakfast plate, dried and crusty, challenging me with beady eyes and a wicked smile. If fish could talk, this one would be saying, "Go ahead. How hungry are you? Desperate enough to eat something like me? I dare you!"

I was as hungry as I could ever remember being, but no matter. I could have been on the verge of death by starvation. I pushed the fish as far away as possible, cradled the small bowl of rice that came with it, and finished it in thirty seconds flat. I sipped green tea and wondered how I would fare under the Japanese grading protocol. I had a record of straight "A's" throughout my Master's program, and I hoped to keep it that way. That was my goal. Whether or not my Japanese professors would cooperate was another question. In any case, it would not be for a lack of effort. That much I could control.

I left the dining hall wondering how I was going to survive on a diet of rice and tea. Language class began at 8:00 a.m., and I followed Moto's directions to a first-floor classroom that would not have been regarded by anyone I knew as a chamber of high inspiration. It was only large enough for ten desks and a chalkboard the size of a beach towel. And, as far as I could see, there was only one piece of chalk. The lighting might have served well for a romantic, candlelit dinner but it left a lot to be desired for things like reading and writing. The room was so chilly that I actually considered returning to my room for a jacket. Too bad I didn't own earmuffs.

The first words out of Pierre's mouth were, "It's like a refrigerator in here. Don't these people know it's winter?"

"Quit your complaining," Mavis said before I could shout, "Go back to Paris if you don't like it."

"I hope you guys slept better than I did," Mitch said, coming through the door alongside Michael and Sandy. He looked at me and shook his head. "I don't know about you, Kai, but my baby crib was bigger than the bed they assigned me."

"I must have gotten an extra large. My feet only hung off the end a foot and a half," I said.

"Poor babies!" said Sherri, who with her short-cropped blonde hair and innocent eyes, looked as fresh as a spring morning. "It's a beautiful day. Stop whining. We're about to find out how little Japanese we know."

"My fear, exactly," Michael said.

I said, "Good morning," to Darlene, but her response was limited to a groan and a nod.

"I know how you feel," I said, even though it was not true. My emotions were an amalgam of nervous energy, boyish eagerness, and those twinges of apprehension the first day of school always brought.

The door opened and our language teacher walked gracefully in. My jaw dropped. Neko Katayama was even more exquisite than I remembered—flawless, stunning, and not a day over twenty-eight. She was taller than most of the Japanese women I had encountered, slender and shapely, with skin like porcelain and hair the color of sable. She wore a conservative business suit that did absolutely nothing to disguise the outline of her hips and breasts. I might not learn a lick of Japanese over the next six months, but I was not about to miss a single class. Our sensei made that a foregone conclusion.

Then she spoke. "Good morning. For those of you who may have for-gotten, I am Katayama Sensei."

"Only a dead man would have forgotten that," Pierre said, with a grin and a leer.

Neko stared at him briefly, and I was preparing myself for a well-deserved reprimand. "In Japanese, if you would, Mr. Trepanier."

I laughed out loud. So did Mitch. "Idiot," Mitch said in Japanese. Then he bowed in the direction of our sensei. "I apologize for my classmate's behavior, Katayama Sensei."

"*Kare mo nanabu desho*," she replied in Japanese. He will learn.

Because I actually understood her, I had to say, "I doubt it."

She smiled. Then she addressed us all in English. "In this class, from this moment forward, you will speak and write only in Japanese, even to each other."

Pierre groaned and Sandy said, "E-gads."

"You gentlemen may have noticed that your roommates are eager to speak only English," Neko continued.

"I've noticed," I said. "And they've already perfected the art of waving me off every time I respond in Japanese."

"You will forgive them, I hope, Mr. Waters," she said, her voice a com-pelling mix of softness and confidence. "They are under enormous pres-sure from their sponsors to return home with a firm grasp of English and a deep sense of western values; a tall order for six months."

She perched on the edge of her desk. "I also understand that some of you have been asking what happened to Professor Yuli Tanaka, the master teacher who was originally scheduled to teach this class. Unfortunately, Tanaka sensei fell ill only two days ago and is still recov-ering in the hospital. Nothing too serious, but enough to keep her in Tokyo. My dear friend, Dean Masami, asked me to fill in. I hope you're not too disappointed. Rest assured I will do my best to fill Tanaka sensei's shoes, as challenging as that might be." Now she pushed away from the desk and took in our faces one by one. "You are asking yourselves what makes me qualified to teach you Japanese. If you are not asking, you should. Why? Because you have every right to know. I was born in Kyoto. My English studies began in elementary school. I placed first in my high school entrance exam and chose Uneo High because the school's language program was second to none. I was President of our English Club and studied English in *yobiko*, which is what we call our after-school university prep program."

"You have to take an entrance exam for high school?" Sandy asked in amazement.

Neko smiled as if our lack of knowledge about the Japanese obsession with education gave evidence of our lack of preparation for our six-month stay here, and she was right. But her voice was much kinder than that.

"Japanese, Ms. Hall. Always Japanese," she said. She then repeated the words in Japanese for our benefit. In English, she said, "The education system here is in many ways a more important molding influence on Japanese young people than their own homes. But it is the home that stresses the importance of education, far more than you do in the U.S., from what I have seen. It is not uncommon for students to travel two hours just to get to the best schools, and we attend those schools based upon high school entrance exam test scores. The best attend the best."

She went on, saying, "We do not drive to school. We take buses and trains. The school I went to, Uneo High, required us to stand on the train to make room for ordinary passengers. We were not allowed to chew gum in public because it might reflect badly on our school. We all wore black uniforms. In Japanese schools, we trade our shoes for slippers. We have as many as fifty students in a class."

"Fifty?!" Darlene finally perked up. "How can you get anything done?"

"It is many students, yes, Ms. Tucker. But it is not like America. We are there to learn, not for babysitting," Neko said without a trace of condescension in her voice.

"I hope your cafeteria at Uneo was more creative than the one we have here," Mitch said with a smile.

This made Neko laugh. "Truthfully? Most students bring their lunches. My mother always packed the same thing: a rice ball, an egg, two pickles, and some type of vegetable."

"Can your Mom start packing my lunch, please?" Mitch asked.

"We spend 240 days a year in school. That is two months more than in America or Canada and many lunches. We also go to school for a half day on Saturday."

"Saturday!" Sandy blurted out. "Poor things."

"The results suggest differently," Neko said kindly, "and when the day is done, we all perform *soji.*" There was a bit of mischief in her smile. "That is what we call cleaning the school: trash, floors, chalkboards, desks, everything."

"E-gads," Sandy said again.

"And we will do *soji* here in our room, as well," Neko announced. She went on. "After school, all Japanese students belong to a least one club, either sports or culture. There are teachers involved in these clubs to a degree, but they are meant to be student run. *Senpai*, the juniors and seniors, mentor the *kohai*, the lower classmen. This is important. In return, the kohai are expected to serve the *senpai*. Nothing serious, just picking up their tennis balls or setting up the theater lights. The *kohai* learn by observing the *senpai* and modeling their behavior. Does that sound at all familiar to you?"

"That's exactly the same relationship that runs through your whole society," I said. "Business, politics, everything."

"So right, Waters-san, so right," she said. There was no praise in Neko's voice, only the fulfillment of an expectation. She looked from one student to the next. "Think of me as the *senpai*. You are the *kohai*. Your success means everything to me."

When she was satisfied that her sincerity was accepted by the eight of us, she continued with her resume. "After Uneo High and graduating first in my class at Tokyo University, I was accepted at Princeton University in New Jersey, in America. Where I studied . . .?"

She looked directly at Sandy, who took the lure and said, "Language."

"Language. After six months with you here at Fujinomiya, I will be returning to Princeton to assume a full professorship."

"So if you can't teach us Japanese," Michael said, "No one can. Ay?"

"Always Japanese, Mr. Frenette, always Japanese." Neko repeated Michael's words in the native tongue and spoke not another word of English the entire class.

Over the next hour, the pecking order among the eight of us became clear. Mitch was practically a virtuoso compared to the rest of us. I was a first grader, not a high compliment. Sandy, Mavis and Michael were kindergarteners and the rest were pre-schoolers without a clue.

Katayama Sensei would use dialogue tapes, repetition, and a dedicated resolve to push us. Always she would say, "Forget English. Forget French. You must think Japanese. You must become Japanese."

I looked at her and thought, I can do that. You talk and I'll listen. In fact, I'll listen all day long. But that was the problem with spending two hours in the presence of a goddess: it was over in what seemed like ten minutes.

I was the last one out the door and said, "Great class. *Domo arigato*."

I considered saying more, but I didn't want to give the wrong impression. She was, after all, our sensei and she deserved our respect.

Japanese Culture—A World View was held in a larger room, almost a mini auditorium, because many of the Japanese students were also enrolled. Kudoh, Moto, and Ikeda were among them. The man standing at the head of the class was one of Japan's most notable authors, Miura Narita. Narita Sensei had been described to me by Takeda as an outsider. Looking at the man, I wondered if it was his shoulder-length silver hair, dark glasses, or the irony in his playful smile.

He gazed up at the class, and the irony in his smile was reflected in his voice, as well. "We call our class Japanese Culture—A World View for a reason," he began. "We will do more than explore the intricacies of our culture, past and present. We will also explore just how our longstanding cultural traits will serve us as Japan's daily interactions—economically, politically, and socially—turn more global."

I looked down the row and saw several of my Japanese colleagues squirm in their seats.

"In the old day," our sensei said, "we would have never dreamed of building anything on the crest of a hill except a Buddhist temple or a Shinto shrine. Is this not true? Now, we think nothing of bulldozing the hill and putting up an apartment house. We are a superstitious people, but are we a religious one? How will this affect our interaction with a growing Islam population in the Middle East? We are the most literate country in Asia, but most of our writers sound more like William Faulkner and D.H. Lawrence than our own Lady Murasaki or Akutagawa Rynosuke. Is this good or bad? We did not eat meat in this country prior to the mid-1900s. Now there are McDonald's restaurants all over Tokyo. Are we better off?"

Now the squirming became discomfort, but Narita didn't back off. "We learn English, but we are hesitant to teach others our language. Why? There might not be another country on earth less willing to teach foreigners like our French, Canadian, and American guests here about their national customs or institutions. Why? Are we being protective of what we have, not wanting to spoil it, or are we embarrassed by our traditions?"

Now Narita Sensei was smiling broadly, not out of cynicism or sarcasm, I thought, but as a way of challenging us. He paused a moment. He removed his glasses and his eyes traveled around the room. I saw something in his face that I had also seen in Neko's: passion, commitment, sincerity. It occurred to me, in that moment of silence, that I had lucked into a class that was a perfect match for the goals I had set for myself.

"Here are your requirements," Narita Sensei said quietly. He replaced his glasses. "I expect perfect attendance. I expect you to stay awake for two hours with your ears pricked and your minds open. I expect questions, participation, and genuine interest. That is all. Do that, and you will earn an "A" in Japanese Culture. There will be no tests. You will write no papers.

But you will come away from this class better able to reenter the world you left behind. If you are in here for any other reason, do not return."

He smiled again.

Neko Katayama and Miura Narita. I was two for two.

Sandy Hall and I walked out of class together and gave thanks for our good fortune. "You don't suppose this guy from Stanford, this Professor Barrett, can stack up to those two, do you?" she asked.

"We'll find out tomorrow," I said. We headed for the cafeteria. "Let's see if they're serving the same fish for lunch as they did for dinner last night . . ."

"And for breakfast this morning."

"We couldn't be that lucky, could we?"

Lunch was less structured than dinner and we joined a table that included Sherri, Michael, and my roommates, Kudoh and Moto. Lunch itself, however, was the same cruel joke, though the humor was becoming more illusive the hungrier I got. I looked across the table at Sandy, and we burst out laughing.

"So much for luck and good fortune," she said to me. "I'll trade you my fish for your rice, straight up."

I gripped my rice bowl theatrically. "Not even if you threw in a thousand dollars and all the tea in Tokyo."

"Darn. I didn't think you'd go for that." Sandy reminded me of Karen in some ways. They were both smart and funny, and, yes, they both had amazing bodies. Sandy was a tri-athlete and Karen could play volleyball and soccer like she was born to the sports. Both were nature lovers, and I was always attracted to women with an interest in the great outdoors. I could see Sandy and me taking a hike up Mount Fuji some weekend. I was still intrigued by the wedding band on her left hand. She had not mentioned a word about a husband pining away in San Francisco and she was not acting unavailable. But I also was not quite up to broaching the subject, at least not in mixed company. Why put her on the spot?

"You're not going to be much more than skin and bones if all you eat for the next six months is rice, Waters-san," Kudoh said in broken English. He ate his own fish *and* mine in two minutes flat, grinning from ear to ear the entire time. "We should lift weights this afternoon and work up an appetite. How does that sound?"

"You're on," I said resorting to English and chastising myself for taking the easy way out.

After sipping tea and listening to Sandy and Sherri discuss Japanese aphrodisiacs, an interesting subject for two women to be laughing about, I went back to my room and spent two hours concentrating on my language tapes. When I could not absorb another word, I changed into a t-shirt and a pair of sweat pants that covered my tattoo. I left the dorm and cut across campus to a small workout room attached to a handball court, a steam room, and a sauna.

Kudoh was already there and he greeted me with a formal bow and a wide smile. I told him that I was still recovering from a recent operation on my left arm—repairing an old sports injury, I phrased it—and we planned my workout accordingly.

The room may have been small, but it had free weights enough for our purposes. Kudoh was only 5 feet 9 inches, tall for a Japanese man, and every ounce was muscle. I could tell he was proud of his strength, but he didn't boast about it. When I complimented him on his bench press, he shrugged and looked slightly embarrassed. He was also shy about the subject of physical health, in general. What he did offer I found insightful.

"We should have this room pretty much all to ourselves this semester, Waters-san," he said. "At least we will not see many of my colleagues here, that I can say for sure."

"Not interested in lifting?" I asked after spotting him on a clean-and-jerk well over 300 pounds.

"Not lifting, not jogging, not much of anything other than golf, and only golf because it is the perfect place to discuss business. Here in Japan, we use the boardroom to discuss golf, and the golf course to conduct business."

We moved to the leg press. We were both pouring sweat, but Kudoh was breathing as effortlessly as a man in an easy chair. He said, "Do you know, Waters-san, that Japan is the only Asian country that has never been conquered or occupied, World War II aside. There is a reason. We think of country first, business second, and family third. Physical health is hardly even an afterthought."

"What about karate or judo?"

"We have hobbies, the martial arts among them. Golf, yes, and tennis maybe. But we learn those skills, and learn them well, mostly as a way of enhancing our positions within our companies. We play tennis or practice kendo to bring honor. You, on the other hand, exercise to clear the mind. Yes?"

"To clear the mind and to stay in shape," I replied after working my right arm with a twenty-pound dumbbell.

"We clear our minds with whiskey, beer, and a trip to the race track or the casino."

Kudoh, I knew, was educating me on an aspect of Japan culture, but he was also venting his frustration. He talked as if the system had gone astray in some way, but there was no denying his tie to the system.

Kudoh headed for the steam room. I put on my running shoes and a sweatshirt, ventured outside, and headed down the hill toward the village of Fujinomiya. A cool, invigorating breeze carried hints of moisture and even snow, but the temperature was perfect for running. The wooded hills that isolated the JIIS campus from the rest of the world made it an ideal place for learning, but the towering trees also lent an air of mystery to the deserted road. The scent of pine blended with the crisp mountain air, and the purity of it gave me an unexpected lift. I picked up my pace.

Beyond the trees, the road widened, now bordering a rambling stream that filled the valley with nature's most compelling music. I could see the village in the distance. I pushed past a rice field and a group of workers diligently preparing it for the growing season ahead. A patch of ground revealed the remains of last season's sugar cane harvest. A stone retaining wall encapsulated Fujinomiya's perimeter. Three school-aged kids were playing with sticks and tossing stones. When they saw the "blue-eyed monster" storming their way, they screamed at the top of their lungs, bolted down the street, and disappeared into a narrow alley. I pictured myself as an albino King Kong in search of fresh meat and laughed out loud.

"It's okay," I wanted to say to them. "Relax. You're going to be seeing a lot more of me over the next six months."

But when I thought about their reactions, I couldn't blame them. I suspected a fear of the white invader had been implanted into their genetic code because their parents and grandparents had lived through the horrors of Hiroshima and Nagasaki. They probably saw an aggressor in every white man who crossed their paths, especially one who seemed compelled to run wherever he was going.

When the town was behind me, I found a dirt road that circled back toward campus. A small farm curled at the foot of the great mountain, a stake of land that brought to mind the first American settlers, or at least my romantic image of them. A diminutive field was dedicated to vegetables like lettuce, beans, and radishes. A dairy cow with sagging skin and dour eyes stood behind a neat white fence. Two chickens that might have been imported from an exotic zoo in South America squawked at me with wild exuberance. A white duck waddled forward, quacked once, and flapped its clipped wings.

There was a meticulous order to the farm that resonated with me: the symmetry of the garden; the perfect right angles of the fence; roof tiles that were neat and tended, if not new. As I saw smoke drifting from the chimney, I imagined a devoted, wise, old Japanese couple living there, and I hoped I would have the chance to say hello some day.

A half-mile from home, I saw Mitch and Mavis headed my way. I noticed that their shoulders occasionally touched and their vibrant smiles suggested a couple testing the waters of a potential relationship. I slowed to a walk, enjoying the chemistry between this beautiful Eurasian woman and the tanned, confident volleyball player from Southern California. I waved.

"Hey, you two. What's going on?"

"Kai. How are you? Did you have a good run?" Mitch asked.

"I'm trying to work off the extra pounds of my new rice and tea diet," I joked.

"Are we supposed to survive on that stuff?" Mavis laughed. "We're going down to the village for some real food. Why don't you join us?"

"Absolutely," Mitch said, though "Absolutely not" would have made more sense to me given the company. I smiled and shook my head.

"Maybe next time. I think I'll head back for a shower." On the one hand, I wanted to respect their privacy. This looked like a couple with definite romantic potential. But I had also put myself on a strict budget that I hoped would leave me with enough money to explore Japan during our semester break and on weekends. "Thanks for the invitation. Have fun."

"Later," Mitch said. I watched them walk away and counted the seconds before Mitch reached for her hand. My count didn't get very far.

My roommates were huddled around the table in the common area when I got back to the dorm. All but Suzuki were poring over their books, scribbling notes, and highlighting passages as if mid-term exams were the following day. Suzuki, on the other hand, was lounging in the room's one lazy chair, smoke spiraling above his ever-present cigarette, and a porn magazine opened on his lap.

"Waters-san! Take a look!" he called. He jabbed a finger at the lurid comic he was reading and snickered. "You will love this one."

Japanese humor, I was beginning to understand, had a dark, sadistic edge to it that was a little over the top for me. This one portrayed a naked woman, two partners, and a flashlight. What Suzuki was amused by I wasn't sure, but I forced a laugh anyway.

"Crazy," I said, using his favorite word. His laughter followed me into the shower.

When I returned, Moto, Kudoh, Ikeda, and the elder Takeda were still buried in their studies. My plan was to confine myself to my room and to focus on my language tapes until dinner, but it was obvious to me that

Moto was struggling with his English studies, so I carried my books into the common area and took a seat.

"How's it going?" I asked of no one in particular.

In return, I received a short nod from Takeda, one that said he would prefer I not break his concentration. No problem.

Ikeda shared a quick bow, but his eyes never left his book. Though all their classes were presented in English, Ikeda seemed the most relaxed and confident about the work he was doing.

Moto, on the other hand, shook his head and grunted. There was no sign of the lighthearted energy that seemed a natural part of his demeanor. Maybe, I thought, it wasn't so natural after all.

"How was your run?" Kudoh asked me.

"Good." I told him about the "blue-eyed monster" and the three kids I had frightened.

"They will get used to you," he said with a wink. "Pretty soon they will be pelting you with rice balls."

"English studies?" I asked.

"American Economics," he said. "Big time important learning on how our competition works and a big time promotion if I graduate with honors."

Kudoh talked with his hands, an unusual habit for a Japanese person. "I bring prestige to Toyota, respect to my family, and for my office mates, a huge celebration."

"And if you don't graduate with honors, then what?" I thought I knew the answer.

"Disgrace," Moto mumbled. It was clear from our conversations that his English skills were lacking in comparison to his colleagues, and frustration was seeping between the cracks of his corporate persona.

I gestured toward his English language book and the copious notes he was scratching out. "Can I help you?" I offered.

A quick and uneasy silence invaded the room. Moto looked embarrassed, and I wished to hell I had phrased the question differently. "I've found that sometimes it helps to talk it out," I said quickly.

After a time, he said, "May I ask a question or two?"

I took this as a plea for help, or at least as close to a plea as a Japanese man could muster. The others kept their heads buried in the books, as if they had not heard the exchange. This, I realized, was their small way of saving Moto from the "culture of shame" we had discussed earlier. Suzuki didn't move a muscle, but he peeked over the top of his magazine and shared the smallest of nods with me, a hint of respect that made me realize the industry heir was not the aloof icon he tried so hard to project.

Moto opened his notebook to the lecture notes from his English language class. As simple and straightforward as it appeared to me, I knew from my own experience with basic Japanese just how much difficulty it presented to him.

I remembered what Neko had said to us in class about becoming Japanese and I extrapolated for Moto's sake. "Forget Japanese, Moto-san. You have to think in English. You have to become English."

"*Hai*," he said. Yes.

While it might have made sense, at some level, to use the afternoon on my own studies, I recognized that this was time better spent. I thought of Emerson and his assessment of successful living: making one life a little easier. Ironic that helping Moto was, at the same time, helping me.

We worked in a methodical fashion that seemed to serve Moto's learning style and certainly worked for yours truly.

Moto's show of appreciation, as demure as it was, made the session worthwhile. For a few minutes he seemed to regain the verve and spirit that I so appreciated in him. Of all my roommates, he seemed the most fragile, or at least the most susceptible to a Japanese mentality tied to performance. Too bad this mentality failed to take into account things like circumstance and reality.

8

The Bombshell

*"One spider's thread
Stretched tight
In front of a lily."*
~ Suju Takano

Organizational Behavior was a four-hour marathon scheduled for Thursday mornings because it allowed the vast majority of the students at JIIS, both foreign and Japanese, to attend. Rumors flew about our teacher, the esteemed Dr. Adrian Barrett, co-author of the textbook we would be using, Stanford professor, and an expert on the intricacies of corporate conduct, performance, and human relations.

I was pumped for the class and I could tell, as I fell in beside Moto and Kudoh, that this was as important to them as was their English language studies. Here was a chance to juxtapose the way it was done in Japan, where unity and an all-for-one attitude prevailed, with America's me-first approach. I was not sure I agreed with that characterization of America, but did have to admit to a certain dog-eat-dog attitude that, while it heightened competition, did little for the spirit of cooperation. Inside, the classroom teamed with excitement. I found a seat next to Sherri and Michael, and Kudoh squeezed into the chair opposite the Canadians.

"Five thousand miles to get the lowdown on Organizational Behavior from a guy who practically lives next door to you, Kai. I like your style," Michael said.

"Hope it's worth it," I replied.

I looked at the wall clock at the front of the room. It was 8:02. By Japanese standards, the esteemed American professor was already tardy. Six minutes later, the door swung open and Dr. Barrett stumbled in. A hush as complete and funereal as a broken clock at midnight swept over the room, and half the jaws in the class dropped. Dr. Adrian Barrett, Stanford's finest, if you believed his press clippings, looked like a hobo after a long journey in the back of a pickup truck. His hair spiked in a dozen different directions and surely had not been washed in days. A stained shirt hung outside his pants as if dressing was something he had done while still in bed. The bandage plastered across his chin suggested a shaving accident of some magnitude, and the pasty color of his skin made me think he had spent a long night with a whiskey bottle. He was tall and gangly in a graceless way. His résumé reported his age as 51, but the kindest thing you could say was that he was aging poorly.

Interesting how many eyes turned my way, as if I might be able to shed some light on the mess of a man standing before us. To call him a disgrace to his home country would have been an understatement. A bigger problem, I thought, was that he looked in no condition to teach any subject, much less make sense of organizational behavior in the corporate world. He made a noisy display of piling his briefcase and several books on his desktop, then dropped gracelessly into his seat at the head of the class.

"Good morning graduate students from far and wide," he said in a voice touched with sarcasm and marked by a tone suggestive of inflated ego. "I am Dr. Adrian Barrett, though I am sure that comes as no surprise to you."

He held up the book he had written. "This is your bible. I abdicate my expertise to the very bright minds who wrote it." This raised nervous laughs from around the room, but I was more interested in Barrett's own reaction to his joke: a wicked smile. "Oh, that's right," he said, peering at the spine. "That's my name. Lucky us."

His tired eyes played over his students. The shock and expectation on the faces looking back at him seemed to spark a modicum of energy.

"Assignment number one: You will read, enjoy, and thoroughly absorb the material in Chapter One of your bible and you will do so by next week. It will serve as the basis for our discussion, and our discussion will be conducted in English, just to clarify, in case some of you were thinking otherwise."

He staggered to his feet, snared a piece of chalk, and placed himself in front of the chalkboard. "Furthermore, we will be separating the class into four equal teams for the rest of the semester. Each team shall create and operate a functioning business with actual product generating real income. This is not a paper exercise. Your business will operate within the confines of our campus and/or the town of Fujinomiya, but you can draw your business from any source. Real dollars. Real yen. You will develop a business plan, present a business model, and implement an action plan. While I will evaluate your team's organization, you will ultimately be graded upon a single factor: earnings generated. Period."

He wrote the words in big letters on the board and then underlined them. When he gazed back at the class, he gave the full force of his attention to the Japanese.

"Understand this. A business organization comes together for a single purpose. It is not the well-being of the worker. It is not the good cheer of the office. It is not 'face.' It is profit."

He spelled it out on the board and underlined it twice. "Profit. All those other things, the good cheer and the high spirits, will take care of themselves if your company is profitable."

Now he smiled, and I could read only bad news into the look on his face. "Therefore, the team with the greatest earnings by the end of the semester will receive an 'A' grade. The team recording the second highest earnings will be given a 'B.' Third highest, a 'C.'"

He paused; it was a theatrical gesture that made me nauseous. Who was this guy? Could this actually be a full professor from a place like

Stanford? It had to be a joke. But what he said next was not a joke. It was a death knell. "And the team posting the worst earnings for the semester will receive an 'F' for their efforts."

The groan that permeated the room was seeped with implications I was just beginning to understand. A "C" grade would be considered completely unacceptable to the Japanese, their companies, their families, and their peers. An "F" would be nothing short of catastrophic, a complete and utter loss of face. I glanced down the row and saw the blood drain from Moto's face. Kudoh's mammoth shoulders sagged. Suzuki had a thoughtful scowl I could not interpret, but I was pretty sure he was thinking: How dare this disgrace of a man come into a classroom filled with committed students and begin spouting American superiority? I had to agree.

Barrett drew four pieces of paper from his briefcase. He said, "Your teams. They were chosen at random."

I shook my head when I heard the word "random." From the little I had already learned, the Japanese did not operate with either an understanding or an appreciation of random actions. Decisions were made in an orderly, explainable fashion. In America, a random selection suggested an unbiased process. In Japan, a random selection suggested a careless process.

Barrett had intentionally assigned two foreign students per team, again randomly selected. I felt it was a stroke of good fortune when Sandy and I were paired together. She glanced at me, flashed an excited smile that brought her oval face to life, and gave me a quick thumbs up. Barrett then went on to call out the rest of our team, giving little consideration and zero respect to the pronunciation of my Japanese counterparts' names. I was furious.

Bad manners aside, I was relieved to hear that Kudoh and Suzuki had been assigned to our team. It would be great having two of my roommates aboard. On the other hand, I felt terrible when I saw that Moto had been teamed with Pierre, the fucking Frenchman, and Darlene, the self-absorbed Texas debutante.

"Good. Very good," Dr. Barrett called, his words edged with an amused cynicism. "Now that everyone is happy, I want you to break up into your teams. You have three hours left to brainstorm ideas. I want concrete strategies on the table by next week. I would suggest you choose a team liaison to report to me beforehand. You have six months to pull this off, not six years, so use your time judiciously. Make it work, people. Make it work."

The esteemed Stanford professor closed his book with a resounding thud, snapped his briefcase closed, and stumbled out. A shell-shocked classroom watched his departure.

"Did that just happen?" I asked of no one in particular.

"Bombshell!" Sherri replied.

"Fucking bombshell," Michael added. "Did you see that guy? Now I know where the term 'Ugly American' comes from, Kai. No offense."

"None taken. I think you hit the nail on the head."

Our distinguished team met in the back of the room, forming a circle with ten chairs and waiting for someone to take charge.

"Let's win this thing," I said eventually. This earned me the attention of nine pairs of eyes. "We need a product that doesn't require major production time or materials we'll have trouble accessing. We have to figure that most of our sales will come from the people here at JIIS. Let's think about what the people here are willing to spend their money on."

"Liquor!" Suzuki called out and didn't receive much resistance.

"Yeah, except we don't have a license, and we won't get one," a youthful Japanese peer in a rumpled suit and pop-bottle eyeglasses said. His name was Kenzo Shinran. In the States, he would have been a member of the Chess Club and head of the Science Club.

"Food," Sandy suggested, but she was already shaking her head. "No. Too much work."

"And not enough margin," said a student who introduced himself as a marketing manager with Sapporo beer.

"Girls," Kudoh said with a wide grin that faded quickly under Sandy's disapproving gaze. "Just kidding, Sandy-san."

"You better be," Sandy said. She wagged a finger at Kudoh, and everyone laughed. Sandy showed no indication of shying away from this male dominated group or the male dominated mentality that was still a major factor in the Japanese business world. Good for her, I thought.

"What about gambling? We set up a casino and play blackjack and poker," I said. I knew the Japanese enjoyed their gambling junkets, and my roommates had made it clear that gambling was a release many men employed in the battle against stress. "Who wouldn't come to that? We could even invite our neighbors from Fujinomiya."

Suzuki was shaking his head. So were several of his countrymen. He said, "Gambling is an escape. Not an honorable business, Waters-san."

"We bet on many things: golf, tennis, horses," Kudoh added. "But it would not be right to build a business around it."

"Okay, then, what about golf or tennis?" Sandy said excitedly. "We have a game or a match that everyone comes to."

"Everyone is playing tennis these days," the man from Sapporo said.

"So we hold a tennis tournament," I said, looking at the faces around me and seeing the idea take seed. I glanced at Sandy and said, "Great idea."

"We plan a day toward the end of the semester," she said.

"And we charge an entry fee," Kudoh said. "Say a hundred yen."

"No, a hundred dollars!" Suzuki said with a grin. That translated roughly into 25,000 yen by my calculations. "Make it special, an event."

"Right. And we sell advertising," I said.

"To corporate sponsors," Kenzo Shinran said, pushing his thick glasses higher on his nose. "We get one of the sportswear companies to donate balls and t-shirts, maybe even new racquets."

"We could put up signs all around campus: 'Sponsored by Toyota,'" Kudoh said, using his own company as an example. "And we could invite people in from the city."

"Does everyone agree?" I asked. "Let's take a vote."

"You have my vote," Suzuki said, jumping to his feet. "I'll be back in a few minutes."

"Where's he going?" Sandy wondered out loud.

Kudoh was laughing. "It's been almost two hours since his last cigarette."

"Poor guy. And all this excitement."

The Japanese lad with the glasses and rumpled suit scribbled furiously on a notepad as everyone brainstormed ideas for the tournament: the time, location, and entry fee; how the event would be structured; prizes, refreshments, and entertainment. The energy of working with a team, all dedicated to a common goal was infectious. I realized that it had nothing to do with culture or country. It was universal. The scent of success and the thrill of the hunt had no borders. They had been driving men and women since the beginning of time. But there was something special in seeing it take root here, far from home, in the company of men we often thought of as our chief competitors in the world market and who, not long ago, had been our mortal enemies in war. Here we were playing on the same team and pointing those competitive juices elsewhere.

Suzuki returned five minutes later with a broad and confident smile on his face.

"Where did you disappear to?" Sandy wanted to know.

"Earning us all an 'A' grade," Suzuki said with his usual smugness. "I just talked to the head of Suzuki's Motorcycle Division, Mr. Hojo Tsuchi. He has committed 12,500,000 yen in corporate sponsorship and advertising to our tournament."

"That's $50,000," I said. I couldn't believe my ears. Suzuki was right. He had just earned us a guaranteed "A." No one was going to be able to match that! A cheer went up from our group and was quickly contained. I could see that my Japanese colleagues were not eager to show up our competition prematurely, but this did not stop two of them from jumping up and pumping Suzuki's hand.

"Great job," I said.

"The division will display all of their new 1984 models at the tournament," Suzuki explained. "In return, we will provide them with banners and flyers promoting the Suzuki name. Does anyone object?"

Of course, no one in his or her right mind was about to object. In fact, the man from Sapporo said in the most sincere voice, "We must make a tournament worthy of their support and we must keep our business plan completely secret. It must not be discussed outside the team. Do we agree?"

"Absolutely," Kudoh said. "Like any business, we hold our cards until the end, including our sponsorship."

"Now that we have a product, we need an action plan," Sandy said.

"And we need a name for our company," I said. "Any suggestions?"

The names came fast and furious and ranged from the suggestive—Nine Guys and a Girl—to the mystical—Tsukini Sah—which, according to my weak translation skills meant, Those Contemplating the Moon. I liked Fuji Ronin, but no one else seemed to. In the end, we chose Kumayama Inc., which meant, Mountain Lion Incorporated.

We all raised imaginary glasses and Suzuki said, "Kumayama. Success and honor."

We talked for another hour, assigning tasks in teams of two. Sandy and Kudoh were charged with seeking other advertising partners. Another pair would work with the school to secure the facilities and to schedule the event for later in the spring. The man from Sapporo beer and a colleague with contacts in the food industry would procure refreshments. While Suzuki and his partner were to arrange awards and prizes and recruit volunteers for the event, we all understood that our instant hero had earned a free pass for the next six months, no questions asked.

I was teamed with Kenzo Shinran. We were given the task of writing our strategic plan and creating an easily understood financial plan. I was appointed chief spokesman, which meant I would intercede with Dr. Barrett and give the final presentation. It made sense, given Barrett's insistence that all work be done in English. It was a heavy workload, but I was pleased to do it. The experience would be invaluable and so would the satisfaction of contributing to a team success.

The most pressing matter fell to Kudoh, our designated Chief Financial Officer, and to Suzuki. While Suzuki had secured a verbal commitment from the motorcycle division of his family's company, we would all feel better about our "A" grade if the money was actually in the bank under the Kumayama name.

"Kudoh-san and I will take my car into Tokyo on Friday and open an account," Suzuki said with his usual casual manner and an unlit cigarette clamped between his teeth.

"Then it's settled," I said. "We'll meet next week and report everyone's progress."

"We can do better than that," Suzuki said. "We must celebrate our early success. I propose our first corporate meeting take place tonight at the Ichiban Tempura in Fujinomiya. Naturally, we will write the evening off as soon as our money is in the bank on Friday."

This proposal stirred the group's enthusiasm even further and the vote on Suzuki's suggestion was unanimous. Good luck had befallen me. Fair or not, Suzuki Motorcycle Division's advertising fee and sponsorship money almost certainly guaranteed me the "A" I was hoping for, even if it was not exactly earned.

It was lunchtime. With my newly found sense of optimism, I found myself believing there would be something on the menu that did not look like a cynical fish with a crooked grin and flaky skin. How wrong I was.

In the cafeteria, I found Moto alone at a table in the corner. When I set my lunch tray down next to him, I realized he was near tears.

"Moto-san," I said. "Are you alright? What's wrong?"

"All is fine, Waters-san. Thank you for asking," he replied in typical Japanese style. "Please join the others. I am not worthy of your company."

"It's Dr. Barrett's Organizational Behavior class, isn't it? His team competition. Crazy, isn't it?" I sipped my tea and pondered my options. There was only so much I could say without embarrassing Moto, and that was the last thing I wanted to do. I wondered if talking about our company would allow him to talk about his. It was worth a try. "We're calling ourselves Kumayama Inc."

"Mountain Lion." He nodded. "We are Mori Kaisha."

I took a guess. "The Forest Group."

"Close enough," he said. He hesitated. This was the moment of truth. "We have decided to open a French Croissant Shop in honor of our French visitor and the head of Mori Kaisha."

I should have known. Pierre, the fucking Frenchman. A croissant shop? Were they nuts? Was there a lower margin product in the entire world than food? And perishable, to boot.

"What's your plan?" I asked because anything else would have come out like criticism, and I had learned enough not to criticize my Japanese friends openly, even with the most innocuous comment.

"We will open a store outside the cafeteria for three weeks toward the end of the semester and an open-air stand in Fujinomiya if we can get a license. We will contract with the cafeteria to use their facilities and charge 250 yen per croissant." Moto shook his head. "I should not be telling you this."

I ran the numbers in my head. Two hundred and fifty yen converted roughly to $1.00. In other words, Moto's group would have to sell 50,000 croissants in three weeks to match the single ad fee we were collecting from the Suzuki Motorcycle Division. If every student, faculty member, and campus employee ate 1000 croissants over a twenty-one-day period, Mori Kaisha would just about make it. Now I had to admit that even the most plain, boring croissant in the world would be a major upgrade from the cafeteria food we were being served, but even I would have a helluva time consuming 1000 pastries in three weeks, and I was a 6 ft. 2 inches, 200 pound, fuel-burning male with a hollow leg. The prognosis was not good.

"Do you even know how to make a croissant, Moto-san?" I asked. I knew the Japanese had expanded their culinary palette over the past three decades, but this was the Japanese countryside, not Tokyo.

"Me? No." This made Moto laugh, though there was no humor in it. "Many pastry chefs here in Japan go to Paris to study: desserts, breads, pastry. But me?"

"Who then? Pierre?"

"Croissants, he says, are simple to make. And one of our team members, Kengen-san, works for Taika, a food supply company. They will provide our supplies, and we will learn. Learn or . . ."

He didn't finish. Learn or fail. Yeah, I could fill in the blank. I was pissed at Pierre Trepanier for forcing a plan doomed for failure down the throats of his teammates. I was also pissed at Dr. Adrian Barrett, an 80s version of the Ugly American, for creating a no-win situation for half his class, all to save himself the challenge of teaching.

Moto's head came up and I could see him reaching out to me with his eyes. I was a *gaijin*, a foreigner, but I had also shown myself to be a friend. At least I had tried. Was that trust I could see him offering me, a place to put his fears? I wanted to say, "Hell, yes, you can trust me!" Instead, I conveyed the message with my eyes and waited.

"Waters-san. For you, an 'F' grade would be unacceptable and damaging to your résumé, a black mark. You are a good student and an 'F' would not look good on your record. This I understand. For me, an 'F' grade would destroy my career. It would bring disgrace to my company, to my fellow workers, and to me. I would bring shame to my family. My wife would never be able to look at me the same. My children would carry the burden of it with them to school every day."

As extreme as this sounded, and as badly as I wanted to assure Moto that it could not possibly be that desperate, I didn't. This was not America, where a black mark signaled a bump in the road, not the end of the world. It might present a hurdle to be overcome, but at least the opportunity to overcome it existed.

I also wanted to say, "Are you the only one on your team who thinks this croissant shop idea stinks? Didn't anyone stand up and say, 'This won't work?'" I didn't say that either. Maybe it was a mistake. Maybe I was trying too hard to respect the Japanese psyche. Maybe a good old-fashioned American tongue-lashing was what Moto needed. Obviously, Darlene, the other foreign student on Moto's team, was either oblivious to problems I saw as obvious or she was too mesmerized by Pierre to speak up. Thank God I had Sandy on my team.

"Listen. I'll talk to Dr. Barrett about his grading system, Moto-san," I said. "He may not understand the problems he is creating. I'm going to schedule a meeting with him for tomorrow to discuss Kumayama's business plan. And maybe I can talk to Pierre about his plan, too."

I honestly did not know whether I was overstepping my bounds or not. I tried putting myself in a similar situation back home. Would I have made the same overture to a new acquaintance in a similar situation? One part of me believed that most of my friends would have taken a stand against such a poorly conceived plan as the one Pierre was proposing. Another part of me understood that the Frenchman had an air of confidence about him a good many people would mistake for leadership. Not much you can do about that, I thought. Some people preferred following. They were just made that way. Darlene, the Texas debutante, struck me as that kind. There was nothing wrong with being a follower, as long as you chose your leaders wisely.

But this was Japan. The Japanese were aggressive, astute business people who held sacred the chain of command. Leaders were not questioned. They had become leaders for a reason and deserved respect for no other reason. Here in Japan, chain of command endured even in the face of calamity. I may have been wrong, but it appeared to me that Pierre had seized control of Mori Kaisha, and now his Japanese teammates were acquiescing in accordance with their view of the business world.

"I would be most grateful," Moto said of my offer. Unfortunately, I heard more hope in his voice than I was prepared to guarantee.

As a matter of fact, I didn't really hold out much hope at all. I really wanted to grab hold of Moto's shoulders and shake some sense into him.

"Forget the Croissant Shop," I wanted to shout. But when I saw his diffi-dent bow and sincere eyes, I knew better.

"You are a good friend, Waters-san. I am in your debt," Moto said as Ikeda, Kudoh, and Takeda set their lunch trays on the table and drew up their chairs.

"Did you get a look at our new cafeteria girl, Waters-san?" Kudoh whispered with a conspiratorial twinkle in his eye. "A real beauty."

"No, I didn't. Pretty, huh?"

"I do not know what she is doing here in Fujinomiya, but we could use two or three more just like her, if you asked me."

Kudoh reached out with his fork to spear my long forgotten fish, but Ikeda beat him to it.

"Hey!" Kudoh protested. "Hand it over, little fellow. I am a growing boy. I need the extra protein a lot more than you!"

Ikeda chuckled. "Fair is fair, my good man," he said, forking the fish into his mouth and offering me a friendly bow. "*Arigato*, Waters-san. I am forever in your debt."

"It's all yours," I replied, seeing that Ikeda was equally as pleased with beating Kudoh out of my fish as he was the bounty of his prize. "You two can fight it out at dinner tonight, too. I may have to open my own auction house. Beady-eyed white fish and slimy beans for sale."

"Not tonight, Waters-san," Kudoh reminded me. "Tonight Kumayama Incorporated will be eating in style at the Ichiban Tempura restaurant in Fujinomiya. We have much to celebrate."

Suddenly, I looked across the table at Ikeda. His face was turning a pale shade of blue, and he started choking. "Ikeda-san! What's wrong?"

The choking turned into a terrible spate of coughing, and his face lost all color. "Ikeda-san!" Kudoh shouted. He jumped to his feet at the exact moment I did mine, but Ikeda had already slumped over in his chair.

"Call a doctor," I shouted to Takeda.

Takeda flew out of his chair and raced toward the door calling for help. Kudoh and I were lifting Ikeda from his chair and laying him on the floor when he went into convulsions. His slight body shook like a leaf. His eyes rolled to the back of his head. He began foaming at the mouth. His convulsions were so powerful that Kudoh and I lost our grip. His chest heaved, desperate for air that he couldn't seem to draw into his lungs.

"Get me a cold cloth. Quick," I shouted though I didn't know who I was shouting at because now there were hordes of mortified people gathered around. I shouted it again, this time to Sandy. "Get me a cold rag. Hurry!"

"He is not breathing!" yelled Kudoh as he ripped off his shirt and used it to wipe the foam from Ikeda's lips. He tried giving him mouth-to-mouth resuscitation while I pounded our roommate's chest. "Nothing!"

"Keep trying, Kudoh," I shouted driving my clenched fists into Ikeda's solar plexus. "Breathe, goddamn it! Breathe!"

Professor Narika, Dean Masani, and Neko burst into the cafeteria even as Ikeda went limp. He was dead by the time I heard the echo of a siren racing up the mountain from Fujinomiya.

The paramedics tried for the better part of five minutes to revive Ikeda, but they had no better luck than Kudoh and I. When they surveyed the scene and realized how completely out-of-the-ordinary Ikeda's death appeared to be, they hailed the police.

The Fujinomiya police were a small town outfit and clearly over their heads. When they discovered that Tatsuo Ikeda was the son of Shadeki Ikeda, the ranking member of the House of Councilors from the Kochi Prefecture and a politician with enough influence to wreck havoc on their careers, the detective in charge of the scene was smart enough to enlist the assistance of the Tokyo police and their world class forensic department. The pathologist from the local Medical Examiner's office was in complete agreement.

So, I thought, covering your ass wasn't a modus operandi reserved exclusively for us supercilious Americans. If only covering your ass could bring someone back to life again.

As a precautionary measure, the entire cafeteria was temporarily deemed off limits, and the police used yellow crime scene tape to insure it stayed that way. There was something so ominous about the tape that a veil of guilt seemed to hover over the entire room. It was a long and sad afternoon.

A helicopter arrived from Tokyo, and two men and a woman aptly dressed in white lab coats quickly took control of the scene. They scoured the area inch by inch. The woman took charge of Ikeda's body and poured over him for thirty minutes, most of that spent examining his mouth, eyes, and throat. One of the men photographed the entire area grid-by-grid. The other bagged everything from the food on Ikeda's plate to the damp cloth we had used on his forehead.

Minute by minute, it struck me more and more like a crime scene even though I knew it was just an unfortunate accident. I was right there when it happened; what else could it have been?

The police focused their inquiry on the four people who had been sitting with Ikeda when the convulsions set in: Kudoh, Takeda, Moto, and me.

I was glad when Neko Katayama, our Japanese language teacher, offered to act as an interpreter for me. I walked the police through the entire day, as if some mitigating circumstance may have transpired during Professor Barrett's ill begotten class or on my one-way trek from the auditorium to the cafeteria.

"I sat down with Moto-san because he seemed a little down after class," I told the detective. "We talked for ten or fifteen minutes before three of our roommates joined us."

"Was Tatsuo Ikeda also a little down after class, as well?" he asked me through my interpreter.

"What? No. Not that I could tell. None of them were. They were admiring the new girl who apparently just started working here in the cafeteria. Just guy talk. There aren't that many young ladies around campus." I shrugged, and the detective seemed to understand our dilemma.

"And then?" he asked.

"Kudoh-san and Ikeda-san were joking around about which one of them was entitled to my fish . . ."

I paused when I saw the uncertain look on the detective's face. "The thing is, I can't bring myself to eat the fish they serve here. Or the fermented beans. My roommates are welcome to it," I explained, and he seemed to accept Neko's interpretation of my words. "Ikeda-san never finished eating. All of a sudden he was choking and coughing and foaming at the mouth. We tried to revive him, Kudoh-san and I did, but . . ."

The detective nodded. He closed his notepad. "That is all for now," he said. "You have had a rough day. *Arigato*."

Then he turned his attention to Kudoh. When he was out of earshot, Neko reached out and touched my shoulder briefly, a gesture that was more comforting than I would have imagined. "It is so sad. One minute Ikeda-san is admiring your new server and laughing, and the next he is dead." After a moment, she asked, "Did you see her, too? The new server?"

"No." I looked at her curiously. "Why?"

"Oh, nothing. I am looking for an assistant, and I thought . . ." She hung her head. "But it hardly seems important at the moment." Then she straightened, as if this show of emotion was unflattering for a sensei. "Will you be alright, Kai-san?"

"Still in shock, I guess."

"You did everything you could, and I will make certain Ikeda's family is aware of your efforts," she said. "You should join your roommates for a while. They seem pretty shook up. I will let you know if the police need to talk with any of you again."

Kuhoh, Takeda, and I watched as Ikeda's body was loaded onto a gurney and taken outside to the helicopter that would transfer him back to Tokyo. An autopsy would be performed in the next 48 hours, we were told, but there were already rumors floating around campus that he may have died from some type of food poisoning.

"That's crazy. We've been eating exactly the same food for the last three days," I said to Kudoh as the helicopter raced toward the horizon. "Why all of a sudden?"

"I do not know, Waters-san. And if it happened to Ikeda, then why not the rest of us?"

"If he was allergic to white fish or those god awful fermented beans, wouldn't he have known that?"

I wasn't really expecting an answer, but Kudoh shrugged and said, "Makes sense. White fish and beans are staples just like rice balls and plums. It does not matter if you are a politician's son or a schoolteacher's; we all grow up eating them."

9

The Tempura Temptation

"Bush clover in blossom waves
Without spilling
A drop of dew."
～ Basho Matsuo

T he entire school gathered in the auditorium just before sunset. Dean
Masani gave a short talk and led us all in prayer. He announced that
Friday classes were canceled and that buses would be provided in the
morning for anyone wishing to return to Toyko for the weekend. He
also announced that the cafeteria would be closed for the night, and
that boxed lunches were being provided for everyone by a church
group in Fujinomiya.

Since Suzuki had already organized Kumayama Inc.'s first company
party at a restaurant called Ichiban Tempura in the Fujinomiya village
square, we decided to honor Ikeda's memory by going forward with our
plans. I was glad we all agreed, because staying on campus seemed the least
appealing idea I could imagine. Better to be with friends, and better to be
as far away from the memories of that terrible afternoon as possible.

I declined Suzuki's invitation to drive into town in his brand new,
two-seater sports car. It just didn't feel right given the circumstances,
and Suzuki understood.

"Another time," he said. "I'll meet you there."

The rest of us bundled up for the brisk twenty-minute walk as the last rays of sun fell victim to Mount Fuji's mammoth shadow. The snow crowning the peak's summit glistened in shades of pink and purple, and I knew I would never forget the sight.

By the time we reached the restaurant, a thousand glittering stars had captured the night sky, a spectacle nearly as impressive as the sunset had been.

I found Sirius blazing at the heart of Canes Major, the Gemini duo of Castor and Pollex, and the Big Dipper. That was the extent of my astronomical knowledge, but only a glimpse at the wonder I felt for it all. Sad to think that Ikeda would never experience another sunset or another star-filled sky. More than sad, I thought, terrible.

We went inside.

The Ichiban Tempura had a rustic air to it, all wood and stone, neatly appointed with simple clay wall pieces and flowers arranged by someone skilled in the art of ikebana. A tiny woman in a white and gold kimono greeted us with a polite bow. She led us into a private tatami room with a sliding door and walls made from delicately painted paper and intricately carved wood, an appropriately "secure site" for our first corporate dinner. Suzuki was already there.

Chairs, as Sandy and I knew them, were conspicuously absent in the tatami room. Instead, pillows had been arranged around a low table. Kudoh invited me onto the pillow next to him. The sight of a rangy blue-eyed America squeezing his long legs under the table provided my Japanese compatriots with endless delight.

"First time at a tatami, Waters-san?" Kudoh asked sarcastically.

"How could you tell?"

The room was suddenly lit with the sparkling presence of four young Japanese women, our servers for the night, and a matronly lady who clearly ruled the roost. Our servers wore matching silver and red kimonos and engaging smiles. They unmistakably knew their jobs. I studied them one at a time as Suzuki ordered Sapporo beer and cold sake all around. No one, I noticed, protested.

My Japanese colleagues were not bashful around our servers, treating them with an air of flirtation that the very poised women embraced as normal. I assumed there were limits to this interaction, and I wondered how the consumption of alcohol would affect those limits.

Beer and sake were served. Before the first toast was raised, Kudoh made certain that Sandy and I understood the rules. He said, "We never allow the man or woman sitting next to us the disgrace of an empty glass or cup. Bad form. And we consider it an insult if a man or woman finds it necessary to fill his or her own glass or cup."

"Two very good rules," Sandy agreed and proceeded to top off the glasses of the men on either side of her, the suave and confident Suzuki being one of them.

He, in turn, raised his glass in the first of what would be a hundred toasts that night. "To our roommate and friend, Tatsuo Ikeda. May his spirit find peace and contentment, and may his memory live long in our hearts."

I listened to the words Suzuki was offering to a young man he had only known for a matter of days and gained a new respect of him. We all raised our glasses. I said a silent prayer for our fallen roommate and then drank.

When the tribute was appropriately culminated, Suzuki asked for the floor once more. His toast this time was delivered with far more gusto. "To Kumayama Inc., The Mountain Lions."

A roar went up in honor of our newly founded company. A succession of other toasts quickly followed, praising the business model we had created, the great game of tennis, Suzuki and his company's generous advertising contribution, and so on, into the evening.

My glass was never empty. Business was not an item on our agenda this night. Bonding was and bonding Japanese style meant the consumption of copious amounts of alcohol. Sentiment ran high with poetry, laughter, and song. When dinner was served, cold sake and cold beer were seamlessly replaced by hot sake, tempura, three sashimi dishes—*mafuro, tai,* and *unagi*—and all the rice a man could eat. The tuna, sea bream, and eel were followed by scallops wrapped in seaweed, raw shrimp, and strips of raw halibut. I lost track of the Japanese names.

Being *gaijin* and male, someone decided that Waters-san required the special attentions of a particularly beautiful server with raven hair, penetrating oval eyes, and delicate features. She introduced herself as Kimiko.

"I am Kimiko," she said in my ear. Her breath was sweet and the gentle scent of jasmine filled my nose. She knew very little English and what she did know was spoken in broken, clipped phrases that somehow struck me as sensual.

"Kai," I said, wondering if she would be offended by the use of my first name.

"Kai," she said shyly. The word rolled off her tongue as if the exchange of given names was a gift, and not lightly shared.

This "arrangement," I realized, could potentially be awkward, but Kimiko was neither overly aggressive nor aloof. She may have been instructed to provide the American with extra attention, but she went about it with grace and what seemed to be genuine enthusiasm. There were unexpected moments when she was fending off the advances of my drunken comrades or gathering dirty dishes and we made eye contact or shared a brief smile. It may have been flirtation, but it was also covert and personal, as if there was a private place in the room where only she and I could go. Either that or the alcohol was having its way with my imagination. It didn't matter; I was thoroughly enjoying myself. In the wake of what had happened this afternoon, it was exactly the escape I needed.

I was only vaguely aware of the parade of food that marched, plate after plate, across our table. What struck me was the extraordinary pleasure of tasting real food again after a week of rice and green tea. But mostly I was taken by the way Kimiko led me from one dish to the next, quietly describing them in words that left me hungry for the sound of her voice. Her delicate hands fascinated me. I found the simplest gestures sensual: the way she ladled soup into my bowl; the way she removed a plate; the way she filled my sake cup.

Her special attention made me the target of good-natured ribbing on the part of my Japanese colleagues, but it did not stop them from wrapping their arms around her waist every time she walked past or playfully squeezing her thigh. All four servers were experts at fending off the hands-on attention. It was so natural and seemingly so inoffensive to the servers that Sandy and I were both amazed.

"Don't try that in an American restaurant, gentlemen," she suggested, "not unless you want to lose a hand or get yourself slapped."

Sandy was right. Flirting with an attractive waitress back home may have been par for the course after a couple of drinks, but the physical contact that our servers here were enduring would have probably gotten you thrown out on your rear in the U.S.

When our plates were cleared, Suzuki called for cold sake, as if any of us really needed it.

"These guys really know how to party," Sandy said to me in a low whisper. "I wonder if they know how to say enough is enough?"

"I don't see you slowing up much," I teased.

"Well, I don't want to be rude. And besides, we have a lot to celebrate." She winked, touched my glass with hers, and shouted, "Kumayama!"

It was easy to see how completely fascinated my Japanese teammates were with Sandy. She had an irresistible sparkle that she shared with them equally. While no one felt deprived of her attention, I noticed that she was not giving any of them false hopes, either. Side by side with Kimiko, the two women may have seemed as different as a rose growing next to a lily, but like the rose and the lily, both exuded beauty and grace. And like the best of women everywhere, each deported herself with strength and pride and each had a firm understanding of her effect on men.

I was pleasantly high but not staggeringly drunk. I listened to Suzuki's low and emotionally charged rendition of *"Ame-moyo Bodaiju,"* "It Looks Like Rain," a heart wrenching love song that opened yet another door on the complicated persona of the Japanese heir. I looked around the tatami room. Tears swelled in the eyes of Kenzo Shinran, the young man in the rumpled suit, and rolled down the cheeks of the marketing man from Sapporo Beer. Kudoh swayed to the rhythm of the melody. Our servers stopped to listen.

My eyes met Kimiko's, ever so briefly. When I smiled, she shyly looked away. Then, when she glanced back, it was so quick and so poignant that only the simplicity of the most skilled Japanese artist could ever have captured the moment. I felt a rush of blood in my neck and head and the swell of something powerful and timeless flooding my body from head to foot. With sake, beer, and the wonders of my imagination racing through my veins, I fell instantly in drunken love with this delicate flower of a woman. Drunken love it may have been, but Kimiko had, in a matter of hours, captured my thoughts and painted the perfect picture of Japanese romance and mystery.

I felt unsteady on my feet as I stumbled out of the restaurant, arm in arm with my new best friends. The cold air struck me in the face and awakened my senses. I was glad to be alive. A moment later, I felt a hand on my shoulder. When I turned, Kimiko was standing in front of me, her mahogany eyes shining brightly. In her hands, she held a small box neatly wrapped in simple brown paper.

"For you, Kai-san. A thank you gift. *Arigato*," she whispered, laying the box gently in my hands.

"I'm honored, Kimiko-san," I said. "*Arigato*."

One of the restaurant's business cards suddenly materialized from inside her kimono, and she pressed it covertly into my hand. Written on the back was a telephone number. "You will call me?" she asked.

It was part question and part request, four words that sent a quiver of excitement down my spine.

I nodded, bowed clumsily, and gently touched her shoulder. "Hai."

Then she was gone and Kudoh was grabbing my arm and guiding me toward the road. "Waters-san, you move quickly, like a tiger," he said with a huge, teasing grin. "Congratulations."

The nine members of Kumayama Inc. stumbled up the hill awash in the headlights of Suzuki's sports car.

"I don't want any of you passing out face down in a rice field," he called.

The mountainside echoed with drunken revelry, the pain and sorrow of Japanese folk songs, and eight men and one woman propping each other up as if sake and beer were all it took to solidify the everlasting bonds of friendship. No one dared think about tomorrow. Our company had just spent its first 50,000 yen, complements of Suzuki's corporate credit card and part of his company's promised investment in our prestigious new enterprise. We had no official revenue. But what we did have was the foundation for a tremendous corporate culture.

Kumayama Inc. had been successfully launched. The future, at that moment, seemed limitless. And when I opened the little package that Kimiko had given me, it contained a cute golden ceramic kitten that created a future of endless fantasies.

The JIIS campus was surprisingly alive when we rounded the last bend. Two police cars were parked at odd angles out front, as if the drivers of the vehicles had been preoccupied with something more important than the lines in the lot, and most of the lights in the dorms were ablaze.

"What's going on, I wonder?" Sandy said to me.

"I don't know," I said though it clearly had something to do with Ikeda's death.

The detective in charge of the investigation was huddled out front of the school's administration office with Dean Masami and most of his staff. I saw Neko Katayama and was surprised when she made eye contact with me. She appeared relieved to see the ten of us coming up the hill. I did wave briefly—something told me it was the right thing to do—and she acknowledged me with a short nod.

I said goodnight to my fellow Kumayama teammates, gave Sandy a hug, and followed Kudoh toward our dorm. Moto and Takeda were sitting at the table in the common area when we let ourselves in.

"You guys alright? You look like you saw a ghost," Kudoh said, and his assessment was remarkably apt. Takeda held a full beer in two hands the way a man contemplating his next chess move might, but his expression suggested someone had stolen the chessboard. Moto was well into his third Kirin, but the textbook resting on the table in front of him was unopened and not one word had been written on the notepad next to the book.

I wished at that moment that I had consumed a little less sake and two or three fewer beers because thinking straight was not coming easily. I pulled up a chair and looked across the table at my two roommates. Kudoh did the same.

"What are the police doing here at this time of night?" I asked.

"They think Ikeda was poisoned," Takeda said eventually.

"Poisoned? You mean food poisoning," Kudoh said.

"Not food poisoning. Poisoned," Moto replied. He took a long pull on his beer as if fortifying himself. "There were traces of Fugu fish in his system."

"Fugu fish?" I exclaimed. "What in the hell is a Fugu fish?"

"Better known as the pufferfish," Kudoh said.

"Poisonous as hell," Takeda said.

"And they found some of that in Ikeda's food? Is that what happened?" Kudoh was incredulous, and I didn't blame him.

"It is just preliminary. It is just preliminary," Moto insisted as if he were trying to convince himself.

"But they are going to inspect the kitchen in the cafeteria this weekend just in case," Takeda added.

"Poisoned? How is that possible?" Kudoh asked of no one in particular. "Could someone have tampered with his food?"

No one said anything for what seemed an eternity. Finally, I broke the silence. "That's the million dollar question, isn't it?" I pushed away from the table and started toward my room. I needed to be alone.

"Waters-san? Are you alright?" Kudoh called to me.

"Just tired, Kudoh-san. It's been a long day," I answered. "See you in the morning."

I managed to kick off my shoes and strip down to my shorts before falling face first on the bed.

I woke up an hour later in a cold sweat; the words, "It could have been me instead of Ikeda," were echoing in my head.

Saying them out loud just made them more real. "It could have been me."

As I laid awake in my bed, a rush of questions flooded my mind. Was the fish actually meant for me, and if so, who wanted to kill me? An image of Kona's severed finger lying in a pool of blood and the fearful look on her face flashed in front of me. Is it possible, Kona could have tracked me down at this mountainside sanctuary? And if it was Kona, how could she have infiltrated and exited the kitchen staff so quickly? Would she think I was dead? Was she still lurking on campus?

These questions led me to the chilling thought that I could have been directly responsible for Ikeda's death. I felt warm tears streaming down my cheeks as I thought about Ikeda's quick smile and eagerness to learn. I heard myself quietly whispering over and over again, "I am so sorry, Ikeda."

The Senseless Sensei

"The air shimmers.
Whitish flight
Of an unknown intruder."
～ Buson Yosa

G iven the amount of alcohol I had consumed the previous night, the bad dreams I had endured, and a general lack of sleep, I probably should have felt worse than I did the next morning.

My first thoughts as the sun peeked through my window were not of home or distant friends, language studies or business plans, or even another breakfast of dried fish and sticky rice. They had nothing to do with the *yakuza* brotherhood, the wail of sirens, or the roommate who had died in front of my eyes the previous afternoon. I would have been forgiven had Ikeda's drawn and ashen face jumped out at me the moment my eyes opened. It didn't.

My first thoughts were of Kimiko, a woman who had captivated me with her sheer elegance, effortless grace, and genuine kindness. Yes, she was strikingly beautiful, and that didn't hurt matters.

I was five minutes into a steaming, hot shower before I allowed myself to think about my 10:00 a.m. meeting with Dr. Adrian Barrett.

I gathered up the notes I had put together with Shinran-san, the young Japanese I was teaming with on Kumayama's business plan, and headed across campus to the faculty building. I knocked on Professor Barrett's office door at 9:58, late by Japanese standards but punctual by mine, and heard a voice call, "It's open."

A musty scent assaulted my nose as I cracked the door, and it hit me flush in the face as I walked in.

"Mr. Waters. Welcome to my abode, humble as it may be," he said with more gusto than he had shown the previous day. Humble, trashy, and in total disarray. The word junkyard flashed like a neon sign in my head, and I was sure it registered at least briefly on my face. "A bit messy, isn't it? I expected maid service when I signed on here, but, alas, that is only one of many disappointments since my arrival."

"Do you have maid service for your office at Stanford?" I asked without letting sarcasm run roughshod over the words.

"You'd be amazed what grad students will do for a bump or two in their grades." He laughed. "Just kidding."

I doubted he was kidding. I saw several signs an optimistic person would view positively, so I tried to ignore the negatives. At least Barrett had tucked in his shirt this morning. His chin was healing from the apparent shaving disaster he had suffered the day before. His color was flush and rubicund, a definite upgrade from pasty and gray. He seemed enthused, if not excited, at the prospect of our visit. How much that had to do with the fact that I was American, as opposed to Japanese, I didn't know.

"Sit down, Mr. Waters, please. Let's talk."

I counted four bottles of Johnny Walker Black, two empty and two full, on the shelf behind his desk. Wouldn't you at least stash them in a cabinet or hide them in a drawer? Apparently not!

He said, "A damn shame about your roommate, by the way. I hadn't met the young man, but no one deserves to die that way."

"No," I agreed. "I still can't believe it."

"The police seem convinced that some malfeasance was involved, but I suggested they take a closer look at the school's menu. I've seen what the cafeteria serves the student body, and frankly I'm not sure I'd put my dog on a diet quite that austere."

If Dr. Adrian Barrett was truly saddened by Ikeda's death, I couldn't tell it by his tone of voice; and it wasn't a discussion I wanted to have in any case.

I said, "Would you like to hear about our business model? We think we have a successful plan."

"I'm sure you do." He offered me coffee. Actually, he filled two mugs from a stainless steel percolator and set the cup in front of me without asking. He reached for one of the Scotch bottles, splashed a shot into his coffee, and offered to do the same for me. "A little something to get the day off on the right foot. What do you say?"

"No thanks."

Barrett hoisted his mug. "To six months as far from San Francisco as possible." He sipped his coffee and struck a thoughtful pose. "Let me fill in the blanks for you, Mr. Waters. Man to man. My agenda here is three-fold. Point one: I came to Japan to mend a broken heart. Mine. She was too young, too beautiful, and too transparent. I would have killed for her. She saw greener pastures and left the esteemed professor without so much as a note. Point two: the revisions of my textbook. My publisher wants something concrete by fall. I intend to use these six months to get it done. Point three: my good friend, Johnny Walker." He waved magnanimously at the Scotch bottle. "He and I intend to spend many meaningful hours together."

He sipped his coffee and sighed. "I didn't choose Japan. It chose me. The job opened up and I jumped on it. I have no interest in Japan, its people, its culture, history, or current business environment. Frankly, the Organizational Behavior class will be student run or it won't be run at all."

He grinned. "So! Now that you're up to speed, let's talk about your company. Does it have a name?"

I told him.

"Boring, but acceptable," he said. "And your business plan."

I explained the tennis tournament, our income model, and the organizational aspects and duties of each company member. I did not mention our advertising commitment from Suzuki.

"You should do well," he said. "The corporate sponsorships and the ad fees have potential. I'll put up my hundred-dollar entry fee along with everyone else. And you'll sure as hell find me at the gala celebration afterwards."

I'm sure we will, I thought, if you haven't passed out by then. "There is another issue I was hoping we might discuss, Professor Barrett."

"Shoot the moon, Mr. Waters. I'm all ears."

"Your grading system, sir," I said gently. "I'm not sure you understand the consequences of an 'F' grade to the Japanese in your class. It would be . . ."

Barrett's feet hit the ground, and a flood of blood turned his face a bright shade of scarlet. "Will be what, Mr. Waters? Disastrous? You're damn right it will be disastrous. What the hell do you think the point of the exercise is? That competition doesn't matter? That if your company falls flat on its ass, it's no big deal because the government will come in, prop you up, and make sure you don't lose face? Is that what you think we're teaching here? Because that's the Japanese way, Mr. Waters. Everyone is so damn worried about saving face. They're all so damn concerned about what everyone will think. They're so consumed with their duty to the company and their obligation to their fellow workers—all that crap— that no one ever questions inefficiency, sloppy work, or falling profits. No one is ever fired and no one is ever forced to retire. Waste is rampant. The Japanese government has been so obsessed with rebuilding their country over the last forty years that they forget what a true entrepreneur really is. They want to compete in the global market, but they're so worried about failure that no one is willing to take risks and all the innovators have become copycats and followers."

He was rambling, and all I could do was sit there and listen. "When you fail in America, it means you didn't have the stuff to succeed. So you pull yourself up, build a better mousetrap, and get back in the game. Here in Japan, failure isn't recognized. No one is motivated by the hard knocks, the bumps, or the bruises that are the seeds of substance, change, and success."

Barrett jumped to his feet. "I might not do much while I'm here in this god-forsaken country, Mr. Waters, but I intend to show the Japanese that the only worthwhile aspects of 'organizational behavior . . .'" He used his fingers to put quotes around the words, ". . . are to promote creative thinking, to push the limits, to dare to fail, and to sing the praises of success. Got it, Mr. Waters? The business world is a pressure cooker, young man, and I intend to turn up the heat on our Japanese brethren."

He finished his coffee, slammed his cup down hard, and smiled. "Now, get out of here, Mr. Waters. Get that tennis tournament of yours up and running. I'm looking forward to it. See you in class next Thursday."

"Thank you, Professor Barrett." I hadn't touched my coffee. I closed my notebook and excused myself. Every fiber of my being wanted to say, "So your 'F' grade is really your way of saying 'Fuck you' to the Japanese and their way of doing business. You think that ruining the lives of seven or eight men in the process is a proper way of effecting change? I don't think so."

I walked out. I was not discounting everything Barrett said. He may have been right on all counts for all I knew, but the method he had chosen to convey the message was terrible, just plain terrible.

The police had reopened the cafeteria, but lunch did not help my mood. As soon as I saw the fish on my plate, I resigned myself to the fact that lunch—and breakfast and dinner, for that matter—was never going to help my mood, so I might as well quit complaining and make do.

As I was pushing my plate away, I saw Neko Katayama walking towards me with a teapot and two teacups on a tray. She wore blue jeans and a turtleneck sweater and her black hair had been drawn back in a long ponytail. I had to remind myself that she was my sensei, not a fellow student.

She smiled and tipped her head in an abbreviated bow. I jumped to my feet. "Katayama Sensei. Good afternoon."

"Waters-san. Good afternoon. May I join you or am I interrupting a moment of meditation?"

"No, not at all. I'd like the company," I said and motioned to the chair across from me.

Neko placed her tray between us and automatically filled my teacup. "I love afternoon tea," she said.

"I seem to be acquiring a taste for it myself," I said.

"I wanted to see how you were doing. It is difficult enough experiencing the death of a friend, but seeing it happen in front of your eyes is something you never completely get over."

"And if the police are right about the way he died . . ." I shook my head. "I woke up in a cold sweat last night realizing it could have been me instead of Ikeda. Want to hear something terrible? I felt bad for Ikeda, but not bad enough to trade places with him. Not very heroic, is it?"

"I think that is called human nature, Waters-san. Not something to feel bad about," Neko said. "It was Ikeda's time. Not yours."

"And if he was poisoned?" I asked her. "Intentionally?"

"That is a matter for the police," she insisted. Then she turned the conversation to lighter matters. "Now tell me, where are your roommates? You have not frightened everyone away already, have you?"

"Hope not," I grinned. "No, I just came from a meeting with Dr. Barrett, our Organizational Behavior professor."

"Ah!" she said, and I could hear the empathetic note in her voice. "And how are you finding his class?"

"How much time do you have, Katayama Sensei? We may need another pot of tea." Her eyes and her posture invited confidence and I accepted her invitation fully. By the time I was done talking, I had replayed our first class with Barrett, with colorful commentary about his dress and demeanor, shared serious reflections on his assignment, and finished with an overview of the meeting I had just finished. Only then did I realize that I had probably said too much, and told her so.

"I assumed this was a private chat," she said simply.

"Thank you."

She sipped her tea. The calm she exuded was almost unnerving. Eventually, she said, "You came to Japan to learn, Waters-san, just as I went to America to learn. And that is what you are doing. Professor Barrett has a point of view. Hear it. File it away in your memory but try to put emotion aside. He is not going to change in six months a way of life that we have been cultivating here since the time of Confucius. Confucius preached obedience, loyalty, and the unquestioning performance of duty. *On* and *giri*. Back then, the vassal owed loyalty to his overlord, the samurai to his master, and the master to the emperor. These basic loyalties even transcended any loyalties to the family, yet within the family, everyone owed loyalty to the father."

She held her cup in two hands. "It is true that many of us, myself included, have rebelled against those tenets, Waters-san, but they are still inbred in our unconscious minds. I might rebel against it, but I still find pride in it. Can you understand?"

"I'm trying," I said sincerely.

"Here in my country, respect is not earned the way so many Americans view it. The child respects her parents because they gave her life; that is reason enough. The student respects her teacher because he or she is imparting knowledge; that is reason enough."

She filled my teacup and I bowed my head. "Here in Japan, we honor the relationship, because the child may one day become the parent, the student may one day become the teacher, and the man in the mailroom may one day be sitting in the boardroom."

"I see."

"In America, I have observed your obsession with acquiring things, as if possessions mark success. You have an expression: 'The man with the most toys wins.'"

"It's kind of sad, isn't it?" I admitted.

"Toys are fine," she replied. "But do toys really define living well or living fully? Do they represent happiness? Japan is a wealthy country and the more we reach out to the world, the wealthier we will become. But if the bottom line, as Professor Barrett suggests, ever becomes more important than things like *on* and *giri*, or more important than the relationships of life, I would consider that regressing. I care more about my students than I do their language skills because I believe that is the best way to help them improve those skills. Have I confused you yet?"

We shared a laugh. "No, Sensei. Like you said, that's why I came here: to learn a few things, maybe expand my horizons. Nice to know I've got a teacher who cares as much as I do. I mean that."

"Then you like it here?"

"Very much."

"Then we should talk again soon," she said honestly. "Now go enjoy your weekend, Waters-san. And do not feel guilty in doing so. Ikeda-san would not want that. He has moved on; he would want you to do the same, I am certain. But do so with a cautious eye."

———

11

The Happy Hoteru

"It looks like rain
The linden flowers
Begin to wave."
~ Ryu Yotsuya

Neko was right. It was Friday. I had two goals for the weekend that I hoped would not look unfavorably on the memory of Ikeda: study and play. I hoped a certain amount of part two of that agenda would include an afternoon or evening with Kimiko. I had memorized the phone number she had given me. Now I just had to work up the courage to call and find a way to communicate my desires without stumbling all over my fledgling Japanese skills. I didn't know what constituted a proper date in Japan, much less how to ask for one. I was an oddity in Japan and I was not sure how appropriate it would be for Kimiko to be seen with me in her community. Would it be a source of scorn or a feather in her cap? Would she be ridiculed or praised?

I needed help. I went down the list of potential intermediaries and Kudoh rose to the top of the list. Good, I thought. I'll consult with him later at the gym.

When I walked into our dorm a couple of minutes later, I was pleasantly surprised to see Sandy huddled with Moto at the table in our common area. Dr. Barrett's Organizational Behavior textbook was open in front of them. Moto was highlighting passages with a marking pen, scribbling madly in a notebook, and listening to Sandy as she patiently explained the introductory message of Chapter One.

"Hey, you two, how's it going?" I asked.

"Your roommate is the worst student at JIIS," Moto mumbled. He looked miserable.

Sandy, on the other hand, looked marvelous in running shorts and a tank top. "I'm trying to get Moto-san used to the concept of a study date," she said, winking at me. "He doesn't get it quite yet, but we're making progress. This is hard stuff."

Then she looked at me and said, "I'm going for a run. Wanna go?"

"After last night, I could use it," I admitted. "Give me five minutes to change."

When I returned, Sandy gave Moto a warm hug and said, "We'll go through it again tomorrow, okay? Thanks for letting me work with you."

"*Arigato*, Sandy-san. I am in your debt," Moto told her.

When we were outside, she looked at me and said, "I don't really want to be in his debt, to be honest."

"Welcome to Japan," I said.

We headed for the green and black of the pine forest blanketing the hills to the east of us. The isolation of the Institute had, I realized, affected me in unexpected and surprising ways. In one seamless moment, it heightened the senses and filled every potential relationship with energy. Here, alone among the trees and under the watchful eye of Mount Fuji, it was as if Sandy and I were the only two people in the world. It might not have been the perfect scenario, but it was close.

A mile into our run, I realized we weren't quite as alone as I hoped. I saw the shadow of another jogger cutting through the forest a quarter of a mile away. Okay, I thought, if we have to share this wooded wonderland, we have to share. Just as long as they keep their distance.

Another mile further on, it occurred to me that Sandy was in a lot better shape than I was. It also occurred to me that I would be lucky to keep up so I left the talking to her and concentrated on my breathing.

Interestingly, the setting, and maybe my company, seemed to relieve her of any inhibitions.

"Katayama Sensei told me that the Japanese planted these forests after World War II," Sandy said. "They wanted these trees to symbolize the unity of their country after the folly of starting a war they knew they could never win. They wanted the forest to represent the orderliness they were striving to restore in their world. That's why every tree is shaped so perfectly. They even seem to move in the breeze as one, don't they?"

"Fascinating. Not one tree too tall, not one tree too beautiful," I said between breaths. I glanced around. Apparently, we were alone again, and I was secretly pleased. I gave my attention back to Sandy and asked, "What about you? Do you like it here?"

"Well, I came here with ulterior motives, to be honest with you, Kai. Yeah, I want to finish my Master's here, but what I'm doing really is running away." We curled into a shaded valley and a cool breeze pricked at my skin. "It's not such a unique story, I suppose. I married my high school sweetheart, and it hasn't worked out. We've known each other since the 4th Grade. My Mom warned me. She said I wouldn't be the same person at 23 as I was at 18. Wow, was she right!"

"What happened?"

"For five years, I let Jeff run the whole show. We lived where he wanted to live, hung out with the people he wanted to hang out with, the whole works. All I had was school, and he even resented that. It was my fault; I could have said something and never did. Then I realized I was suffocating. Suddenly, all I wanted was to be somewhere else, anywhere else, with anyone else or even alone. That's why I'm here. I'm trying to reclaim the real Sandy, trying to discover what the hell I really want out of life."

"That doesn't sound like running away to me," I said. She glanced over at me and a look of gratitude touched her eyes. Actually, I felt thankful myself. Sandy was confiding in me, sharing thoughts that were both personal and conflicted. She had willingly placed herself in a position of vulnerability. It made me feel good about our budding friendship. "Do you still love him?"

"I don't know if I ever really loved him, Kai," she admitted. "Young love, sure. Physical attraction, yeah. He was kind of obsessed with me, you know, and I liked that. I liked having that effect on a man. Does that sound like the shallowest thing you've ever heard?"

"Hell, no. We all like having a positive effect on a member of the opposite sex. Anyone who says otherwise is lying. Physical chemistry between a man and a woman is a pretty spectacular thing. Of course, that's just the beginning. Then comes the hard part," I said.

"Don't I know it! Like getting to really know and respect each other. I don't know how I was expecting that to happen. I didn't really know myself and I sure didn't have a clue about self-respect. I know I was never able to talk to him the way I'm talking to you."

"Sounds like you've come a long way," I replied.

"I'll make you a deal," she said with a wide smile. "I'll be here for you if you'll be here for me, day or night. Deal?"

"It's a deal," I said, though I wasn't sure whether this open-ended exchange suggested a simple friendship or a bridge to something deeper. As I watched Sandy out of the corner of my eye, I thought about whether I would be open to such an eventuality and realized I might be. Time would tell.

"Great run," I said as we left the road and returned to campus. "I hope I didn't hold you back."

"I have to admit that I was showing off some," Sandy said, and I noticed a hint of flirtation woven in and among the words. Then she smiled one of those irresistible smiles that all women seem to have in their repertoires. "Trying to make a good impression, I guess."

"Well, for what it's worth, I haven't enjoyed a run that much in a long time," I said truthfully. We hugged. It was a hug between friends, and I was comfortable with that.

"Next time I want to hear all about your love life," she said playfully.

I took the stairs back to my dorm. It was 4:00 in the afternoon, and my roommates were already proving that happy hour wasn't a tradition held sacred only by Americans.

"Waters-san. Banzai!" Kudoh called to me.

The bottle of beer in his hand wasn't quite a quart, but it was significantly more impressive than the standard 12-ounce bottle from the standard American six-pack. My first day at JIIS, I had discovered that the vending machine outside our door served Sapporo and Kirin, just like vending machines all over Japan. Deposit 350 yen and the same machine would deliver a bottle of cold beer to anyone with the money to spend. No ID necessary. I found it amazing, but I was already getting used to it.

"In America, we would have kids crawling drunk through the streets," I said. "Every machine in the country would have to come with a bodyguard, a babysitter, or both."

"Not here," Moto said. There was already an empty beer bottle in front of him and he was halfway through a second one. "Children here do not misuse the machines. It is just not done. No safeguards or ID checks are necessary."

"I don't get it," I admitted.

"There is a social trust built into the system that prevents abuse, Waters-san. Once we come of age, we expect our younger siblings and younger classmates to honor the system just as we did. And it works."

Suzuki cracked the seal on a liter bottle of something called Ocean Whiskey. He took a swig, grimaced, and passed it on to me. "Waters-san, to the weekend!"

The moment the whiskey touched my lips, I understood Suzuki's grimace. Foul the way a shot of Old Crow was, I imagined Ocean was just as effective. In fact, the second swig didn't taste nearly as bad as the first. "To the weekend!"

"To our *gaijin* roommate," Kudoh called. "Kanpai!"

"Kanpai!" Takeda replied, as if no toast should go unanswered.

After one beer, I was inspired to call Kimiko and invite her to the growing festivities. I cornered Kudoh, put the telephone in his hand, and shared my inspiration.

"A first-class idea, Waters-san," he said and showed no apprehension about dialing her number. I was only able to recognize a dozen or so words from his conversation, but the devilish look on his face told me our invitation was being considered. When Kudoh hung up, he flashed his now familiar grin and said, "She will be here and she is going to bring friends."

Excellent, I thought, and felt a swell of excitement at the idea of seeing her again. I slapped Kudoh on the shoulder. "Thank you, my friend. *Domo arigato.*"

By 6:00 p.m., I was into my third Kirin and ready for some Motown. When Wilson Pickett started singing "In The Midnight Hour," Kudoh jumped to his feet and turned the common area into a dance floor. I may have found his technique wanting, but I could not fault his energy. When Wilson gave way to Smokey Robinson and the Miracles' "My Girl," I was ready to show off my singing skills to anyone willing to listen. I was also willing to endure my roommates' laughter because laughter was the common bond that would make this first party memorable.

"Too bad Ikeda is not here to enjoy our American roommate's bold interpretation of Motown," Takeda said with a smile.

"I do not know," Suzuki said, shaking his head, and feigning a tortured grimace. "I am about ready to trade places with him right about now."

This, I realized, was the best way to remember Ikeda; listening to the music he loved, laughing, and drinking a beer or two in his honor.

By 7:00, Dorm 6 had attracted a dozen classmates and happy hour evolved into a full-fledged party. Mitch and Mavis arrived with a bottle of red wine they had acquired in Fujinomiya. Red wine as their drink of choice seemed to fit the now inseparable lovers, just as they seemed to fit one another. They just seemed right for each other. I could see it in their eyes.

"Welcome," I called when I saw Sherri and Sandy walk through our door. The sound of their laughter was as engaging as their infinitely curious smiles. They were holding hands and were two or three drinks into a party that had obviously started long before their arrival. We hugged.

"Welcome to party central."

"So this is where it's all happening," Sandy said.

"You better believe it," I said. "Where's the rest of the gang?"

"I know Michael took the bullet train into Tokyo for the weekend," Sherri said. I didn't know if it was the alcohol or the company, but Sherri was flush with color and her eyes sparkled.

"Darlene's not feeling well," Sandy said. "She's bundled up in bed with a cup of tea and her journal."

"Sick or homesick, I'm not sure," Sherri said. "But our Texas debutante is having trouble acclimating to her new home, I'm afraid."

"What about Pierre? He too good for us?" Sandy asked with a devilish grin.

"You know how refined his tastes are," I said sarcastically.

"Ladies, ladies, ladies!" Moto stumbled over and embraced the women as if two long parted friends had suddenly appeared at his doorstep. Ah, the wonders of alcohol, I thought. Moto had finally put aside his textbooks and the pressures of our first week in the classroom. His escape had been manufactured with the aid of several Sapporos and two or three shots of whiskey. "Two women far too beautiful to be left alone in the company of an uncultured American. Come, let me buy you a drink."

"Uncultured," Sandy teased. "Now I'm getting the real picture."

"Damn. Unmasked," I said, snapping my fingers in mock dismay.

"We still love you," Sherri said.

She accepted Moto's offer of cold sake, tossed it back like a shot of Tequila, and winced. "Good stuff. I'll have another."

"Poison," Sandy said. She watched Moto stumble away. "Is he all right?"

"You know how the song goes," I said. "Some people drink to remember; others drink to forget."

"Well then, here's to forgetting," she bellowed, clinking her bottle against mine and taking a drink.

Kimiko's arrival a couple of hours later struck me two ways, both exceptionally positive. In the first place, just the sight of her took my breath away. In the second, the smile she shared with me suggested that her primary motivation in coming might just have been to see me. True or not, I was willing to believe it. I guess my Japanese cohorts didn't see it that way, because they swarmed over Kimiko and her friends the second they walked in. The girls' hands were instantly filled with cups of sake and bottles of beer. Each of them suddenly had the undivided attention of two or three men starved for female companionship. It didn't seem to matter whether or not the girls were available.

"The thing is, Japanese men just need someone to listen to them," Takeda explained to me before joining the stampede. "Someone other than their wives or their girlfriends."

"Like the geishas," I said falling back on the old wives' tales most Americans used in describing Japanese life.

Takeda laughed. "You people in the West are fascinated by our geishas. I guess I cannot blame you. Unfortunately, an ordinary Japanese man might glimpse a geisha getting into a limousine or being escorted into an exclusive nightclub, but that is as close as he will ever get to one. No. For us, it might be a barmaid at the local tavern, a secretary at work . . . or our servers at the tatami room in Fujinomiya. Anyone we can regale with our success stories or bore with our failures. So forgive us if we seem overly obsessed with your Kimiko and her friends. We mean well."

I almost blurted out, "She's not *my* Kimiko." But instead, I said, "Thank you for sharing that, Takeda-san."

He bowed, and I noted just a hint of sarcasm in his eye. "You are not the ordinary foreigner, Waters-san. We are not just a curiosity to you or a spectacle, are we?"

"No," I said. "More like friends."

Takeda nodded. "As long as you do not expect the same in return from every one of us. You have seen that already, I suspect."

"I have no expectations of you," I told him, "only of myself."

"That is wise."

The sound of a cow mooing echoed down the hallway outside our dorm and became stronger with each passing second. I blamed my imagination, alcohol, and a poor diet. Then the huge beast poked its head into the doorway and I heard Dr. Adrian Barrett's drunken laughter.

In his advanced state of inebriation, he had herded the cow all the way from the farm on the outskirts of campus into our dorm. And he was proud of himself for having done so. The cow stuck its huge head, with dour and innocent eyes, further into the room. Whether it was the sight of two dozen drunken revelers or a desire to join the festivities, he raised his head and filled the room with an imploring, tremulous moo. Everyone rolled with laughter.

"Leave it to Barrett," Sandy whispered in my ear.

"You don't sound surprised," I said sarcastically.

I watched the Stanford professor relieve Suzuki of the whiskey bottle and was amazed at the amount of Ocean he consumed with a single swallow. He staggered into the room and left the cow to fend for itself. Brilliant. He wouldn't know how inappropriate this behavior was, that a sensei did not socialize with his students. And if he knew, he wouldn't care.

He shouted, "My kind of party," and took another drink. Suzuki had to pry the bottle from his fingers.

"I think I'll escort our bovine mascot back to his pasture," I said to Sandy and Sherri, "before our esteemed professor starts plying it with whiskey."

"Good idea," Sherri said. "Want some help?"

I shook my head. "I'll recruit a couple of my roommates."

My recruits turned out to be Kudoh and Moto and both seemed more than willing, not that the unexpected arrival of Professor Barrett had anything to do with it.

"Oh, no," Moto said sarcastically. "Not at all."

"Bad form," Kudoh said. "What is his problem?"

"Forget him," I said as we steered the cow out the door and across campus. I had no intention of explaining Barrett's checkered past or his many problems, not on a night as beautiful as this. We laughed the entire way, just three perfectly high grad students leading a thousand-pound cow back to the safety of its corral. Or maybe he was leading us; it didn't matter.

We were weaving our way back up the hill toward campus, arm in arm, and listening to Kudoh croon a rueful love song, when a car pulled up alongside us. When I saw Kimiko lean out of the driver's side window, I wanted to reach in and hug her. What a sight! I think Kudoh and Moto had similar thoughts about her three friends. I was only able to decipher every third word of Kimiko's exchange with Kudoh, but the gist of it was an invitation to join them in town for a drink. It was an invitation we did not hesitate to accept.

I piled into the front seat next to Kimiko, and Kudoh and Moto squeezed into the back. We joked and laughed all the way into town, mostly at the expense of Kimiko's driving, and when Kudoh saw the flashing sign outside a hotel called the Happi Hoteru, he shouted. "What better place than here. Of course! Waters-san, your first visit to one of Japan's famous love hotels. Banzai!"

"Banzai!" Moto called. The girls covered their mouths with their hands and giggled. "This is an important cultural lesson for you, Waters-san."

He went on to say that we would rent a room for an hour, order food and drinks, and the ignorant American would be educated to the subtleties of Japanese sexual mores. Of course, the way Kudoh and the girls laughed, I assumed his explanation was filled with innuendoes and implications I did not understand. Maybe it was just as well.

There was really nothing subtle about the Happi Hoteru. From the lounge to the private suites, every room was lavishly decorated and devoted to individual themes as diverse as 1920s Art Deco, ultra-Vegas, and the Roman bathhouse. Kudoh choose the Dragon's Lair, a single room painted in rich shades of red and black, with images of flying creatures reaching out from the walls. The bed was the most prominent piece of furniture in the room. Beer was served along with nuts and candies. Kudoh and Moto kept Kimiko's friends in stitches while she and I struggled with the intimacies of a conversation relying more on gestures and expressions than well-spoken phrases.

I found it exciting and energizing, but I also found it educational. Fujinomiya may have had its love hotels and one or two fine restaurants, but most of its residents eked out their livings farming rice or sugar cane or working in the Toyota plant across the river. The girls were probably dressed in their best dresses, but their best dresses suggested simple lives without an abundance of luxuries. Kimiko drove a car that was seven or eight years old and probably her family's sole mean of transportation.

Kimiko carried herself with dignity. So did her friends. I wanted to know more about the life she led, but the language barrier and setting prevented it. Though I didn't know what was proper given the setting, I could not deny the urge to kiss this extremely attractive woman. Instead, I gently touched her hair. When she neither slapped me nor called me a disgusting pig, I assumed I hadn't stepped over the line and did it again.

Then the hour was over. Kimiko drove us back to campus. Before I opened the car door, she reached across the seat and took my hand. The look in her eye was as gentle as it was provocative. She whispered, "I would like to see you again, Kai-san. Soon."

"*Hai*," I said. I was clearly out of my depth and if Kimiko's shy smile told me anything at all, it was that she knew I was out of my depth. Well, I thought, nothing ventured, nothing gained. "Soon."

It was nearly 2:00 a.m. and all was quiet across the JIIS campus when Kudoh, Moto, and I tiptoed back into our dorm room. For a brief moment, I thought I had been transported back in time to my days at the University of Iowa and I almost started laughing. There were bodies strewn over every piece of furniture and propped up in every corner, fallout from some very heavy partying. Some things, I thought, never change. I stepped over two snoring Japanese, crept down the hall, and opened the door to my room. I stopped dead in my tracks. Sandy and Sherri were lying on my bed, naked and panting, exploring each other the way new lovers had been doing for centuries. They were neither startled nor embarrassed, and only paused long enough to take in the stunned look on my face and giggle.

"Sorry," I said. "Excuse me. I mean . . ."

I didn't know exactly what I meant, so I backed out of the room and quietly closed the door behind me. Wow! Were there really two naked women making love on my bed? And hadn't I been flirting with one of them earlier in the afternoon? I shook my head and blamed it on the amazing dynamics that this isolated corner of the world seemed to be producing. Maybe there was an understanding that the comings and goings of our six-month hiatus in the Japanese countryside were somehow secured by an unspoken right of privacy. Why not explore?

The floor did not look particularly appealing. This was too much like my days at UI. Unfortunately, I was exhausted and my options were limited. I did not imagine that barging into the women's dorm and demanding equal rights would go over well, so I grabbed a seat cushion from one of our chairs, found an available corner on the floor, and used my coat as a blanket. The image of two women having sex on my bed and the enticing smile on Kimiko's face were the last things I replayed in the theater of my mind before falling asleep.

I awoke with the sun, suffering a serious dearth of quality sleep. I wondered what I would find when I opened my bedroom door and gave some thought to heading straight for the cafeteria and a cup of hot tea. Curiosity and exhaustion got the better of me and I turned the doorknob as gently as I could. The room was empty. The bed was perfectly made.

For a brief moment, I wondered if it had been a dream, but the subtle scent of perfume and the pink panties I found under my pillow suggested otherwise. I fell face down on the bed and heard myself chuckle in amazement. I had to give Sandy credit. She had taken her search for fulfillment to a new level.

Wow!

Revenge

"Even a wild boar
With all other things
Blew in this storm."
~ Basho Matsuo

O n Monday of the following week, a short, very formal service was held at the base of Mount Fuji in honor of our fallen classmate, Tatsuo Ikeda.

No more idyllic and powerful setting could have been chosen for the ceremony. I looked for Neko, but she was nowhere to be found. I didn't blame her. Hell, I wasn't exactly looking forward to it myself.

It was not, however, a sad occasion, as it turned out. The Buddhist monk who presided over the ceremony had the kind of gentle expression and blissful smile that made me think this was a moment to be celebrated, not an event laden in grief.

Miura Narika, our professor of Japanese Culture, presented the eulogy, and I was pleased to see he possessed the same calm expression and peaceful smile as the holy man who had gone before him.

The Buddhist overtones of his talk had a positive, optimistic ring to them, and the implication was that Ikeda was in a better place today than he was that fateful day the previous week.

I was glad to have Moto-san serve as my interpreter, mostly because the sincerity I heard in his voice was a quiet, welcome contrast to the agony he had been experiencing with his studies.

Narika Sensei talked about death and the impermanence of life as if they were one and the same subject. "Death," he said with a complete sincerity, "is not the end of life, my good friends. Not to the Buddhist who really believes or the man who understands the temporary nature of this life we lead. It is merely the end of the body we inhabit in the here and now. Our spirits remain, always. As does Ikeda's spirit. And as our spirits will do when this life ceases in us, Ikeda's spirit is right now seeking a new body to inhabit and a new life to attend to."

He went on to says, "Where, when, and with whom our spirit is reborn is a matter of Karma, what we Buddhists see as the positive and negative result of our actions. The same is true for Ikeda's spirit. Hard to think of his short 23 years as having been anything but positive, is it not?"

"There are six realms," Moto said to me quickly. "Six realms in which the spirit can ascend or descend depending on our Karma. The highest realm and the last step before Nirvana is heaven. The lowest is hell."

"Sounds familiar," I said.

"Of course, there are 37 levels to our heaven, Waters-san."

"Oh!"

"In between heaven and hell are four other realms: human; Asura— not a particularly happy place to be; hungry ghost . . ."

"Sorry?"

"A spiritual realm for those of us who have an excessively evil side," Moto explained.

"Ah."

"And closest to hell is the animal realm."

"That's a bad thing?"

"I'll explain later," he assured me. "For now, we should listen."

And listen we did as Narika Sensei asked, "Can any of us believe that Ikeda 's Karma could lead him to any other than the human or heavenly realms?" Narika punctuated this with another soft smile. "But does it really matter? None of the stages of our lives are permanent, and all lead to the highest of places. Nirvana. How can we fear death if we understand that our existence continues? Ikeda's journey has just begun, my friends. We know this."

I didn't know how Narika's talk struck Sandy or Sherri or any of the rest of the foreign student contingent, but I found it uplifting.

"Christians grieve," Kudoh said to me as we made our way back down the hill to the bus. "Buddhists accept. Shinto gives praise. No one view of death is better than another."

"It depends on the circumstances, don't you think?" I said. "Ikeda was young and he didn't exactly die of natural causes."

"True," Kudoh admitted. "No matter how strong your beliefs are about an afterlife, I suppose we are all hoping to find out whether those beliefs are true or not when we are about 70 or 80."

"Better than 23."

"You know what I think?" Sandy said. "I think Ikeda is probably looking down at the two of you and laughing his head off."

By the time we returned to campus, the sun was high in the sky, and I was of two minds about how to spend the next couple of hours: to study or to run. I didn't suppose my Karma would be affected one way or another, so I decided to run first and study later.

Before heading out, I took the last of my antibiotics. I had already forsaken my painkillers, convinced that the wound on my arm was healing faster than I had expected. I had used the last of the aerosol spray on my tattoo, satisfied that the occasional twinges were just the nerve endings healing. I didn't know if I was actually getting used to the idea of a tattoo, but I was becoming more and more fascinated with the design. A tiger breaking through a Yin and Yang sign didn't strike me as the massive contradiction it had that first day. It was beginning to make sense, and that was a scary thought to a midwestern boy with a midwestern view of the world.

As I set out, I focused on the odd hypocrisy of the tattoo juxtaposed against the backdrop of organized crime. The image of balance and symbiosis represented by the tattoo as compared to a world ruled by violence. The dedication *yakuza* members showed for family given their rebellion against the cultural mores of the society they lived in. Freedom in light of conformity. Justice as seen in the shadow of manipulation and exploitation.

The contradictions were confusing enough, I thought, but, in the end, it was probably more about belonging than anything else. Even in the light of criminal activity, if a man felt he belonged, he could and would entertain the corruption of his values. After all, who didn't want to belong?

I was sweating by the time I entered the forest. I dropped into a narrow valley and a layer of misty fog painted the path ahead of me and wrapped around my feet. The cool of a world perpetually in shade touched my skin and made me realize how glad I was to be alive.

I liked what I had heard that morning from Narika Sensei. I liked the idea that our actions, positive or negative, dictated a future marked with either happiness or suffering, but I also knew I wasn't quite ready to go there. My goals were simpler than that at the moment, and at the top of the list was an hour or two alone with a beautiful woman named Kimiko. Now if I could just get up the nerve to make it a reality.

I was halfway to Fujinomiya and deep in the forest when I heard the echo of footsteps sounding from some point behind me. I couldn't judge the distance or the direction and blamed it on the breeze filtering through the trees. I glanced over my shoulder hoping to see Sandy in her gym shorts and tank top, but now the footsteps were coming up fast on my left. How had that happened?

I turned my head to the sound, but the angle of the sun created a line of shadows that hid the fast-approaching runner from my view.

"Sandy? Is that you?"

Not two seconds later, the runner burst out of the trees at a full sprint. I froze, my feet suddenly glued to the forest floor as if the apparition had appeared out of thin air. But it wasn't Sandy. It was Kona.

She was dressed in black from head to foot, and her eyes burned with the fire of revenge. I caught sight of something metallic and glistening in her right hand and realized it was a blade much like the one she had used in her attack against *Oyabun* Yamaguchi.

She screamed my name with the same guttural voice I had heard the night of the attack and then the words, "You destroyed my dreams and now I will destroy you."

"Kona!" I shouted. She was closing the distance between us with remarkable speed. "No!"

I backpedaled, tripped, and fell. I was scrambling to my feet ready for a fight to the death when a second figure flashed from behind a tall pine tree. I couldn't tell who it was because the hooded apparel hid the face, but the diminutive size of this unexpected warrior made me think it was a woman. The speed of her entrance spoke of a highly trained fighter, but these were impressions that accumulated in my brain in less time than it took her to cover the distance between the forest and my attacker.

Like a seasoned martial arts expert, she rose into the air and struck Kona with a leg kick that was more a blur in the misty light than a person attacking a knife-wielding foe.

The blow stunned Kona. She spun as she fell, a look of shock and dismay creasing her anguished face. She hit the ground with a resounding thud, impaling herself on the very knife she had intended for me. The sound that rose up from inside her was part surprise, part futility, and part resignation; and it was the resignation that struck me as most poignant. It seemed that nothing in her sad, difficult life could have saved her from this tragic end.

Her legs trembled, quivered, and then fell silent. Blood rushed from the wound on her chest and the ground absorbed it. Her startled eyes stared with empty wonder as she died.

I ran to her, dropping to my knees and saying, "God, no!"

I turned her onto her back hoping there was still a breath of life in her. Please, I thought, she didn't deserve this.

My savior, still hooded and poised for a fight, stood over Kona until her final gasp. Then she looked down at me and said, "She is at peace now."

"Peace?! This isn't my definition of peace," I said. Then I mouthed what I had been thinking moments ago. "She didn't deserve this."

"You show yourself a thoughtful, compassionate man, Waters-san, for one who was moments ago staring death in the face."

Now I recognized her voice. "Neko?"

She drew back her hooded mask. I didn't recognize the intensity in her eyes, but it was Neko just the same; beautiful, focused, and calm.

"Yes, it is me, Waters-san." She knelt down beside me and used her fingertips to close Kona's eyelids. "And you are right. By western standards, she deserved better. We believe differently."

"The impermanence of life," I said, quoting Professor Narika from his eulogy of Ikeda. "Rebirth? Karma? Cause and effect? Is that it?"

"Yes, Waters-san. It is." Neko extracted the knife from Kona's chest. There was so little blood that it was as if she had been here one moment and the next her spirit had fled with the swiftness of a passing thought. "She died quickly. Perhaps we have that to be thankful for."

I was watching Neko. The fighter had transformed into a woman of purpose. I said, "You saved my life."

"One never knows. You had strength and size on your side. She had the element of surprise and purpose of will on hers," Neko said without emotion. "What is important is that you are alive. Now we must act. And quickly. Help me."

"What were you doing here?" I wanted to know.

"Quickly. And without questions, Waters-san. You will have your answers. But for now, we must move her. And I know a place."

Neko used her hooded mask to cover Kona's snow white face. She used the sash from around her waist to secure Kona's hands and to bind her legs. "We will take turns carrying her."

Neko began hoisting Kona to her feet, but I intervened. "Me first," I said, slinging my attacker's limp body over my right shoulder.

She was feather light, and I wondered how long it would be before rigor mortis set in. An hour? Two? Surely it wouldn't take us that long to get her body back to campus or into town. But Neko was not intent upon following the road. Instead, she turned into the forest and immediately cut a course away from both the school and Fujinomiya.

"Where are we going?" I asked.

"A place I know," was all she said.

It was slow going, mostly because we were ascending the low hills surrounding Mount Fuji, and because the loose groundcover made gaining traction difficult. Twice Neko offered to carry Kona's lifeless body and twice I declined.

"I'm fine," I said on both occasions.

My shoulder was about to give out when I saw the small wooden hut crowded among three towering pine trees and not a stone's throw from the great mountain.

"We are here," she said.

"What is this place?"

Neko didn't answer. She gestured towards the direction of a grassy knoll and said, "First we will give Kona a proper resting place. Lay her there."

She entered the hut through an unlocked door and reemerged moments later with a small shovel. We dug a shallow grave, laid Kona's body inside, and covered her with dirt and sod. Neko used eight or ten rocks to construct a small structure at the head of the grave, part headstone and part cairn. I was impressed with the reverence she showed but not surprised.

"Rebirth," she said simply.

"A safe passage," I added without knowing exactly why.

"Come," Neko said, leading me into the hut.

As rudimentary and broken down as the one room was, it did have a stash of firewood, a fire pit, and a cast iron teapot. Tea leaves filled a wooden urn next to the pot.

Neko lit a fire and stoked the flames until they were tinged with blue. She boiled water silently and prepared tea.

"What is this place, Katayama Sensei?" I asked again.

"A retreat. A sanctuary. A safe house."

"A safe house? For who?"

"Sit, Waters-san. Drink your tea. I have something to show you."

There were no chairs, so I found a place on the floor near the fire. I held my teacup in the palm of my hand, sipping gingerly, and feeling the heat of the liquid penetrating my body.

I watched Neko kneel with exceeding grace next to the fire. The flames colored her face in vivid shades of orange and red and turned her beauty into something ethereal and hypnotic. She turned her back to me, carefully unbuttoned her tunic, and allowed the garment to fall away.

Her back was lean and muscular and emblazoned with the same magical tattoo that I had seen, touched, and caressed on Liliko's back as we made love on an airplane—what seemed now to be an eternity ago.

The Bengal tiger flashed orange in the hut's pale light and the circular Yin and Yang sign seemed to hover like a living entity. The tattooed flames encircling the motif burned nearly as bright as the ones in the fire pit.

I had to resist reaching out and touching her skin with all my will power. "*Yakuza*," I uttered, a whisper bathed in awe.

"Yes," Neko said simply. She raised her tunic and wrapped the garment around her shoulders. Now she turned and faced me. "I was sent by *Oyabun* Yamaguchi to keep an eye on you, Kai. He thought Kona might follow you to Fujinomiya, and he was right. He arranged for me to replace your language teacher and paid her handsomely to take the semester off. Dean Masami is, as I said, a friend, and I convinced him that he could find no better last minute replacement than me."

"The Fugu fish poison was meant for me, wasn't it?"

"Yes, Waters-san. It was."

"And the new cafeteria girl Kudoh was so impressed with was Kona. But I never saw her. And it never occurred to me, not in my wildest dreams."

"She moved quickly. I could not prevent Ikeda's death. So, in part, I failed my *Oyabun*." I could see the sorrow creeping into Neko's eyes. "I will atone for my failing before returning to the States."

I sat up. "No! Please. Not that. Not *yubitsume*. Liliko said there were no women in the *yakuza*. How can you be held to their rules?"

"That is not exactly what she said, Waters-san." Neko smiled, but it was an empathetic gesture, not a mirthful one. "The *yakuza* is 150,000 strong in Japan. Be assured that women have their influence."

"But you? How is that possible? You're a Princeton graduate, a teacher, a mentor. How is that possible?"

Neko refilled our tea. She put a log on the fire and stoked it with a fire iron. Then she said, "My great, great grandfather was born in 1818 to a peasant woman and a man accused of stealing bread and vegetables during an earthquake that ravaged most of Honshu. He could not convince the authorities that he was distributing the food to people who were starving in the streets. I happen to believe it was true. He was labeled a ronin, a gurentai, and that was a tough label to dispel back then. It still is. And once outcast . . ."

She let the words linger, then continued, saying, "My great grandfather was a machi-yakko in the Genyoshi Society at the turn of the century, a servant of the city who actually fought against the ronin. My grandfather helped organize the labor movement on the docks in Tokyo after the war. He made many enemies. My own father took over for my grandfather and joined with *Oyabun* Yamaguchi because both of them opposed the narcotic trade. They were in the minority, and it cost them both a lot of friends, but also earned them the respect of some rather powerful ones. My mother fell ill when I was only six and we thought she was going to die. So did the doctor who diagnosed her. *Oyabun* Yamaguchi intervened. He made certain she got the medical treatment she needed. The best hospital. The best doctors. She lived another nine years. It was my mother who insisted I go to America to study even though my father opposed it."

"I can't tell if you're proud of your roots or ashamed," I said honestly.

"My family has survived many centuries with very little. We pride ourselves on loyalty. Do I approve of everything the *yakuza* do? No. Will my sons be a part of it? No." She looked at me. "And you? How do you feel about your honorary membership?"

"All I know is that I like Liliko and I like her father. I like you. I respect you. And I'm glad you were there for me today." I shrugged. "Do I wish a man who tricked Kona into leaving her village in Malaysia is the one lying in that grave we just dug? You bet I do."

"On that we agree," Neko said. "But it is, unfortunately, a matter that must not leave the walls of this hut, Waters-san. I must insist upon it. And so, I am sure, would *Oyabun* Yamaguchi."

I stared at the flames of the fire until my vision blurred.

Finally, I said, "We know who killed Ikeda-san. And we know why. Shouldn't his family know? Don't they deserve that, at least?"

"And who would it serve? Will it bring Ikeda-san back or Kona? Of course not. But Ikeda's father is a very powerful man, and if he believes the school was at fault in his son's death, he may take his anger out there. If he feels the *yakuza* was to blame, he may insist on a crackdown. Which is the lesser of two evils?"

"I don't want to see the school affected, I know that," I said.

"But?"

"But *Oyabun* Yamaguchi went out of his way to protect me, and I owe him the same."

"And the solution?"

"What if we assured Ikeda's father that what revenge could be extracted on behalf of his son has been extracted? What if *Oyabun* Yamaguchi delivered the message himself? And what if he could create a scholarship fund at the school in Ikeda's name?"

"That is very inspired thinking, Waters-san." Neko smiled at this. "I will share your proposal with the *Oyabun* myself. Will you be satisfied with his decision?"

I shrugged again. "That would be the Japanese way, wouldn't it? And since I am a guest in your country . . ."

I didn't have to finish the thought. Neko knew that I might not be satisfied with his decision, but I would respect it. In the meantime, I had to prepare myself to take Kona's death to the grave with me. I wasn't satisfied with that either, but I would respect it.

———

13

Pairings

"On the surface of the spring beach
A circle
Is largely drawn."
~ Kyoshi Takahama

Katayama Sensei joined me in the cafeteria after lunch the following Friday, as if we had planned the rendezvous. We were no longer merely sensei and student. We were conspirators. We were *yakuza* brethren. We were the bearers of a terrible secret. But we would carry on as sensei and student. This was not a spoken pact, but one that the last week had solidified. Our Friday teas were seen by the rest of the school as a sensei taking a special interest in one of her students, just as Neko did with Sandy and Sherri at breakfast on Thursday, and Mavis and Mitch after class on Wednesday. It was part of Neko's cover, to be sure, but it was also the teacher in her doing what the teacher in her would do in any situation. It was the real thing, which made her cover impenetrable.

Neko filled my cup. We had spoken not a word about the events of the previous Monday. I didn't doubt that we ever would again. We drank in silence for a moment, and then she said, "Let me tell you a story, Waterssan, a history lesson with a moral. You have heard of Marco Polo. He was the first European of any note to introduce Japan to the outside world. This was in 1298, and our country was already 5,000 years old. He called Japan 'Zipangu.' He nicknamed our islands the Land of the Rising Sun."

"Very poetic."

"He told the world that we were civilized in our manners and completely independent of any foreign power. Both true. He then got a little carried away and said that any visitor who did not have enough gold to buy his freedom could expect to be roasted alive on a spit, suggesting that we had a penchant for the taste of human flesh. These falsehoods were a little hard to shed, so we did not get many visitors after that, but were not all that disappointed by our lack of popularity."

"I can imagine," I said, happy that she was smiling.

"No one here gave it a thought," she assured me. "The Portuguese came in the 16th century and found our customs the most civilized they had ever encountered, even if we did not welcome them with open arms. The Christian saint, Francis Xavier, wanted the rest of the world to know that we excelled in piety. I think that is how he put it. He also said that we placed considerable emphasis in our daily lives on honor and reputation. You can see that little has changed over the centuries, Waters-san. We still value honor and reputation and we still undervalue the opinion of our neighbors. That, however, is changing."

"And after the Portuguese?"

"By the mid-1700s, people were describing Japan as a self-contained world with few outside interests and almost no outside influences. For 5,000 years, we were unconquerable. Our only wars were with each other. Half the people who came here thought we were barbaric or backward because we valued our isolation so strongly."

Neko drank her tea and contemplated. "I am not sure what prompted us to resort to colonialism a century or so ago but, like almost every other colonial power, we failed miserably. We invaded China, Formosa, and Korea. The only explanation that makes any sense of this is that we had begun to adopt a more westernized model of living and governance. You see, a hundred years ago or more we began to support foreign trade and, consequently, began to be influenced by foreign behavior."

"Maybe expansion was part of that new mentality," I ventured.

"Maybe your rulers couldn't see how futile colonialism had always been. And probably always will be."

Katayama Sensei smiled. "Thank you for taking my point, Waters-san. Conquering others has never worked, has it? Eventually, the conqueror tires of war, but the conquered ones have nothing for which to live but reclaiming their freedom."

She held my eye. "Business is the one factor that can truly bind us together. Economics. Mutual interest in profits. When people prosper, they recognize the advantages of getting along. It is simple. That is why Japan and America have turned so completely from enemy states into allied nations, and that is why your presence here is so important. Do you see, Waters-san?"

"I do," I said. I filled her teacup. "And that is why your presence in America is so important."

"Out of war came mutual admiration. How ironic," she said.

I could hear in her voice that our session was almost done for the day, but I needed to know where things now stood since the threat posed by Kona was now behind us.

"Will you be leaving us soon?" I asked.

"How would you feel about that, Waters-san?"

"As a grad student forking over untold amounts of money in pursuit of my education," I was smiling when I said this, "I would be very disappointed. As a friend saying goodbye to a confidante—and I know that's completely against the sensei/student rules—I would be sad. But I would also understand. You have fulfilled your promise to *Oyabun* Yamaguchi."

"My commitment to the school is for six-months, Waters-san. But my commitment to my students has no bounds—that is why I became a teacher. And we have a lot of work left to do. On the other hand, my commitment to *Oyabun* Yamaguchi is for a lifetime." She lowered her voice slightly. "You saved the *Kumicho*'s life, Kai. As long as you are in Japan, you can expect the clan's protection. That is what the tattoo on your leg symbolizes: commitment and loyalty. And you will always have mine."

I was moved, but I was also overwhelmed. Nonetheless, I said, "And you mine, Katayama Sensei."

She bowed slightly. "*Arigato.*"

And then she gathered up our teacups and was gone.

I walked back to my dorm. Kudoh and Moto both had books sprawled across the table in the common area, but Kudoh's head was cradled in his arms, and he was snoring softly.

"Now there's a student after my own heart," I said to Moto with a wide grin.

Following Ikeda's death, I had grown closer by the day to Kudoh and Moto. Of my four remaining roommates, they had accepted my natural offer of friendship most readily. We shared some of the same classes and had similar interests. Moto and I studied together for many long hours. There was a gentleness to the man that I could not help but embrace and his sense of humor was irresistible. I was slowly regaining the strength in my left arm and shoulder, as Kudoh and I worked out every other day. His good-natured outlook meshed perfectly with my gregarious nature.

Thursdays brought Kumayama Inc. together. We waded through Dr. Barrett's lackluster classes, relying on personal initiative to cover the demands of his textbook, and then used the rest of the day to solidify the details of our spring tennis tournament. By design, word had leaked about our plans. Suzuki had seen to that. Interest was already fermenting. We had $50,000 in the bank and an insurmountable lead on our competitors.

Thursday nights we held our weekly corporate dinners at the restaurant in Fujinomiya. Our tatami room was now on permanent reserve. I was finding Kimiko even more irresistible and the special attention she showered on me was now well in excess of the parameters set for her that first night. More and more, we were seen as the center of a budding romance. I didn't fight it. The problem I faced was calculating the boundaries.

This was not Chicago or Iowa. It was like navigating a minefield and I was more concerned about Kimiko's good name than my own, despite the fact that she was often the aggressor.

Notwithstanding the language barrier, I was learning more about Kimiko with every meeting. She was intelligent and sweet and, I thought, starved for stimulation beyond her day-to-day life. The more I interacted with her, the more Kudoh and Moto took an interest in our relationship. Because they did not face the same communication problem that I did, their conversations with Kimiko and her friends allowed them to explore in more detail what it was like living in Fujinomiya.

It was, they told me, a simple life, but also a difficult one to rise above and move beyond. Farms were deeded from father to son. Marriage within the community was an expectation and often arranged. Education was not the priority it was in Tokyo. The high school here was not of the same college preparatory variety that the kids in the city fought to attend. There were no entrance exams because there was only one choice. Escaping to Tokyo or Kyoto was the quickest way for a young woman to find herself ostracized from family and friends and once outcast, the return of the prodigal child to the open arms of those who had cast them out was rare. Nonetheless, Kudoh told me, teenagers and young adults in Fujinomiya were always looking to escape. Few ever did. The pressures were too great and the potential ramifications too grave. In the Japanese mentality, ostracism was nearly akin to death. The rewards had to greatly outweigh the risks.

Friday at four o'clock in the afternoon—you could set your watch by it—the shackles of a long week of duty and obligation were cast aside by the promise of the weekend, and this promise was best realized by our dorm's weekly party. Come one, come all. It had become an expectation, a promise, a given. Dorm Six had solidified its place as party central, and the legend was growing quickly. A Toga party one Friday, complete with white sheets and as much debauchery as possible. Another Friday, a Super Bowl party engineered by four Americans who thought the world revolved around Super Bowl week. Yet another Friday, a Samurai party with less than authentic costumes but no shortage of dramatic acting and shouts of "Banzai!" echoing across campus for hours.

Kimiko and her friends from town were now regulars and always greeted as honored guests, not surprising for a population dominated 10 to 1 by males. Sherri and Sandy, two of the most prominent, sexy, and alluring females on campus had already been scratched from the roles of available women.

Mavis and Mitch were inseparable. Two weeks into the semester, Mitch had taken up permanent residence in her dorm room. I was amazed at how well they fit together. Sometimes you looked at a couple and everything about them worked. Mavis and Mitch were like that. The physical pairing was undeniable; they just looked like a couple. The aesthetics matched perfectly. They shared a love of travel and adventure. Come the weekend, we rarely saw them. Mavis came from a wealthy family and, though she didn't flaunt it, the money allowed them the luxury of travel. They visited the hot springs of the Izu Peninsula one weekend, the plush resort at Shuzenji the next. We heard talk of a traditional Japanese hotel in Shimoda called the Ryokan. I could share in their excitement, the thrill of new love and the prospects of something meaningful if not long lasting because I had been there. Karen and I had spent the better part of three years exploring that dynamic and though we had gone our separate ways, I wouldn't have traded a minute of it.

I wondered how Sandy and Sherri fit into this relationship equation. The thrill of new love was certainly there, but whether either of them was giving any thought to something enduring, I didn't know. Here were two attractive women who had garnered the attention and interest of almost every man on campus, mine included. I swore that both of them had flirted with me, if not with serious intent, then with enough intent to keep me interested. I was also known for my ability to read more into a passing glance than really existed, but better that than reading nothing at all, I thought. Now these women were a serious couple who, like Mitch and Mavis, were sharing the same dorm room and the same bed. Their living arrangement had become the talk of the campus, leaving amazement and bemusement solidly in their wake.

The previous Friday, when Sandy and I set out on our regular run, she had confessed to me her awakening. She was, in her words, "Happier than I have been in five years, and maybe the five years before that." She added, "It scares me how fast it happened, Kai, but the feelings don't scare me at all. Sherri is just the most beautiful person and she knows what it means to treat me with respect. She views me as her equal, the way partners are supposed to. Her love is so deep and so genuine that it kind of frightens me. I've never known anything like it. And the way she touches me, I have to tell you . . ."

She left me hanging with that, but I knew what she meant and said so. "I'm really happy for you," I said. I couldn't possibly listen to her describe this new relationship without feeling good for her, as surprising as I may have found the relationship.

"I never got that from my husband," she said. "Not the respect or the love or the . . . satisfaction."

Sandy admitted to ambivalence, too. All I could advise was to take it slow and enjoy the moment; a cliché, yes, but still a sound approach. Who knew where or when love might strike?

The relationship was not a problem for the Japanese at JIIS, not the way Kudoh explained it to me.

"It does not matter," he told me that day in the weight room. "Sexual pleasure is sexual pleasure here in Japan. There are no laws against two men or two women being together. And there is no guilt, either. We enjoy sex. We do not obsess over it the way you do in America. There are too many of us living too close together to do otherwise, Waters-san."

Sandy and Sherri were glad to hear this because they did not want their situation to be in the spotlight. They wanted to be free to let the relationship guide them where it might.

Darlene, our Texas debutante, was another subject completely. She had found her Japanese experience neither enlightening nor endurable. All cocky and outspoken when she arrived, life in the Japanese countryside had finally gotten the best of her. It was, to be sure, partly the solitude and partly the lifestyle. Darlene had come to accept opulence and being on center stage as a way of life. The problem was that center stage was more or less a foreign concept in Japan.

The Japanese culture was built within high and insular walls. Penetrating those walls was not simply a matter of personality or even good intentions. On the surface, the Japanese were friendly and accommodating. They could be scrupulously polite to a guest. They might go out of their way to ensure your comfort. They would even project an air of self-effacement to honor your place in their home. But this was not necessarily done in the name of friendship. Friendship suggested obligations that the Japanese took extremely seriously. Granting a foreigner anything beyond a cordial relationship was rare. Most of the Japanese at JIIS had enough on their plates. They were not unfriendly, though they must have seemed aloof to Darlene. They were not thoughtless, though they may have seemed preoccupied to her. They were too preoccupied with family, business, and the pursuit of excellence to pamper a rich Texas girl. In Darlene's eyes, the Fujinomiya campus must have seemed like a self-inflicted prison camp and fifty Japanese businessmen with self-imposed agendas provided no hope for escape.

Darlene had probably surveyed her bare-bone dorm room and shuttered with disbelief. She had reacted to the cafeteria's menu of fish and rice with less enthusiasm than even I had. I could not imagine her dismay when she discovered there was not a single television on campus and only one telephone, the phone in the Dean's office. Darlene didn't stand a chance, poor thing.

Three weeks into the semester, a bus pulled up in front of the school and hauled away Darlene and her collection of over-sized trunks. We all shared a farewell hug and offered polite comments like, "We'll miss you," and "The place won't be the same without you." There was really only a certain amount of truth to those statements. It was nothing personal. Darlene had rarely socialized and had never integrated. I felt bad for her, but she was better off back home.

When I looked around me, I realized that I, more than any other visiting student, was forging meaningful relationships among the Japanese. The friendship that Kudoh and I were creating was special to both of us. It didn't hurt that he was thriving at the Institute. English seemed to come naturally to him and he spoke it almost exclusively. The sound of his own voice speaking English seemed to make him laugh, or at least his delight in mastering the language brought him huge satisfaction. It also allowed him to breeze through his course work. He and I spent every other day in the weight room and I don't know which one of us looked forward to it more. We pushed each other. We laughed. We talked about women and sports and business. Kudoh did not hide the fact that he considered his six-month hiatus here a welcome reprieve from the frenetic day-to-day pace of Toyota's corporate offices.

"There is something about the air here," he would say. "Fresh and clean and breathable. It's like a gift from the mountain. I could retire here, Waters-san."

When I suggested that it was the three square meals the cafeteria fed him without fail everyday, his eyes twinkled. "I am in heaven. I admit it. But I am a bachelor. What more could a bachelor ask for than a live-in chef?"

Moto, on the other hand, was a picture of pure misery. Where English came naturally to Kudoh, it was as foreign to Moto as something from another planet. He struggled, but not from lack of effort. He studied tirelessly. He crawled out of bed at 5:30 every morning and fell back into bed exhausted, frustrated, and disconsolate at 2:00 every night. Sandy and I tutored him nearly every day, she on organizational behavior and me on English studies. If he was frustrated with his own lack of progress, I was frustrated with him and his Japanese cohorts for allowing the fucking Frenchman to impose his will so completely on them with respect to their croissant business. From the few whispers I had heard about the other teams and their business models, Moto was in serious trouble. His company, Mori Kaisha, was on a collision course with an "F" grade unless something miraculous occurred, and I thought Moto knew that.

I had extended the hand of friendship to Moto because I liked his energy, respected his honesty, and took true pleasure in his sense of humor. He had reciprocated by exposing a side of himself that no other foreigner had ever seen: fear and insecurity, to be sure, but also a gentle humanity.

One day, after our books were closed and we were both sipping a cold Kirin, long after everyone else had gone to bed, he fell into an emotional discourse about his lovely wife, Nobuko—"my rock," he called her—and their two beautiful daughters. Mariko was four and Tomiko was seven. "They are my jewels, Waters-san. I would give them the moon and the stars, gladly and with my whole heart. And I would never in ten thousand years bring them dishonor."

"I'd love to meet them," I said.

"Then you would agree to accompany me to Kyoto for a visit perhaps," he said hopefully.

"In a New York minute," I replied. When Moto's brow furrowed in confusion, I simplified my response. "I'd love to meet Nobuko and your daughters, Moto-san. It would be an honor."

"Semester break then," he said. "We will take the bullet train to Kyoto and be there in two hours."

Our visiting student numbers dwindled even further the following week with the departure of Michael Frenette, the Canadian whose most memorable contributions to the JIIS campus were his sudden disappearing acts every Friday morning. He would throw a light duffel bag over his shoulder, trek into Fujinomiya, and catch a bus into Tokyo. Michael was a fan of Japan's infamous bullet trains and he had taken advantage of their instantaneous delivery system to visit Buddhist temples as far south as Nara and Shinto shrines as far north as Miyagi.

Michael did not claim a profound interest in eastern religion, per se, but to hear him describe the Temple of Haryuji near Hara, you were left believing that something mystical had occurred there.

"Profound," he told me over tea one afternoon. "The temple's buildings are the oldest Buddhist structures of their kind in all Japan, and might be the oldest surviving wooden buildings of their size in the world. Their history is what astounds me, Kai, as well as the devotion that makes the history so important today."

I still was not sure whether it was boredom that drove Michael away or his self-proclaimed lust for travel and discovery. Sherri told me that Michael didn't need the credits to get his Master's Degree. Pure experience was what he sought. He caught a bus one Friday, with all his bags in tow, and never returned. He wanted to compare Japanese culture with the competing forces throughout Southeast Asia, he'd told me, and mentioned stops in Hong Kong, Thailand, and South Korea.

Michael's departure made me wonder how I would react if the semester credits were no longer necessary for graduation. It was a good question. The isolation of Fujinomiya and the JIIS campus had its positive side. It had brought me closer to myself, and that was a good thing. Here, I was Kai Waters, as few people had ever seen me. My identity was not tied to friends or family. It was not influenced by a need to perform or a desire for acceptance. It was not the product of the environment the way it was in the suburbs of Chicago or the university life in Iowa. Back home, I was often who I thought I should be, knowingly or not. Succeeding was often tied to making an impression. Here, among the endless forests of pine and fir, I was not projecting an image. The Japanese might have been observing me as a stranger from a strange land, but I felt they weren't overtly judging the man or the image behind the man at the current time. I knew the depth of their personal analysis would grow deeper as we spent more time together.

For now, it was good to just be Kai. I was not willing to give that up yet. In fact, I wanted to practice being just Kai until I could break free of the image and return home as the authentic man I was becoming. I could see myself being a better man, a more realistic partner, and a more self-assured business person. Sure, there was an esoteric element to this thinking, but I had come to Japan in search of new ways of thinking and I was finding them.

No, I wasn't going anywhere, not quite yet. I was learning too much.

———

Sumo

"Bush clover in blossom waves
Without spilling
A drop of dew."
～ Basho Matsuo

N eko Katayama delivered the invitation personally. She also kept it very private, waylaying me as I headed for the weight room and my Friday afternoon workout with Kudoh.

"For you, Waters-san," she said, laying the embossed card in my hand.

"*Arigato*, Sensei. What is it?" I asked.

"Open it. I believe there may be a bit of Japanese culture in your future," she said with an enticing smile. "You might want to keep the name of your benefactor to yourself, however."

I could only imagine one reason in the world for Neko to make such a covert statement: our mutual friends in Tokyo. I opened the envelope. The words were written in Kanji. I stared at the Japanese script and could decipher about half the words. Neko opened her hand and said, "May I interpret?"

I bowed slightly and said, "*Arigato*."

"It says, 'Mr. Kai Waters. Please join me Saturday for a night of Sumo wrestling at the Arena of the National Sport. I will send a car for you at 5:00. Regrets Only.' It is signed, '*Oyabun* Ter Yamaguchi.'"

Neko was smiling the way a teacher smiles when she knows a student is on the verge of a pleasurable discovery. Or maybe she was smiling because she knew there was no way I could refuse such an invitation. A night of sumo wrestling was something I had come to Japan hoping to see. Sumo ranked with American baseball as the country's most important sport. I wouldn't miss it for anything.

"Sure. Sounds good," I said as casually as possible, and realized my heart was drumming the inside of my chest like a hammer on a drum, a sign of anxiety, but also one of pure excitement. "Is there anything I need to do? Should I call or write or anything?"

"That is not necessary. Just be ready on Saturday," she suggested. "If the *Kumicho* said there would be a car here then, it will be here."

And indeed it was. I was waiting in the parking lot when the black limousine, with its smoked windows and high gloss finish, pulled up. My faithful friend Tonto jumped out of the front seat, said *"Konbanwa,* Waters-san," and opened the rear door for me.

I heard a pleasant giggle even before I stepped in and realized I had been provided with female companionship. Not one, but two. "Meet Rika and Izumi," Tonto said in broken English. To the girls, he said, "Kai Waters. Our honored guest."

The interior of the limo smelled of Lily of the Valley and hints of cinnamon. Intoxicating. The women were like those I had seen in the private club in Tokyo: young, but regal. Rika reminded me of a perfectly fired piece of porcelain, pale and painted and sculptured with the kind of delicate features that made a man think he was in the company of a teenage girl with the eyes of an expert negotiator. She wore a schoolgirl's pleated plaid skirt and a white blouse.

"Rika." I held out my hand, and she coiled her fingers gently around it. Our eyes met, and I knew the meaning of star-struck. She withdrew her hand and dropped her gaze.

Izumi ignored my hand and moved over next to me. She wore an obscenely short black cocktail dress. Her body would have stopped traffic. The amount of cleavage she was showing was almost sinful, and I couldn't help the flood of energy coursing through my system.

"Comfort women" was how Liliko had described them at the club. Their bodies were not for sale. They were works of art to be appreciated. They were status symbols, sounding boards, and what the Japanese male viewed as the ultimate companions.

"Drink?" Izumi said in Japanese as the car returned to the highway. "Sake? Scotch? Beer? We have it all."

"Sake," I said. "*Arigato.*"

I would have been lying if I said I was not fighting the urge to reach out for her. I'm not sure what stopped me. Liliko? Kimiko? Just good common sense? So, instead of making a fool of myself, I sat back and allowed them to spoil me with unbridled attention that included offers of marijuana, cocaine, and opium. I got tired of saying, "Just sake," and they finally stopped offering.

We drank and toasted and pretended not to have a language barrier. I practiced my Japanese, and they laughed at my accent as if I were the last great American comic. They spoke slowly, used their hands to illustrate, and became more animated with each glass of sake.

Along the way, I did get some insight into the ancient world of Sumo. Izumi called the wrestlers *sumotori*. Rika referred to them as *rikishi*. She stood up in the middle of the moving limo, flexed her slender arms in an exaggerated muscle man pose, and shouted, "Strong man!"

I nodded the prideful smile of a linguist extraordinaire with a nice buzz and said, "Ah! *Rikishi*. Strong man."

Rika clapped, and Izumi filled our sake glasses. She said, "Fifteen hundred years ago, possession and rule of the Japanese islands was determined by a sumo match. Back then, it was a fight to the death. No longer. Still serious though. And big money."

"Do women attend sumo?" I asked.

"*Hai!* Women are big sumo fans," Izumi said. "I have attended many."

The girls tried to explain the rules using the interior of the limo as the ring.

"*Doyho,*" Rika said and used her hands to make a big circle. Watching them pantomime the exaggerated rituals of the *sumotori* was sensual and

funny and more instructive than I would have imagined. It was a simple
sport if I understood them correctly. The object was to force your opponent out of the *dohyo*, something that might take as few as two or three
seconds or as long as two or three minutes, if my personal demonstration
meant anything. I also got the impression that you could win by throwing
your opponent to the mat, which Izumi did to Rika in a playful move that
looked more like ballet than sumo.

When the pantomime ended and we were finally able to contain our
laughter, we sat back and watched the city lights of Tokyo sweep past us.
We entered the Ryogoku neighborhood in southeastern Tokyo and Izumi
pointed to the magnificent sporting arena that filled our window.
"*Kokugikan*," she said.

The limo wound its way past parking lots and parking garages to the
VIP lane in front of the entrance. The girls wished me a good time but did
not accompany us inside. I walked between Tonto and the Lone Ranger as
if the VIP moniker had been invented just for me. We did not enter the
complex with the masses. We shuttled along a roped off corridor and in
through a pair of well-monitored glass doors. The Lone Ranger flashed a
VIP card that opened the way to a bank of escalators and a sign that read
"Club Seats" in three languages. I could have been a rock star or an alien
from a neighboring galaxy given the blatant stares I was eliciting.

Ten seconds later, I caught sight of *Oyabun* Ter Yamaguchi and his
saiko komon, Uncle Kohji Yamaguchi. They were standing in a tight group
of fifteen or so men, crowded around a private bar and a mini-buffet.
Their laughter traveled across the corridor and made me think they had
been partying for some time.

"Ah! Waters-san, my good friend. *Konbanwa!*" The *Kumicho* hailed
me.

His group turned in unison as I approached and watched with tight
smiles as the *Oyabun* encircled me in his arms. Nothing quite like saving
a guy's life to get in his good graces, I thought. The clan boss was in a jubi-
lant mood and proceeded to introduce me to his party the way he might

a son. I shook a dozen hands, received several slaps on the back, and a second hug from Uncle Kohji. I bowed and smiled and actually felt welcome.

I was given a drink and a small plate of *yakitori*, strips of chicken served on a stick and very tasty. I had no idea what they were talking about before my arrival, but now the talk turned to sumo.

I got the impression that the *basho* we were attending was one of six Grand Sumo tournaments held every year in Japan. It was a two-week affair that opened this night and featured the *Yokozuna*, the pinnacle of sumo and a rank held by only 65 men. I was feeling more elitist all the time.

But I had no idea how elite the company I was keeping was until the *Oyabun* and his group filed into the arena, a huge and boisterous hall built around the fighting ring, or *dohyo*, that rose up at its heart.

An usher, female and beaming with recognition, led us down a set of stairs to a private box in the first tier of seats.

"Great seats," I said in English to no one in particular.

It was Uncle Kohji who responded. He said, "The *Oyabun* would be honored if you sat with him. As would I."

I lowered my head slightly and said, "*Arigato.* I would be honored."

The buzz that followed the passage of the Yamaguchi clan to "our" box was unmistakable. There were hushed whispers, animated greetings, and envious eyes. The *yakuza* may have been similar in certain respects to the American mafia, but it was apparently more visible. The *Oyabun* could have been a sports figure or an entertainer given his reception, and I couldn't decide whether to puff my chest out or hide my face as we took our seats.

Most curious was the empty seat to the *Kumicho*'s left.

"Is Mrs. Yamaguchi expected?" I asked his senior advisor, my gaze turned toward the empty seat.

Uncle Kohji shared a brief smile. "Mrs. Yamaguchi prefers the theater to sumo, Waters-san. No, the empty seat is an invitation."

He held my eye and waited for me to fill in the blank. "To talk business?" I ventured.

"Indeed," the *saiko komon* said. "The propositions the *Oyabun* fields here are like seeds in a garden. Some will sprout. Others will flower. And yet others will never see the light of day. In fact, most. He is not being rude to you or I; we are his brethren and inviting us tonight is a sign of respect. The business he does here is another way he protects his brethren. Can you understand?"

"I think I can."

"Excellent. Now enjoy Japan's national sport. Watch and learn."

Watch and learn? I wondered what that was supposed to mean, but I didn't need to wonder for long. The *saiko komon* could have described it in one word: ritual. Sumo was nothing if not ritual-filled.

The lights dimmed, and silence fell over the arena. The basho began with a ceremony that was almost religious in nature. I watched as a man with a priestly presence carried two small wooden vessels into the center of the ring.

"Salt and rice wine," Kohji Yamaguchi whispered to me as the priest christened the ring with sprinklings of salt and wine. "He is blessing the *dohyo*. The salt purifies the ring and the wine rids it of evil spirits."

"*Hai*," I said.

When this first ceremony was complete, a man clad in a most elaborate and luxurious kimono and wearing a strange hat that reminded me of a square, black fez took the priest's place in the ring.

"Our referee," the clan's senior advisor said quietly. "A very prestigious position. Highly respected."

A moment later, a hush and a stir swept through the crowd as the first two *rikishi* entered the ring. They wore exquisite silk dresses with elaborately sown designs that were truly works of art in their own right. Then a mighty roar crashed through the hall as the sumotori were introduced. With great attention and obvious ceremony, two attendants helped the wrestlers remove their gowns. Underneath were two huge men with rolls of fat hanging from their stout frames, disguising immense strength and, I imagined, remarkable dexterity. They were Japanese heroes. I could tell it just by the energy throughout the arena.

They wore thick silk belts around their waists and thongs that covered their genitals; that was all. The ritual continued as each man filled his mouth with water, swished it from side to side, and then spit it out.

"To cleanse their mind and bodies," Kohji Yamaguchi said.

I then watched each man toss a handful of salt over his shoulder.

"To please the gods. Very important," he whispered.

The two combatants immersed their hands in white powder, clapped away the excess, and then took their positions in the ring. They bowed in unison to the referee, then bowed to each other.

They stomped their feet like great ships rolling from side to side, set themselves in combat-ready positions, and vouchsafed their opponent with the most intimidating glare each could muster.

A moment of electric silence filled the hall, a signal from the referee initiated the combat, and then the thunderous clap of two larger-than-life men charging into one another echoed in my ear. The crowd exploded.

The exertion of two sumotori using every ounce of their strength to move the other out of a ring not five yards across was a physical sensation I could feel all the way up to where I sat. I had never experienced anything like it. And that one of the wrestlers tumbled out of the *dohyo* less than ten seconds later only amplified the feeling.

I watched as the victor and the loser finished their match with respect-ful bows that reminded me of the handshake that ended every tennis match or football game I had every played. They called it respecting your opponent here. We called it sportsmanship. A rose by any other name, I thought.

I cheered right along with the *Oyabun* and his clan members simply because the pent up energy had to go somewhere. My first sumo match. I would never forget it. How could I?

An hour and five matches passed and the excitement never abated. I tried not to pay attention to the men who came and went from the empty chair at the *Oyabun's* side, but I couldn't help myself: a man in a per-fectly tailored silk suit that must have cost him a couple of thousand dollars; a bulbous man dressed from head to foot in white with an unlit cigar clamped between his fingers; a serious, bespectacled young man who presented the *Kumicho* with a small, gilded box; a Caucasian man with an open shirt and gold chains dangling from his neck. As far as I could tell, *Oyabun* Yamaguchi received each of them with the same reserved demeanor and very few words. Mostly, he listened.

I calculated that each visitor had three minutes to make their pitch, always between matches, and speaking in a voice that carried no further than the man next to me.

Only one man, the bespectacled youth, earned a second audience with one of the *Oyabun's* associates, but I could not tell if that was a good thing or not. I was fascinated by these interactions and couldn't really say why. I was aching to know what each man was proposing to the Yamaguchi boss. Was it legal or illegal? New business or old? Violent or peaceful?

I told myself it didn't matter. It had nothing to do with me. I was an honorary member of the clan. The rules did not apply to me.

"Are you enjoying yourself, Waters-san?" The *Oyabun* shifted in his seat and spoke to me for the first time in an hour.

"Very much. It's quite a spectacle."

"Interesting, do you not think, how sumo reflects life itself?" he said unexpectedly.

"How so, *Oyabun*?" I asked knowing he was eager to share a philosophical slice of life.

"The *sumotori* belong to teams. They live communally. It is their way of life as well as a sport. Each wears the traditional *mawashi*, the thick belt that you see, no matter what their rank. And yet, each man carries his own rank. Sumo is strictly merit based, Waters-san, as truly as life itself is. They must earn their place. They gain rank and pay only by winning, not for style or show. Lose and you drop in rank. A *basho* includes 15 bouts for each contestant, and rarely does a man win every bout. But each *rikishi* seeks what is called *kachi-koshi*, 8 wins out of 15. That is enough for victory."

"I see."

"Every man has failures, Waters-san, whether it is in his business life or his personal life. Is this not true? But it is the man that pulls himself up and shows a willingness to play the game again and strive for *kachi-koshi* who stands out."

The *Oyabun* nodded toward the ring as the wrestlers went through their traditional pre-bout ritual. The water, the salt, the bows.

"But victory without respect means nothing, Waters-san. We honor our opponents even when our goal is to crush them. In sumo, the *rikishi* do not pull hair or gouge eyes or strike with a closed fist. Boundaries. Healthy boundaries, just like those we set for ourselves in life if we want to maintain our self-respect."

"Agreed," I said feeling good about holding up my end of the conversation.

"But," the *Kumicho* said, emphasizing the word with a raised finger. "Pushing, tripping, throwing, even slapping an opponent are accepted techniques. The *sumotori* who chooses not to apply every technique and trick available to him is a fool. Sumo is about creating advantage and opportunity. Why? Because the match is over in the blink of an eye, Waters-san. If you are not prepared for the moment, you are letting the circumstances rule over you instead of taking charge of the circumstances. All life—business, love, sport—is the same."

"And then . . ." He gestured toward the *dohyo* as the bout ended, and we watched as the wrestlers bowed to each other once more. "Maintain your dignity, win or lose. Do not bask long in your glory nor revel in your opponent's defeat. Instead, prepare again for what lies ahead, for whatever life has in store for you."

He held my eye long enough to make me uncomfortable, smiled as if he was satisfied, and then turned and greeted one last visitor.

We didn't stay until the end. The *Oyabun's* bodyguards were eager to see him out of the hall before the crowds descended.

I said my goodbyes to the clan's boss and his senior advisor before the two men were ushered out. "I enjoyed it immensely," I told them. "Thank you for the invitation."

"Not at all," the *Kumicho* said. "You honored us with your presence. I hope you found our national sport mildly interesting."

"I enjoyed the entire night, *Oyabun* Yamaguchi. *Domo arigato.*"

I was not exaggerating. I had enjoyed it. It was a good time, but it was also an educational time, and one of the things I learned was that a steady diet of the *yakuza* way was not something I desired. Too much high drama, I thought as I followed Tonto outside. When I went to a baseball game at Wrigley Field or a football game at Soldier Field, I wanted to escape from reality, not be reminded of it everywhere I looked.

The limousine was waiting for us out front. Izumi and Rika were not part of the return trip package and I was secretly grateful. I just wanted to lean my head against the seat back and close my eyes. By the time the Lone Ranger had fought the traffic to the expressway, I was sound asleep. Why my dreams returned me to Mount Fuji and the same dragon who seemed determined to hunt me down, I didn't know. I was glad when Tonto shook me awake. I was even happier when my head hit the pillow on my undersized bed and a dreamless sleep carried me through the rest of the night.

15

No Problem

*"I grew up
Bathing in the emerald sea
Of everlasting summers."*
～ Hisajo Sugita

M y learning was less about the classroom than it was about expand-
ing the walls of my mind and heart, but there were positives
resulting from my classes, too. Katayama Sensei's Japanese language class
had been pared by two students, so the one-on-one attention we received
felt almost like personal tutorials. Neko infused her classes with philosophical overtones that were nearly as valuable as our language studies.
Her theme was simple: understanding Japan's idiosyncrasies brought
color to the language, but it also provided insights meant to inspire us
into being more productive citizens of the world.

"Do not expect the rest of the world to be like you," she said. "Do not
think that everyone longs to be a Californian or a New Yorker. Do not
think that people in Japan, Africa, or South America desire your lifestyle;
as if there is something wrong with the way they already live their lives. It
is not true. Instead, embrace the way we live here or the way they live in
Brazil or Nigeria, and you will create bridges instead of walls."

I loved listening to her. She was, more than anything, authentic. She
used failure as well as success to instruct. She preached balance, even as I
could imagine her struggling to achieve balance in her own life. I wouldn't

have traded our Friday afternoon tea sessions for anything. I would have stayed in Fujinomiya just for those precious hours. Our discussions touched on subjects as diverse as politics and business, but also explored things like relationships and religion. The *yakuza* was not off-limits, but we only talked about it in general terms. If Neko asked, "Did you enjoy the *basho*?" it was her way of allowing me to explore the dynamics of the sumo tournament in light of the company I had kept that night. But if I crossed the line by asking about the "business" proposals the *Kumicho* had entertained that night, she simply smiled and said, "I'm hardly privy to that kind of information, Waters-san," and that was that.

Professor Miura Narita's Japanese Culture class was most instructive in the ways in which he made my Japanese colleagues uncomfortable. He pushed them unmercifully to understand that they had to break away from the shackles of duty, obligation, fealty, and shame if they were to maximize their business relationships with the outside world.

"Do you think an oil merchant in Dubai or Riyadh really gives a damn about whether you and Sony or you and Toyota come away from a business deal wearing a robe sewn of integrity or honor? They only want to know the color of your money and whether or not you can fatten their bottom line," he would shout. Then he would lower his voice and peer over the top of his dark glasses. "It is your job to seal the deal without drowning in the cesspool. It is not your job to clean up the cesspool. See the difference, my friends?"

Narita Sensei did not want me to think like Kudoh, and he did not want Moto to think like me. "That is not the answer. You are Japanese, Moto-san. Embrace it. You, Mr. Waters, are American. Embrace that." He would take off his glasses and jab them at me like a pointer. "You do not have to think like me, but you sure as hell must understand what makes me tick. You do not want to waste your energy trying to change me. This is the business world. Use your energy to get inside my head and satisfy my needs, and I will use my energy to see that your needs are met in return."

He would take in the class, one student at a time. "You are a product of your society, but you are not a slave to it."

The disaster on my schedule was the disaster on everyone else's schedule, too: Organizational Behavior and the drunk teaching it. Dr. Adrian Barrett demonstrated all the traits of a full-blown alcoholic. The bottle controlled his life—as he had told me very plainly that first Friday he wanted it to do—morning, noon, and night. If he didn't stumble into our classroom stinking of whiskey, he strolled in sporting a major league hangover.

Barrett always did two things to sustain his ability to get through class. The first of these was to query us for feedback on the previous week's reading assignment. He had neither the energy nor the forbearance to ask specific questions of individual students. That would have required interaction, and he loathed the possibility of interaction as much as we did. The second thing he did was to always focus his lectures, the longest of which might approach ten minutes, on the same theme: the fallacy of the Japanese work ethic. He would use his ten minutes to debunk the myth that all industrial Japan operated with the precision, savvy, and profitability of Toyota or Sony.

"They are the exceptions to the rule of an unproductive system bloated with staff, slowed to a crawl by a follower's mentality, and most competent at pirating ideas from others," Barret said.

No one challenged him. There was something in the air that reeked of at least some truth, and Barrett didn't hang around long enough to hear debate on either side of the aisle.

"All right then. Chapter Four next week. Come prepared. Now go to your corners and get those businesses up and running. The clock is ticking. Make it work. Team leaders will update me with your monthly reports before noon on Friday. Whatever day you do come in, make it before 1:00 p.m. but not before 10:00 in the morning. *Sayonara*," he would say and haul his briefcase, which was never opened, back to his inner sanctum.

Using the Japanese farewell, *Sayonara*, was not a tribute to his hosts. I could hear the sarcasm in his voice. No, it was another less than subtle dig, and it only perpetrated a spiraling decline of respect for him among the student population.

I was fairly certain that Dr. Adrian Barrett, broken hearted Stanford professor, would take immense pride in that decline. He would consider it a building block in U.S.-Japan relations.

In our last one-on-one meeting, he had said to me, "This isn't a love fest, Mr. Waters. This is a battleground. I don't want the Japanese to like us. I want them to have an insatiable desire to stomp us to death in the industrial arena. I want them to be thirsty for our economic blood. Why? Because that will drive them to make better cars and better toasters. That's the way, young man."

"You mean if we piss them off? You're kidding?" I said this even though I found myself listening to his argument.

This made Barrett laugh. "The last things we need from the Japanese as business partners, Mr. Waters, are their aloofness or their complacency. Don't you see? Look back in time, World War II and before. For thousands of years the Japanese lived on their little islands, alone and isolated. They were cultured enough, no one denies that, but hardly progressive. Then they got a taste of western excess, a taste of wanting more just for the sake of *having* more. Get it? Conquering China or Formosa or Guam couldn't possibly have served them in any constructive way; they just got a taste of conquering. And they liked the taste."

Barrett stared at the ceiling before continuing. "We don't want them to lose that taste for bigger and better things, Mr. Waters, because that's what will make them better business partners."

When I shared this point of view with Neko, she said, "Can you find the threads of truth that run in and out of the good professor's ramblings, Waters-san? They are there. It is your task to find them despite your dislike for the man."

Neko had, in many ways, become more than my teacher and counselor. She was also more than my secret. She had evolved into a confidante and a friend. I trusted her. So when she suggested I keep an open mind about Professor Barrett and his half-baked ideas, I did.

For me, it became a question of motivation. What motivated people to act, to be creative, to be constructive? Were they the same motivating factors that caused them to be destructive, reactionary, and aggressive? How much did culture play into that? Did a melting pot culture like the one we had in the States breed different motivational proclivities than those in Japan? Did we care less about the man standing next to us because we shared less history with him than the Japanese man did with his fellow countrymen? Were we more willing to throw our competition to the wolves than the Japanese were theirs because there was less history to fall back on, a less refined code of conduct, and less respect? The answers were obvious and not altogether complimentary. The bigger question was this, however: Were these new motivational influences, ones that seemed to permeate western thinking, a good thing? Were they positive steps for mankind?

When I felt myself becoming philosophical, I gathered my books together and went in search of my fellow members of Kumayama Inc., entrepreneurs extraordinaire and promoters of one very historic tennis tournament. Here, the energy was high. And why not? Kudoh and Suzuki had traveled to Tokyo some weeks earlier and had finalized the Suzuki Motorcycle Division's advertising contribution. The $50,000 ad fee had been deposited in full into an account at the Edo National Bank in the Kumayama name with Kudoh and Suzuki as joint signatories. We were officially up and running.

While they were there, Suzuki arranged for the delivery of his company's ten latest, groundbreaking motorcycles—models the public had yet to see—for unveiling the week of our tennis tournament. This was a feather in the cap for him and a coup for Kumayama Inc.

Every time our group came together, I made a point of cautioning my fellow teammates against complacency. There was a feeling among us that we had an "A" grade sewn up, but there were no guarantees.

"We still have plenty of work to do," Sandy said, reinforcing my point and making me look less like an overbearing, reactionary American. She turned the meeting over to the young man from Sapporo Beer and his colleague from the food industry.

"Gojo is a leading sports drink here in Japan. You may have heard of it," our food industry colleague said for Sandy's and my benefit. "They have committed 600,000 yen in sponsorship money to our group."

"That is around $2,500," the Sapporo man clarified.

"And all the refreshments for our tournament," added his colleague.

A cheer went up. This was exceptional news. "Terrific," Sandy said, hugging them both.

"What about food?" Kudoh asked the pair.

"We are still working on that, but we think the Ichiban Tempura restaurant in Fujinomiya should get the gala dinner job since they have been so good to us. How does everyone feel about that?"

"Great idea," Kenzo Shinran, my perpetually rumpled colleague, said.

"Sure thing. As long as Kimiko does not have to work that night," Kudoh said with a huge grin and a factitious wink. "I do not think Waters-san would be too pleased with that."

This brought a well-deserved round of jeers and laughter, but I took it well.

Thursday nights at Ichiban Tempura became increasingly special. Our corporate dinners were like a growing addiction for a man trapped in the body of a wide receiver and who, for six of every seven days a week, had no visible means of nourishing that body. I had already made myself two promises. If I ever escaped this culinary-deprived campus, I would never consume another grain of white rice for as long as God allowed me the ability to eat. The ubiquitous green tea, however, I had grown unusually fond of, and I told myself I would return home well supplied in the genuine article; no imitation green tea for me.

The food in the tatami room was a virtual lifesaver. It not only filled my stomach, but it reassured me that the gastronomic palette beyond the JIIS walls also had not been reduced to rice and beady-eyed white fish. Hallelujah!

Our dinners were also furthering my understanding of my Japanese colleagues. We were becoming comfortable with each other. If not close and not completely open, we were at least less guarded. We were quickly finding the depth of our relationships, even if that depth was often regrettably shallow.

I tried to draw a comparison between this situation and a similar one that might arise back home. It was not, I concluded, as different as I might have expected. Take ten guys in Chicago, throw them in a room once a week to guzzle alcohol and eat to their hearts' content, add yourself to the mix, and you might make a real connection with two or three of them. Two or three others you might find interesting enough to engage in light to moderate conversation. Another two or three would be, at best, part of the landscape. You might even find a reason or two for actually disliking one of them. This was human nature, the roll of the dice, the turn of the cards. It was not cultural bias. I could have gone through the Kumayama roster and slotted my teammates nicely into each of those categories. Actually, my luck was better than that. Sandy and Kudoh had become good friends, and there really was not a guy in the room I disliked.

The prize that made Thursday nights more than a night out or a chance to eat real food was the illuminating presence of Kimiko. I could hardly contain my excitement beforehand, and I really didn't know what to do with my excitement once I arrived. Bow, say *"Konbanwa,"* touch her hand, hold her eye for one perfect moment, and feel my heart pound in my chest.

For some weeks, I had assumed my infatuation with this sensual, very delicate woman was a means of distancing myself from the romantic chapter I had recently closed in my life with Karen. Then I discovered that sadness or relief or whatever it was I was feeling had nothing to do with it. The spark of young love had grabbed me with two hands and thrown me into the deep end of the pool. It was an amazing feeling.

As it did every Thursday, a charge of electric energy ran through my veins when the Mountain Lions filed into our reserved tatami room. Strict rituals had been established and the first of these was the seating order we observed. Sandy, now resigned to the order of things, sat beside Suzuki. My roommate had been luckless in wooing this California Girl, as he had taken to calling Sandy, away from the Canadian Chick, as he playfully referred to Sherri. Suzuki took the rejection well.

Sandy's fallback line was always, "You're just too much man for me, Suzuki-san."

This, at least, was a face-saving rebuff, and I had to credit Sandy for that.

I squeezed in between Kudoh and Kenzo Shinran. We started the evening with a cold Sapporo, no exceptions. Kimiko always served Sandy first and me second, still referring to us as "our honored visitors" after all these weeks. Suzuki always made the first toast and it always anointed the growing bond of Kumayama Inc.

On this particular night, he came to his feet and said, "Ten roaring mountain lions. Kumayama Inc. Kanpai! Cheers!"

Now we were rolling. By the time our traditional yakitori appetizer was served, the toasts had traveled around the table.

I always tried to give a plug to Suzuki and his company because I had now come to realize that my cocky roommate was under as much pressure as any of my other colleagues. It was not easy being the heir apparent to any monolithic company, much less a Japanese one with your name on it, and his bluster was as much defense mechanism as true boasting and swagger.

"To the best motorcycles on the entire planet—Suzuki—and our very own corporate representative, marketing wizard, and roaring mountain lion, Suzuki-san. Hear, hear!"

"*Arigato*, Waters-san. Banzai!" Suzuki was not shy about toasting his own status, and I had to give him credit for that.

It was a given that we all had a nice buzz going by the time the shrimp tempura and rice were served, and the meal would never have been complete without copious amounts of hot sake.

Kimiko and her three co-hosts had long ago been made honorary members of our fine company, and for every shot of sake they politely refused, my Japanese cohorts felt obligated to drink in their honor. Every shot emboldened them and made them more gregarious. The girls spent the better part of the evening fending off their advances and giggling as if a hand on their bottoms was just the cutest thing in the world. I admired their poise and the deftness with which they handled this drunken groping. There was never a scene, never a sharp retort, and never any indication that an impropriety had been committed. Only in Japan, I thought with equal parts admiration, astonishment, and dismay. We would have called it harassment back home. Here, they called it the status quo.

Interestingly, a part of me wanted to protect Kimiko from this overt groping. That was surely a guy thing, but I also suspected it was an American guy thing, standing up for your woman and all that. In an age of burning bras and women's liberation, that could be a double-edged sword.

The sexual revolution and equality of the sexes were still a long way from making in-roads here in Fujinomiya. Maybe it would hit the Japanese countryside about the time Kimiko's daughters were her age. For now, all I could do was treat Kimiko the same way I treated Sandy, Sherri, or any other woman. It was a small gift, but if I believed even half of what I had seen since coming to Japan, then I could safely say that even the smallest of gifts could make an impact.

Dinner wasn't dinner without the cold sake that came once the shrimp had been devoured and the green tea ice cream savored. We sang a song or two, cried a few tears, and laughed until our sides ached.

I could not get enough of Kimiko's company. She did more than tend to my every need, which was the job she had been assigned our first night in the restaurant. She touched my hand in a most subtle, sensuous way, brushed up against my shoulder, very discreetly rubbed up against me the way only lovers do in the presence of others, and made eye contact even as she was serving someone on the other side of the table.

Another Thursday night ritual was the handwritten note Kimiko always slipped into my hand as our group was leaving the restaurant. Penned in broken English, they read like Hallmark cards, sincere and touching and straight from the heart. Each was written on Hello Kitty stationary, with a baby kitten leaving footprints across pink paper.

She made me laugh and sigh at the same time with lines like, "I am happy just to be with you." When she wrote, "I am very grateful to meet with you, Kai-san," I could see her straining for the right words and knew how painstaking the task had been for her. She always wished me "good luck" and reminded me that she was waiting anxiously to see me again.

There was something different about the letter she tucked into my shirt pocket this particular night. It was not the envelope or the printing, but the innocent, alluring sparkle in her eyes as she slipped it into my hand. I was eager to return with it to the privacy of my dorm room.

When I was stretched out on my bunk, I glanced at the front of the envelope. My name was written in both English and Japanese, the second in graceful calligraphy. I opened it. The stationary inside was neatly folded into fourths. The note was simple and short, but it pushed our relationship in a new and exciting direction. It read:

> Dear Kai-san:
> Your eyes like ocean, deep and blue.
> I like to meet you.
> Meet me at Happi Hoteru. Tomorrow night, 9:00. Room five.
> My love is like cherry blossoms.
> Love, Kimiko.

I stared at the paper as if it had mysteriously fallen from the sky, felt its soft texture, and then read the words a second and third time. I was surprised at the range of emotions six simple lines could express. The excitement was instantaneous; a physical rush that had the effect of kicking my blood pressure up a notch, leaving me a little breathless, and creasing my face with a wide smile. A haunting and almost helpless voice within questioned how I was supposed to respond. It was not as simple as, "Yes, I'll be there. As a matter of fact, Kimiko, I'll be there with bells on and probably a half hour early." And it was not a matter of, "No, sorry, I can't make it. You're just too beautiful, and I wouldn't want to do anything to ruin this nice little friendship we have going."

Hell, yes, I would meet her. That was not the issue. The issue was how to properly handle this "foreign affairs crisis," because I did want to handle it well. How often did I run into a woman who said things like, "My love is like cherry blossoms"? Not often, at least not in my very limited experience. To date, our conversations had been warm and friendly, but also almost infantile. "It's a beautiful night, isn't it?" "You look pretty." "The yakitori is delicious." Matters of love and sex were not part of my Japanese repertoire.

I was probably making more of it than I should have. After all, she was a beautiful young woman and we were obviously attracted to one another. I knew one thing. The Happi Hoteru was designed with one thing in mind: clandestine meetings of the sexual kind.

But Kimiko was different from the other Japanese women I had met. Comparing her background to those of Liliko or Neko was like comparing two different planets. How should I treat her? Was there a love hotel protocol in a small town like Fujinomiya? Did it require the man to be the aggressor? Were we expected to shed our clothes the minute the door closed? After all, we only had an hour. Did I bring flowers, a chilled bottle of wine, or massage oil? All sounded plausible, silly, and exciting at the same time.

If I was going to meet Kimiko for an hour at the Happi Hoteru, I wanted it to be memorable. I needed advice, but I also needed confidentiality. I could talk it over with Sandy during our run the following day. We had developed both a comfort level and a measure of trust between us that allowed us to discuss almost any subject. But there were two problems: one, Sandy knew even less about Japanese love hotels than I did; and two, she might pledge her silence, but vows of silence rarely extended to one's primary mate. Sherri would probably know about it after one drink, and who knew how far it might spread after a shot or two of Ocean whiskey? I considered talking it out with Neko because I had no qualms about the confidentiality of our Friday afternoon conversations. But I was really not ready for a sexual discussion with my sensei.

I needed a man-to-man conversation, and Kimiko's note was going to burn a hole in my pocket until I decided on the best candidate. Moto, it seemed to me, was too preoccupied with his own set of troubling circumstances. He was also very married. Suzuki was also married, but this did not seem to hamper either his need to flirt or his apparent willingness to play the field. I would also question the confidential nature of any discussion I had with Suzuki. Sometimes words just tumbled out of his mouth like a gumball machine on automatic pilot.

I felt confident I could trust Kudoh. He also spoke fluent English and brought out the best in my limited Japanese. Kudoh's status as a single man was still a curiosity, but that did not seem to reflect a lack of interest in the opposite sex. He did strike me as somewhat conservative when it came to women, and this might be another reason for trusting his advice.

We were halfway through our Friday workout when I shared Kimiko's letter and explained my dilemma. "This idea of a love hotel is new to me," I said to him, "and Kimiko and I lack the language skills to communicate well."

Kudoh looked up from the letter and smiled like a wise old sage who found both humor and insight in the situation.

"Kimiko has shown her willingness to take the lead in this affair, has she not, Waters-san?" he asked, sitting across the bench press from me. "I would allow her to continue to do so, though I doubt she has much more experience with the Happi Hoteru than you do. She does not seem the type."

I was glad to hear Kudoh say this, not that I needed to be the first. I guess I just didn't want to be just another in a long line of men.

He said, "Kimiko has obviously thought this out, if her letter means anything. She must have a plan for the night. I would follow her lead,

Waters-san. If she says anything you do not quite understand or asks a question you cannot answer, just remember two magical words."

This sounded good: two magical words. I said, "Okay. I can do that. What are these two magical words?"

"*Mondai nai.*" He smiled his huge, wily smile.

I repeated them. "*Mondai nai.* Which means?"

"*Mondai nai* means, 'No problem.'" He pursed his lips and nodded. "If Kimiko is desiring the sexual adventure that you are hoping for, '*Mondai nai*' will open the door for you both. Let us practice, Waters-san. I will be Kimiko." He laughed with glee, then raised his voice an octave and said, "Oh, Waters-san, will you help me unsnap my bra, you big blue-eyed American?"

I nodded convincingly, playing my part, and said, "*Mondai nai,* Kimiko. *Mondai nai!*"

"You got it," Kudoh shouted. "You are ready, my friend."

Great. Terrific. Two words guaranteed to solve all my problems. I was in the throes of a wonderful dilemma. One part of me was far more nervous and anxious than I had ever been on my first date—homecoming my freshman year in high school with Mollie Wagner, easily the sexiest 15-year-old on the planet. Another part of me was overwhelmed with anticipation and the wild ride my imagination was already taking me on.

I had two words in my arsenal. I played them over and over in my head that afternoon until they sounded natural, casual, and true. At least in my own mind: "*Mondai nai.*"

———

Kimiko

*"The storm
During half day
Has broken the stem of mallow."*
～ Shiki Masaoka

I started toward town at 8:30 that evening, absorbing the cool breeze and doing nothing to dampen my imagination. Sexual anticipation is one of the great gifts of the universe and the best way to honor it is to allow it to sweep you away. And so I did.

The Fujinomiya streets were peaceful and quiet by this time of night and I was grateful for the anonymity. I entered the hotel through a gaudy front entrance. There was nothing subtle about the Happi Hoteru or its purpose and a moment of discomfort reminded me that while we Americans were largely obsessed with sex, we were also slightly embarrassed by it. We liked our hotels and motels disguised as way stations for weary travelers, façades of propriety and practicality. Not the Japanese. They embraced sex. They did not try to hide the fact that some hotels were reserved for that purpose only. Why not go for it?

Though I tried to avoid acting like an American *gaijin* when I asked for Room Five, the raised eyebrows of the hotel manager suggested I had failed. She did bow politely, however, and used an open palm to point me in the direction of the room.

I paused in front of the door, pushing aside a trace of anxiety and a flood of excitement by taking a deep breath, and knocked lightly.

A magnificent princess answered and the breath I had just taken was stolen, totally and completely. Kimiko was dressed in a beautifully embroidered kimono made of ivory colored silk. Every curve and valley of her petite, sensual body—a body I had dreamed about for weeks—came alive beneath this sheer material. Her charcoal black hair fell in waves across her shoulders and down her back, glistening like a moonless night. It highlighted her angelic face like the first light of a beautiful sunrise, elegant and graceful. But it was her smile that most captivated me. Gentle, warm, and inviting, it swept away every trace of anxiety and any concern I might have had about language.

"*Konbanwa*, Kai-san." She bowed slightly.

"*Konbanwa*, Kimiko-san. *Anata wa totemo kirei desu.*" I hoped I had been successful in telling her how beautiful she looked.

"And you are very handsome." I would never grow weary of that accent or that ability to turn my language into something beautiful. "Come in, please."

When I stepped past her, a scent rose from her flawless skin that was so evocative of jasmine I wanted to reach out and touch her right then and there, just a hand on her shoulder to tell her how glad I was to be there. She curled a hand around my arm and led me into the room.

The room's theme bespoke ocean. Under a soft pink light, walls painted azure blue and accented with shades of myrtle green and turquoise seemed to move in waves around the room. Meticulously tended aquariums formed a cincture from wall to wall and each came alive beneath muted green light. Out of the light swam exotic fish of every size and color. If a room could feel like a private beach at sunset, this one came close.

Music so classically Japanese—a meld of strings, wind instruments, and subtle percussion—drifted from the speaker of a portable tape player, and I knew that Kimiko had chosen it just for this occasion.

Yet the exotic fish, the atmosphere created by soft lights, and the music paled under the glow of Kimiko herself. She was radiant, as if a light emanated from deep inside her.

"Sake?" she asked.

"*Hai. Arigato,*" I replied.

A porcelain sake set sat atop a small side table, and she carefully filled two small cups. She took my hand and led me to the side of the bed. We sat.

I said, "*Kanpai,*" and hoped I didn't sound too foolish.

She said, "Cheers," in her broken English, and we both laughed. The sake was hot and powerful. It exploded in my stomach and branched out through the veins of my chest and arms. I could feel the heat on my face. I wanted to tell her again how amazing she looked and said, "*Anata wa kirei desu,* Kimiko-san. So beautiful."

She smiled again, and the last of my fears evaporated. I kissed her cheek and ran my fingers through her hair, breathing in the clean scent of it. Kimiko drew a folded piece of paper from inside her kimono and gently handed it to me. The note was penned in beautiful calligraphy, the Chinese characters like a work of art. Later, I would discover that the note simply said, "Kai-san. I give you a massage," but for now the words were completely meaningless to me.

I tucked the note into my shirt pocket, kissed her hand, and said, "*Mondai nai,* Kimiko-san."

Kimiko giggled when she heard this. Excellent, I thought with a smile. Kudoh had given me a universally correct phrase.

She reached up and began unbuttoning my shirt, her graceful fingers moving slowly from one button to the next. When my shirt was opened, she ran her hands over my chest and whispered words in Japanese that I did not understand but took as an invitation to undress and join her on the bed.

While I kicked off my shoes, socks and pants, Kimiko turned down the bed. I was naked and not quite sure what to do next when she invited me to lie on my stomach and motioned to the oil on the nightstand. When I stretched out on the bed, she opened her kimono, joined me on the bed in one fluent movement, and straddled me from the back. I could feel the heat of her thighs against my legs and the warm touch of her pubis told me she was naked beneath her gown.

She whispered my name and two or three softly spoken Japanese words. She poured oil into the palms of her hands, warmed it between them, and then began massaging my back, gently and rhythmically, but also with strength and confidence.

I felt her long hair graze my skin as she leaned closer. Her words purred in my ear and I felt her lips on the back of my neck. The heat spread, and I fell into a warm world of pleasure.

I could think of nothing more sensual, nothing I had ever experienced, nor a woman with whom I wanted to be with more. I whispered her name, but we both knew that words were unnecessary.

Her hands moved down my back and along my thighs. I felt the pressure building, and Kimiko must have sensed it too. She used her long fingers and gentle touch to invite me onto my back. I had forgotten all about the tattoo on my thigh and Kimiko hardly glanced at it. She mounted me. Our connection was immediate and powerful, and the sounds that filled our tiny room came from places deep within us. I had never felt anything so erotic and the sight of Kimiko above me transported me to a world far, far away. She moved with the rhythm of the background music and her eyes fixed on mine, linking us further. Her kimono parted, exposing small, firm breasts. I reached out for her.

Her hips churned, bringing our connection to a climax as powerful as any I had ever experienced. Kimiko's entire body shuttered, peacefully and completely, like a tree quaking in a cool spring breeze.

I drew her near and kissed her. I wanted to tell her how priceless the gift she had just shared with me was, but I knew my touch could say it far better than my words and her gentle smile, as I caressed her, told me she understood. She drew herself near to me, her fingers tracing the lines of my face, and whispered in my ear. "*Watashi to kekkon shite kudasai.*

Shochi shite kudasai." I would not learn until later that she had said, "Would you marry me, Kai-san? Say you will."

I kissed her ear and whispered in return. *"Mondai nai."*

This caused a moment of glee and laughter so sweet that I was left believing that "no problem" was the perfect answer to whatever it was she had said. Thank you, Kudoh, I thought. Thank you.

I held her, absorbing the scent of her skin and the sweetness of her breath. When there were only two minutes left in our hour, I reluctantly released her. We dressed, and even this was an act of intimacy, for I traced her body with my hands even as she covered it again with her Kimono. I wanted to remember the curve and shape of her body with my hands and stopped only when I heard a quiet tapping on the door.

"We go," Kimiko said. "You first. Then me."

She led me into the hall and directed me toward a rear exit. This, I realized, allowed her a less conspicuous departure from a side door, out and into the silent streets of Fujinomiya.

This surreptitious parting confirmed my earlier suspicions that it might not be in Kimiko's best interests to be seen with an American *gaijin* in a place of intimacy. I did not want anything to jeopardize her place in the community or with her family, but I also reminded myself that she had initiated our rendezvous. She was surely aware of the potential consequences and she was, after all, a grown woman—grown, beautiful, sexy, and exotic.

What an amazing, memorable hour I had just experienced and my wish was that she found it so, too. Whatever we had shared was priceless, I thought. Few words had passed between us and none were really needed. It was beautiful and ineffable, and no one could take that away from us. It was hard to believe that it had been only an hour. While it had passed quickly, there was also a sense of timelessness to it.

I walked up the hill and through the forests protecting the JIIS campus from the rest of the world. The cold air tingled. I tried to assess my own feelings and ended up trying to assess Kimiko's. We were lovers, but did she feel love? Her short notes had confessed as much, but were they real? It could just as easily have been an adventure in her eyes, a fling with the blue-eyed foreigner. A part of me hoped this was the case, that it had been only a foray into the unknown before settling into the life for which her years in Fujinomiya had really prepared her: a husband, kids, and ten or fifteen acres of farmland. I did not want to complicate her life, a life I knew I would only be a part of for a brief time.

I liked Kimiko. I wanted to be with her again. I had fantasized about a foreign romance and had to admit that the fantasy had not come close to the reality of my experience with Kimiko. That was not so much a comment on my imagination as it was on the amazing hour we had just spent together.

I was sure I was smiling as I walked into the common area of our dorm room. The Friday night party was well underway and the smell of beer and whiskey hit me like smelling salts bringing a boxer back to life after a knockout punch. Someone had dug up an old Beatles tape, and "I Want to Hold Your Hand" caromed off the walls. The crowd was mostly male and almost all Japanese. When I saw Dr. Adrian Barrett, flushed with Johnny Walker Black, I decided my Friday night had been too extraordinary to soil with his company. I was halfway to my room when Kudoh caught up with me, a half-empty Kirin in his hand.

He threw an arm around my shoulder and whispered drunkenly in my ear, "So how was your evening walking through the forest filled with cherry blossoms?"

I put a finger to my lips, hoping he would take it as a sign of confidentiality. "*Mondai nai*," I said.

Kudoh broke up laughing. "No problem."

"Let's keep it between us, Kudoh-san. Okay?" I said, hoping I was not relying too much on subtleties.

"A-okay, boss. *Mondai nai*." He used two fingers to seal his lips and laughed again.

I opened the door to my room and hoped to hell Sandy and Sherri weren't curled up in my bed again. Not this time, thank God. I stretched out on my bed, thumbed through a couple of books, and never got past the first paragraph. Then I made a halfhearted attempt at writing a letter to my parents. Later, I wouldn't remember falling asleep.

———

17

The Trip

"Depth of the valley
How high a butterfly
Passes."
~ Hisajo Sugita

I awoke feeling both energized and confused. I attributed these conflicting states of mind to the remarkable hour I had spent with Kimiko. I was energized because I had never engaged in a more erotic evening. I was confused for the same reason.

Moto and I would be traveling to Kyoto that morning and I was excited to be spending time with my good friend over a holiday weekend that extended through Monday. I was thrilled at the opportunity to explore one of Japan's oldest and most beautiful cities, especially with a Kyoto native as my guide. I was also looking forward to meeting his wife and kids and sharing a home-cooked meal. But I was also anxious to break away from the confines of the JIIS campus. The walls had been closing in of late and a road trip was long overdue.

I realized that I could also use a few days to distance myself from Kimiko. I had some thinking to do about my feelings toward this remarkable woman. I didn't want to lead her on in any way but I also knew that stranger things had happened than two complete strangers meeting in a foreign land and living happily ever after. Mitch and Mavis were the perfect example. Why not Kai and Kimiko?

The bus ride into Tokyo took longer than the bullet train south, 180 miles to Kyoto. Before I knew it, I was gazing out at Biwa-ko, the largest lake in Japan and a stretch of vitreous cobalt that almost seemed surreal to the naked eye.

Moto talked and I daydreamed. I was impressed with the personal impact of my short stay in Japan. I had not had time to be homesick, and I had spent as little time as possible reminiscing about the demise of my relationship with Karen because it brought such a deep sorrow to me. Demise, however, was not the right word. She and I had just run our beautiful course as a couple and our parting had created a painful void the likes of which I had never before experienced. We had given each other stability and security during those crazy, chaotic college years when the instability and insecurity of having left home and being on one's own for the first time could play real havoc on the psyche. Now the anchor provided by our relationship was not as important or as necessary, but our love for each other would always burn brightly.

Interestingly, my first months in Japan had solidified this newfound security. Stability was now something I had no doubt about achieving. *When* I would achieve it might be in question, sure, but that didn't frighten me. For now, traveling a path of personal discovery felt more urgent and more satisfying.

I looked over at Moto, who was telling me about his seven-year-old daughter, Tomiko, and her love of the piano. He suggested that she might be willing to give us a brief recital if we begged just a little and seemed to take a certain pride in the fact that he felt strongly enough about our friendship to invite me home for a visit. This was a significant demonstration of affection for a Japanese business executive.

I guess you do have something to offer, Kai, I thought. Kimiko apparently thinks so and so does Moto. When I was just being myself, I seemed to have something to offer others. It was an important lesson and I told myself to remember it. Yeah, that sounded like something my dad would say. But, like most of life's lessons, it was something I had to learn for myself.

"Kyoto," Moto was saying, "was once the capital of Japan. It was not until sometime in the late 1800s that the Emperor Meiji moved to Tokyo—which means 'Eastern Capital' by the way—so the history of my home town is extremely rich. The Imperial Palace built by Emperor Kammu in 794 is still standing, if that tells you anything. You will see Buddhist temples nearly 1500 years old, Waters-san. Not only that, Kyoto is home to some of the oldest Geisha houses in Japan, and many of them are still operating. Not that I have spent much time there," he added with a wink. "I doubt Nobuko would approve."

"You might have a point, my friend," I agreed.

We stepped off the bullet train and hailed a cab. There was an orderliness and a simplicity to Kyoto that made Tokyo look chaotic and I found myself enchanted by the sheer age of the buildings.

"Kyoto was built according to the block system of the ancient Chinese capital of Chang-an," Moto said with pride. He pointed to a slow moving river occupied by skiffs and pontoons. "The River Kamo bisects the city almost perfectly, and the hills surrounding us on four sides have kept Kyoto from growing too much. We still have our share of less than beautiful apartment buildings, though, I am afraid."

The cab entered the area of the city called Gion, and I thought I had been transported back in time. The alleyways and many of the streets were too narrow for cars, but not, I noticed, for a bean curd man's bicycle. A kimonoed lady carried an open, gaily colored parasol. Public bathhouses occupied every corner, and a man in a bathrobe padded along the sidewalk as if nothing could be more natural. A woman leaning out a store window beat a tatami mat with a long stick.

We had to walk the last block to an ancient, classically appointed Japanese inn called Nioman. It was as spotless as it was old and the owner was also the concierge. She bowed as if Moto had been a guest there many times. She led us to a pair of tiny rooms on the main floor and made certain I knew how to use the small hand pump attached to the sink.

"Put on a robe," Moto said. "I will take you to the hot springs for a soak."

I dropped my luggage on the floor, found a guest robe laid out on the bed, and squeezed my feet into slippers that were two sizes too small. I met Moto outside our rooms five minutes later. Off the back of the inn, a macadam path coiled in and around perfectly raked Zen gardens and neatly trimmed junipers. A drum bridge arched above a churning stream. The path narrowed among a forest of bamboo and the hot springs were nestled among the trees.

We disrobed. I was about to slide into a pool of steaming water when I realized that Moto was staring at the tattoo on my thigh. I tried to cover it with my towel, but it was too late.

His eyes were as large as saucers and there was a note of disbelief in his voice when he said, "Kai-San! Your tattoo! Do you realize what the sign of the tiger and the flames symbolizes?"

"It's just a tattoo, Moto-san," I said, casually submerging myself in the tub.

Moto took his place in the spring next to me, but his eyes were still wide with amazement and concern. His voice was a low, guttural whisper when he said, "You wear the sign of the *yakuza*, Waters-san. Did you know that?"

"It's a long story, Moto-san."

"Have you any idea what that means? The power of that sign here in Japan?"

I looked at him, taking in his gaze, and trying to convey both sympathy and discretion. "I do. And I also know what you must be thinking. But I don't want you to be concerned. Everything is fine. I have nothing to do with the *yakuza*. I met some people in Tokyo and helped a man out of jam."

"What kind of a jam?"

"The kind of jam that I wish I could have avoided. The tattoo was his way of thanking me. That's all."

"That's all!"

"Yes. I need you to believe that, Moto-san. You are my good friend, and your friendship is important to me."

"I do believe you, Waters-san. A tattoo does not change our friend-ship." Moto leaned closer, a confidante dispensing pearls of wisdom. "But I would advise you to be very discreet about who sees it, Waters-san. If I understand its meaning, you can imagine how many other people will, as well. And some of those people might not look upon it favorably. Can you see that?"

"Yes, I understand that. Thank you for the advice. I was careless. It won't happen again." I nodded emphatically. "But I must ask you to keep this between us, Moto-san. I know I can trust you to do that."

"You have my word, of course," he said, but I could see that there was more on his mind. "But I must ask one thing, Waters-san. "

"Anything," I said.

"Does this . . . this tattoo and the people . . . the people it represents, this man . . . do they pose any kind of threat to you? Any danger?" he asked.

I held his eye, surprised at how calmly I took his question. "No," I said, "None."

Moto breathed a sigh of relief. "Oh, Waters-san. I am so glad. I should not have asked, but I want you to know that I am here to help you in any way."

"No. You had every right to ask," I assured him and appreciated his gesture of friendship. I wondered briefly if my *yakuza* brethren knew of my presence in Kyoto. I had mentioned the outing to Neko, but it never occurred to me that she would share the information. On the other hand, *Oyabun* Yamaguchi had pledged his protection while I was in Japan. I had assumed the death of Kona had tempered that pledge, but maybe not.

I didn't want to think about it. I lowered myself further in the water, closing my eyes, and hoping this would bring the conversation to a close. The hot water roiled around my legs and chest and I settled on a wooden bench anchored to the side of the pool.

"This is incredible, Moto-san," I said as the water broke above my shoulders and settled below my chin. A cool breeze shook the bamboo stalks, their fluted sound as melodious as any song, filling the air. Whatever tension I had been carrying over the last months evaporated. When I opened my eyes again, I could see that Moto had immersed himself in the spring, as well. His eyes were closed, and the lines on his face had softened. He sighed as if we had discovered an oasis, free of tension and expectations. My friend was clearly in his element here. Within minutes, he was more relaxed than I had ever seen him.

"I have been longing for this, Waters-san," he said, explaining that a short reprieve before joining his family and reclaiming his role as father, husband, and head of the Moto household was commonplace among traveling executives. "This way we do not carry the pressures of the work world home with us. Or, at least, less than we might."

"Great idea," I said.

"My family sees little enough of me as it is," Moto said in fractured, heavily accented English. My native tongue would never be his strong suit, I decided, and I had to wonder why Moto had been selected to represent his company at the Japan Institute of International Studies.

As if reading my thoughts, Moto gazed across the pool at me and said, "I am a lucky man, Waters-san. Who would have imagined Homare Moto ever being chosen for such an honored task as representing the Sony Corporation for six months at the prestigious Fujinomiya campus? I wish the honor had gone to someone else, to be frank."

This did not sound like modesty, though Moto was surely a modest man and not likely to tout his status as a rising star at the internationally renowned Sony. It sounded more like a plea.

"How did you get started at Sony, Moto-san?" I asked, my interest genuine.

"I graduated third in my class at Tokyo University. I was highly sought after. I studied international marketing because a friend of my father advised me in that direction. I pictured myself as an artist or a poet when I was growing up, but my family does not see those as legitimate professions. Hobbies, maybe."

Moto closed his eyes again and sank deeper into the water. "I was lucky," he said. "It was at school in my junior year that I met Nobuko. I fell in love the moment she said my name. Her father is a very powerful man. He owns a large accounting firm and plays golf every week with Kudo Sugiyama."

"That sounds like a name I should recognize," I said lamely.

"He is Sony's Chairman of the Board."

"Oh," I said even more lamely. "Now I'm getting the picture."

"Yes. 'Two plus two' as you would say in America. I married Nobuko. Her father introduced his new son-in-law to Mr. Sugiyama and I found myself the recipient of a lucrative job offer, one I could not turn down."

No, I guess not, I thought. The would-be artist was thrust onto a career path lit with potential but also littered with the hazards of a glaring spotlight and more expectations than he could have ever imagined, much less sought.

"Great things are expected of me at the Institute, Waters-san," he said, again reading my thoughts. He chuckled, but there was a decided lack of humor in it. "I am expected to return to Sony versed in English and filled with nuggets of Western insight. They do not know that my future hinges on a Croissant shop and the volume sale of $1.00 pastries." He chuckled again. "Not to worry. I am about to introduce my American friend to my wife and daughters, a great honor for me."

"And a great honor for me," I said, though I was still hearing him say, "Great things are expected of me at the Institute."

I could hardly walk when I dragged myself out of the hot spring. My legs felt like rubber. That's what comes from being boiled alive for an hour and twenty minutes, I told myself. I stumbled back to my room, showered, and put on the dinner robe I found perfectly folded on my bed. When I was dressed, I met Moto among the flowers and trees of the inn's garden. A slight man attired in Japanese robes held a wide rake that he ran through a sea of pure white sand, creating island mounds among waves that seemed to have no end.

"He is a Zen monk," Moto said. "The sand represents the ocean. The mounds represent the many hundreds of islands of Japan and the unity that has always been our country's goal. We are closer to it now than we have ever been, but there were many bloody times in our history, Waters-san."

"I have read about your civil wars," I said.

"It was not until the fifth century, when the greatest of the Chinese influences swept over our country, that we began to record our history. Chinese script, classical literature, medical techniques, and elements of Confucianism impacted us greatly. But we have never lacked for boldness, courage, or the willingness to die for a cause. Sadly, we sometimes failed to conduct our due diligence over the cause at hand, though."

"That is a problem all human beings seem to have on occasion," I added.

Moto laid a hand on my shoulder. "But enough history. We have a meal awaiting us that you will never forget, Waters-san. Follow me."

He led me back inside, down a narrow hall, and into a tatami room enclosed by paper walls decorated with delicate drawings of bamboo, birds, and mountain vistas shrouded in fog.

When Moto declared this an event I would never forget, he was not exaggerating. The delicacies came one after another, each more exotic and flavorful than the last: battered albacore; raw shrimp; unagi; scallops wrapped in seaweed; salmon that literally melted in my mouth; chicken lavished in teriyaki; marbleized beef; and agi-dasi tofu. There were nine courses, testing my sense of culinary adventure and challenging my taste buds like no meal ever had. It kept two servers going full steam for nearly two hours. Hot sake flowed freely, drawing out Moto's generous sense of humor and tapping a sense of freedom I had yet to see in my friend.

"Ah, Waters-san. And now the highlight of the evening. Dessert."

Our servers made the presentation jointly, and it took all my self-control not to flinch, faint, or excuse myself from the table.

"Baby squids soaked in sugar, a delicacy like no other," Moto announced with the same alacrity and enthusiasm one might announce the birth of a child.

I was presented with a different side to this "meal of a lifetime." This side, unfortunately, I could have done without. I had learned that the Japanese will go to the ends of the earth to make a guest comfortable. It was Moto's duty to make me feel special; it was his responsibility to put me on a pedestal. In return, it was my obligation to express my appreciation for his hospitality, even as he discounted it. One way of accomplishing this was to swallow every morsel of baby squid as if consuming my favorite ice cream. This I did.

"Wonderful," I said without gagging.

A last cup of sake saw us to our feet, and we walked arm in arm back to our rooms. I lost track of the time, but we completed the journey with a minimum of wrong turns.

We stopped in front of my room. Before I opened the door, I put a hand on Moto's shoulder. "My good friend, I thank you for the unforgettable meal and a fine day," I said. "I hope you know that I will do everything I can to help you with your studies once we return to campus. Day or night, I'm there for you, Moto-san."

Tears pooled in Moto's eyes when he heard this. They spilled over in endless torrents and drenched his cheeks and chin. These may have been tears of gratitude, but the sobs that followed were heavy with sadness and weighted down with inevitability. Nothing is more painful than helplessness.

"You are Sony's rising star. You make them proud every day. Your success will be their success," I said.

Moto threw his arms around me. "*Domo arigato*, Waters-san. *Anatawa yoi tomodachi desu.*"

"I can't wait to meet your family tomorrow," I told him truthfully. "I can only imagine how proud they are of you."

I walked him down the hall to his room, pushed open the door, and guided him inside. "Get some sleep. It's been a fine day."

Back in my own room, I only managed to kick my slippers off before falling flat on the futon. Sheer exhaustion carried me into a restless sleep torn by sound-bite dreams and the tortured ramblings of the unconscious mind.

I awoke with a start two hours later, and all I could see was Moto's tormented face. A man of such generosity and kindness, yet I saw him cracking at the seams and felt unsure how to prevent this seemingly inevitable rupture. The confluence of corporate stress and his spiraling decline at school could well be a bellwether of something more serious, but I refused to believe he was beyond my help, even if I had to enlist the entire foreign contingent of JIIS to get him through the semester.

The following morning, they served coffee especially prepared for the American *gaijin*, and I savored every sip. Moto hailed a cab. Our first stop was Ginkakuji, the Silver Temple, a graceful two-story pagoda with sweeping eaves and a wide deck. It was simple and elegant, surrounded by meticulously tended gardens and a pond alive with water lilies.

"It was built 600 years ago by the Shogun Yoshimasa, a devoted Buddhist," Moto said. "Buddhism came to us from the Chinese, Waterssan, though Shinto is our original religion."

"Shinto. The Way of the Gods." I was showing off now, but Moto only nodded with increasing gravity.

"Now Shinto and Buddhism are equally accepted and mingled in many ways. You often see Shinto shrines and Buddhist temples on the same block, but when I want to feel the peace of my Buddhist roots, I come here to the Silver Temple. I will spend a few minutes, if you do not mind."

"No, not at all. Spend as long as you like, Moto-san."

Moto entered the temple and I toured the gardens. I was glad we had come, for Moto's peace of mind more than anything. Religion, at least organized religion, was not a big part of my life. If pressed, I might refer to myself as a Christian. My problem with organized religion was the division it caused. The way I saw it, the very first moment one religious sect deemed itself more important or more righteous than the church down the street, the most basic messages of Jesus or Buddha or Vishnu went right out the window. "Love one another" was the one central theme that made real sense to me, and it seemed that the minute the Catholics proclaimed themselves the one true religion or the Hindus claimed their beliefs to be the most direct route to salvation, compassion and open-mindedness were lost.

According to Moto, when the Jesuits landed in Japan in the 16th century and set about trying to convert the people from their Shinto roots or their Buddhist lifestyles to Christianity, they employed the Portuguese and the Dutch to burn Buddhist temples to the ground and slaughter their priests. I didn't imagine that Jesus or Buddha would have approved.

The gardens surrounding the Silver Temple, with their quiet flow of water and natural beauty, spoke to my view of what religion should be: an influence that touched the soul in simple, gentle, and profound ways. I might believe in a higher power, but my vision was no more correct than Moto's nor any other man, woman, or child. Freedom of worship was great, but when it began pitting men against one another, it was no longer about freedom; it was about control. I could not remember anywhere in the Bible, the Rig Veda, the Pitaka, or any other articles of faith where control was the virtue of choice. But what did I know? At age 23, I was still seeking an understanding of these things.

As soon as we arrived at Moto's house, I did know one thing. I knew that when Moto introduced me to his wife, Nobuko, and the two beautiful daughters who would throw their arms around him the minute we walked in the door, he would feel it was worth all his hard work, stress, and anxiety.

Their house on Keio Dori in Kyoto's old section was tiny by American standards, but pristine and welcoming. Built of wood and stone with a tiled roof, it was a single story that might have been called a bungalow in Deerfield, Illinois.

Nobuko was a petite, lovely woman who spoke volumes with her eyes.

There was unmistakable warmth and quiet grace in the way she bowed and her voice had a resonant tone to it that struck me as both humble and strong.

"You honor us with your presence," she said in Japanese.

"Your hospitality is most generous," I replied. "Thank you for having me. Your daughters are beautiful."

Mariko, a wisp of a girl with mahogany eyes and thick black bangs, held tightly to her mother's leg as the blue-eyed monster smiled down at her. Tomiko, at seven and older by three years than her sister, had taken up a similar pose alongside her father. Tomiko's green eyes reminded me of the ocean: wide, fluid, and missing nothing. Both girls had donned impeccable, if simple, kimonos. I felt sure they had been forced to wear them in honor of the American *gaijin*.

"It's a pleasure, Tomiko-san," I said to her in broken, unpolished Japanese that made both girls laugh. I decided to laugh, too. No excuses. "Your father tells me you play the piano."

The piano, an old upright with ivory keys, sat in one corner of the family room and the music was opened on the music shelf. "You will play for me later?"

Her eyes widened when she heard this, an arm encircling her father's leg, but a small smile told me there was a slight possibility that she might. What more could a guy ask for?

Throughout the evening, I watched Moto's interaction with Nobuko. The respect he showed was no less impressive than the playful affection he demonstrated. He complimented every dish she served at dinner, and he listened to every word she spoke as if they had been engraved in stone. In return, she took considerable pride in, of all things, his special sense of humor. The night was filled with laughter that did not appear to be anything reserved for special guests or special occasions. Laughter, I guessed, was part of their lives.

I got in on the action myself. All it took was a few ill-spoken Japanese phrases to give the girls the giggles. Hearing them laugh inevitably got me going, and by the end of the night, the blue-eyed monster had made a couple of special friends. Very special!

I was rewarded with two small origami animals that the girls had folded, a giraffe from Tomiko that was remarkably lifelike and a peacock from Mariko that could have passed for a beaver or a turkey. I was honored.

"*Dai ji ni shimasu,*" I said. "I'll treasure them." I accepted their gifts with as formal a bow as I could produce. I don't know who was more proud, the girls or their father, but it was clear to me that nothing in this world meant more to Moto than his daughters.

I did get my piano recital, a short and simplified version of an old Japanese folk song. After an encore of Brahms' Lullaby, the girls were ushered off to bed.

While mother and father were tucking in their daughters, I sipped the green tea Nobuko had brewed for dessert. I played the evening over in my head and realized that Moto had skillfully hidden the enormous fear he was harboring. I wondered if Nobuko was aware of the difficulties he was facing at JIIS. If she was, the signs were not obvious to me. If she wasn't, well, it suggested another piece in the complicated puzzle that was the Japanese psyche.

The following day was no less pleasant or instructive. Moto and his family gave me the tour of historical Kyoto: shrines, temples, gardens, and palaces. Nobuko had studied Japanese history and she talked, with the assessment of an objective observer, about its evolution from the feudal state to the current capitalist monarchy.

"Our spirituality has never waned. We are still a culture that values the human spirit. We teach our children respect by example rather than words. We teach them that all living things deserve respect simply because they exist and that their existence means everything to our own existence."

"Sure," I said. "Yin and yang. Finding the balance."

"Yes, but first, recognizing what is balance." When Nobuko stopped and held my eye, I knew this was of particular importance to her. "Men cannot impose their will on the universe, Kai-san. The universe imposes balance and harmony no matter what man does. I believe this. Our place is small and humble in the larger scheme of things. Recognizing this, we can live in peace. If we attempt to impose our will on the world, the universe will eventually right the wrong. If we destroy ourselves in the process, heaven and earth will continue on as if we were never here."

This was a most revealing point of view, here among the manicured gardens of Kyoto with their perfectly pruned Bonsai trees and ancient Koi fish populating the waterways. It was also particularly revealing in light of the turmoil Nobuko's husband was experiencing at the Institute, even more so if he was concealing it from her, and I was certain he was.

I gazed out over the glassy surface of the pond and saw the mirror image of Japanese society right in front of me. To the foreigner, the water told the story of a calm and peaceful world. Below this tranquil surface, however, were churning currents—a raging fear of failure.

18

Taketomijima

"Petals of chrysanthemum
Curve in their whiteness
Under the moon."
~ Kyoshi Takahama

The day we returned from Kyoto, spring gave birth to cherry blossoms more beautiful and elegant than any photograph could ever depict. A breeze soughing through the leaves brought the blossoms to life. With the breeze came a scent so fragrant that any negative energy a person might have been harboring disappeared, at least for an hour or a minute or a fleeting moment. It was worth it, in any case, I thought.

"Here's the plan," Mitch said as we walked from the cafeteria toward our Wednesday morning language class. "Mavis and I are planning a trip to the island of Taketomijima during spring break."

"I don't think I've heard of it."

"That's what makes it special. No one has. It's the southernmost island in the Japanese chain and like nothing the imagination can fathom: lush tropics, star-shaped sand, and beaches that stretch on forever. Paradise, my friend, five days of paradise. When you see the color of the water—I'm telling you, man, it's an aquamarine like nowhere else in the world—you'll be astounded," Mitch said.

"If you're trying to sell me, you're not doing a bad job," I admitted.

"I've put the word out to Sandy and Sherri, too. What do you say?"

"What about Pierre?"

"Not in a million years!"

"Then I'm in," I said. Was he kidding? I wouldn't miss it. With that on my calendar, I could just about get through the next four weeks.

I sat down with Dr. Adrian Barrett that afternoon for our weekly update.

"So, how goes the progress of the Mountain Lions?" he asked with a touch of sarcasm in his voice. He wasn't drunk yet, but neither was he trying to hide the cocktail he was nursing: Johnny Walker Black on ice. What else? He had gotten into the habit of pouring me hot coffee without asking and I had grown accustomed to drinking it black.

"I've finished our strategic plan and brought our financials current," I said, offering him two neatly prepared folders.

"Let's see how the tennis tournament is progressing." He steadied reading glasses on the tip of his nose and actually pored over the papers with an uncharacteristic interest; that was to say, he gave them slightly more than a cursory glance.

"It says here that you've signed advertising deals with Toyota, Sony, and Gojo Beverage as well as your initial deal with Suzuki. Am I reading this right?" He peered at me over the rim of his glasses.

"Signed, sealed, and delivered," I assured him. "The money has been deposited into our account in Tokyo."

I helped him find the banking information and resisted drumming a finger over it for emphasis. "Outstanding," he said. "And how is your early sign-up going?"

"We have fifty participants already on board at $100 a crack," I said. "Kirin Beer has agreed to sponsor the trophies and the refreshments. Catering will be done by the Ichiban Tempura restaurant in Fujinomiya."

Barrett took off his glasses. "Bravo, Mr. Waters. A bank balance of $65,000 puts you about $60,000 up on the competition, though of course you'll keep that bit of information between us. Actually, that silly croissant operation is running in the red. I still have not figured out their business model, and as far as I can tell, they're still searching for a bloody manufacturing source for their pastries."

"I think they have a leadership problem," I said.

"Don't blame your French counterpart, Mr. Waters. It doesn't look good on you. Better to wonder why he was left in charge to begin with, don't you think? And please, don't give me your philosophical mumbo-jumbo about duty and obligation and how hard it is for the Japanese to impose their will on a guest."

"I wouldn't dare," I said. In this case, I had to admit that Barrett was probably right. There were nine Japanese businessmen about six weeks away from an "F" grade because they wouldn't step up to the plate and tell the fucking Frenchman to fuck off. Were they really willing to let their business fail out of a sense of duty to a man who couldn't care less about their well-being? I didn't get it.

I was of two minds about our corporate dinner the next night, our first since my return from Kyoto. A part of me couldn't wait to lay eyes on Kimiko. I missed her smile, her mesmerizing eyes, and the way her kimono followed the curves of her amazing body. But I also knew that our rendezvous at the Happi Hoteru had changed our friendship forever. I really didn't want my Kumayama business partners wondering what that change was about, even though I had already confided in Sandy and Kudoh.

I also felt a responsibility toward Kimiko's place in her community. I did not want her to lose face with her friends or family either. In two months, I would be on my merry way. If Kimiko found herself exiled from the community of her birth or outcast from her family, it would hardly be a fair trade-off. The flaw in this very idealistic argument hinged upon the fact that Kimiko was an adult; no one was twisting her arm or forcing her into a relationship with me. I was no more responsible than she was. I wanted to respect Kimiko for who she was, her strengths as well as her weaknesses, but I also didn't want to see her hurt.

Kimiko probably doted on me more than usual during our dinner

and her smile was dazzling in a way that only a secret lover's smile can be.
Interestingly, I really didn't care what my teammates thought after I'd finished a beer and a cup of sake. If they wanted to speculate about Kimiko
and me, well, I didn't imagine it would go any further than speculation
anyway.

As for me, I could picture her slender body so clearly under her
kimono that I thought we were back at the Happi Hoteru. I found myself
fighting the overwhelming urge to reach out, take her in my arms, and kiss
her lips. We were lovers; that was what lovers did. I resisted the urge.
Instead, I tried to communicate the thought with my eyes and the tone of
my voice, the most sensual communication of all. We were two lovers,
hiding from the world but refusing to hide from one another.

The note that Kimiko placed in my hand that night read:

> *Kai-san,*
> *My lover. Did you miss me?*
> *I missed you terribly.*
> *Love and kisses, Kimiko*

One part of me was actually relieved by the innocuous tone of the
note—no covert invitation for a repeat performance at the Happi
Hoteru—while another part of me felt slightly cheated. Could it be that
she was now waiting for me to initiate a return rendezvous? I had no way
of knowing.

I saw Kimiko a half dozen times over the next few weeks, but only
once were we able to spend any significant time alone. There always
seemed to be friends or classmates nearby. They may have caught glimpses
of us touching in ways that suggested something more than friendship,
but Kimiko was careful to maintain a certain decorum. Despite urges to
the contrary, I resisted saying, "To hell with decorum."

She would whisper things like, "I miss your touch."

That may not have been as good as sex, but it was sensual enough to
keep me fantasizing. The few times we were able to kiss without wondering if anyone was looking, there was no containing our excitement. Most

of the time, however, the complications created by life in the Japanese countryside left us to our imaginations. School was sometimes almost an afterthought in comparison to my growing infatuation with this remarkable woman, so different from anyone I had ever dated before. True, Kimiko and I were not actually dating by conventional standards, and that may have fueled the infatuation.

With the semester winding down, I did three things during the weeks prefacing our trip to the island of Taketomijima. First, I forced myself to spend 90 minutes a day on my Japanese language studies, only to be frustrated by the insistence of everyone around me that I speak only English.

Next, I huddled on a daily basis with my teammates from Kumayama Inc., as the date of our tennis tournament grew closer. This was a clear-cut "A." I knew that because Professor Barrett couldn't resist telling me about the "abject failure," as he put it, of our competition.

The third item on my semester agenda, and the one I spent the most time and energy on, was the daily English language tutoring of Homare Moto, my increasingly depressed roommate. Sandy spent nearly as much time dragging him kicking and screaming through Professor Miura Narita's class, Japanese Culture—A World View.

Moto progressed the way a small child progressed with his multiplication tables, slowly but surely. English was never going to be his forte, but his unique grasp on the relationship between industrial Japan and the rest of the world reminded Sandy and me why he was so highly regarded at Sony. It was unfortunate that he didn't see it the same way.

The millstone around Moto's neck and the source of his depression was the lack of progress in his Organizational Behavior team, Mori Kaisha. The company had only that week secured a manufacturing source for their croissants. Their campus store was scheduled to open over the weekend. It was a start, but almost certainly a futile one, given the dwindling semester. Their plan included a second store—actually an open-air stand—in Fujinomiya, but they were still wrestling with the town on a license.

"Even if they do grant the license, we will only have a month to sell our product. And a product like ours requires the building of a loyal customer base," Moto said, wisely. "We should have been operating two months ago."

Moto knew the marketing world as well as anyone I had ever discussed the subject with, and he recognized it as a lost cause. That did not stop him from putting six or seven hours a day into the project. When I approached Pierre with the realities of his group's marketing woes, he called me "an ignorant American."

"Our business has something your tennis tournament will never have, pal, and that is sustainability. It's a real business. And if bloody Adrian Barrett, drunkard extraordinaire, can't see that, then he should be replaced. So why don't you fucking go away and mind your own business, Waters-san!"

The Mori Kaisha Croissant Shoppe was set up as a permanent booth outside the cafeteria. Once it was operational, I bought as many croissants as I could stomach without depleting my travel fund, which was untouchable. Instead of my ubiquitous rice-and-green-tea diet, I adopted an equally nutrition-less diet of pastries and green tea. I could say, without equivocation, that the croissants tasted a helluva lot better than the rice. Had I only been in a position to substitute honest to goodness coffee for the tea, I would have taken a definite step up the culinary ladder.

Quality was not the problem at the Mori Kaisha Croissant Shoppe, volume was. They were not going to make it. I could help Moto with his English and Sandy could tutor him all day long in his Culture class, but there was only so much we could do for Mori Kaisha.

Mitch pulled me aside one Friday morning, after we had both dropped $4.00 at the Croissant Shoppe. A true Californian at heart, he said, "They missed the boat when they didn't put in an Espresso bar to go with their pastries."

"They missed the boat in a lot of ways, I'm sorry to say." I wolfed down two croissants in less than a minute, and they hardly made a dent in what had become a perpetual state of hunger. We sat on a bench next to a flowering cherry tree and sipped hot tea. "I can't wait to get out of here for a few days."

"Listen. Just between you and me, I've decided to propose to Mavis while we're in Taketomijima," Mitch said with a broad, if mildly anxious, smile.

I looked at him in amazement. "That is fantastic," I said, and shook his hand. "Congratulations!"

"She hasn't said 'yes' yet. Don't jinx me."

"She's an amazing woman, Mitch."

"She is. I've never met a kinder, more generous person."

"Yeah. And it doesn't hurt that she's brilliant and beautiful, to boot." This made him smile again. "Can you believe I had to come 5,000 miles to meet the girl of my dreams? I'm a lucky man."

"She's pretty lucky too," I said. "What about a ring?"

"Ah! The ring." A tiny velvet box materialized from the inside pocket of Mitch's coat. He cracked open the lid. There was a simplicity to the ring's design that caught my eye, though it occurred to me that the diamond setting might have been of more interest to Mavis. "What do you think?"

"Are you kidding? She's gonna love it," I replied.

"I also bought her a strand of Mikimoto pearls. Mavis has a thing about pearls," Mitch said. He slid the ring back in his pocket. "This is just between you and me, right? I want it to be a surprise."

"Wild horses couldn't drag it out of me."

In the end, only four of us—Mitch, Mavis, Sherri, and I—boarded a plane the next morning, en route to Taketomijima.

"Sandy couldn't make it," Sherri explained. "She needs every spare minute and then some to finish her thesis."

Our circuitous journey eventually took us to the island of Okinawa. For an American, a pall of shame hung over the capital city of the same name. The U.S. military had, since the end of World War II, been a less than stellar presence on Okinawa. The most recent in a series of disturbing incidents clouding this presence was the rape conviction of a U.S. Marine. His victim was a young Okinawan schoolgirl, reported to be 15 years old and still recovering in a nearby hospital. The Marine had been sentenced to life in prison by a military tribunal, but the wounds created by our ongoing occupation of the island continued to fester.

The animosity against the U.S. was so tangible, it permeated the Okinawan air like the sickening smell of death. The three hours we spent on the waterfront waiting for the boat that would ferry us out to Taketomijima were some of the longest of my life.

It was early evening and the sun was taking its final bows when we boarded a huge ferry packed with people and set out on our 14-hour trek for Taketomijima. I didn't look back.

The four of us stretched out on the upper deck and watched a glorious sunset materialize over the China Sea. It was nearly midnight when we made our way to the ferry's designated sleeping area, really nothing more than an enclosed deck covered with tatami mats. A mass of humanity lay head to toe. Japanese of every age huddled together, and the sounds of snoring old men melded with the whimpers of young children. This was not my idea of a vacation. I snared a paper-thin blanket, climbed back up the stairs to the ship's upper deck, and curled up on a hard wooden bench. The only sound was the restless ocean, churning off the ferry's stern.

Five minutes later, Sherri, the famous partner of my friend Sandy and a complete mystery to me, came up to the upper deck and whispered in my ear, "Would one very sexy American allow a lost Viking the pleasure of joining him on this beautiful evening?"

"Absolutely."

Her eyes glimmered in the starlight, and she quickly crawled under the blanket with me and cuddled up to my warm body like a little kitten.

Sherri said, "I am really uncomfortable being alone. I have been living with this fear of being stranded since I lost both my parents in a fire at the paper mill they worked at in Fort Frances, Ontario. I was only five years old at the time. After that, I was passed from relative to relative my entire childhood and never really felt loved or wanted. I know it may sound self-serving, but the only time I feel at peace and protected is when I am next to a lover, Kai. But I know I can trust you to keep me warm and protected tonight."

"You can," I said, wrapping my arms around her.

"And I will always be indebted to you for sharing this night with me. Here on this great voyage across the China Sea."

The star-strewn sky provided us with a peerless light show. Sherri and I snuggled together for six hours. It was strange to be cuddled with Sandy's lover but Sherri made it feel like we had been holding each other our entire lives. I awoke, stiff and content, an hour before the island of Taketomijima appeared above the horizon.

Once there, a motorized boat ferried us to a small, narrow pier and our first glimpse of paradise. No cars, no telephones, no television. If communing with nature and getting in touch with yourself was not the goal, then you had come to the wrong place. It seemed almost natural the way Sherri and I paired up. Despite her recent fling with Sandy, an unexpected experiment for both women, I still found Sherri irresistible. There had always been something seductive about her little girl features—the innocent smile and short-cropped golden hair—but I was determined to respect her newfound relationship with Sandy. Friends? Well, it didn't have the same ring as island lovers, but that was perfectly okay with me.

I did not try to compare Sherri with Kimiko. I had enjoyed the physical chemistry with Kimiko, and there was an irrepressible sweetness to her that brought a smile to my face. But I was happy to be putting some distance between myself and that rather confusing relationship. The semester was into its final stretch and I was already preparing for life after Fujinomiya and a return to the States. I wouldn't be terribly disappointed if this week long hiatus proved to be the break both Kimiko and I needed to put the relationship behind us. I would miss her, but that was all part of a short-term romance.

We checked into our inn. We were assigned two open-air huts with sod walls and grass ceilings. Mitch and Mavis quickly threw their gear into one hut, as if nothing could be more natural.

I looked at Sherri and said, "Need a roommate?"

"As long as he's tall, dark, and handsome. Wait! Make that tall, blue-eyed, and handsome," she said, flashing a smile that could set a grass ceiling on fire.

We shared a small tatami matted room with two small futons and small white pillows lying side by side. That was about it. The showers, we discovered, were communal.

"And people do not drink the water," the inn's manager joked. "They drink cold beer, delivered daily. It is our most important import."

"*Mondai nai*," I said to him.

"Beach time," Sherri called once we were settled. She changed into a bikini without a trace of embarrassment and looking nothing short of sexy doing it. I was the puritanical one in this hut, but I managed to get my swimming suit on without blushing too profusely. It made no sense, I realized, to try and hide my tattoo here and it would have been impossible in any case. When Sherri caught sight of it, her eyes widened.

"My, aren't you full of surprises," she said with a smile. "I would have never pegged you as the tattoo type."

"I lost my head one night in Tokyo and ended up in a tattoo parlor. Too much sake," I confessed.

Sherri took my hand and led me outside. "Well, tiger, now that you've got it, you might as well show it off. Let's go get some sun, shall we?"

We requisitioned two six packs of beer, a cooler, and beach towels from the inn's front desk. We met Mitch and Mavis outside their hut. I waited for another round of comments on my Bengal tiger, but no one said anything. I was grateful. I was tired of lying.

We followed a narrow path through the jungle, stepping out onto a setting more breathtaking and pristine than anything this midwestern boy had ever seen.

Unspoiled beach stretched in either direction. Snow white sand pearled at the foot of water as clear as crystals. Sherri scooped up a handful of sand and we marveled at each grain's star shape.

"They say it's caused by the coral reef that surrounds the island," Mitch explained. "There is something about it you don't see anywhere else in the world."

"Magical," Mavis said. She gazed down a beach completely void of people. "And the best thing is, we have it all to ourselves."

"I planned it that way," Mitch told her, "just for you."

"Romantic bastard," I teased.

"Look at that water," Sherri said. "It's like a Monet painting, isn't it?"

She was right. The overlapping hues of aquamarine that rippled in waves out to sea were alive with tropical fish that had discovered the bounty of the Taketomijima's indigenous reef. And by my eye, they seemed to be inviting us to join them.

We laid out our towels and toasted our good fortune with icy beer.

"To paradise," Mavis said. In the spirit of all truly liberated French women, she tossed aside her bikini top with unabashed flare, and Sherri didn't think twice about doing the same.

"Ah, freedom," she called.

"I'll drink to that," I said, feeling like a shipwrecked sailor who has been washed ashore on an idyllic island populated by beautiful women. And like that sailor, a return to civilization was the very last thing on my mind.

I drank two beers and then took my first plunge in the warm waters of the China Sea. My companions followed, one after another, but I outlasted them all. When I dragged my waterlogged body back to dry land, I discovered that Mitch had procured a carafe of cold sake and four umbrella drinks from the cabana down the beach. At that moment, my only concern in life was which beverage to drink first. We toasted with sake and sipped our exotics.

Lunch was fresh vegetable sandwiches, fruit cups, and orange sherbert. I waited an hour before talking Sherri into a game of Frisbee. She was a natural.

We took a last swim before heading back to the inn for a shower, a change of clothes, and a short nap. The beach cabana served swordfish, shrimp, and fresh pineapple for dinner. We drank a Mai-Tai before, cold beer during, and hot sake after.

After dinner, we carried our drinks down the beach and found a crudely built fire pit. Within ten minutes, Mitch and I had a small fire burning. The sound of the gentle waves breaking across the sand echoed on the breeze and ten thousand stars charged the air with electricity.

"Now that's a light show," I said, gazing toward the sky.

"Could we ask for a better night?" Sherri asked. "Great food, great friends, and our own corner of paradise."

"Hear, hear." I saw Mitch reach into his pocket. He came away with a sheet of neatly folded stationery that caught everyone's attention.

"What's that?" Mavis asked.

"It's something I want to read to you, something I wrote. Do you mind?" he asked, moving closer.

"Oh, goodie!" Sherri said. "Poetry."

It seemed almost natural that she moved closer to me at the same moment, and suddenly I felt her hand on my arm. It was as if she knew something special was about to take place and she was right.

Mitch was suitably buzzed for the occasion but there was a clarity in his eyes and voice that suggested how important the words on the page were to him.

The poem began:

> One day I was moving down the river of life alone,
>> At peace with my place in the world.
> I arrived in the Land of the Rising Sun expecting the river
>> To twist and turn and carry me onward.
> What I didn't expect was to meet a goddess along the way,
>> Beautiful, glowing, gentle, and kind.
> Suddenly, I couldn't see traveling that river alone anymore . . .

By now, tears were flowing down Mavis's cheeks, and she was clutching his wrists. Sherri's grip had tightened on my arm and a single tear trickled down her cheek, as well. The tear glistened in the reflective glow of our campfire, a stream of gold and orange that seemed very magical. As for me, I was thinking how lucky I was to be in this place at this time and marveling at the unexpected paths my decision to come to Japan had led me down.

Mitch read on:

> If the flow of these turbulent waters
>> Strikes you as an adventure worthy of a lifetime,
> I would ask you, Mavis, my lover, my confidante, and best friend,
>> To be even more than that.
> I would ask you for your hand in marriage,
>> To be my partner for life, to be my wife . . .

He looked up at her. Mavis was sobbing, but the sobs were filled with passion and love; that was easy to see. And she was nodding her head with every word.

The poem ended:

> I promise to challenge you, to help you seek your passions,
>> And to support your dreams.
> I promise to share my strengths and allow you to support me
>> in times of uncertainty.
> I promise to give you, Mavis, the best of me. Forever.
>> Will you marry me?

"Yes!" Mavis blurted. She jumped into his arms, showering him with kisses and holding him with all her strength. "Yes, I will marry you, Mitch Palmer. I will."

The velvet box was now in his hands and he was opening the lid. He showed her the engagement ring. "This is for you."

He slid the ring onto her ring finger and Mavis burst into tears of happiness. Sherri knelt down beside her.

"Show me, show me," she said excitedly. The flames of our fire danced across the diamond, bringing every facet to life. "Oh, my gosh. It's beautiful, Mavis. I'm so happy for you guys."

I reached out and shook Mitch's hand. "Absolutely beautiful. Congratulations."

"Thanks. Glad you were here."

"Now I can borrow that poem when my time comes, right?" I teased.

"Sure, absolutely, if the price is right." We laughed.

"A toast," I shouted, filling four sake cups to the brim. "To a beautiful and magical couple!"

"And a lifetime of happiness," Sherri added.

We kept the fire stoked and the sake flowing until the full moon dropped far into the western sky. When the last drop had been drunk, we stumbled back through the jungle to our huts.

Sherri was out of her swimming suit in a matter of seconds and leading me into her bed before I had a chance to wonder whether or not it was a good idea.

"What about Sandy?" I managed to ask as she helped me off with my shirt.

"She's the one who recommended it."

"Nice of her."

"Don't get me wrong. I love Sandy. I only want you for the pure pleasure of the sex."

I wasn't about to argue with that and there was no turning back anyway.

I experienced five days and five nights of pure pleasure. We left the island by the same boat that had delivered us there, and I realized I had just experienced a holiday that would never be duplicated nor easily forgotten.

Four weeks remained in the semester. I felt refreshed and ready to host a tennis tournament like nothing Fujinomiya had ever seen.

Sherri and her uninhibited thirst for sex had weaned me of my obsession with Kimiko. It was a good feeling; I was ready to move on. I only hoped that the week away had given her the chance to put me behind her, as well.

The Real Sensei

"Flowers of morning glory
The sky above this street
Begins to overcast."
~ Hisajo Sugita

I t was not to be.

When I walked into my dorm, Kudoh and Takeda were huddled at the table in the common area with textbooks and notepads opened in front of them. Suzuki was hunkered down in his usual spot, the easy chair, blowing smoke rings toward the ceiling, and—big surprise—perusing a new porn magazine.

All three had returned to their respective homes during spring break and used the time to reacquaint themselves with friends, family, and real food. Moto had not. He had spent eight hours every day working at the Croissant Shoppe in Fujinomiya and the rest of his time losing even more ground on his studies. I could see it in his eyes. The gray pallor of his face was shocking to someone who had been away for a week. He could barely look up when I walked in.

"Waters-san, welcome home!" Kudoh called to me.

"Thanks. It's good to be back. I missed all of you," I said.

"Sure you did."

"Did you find Taketomijima the paradise you had hoped for?" Takeda asked.

"Amazing," I replied.

"Good," Suzuki said with a broad, sarcastic grin, "because someone here has missed you a lot more than we did, and I am not talking about your good friend, Professor Barrett."

"What are you talking about?" I wondered aloud.

Kudoh could not contain his laughter. "Your bedroom has received a serious face lift thanks to a beautiful woman," he said. "Take a look."

My heart sank.

I carried my bag down the hall, opened the door to my room, and found it decorated floor to ceiling with crepe paper, balloons, and hand-made posters.

"What the hell happened?"

Kudoh had followed me inside, grinning from ear to ear. "Moto informed us that Kimiko came by every evening and left you a welcome home present. I think she is in love, Waters-san."

Five neatly wrapped boxes were arranged on my bed. A pink envelope with my name surrounded in hearts lay on my pillow. I started with the card, wondering if my deepest fears hadn't been realized. The card told me they had. It read:

> Kai-san:
> I missed you very much while you were gone.
> I like you to meet my parents!
> Okay? When you return.
> Love and kisses, Kimiko

"Oh, no." I handed it to Kudoh.

He read the words out loud, and his eyes widened.

"Not good, Waters-san. Not good at all," he said. "This is serious business in Japan. An invitation to meet a girl's parents suggests a committed relationship. It is like a step away from being engaged."

"Oh, no," I said again. I was dumbstruck.

Kudoh studied me. "Did you say something to Kimiko that might have given her that impression?"

"What? That we were engaged? Are you crazy? I said, 'Mondai nai' a couple of times without knowing what the hell I was saying it to," I admitted. "Now what?"

"It is my guess that she took your rendezvous at the Happi Hoteru more seriously than you did. Can you remember anything she might have said, something in Japanese that you did not understand or anything you said in English that she might have misunderstood?"

I replayed that night, frame by frame, and realized again how limited our conversation was. When Kimiko did speak, it was mostly in English, or her very courageous attempt at English.

I remembered her falling back into Japanese after we had made love. The words were not familiar, and I had taken Kudoh's advice and replied, *"Mondai nai."* Kimiko's reaction had been instantaneous and more enthusiastic than I would have expected from a simple, "No problem."

I looked at Kudoh and tried to reconstruct her words. "She said something like, *'Watashi to kekkon shite kudasai.'* I didn't understand all of it, so I said, *'Mondai nai.'*"

Kudoh's jaw dropped. "Great. Just great. *Kekkon* means 'Marry,' Waters-san. *Watashi to kekkon shite kudasai* means 'Would you marry me?'"

"You're kidding?" I stared at him. "In other words, she proposed, and I said, 'No problem?'"

"Right," Kudoh said miserably. "And I am to blame. I told you to say *'Mondai nai.'* It was my idea."

"It's not your fault, Kudoh-san. I'm a big boy. I got myself into this mess. Now she wants me to meet her parents." I sat down on the edge of the bed. "I can't do that. I'm not quite ready for marriage, Kudoh-san. I would not do anything to hurt Kimiko or to dishonor her, but I didn't come to Japan to find a wife."

"But dishonor her you will, Waters-san," Kudoh said. "It is inevitable, no matter what you do. But if you really have no intention of marrying Kimiko, you cannot accept this invitation." Kudoh gestured to Kimiko's note. "That would bring dishonor to her entire family, not just to Kimiko. Do you understand?"

I nodded. I was already way ahead of him. There was no chance I was going to accept her invitation, but there had to be an alternative to flat out rejection. Katayama Sensei, I thought. If there was one person who could look at this situation from both sides and advise me, it was Neko. She would probably see me as a bumbling, insensitive American who had taken advantage of a short-term liaison before escaping back to the States, but I had to risk it.

"I have an idea," I said to Kudoh. I stood up and put a hand on his shoulder. "Can we keep this between us, my good friend? I doubt Kimiko would appreciate this getting around campus."

"You can count on me, Waters-san. Word of honor," Kudoh said sincerely. I could not have believed him more completely. I wondered for a moment whether the phrase, "word of honor," meant more in Japan than it did in Chicago. I certainly wanted to believe it. But Japan was thousands of years old and the subtleties of duty and honor were more ingrained. So, I supposed, were the repercussions of breaking your word. Hopefully, my rate of learning about these things had increased during my time here. If so, that alone would make the trip a rousing success.

After language class the next day, I stopped by Neko's office and knocked lightly on the door. She glanced up from the pile of essays we had turned in that morning.

"Waters-san. *Konnichiwa*," she said in strict Japanese. "What can I do for you? You seemed a little distracted in class today. Was I wrong?"

"Actually, that's why I dropped by. I was wondering if we could have tea later," I replied.

"You are having problems with your latest assignment?" I could see on her face that she knew better.

"It's a little more personal than that, Katayama Sensei," I admitted.

"Come by after lunch and I will brew a pot of my family's special tea. It is brown and very strong. We will talk."

"Thank you. I'll see you after lunch."

I hardly heard a word Dr. Narita said during our Japanese Culture class. This was rare. Normally, I prided myself on my attentiveness. When you're responsible for half your college tuition, you learn to be attentive fast. Ownership does that, my father would say. It makes you more diligent and diligence leads to success. Not on this day.

When I returned to Neko's office, it smelled of brown tea and cinnamon. She had changed into blue jeans and a cream colored blouse and had tied her magnificent black hair into a ponytail.

"Come in," she said when I knocked. She invited me to sit in the office's one and only overstuffed chair. She served tea in porcelain cups and seemed pleased when I declined honey and sugar. "You are becoming more Japanese all the time."

"I'll take that as a compliment."

"I hope you had a good time in Taketomijima. Quite beautiful, is it not?" she said.

"Yes, very," I said though I didn't remember telling her about the trip. Well, I thought, if the *yakuza* really thought it was necessary to keep an eye on me in a place as remote as Taketomijima, maybe I should be grateful.

"They were there?"

"Of course," she answered almost rhetorically. "A promise is a promise."

For nearly a minute, we sipped tea together in silence. I waited for her to open the conversation.

"I am honored that you feel comfortable discussing a matter of a personal nature with me, Kai-san," she said in English.

"You're not the average teacher, Katayama Sensei."

"Nor are you an average student," she replied. "What is on your mind?"

"I met a girl in Fujinomiya when I first arrived, back in January. Her name is Kimiko Makita. She works at the restaurant in town. Now I think I've misled her, and, well . . ."

"Please start at the beginning."

I did. I committed myself to telling her every detail, including our rendezvous at the Happi Hoteru. I shared all of Kimiko's love letters and knew without asking that Neko would respect their confidentiality. The gentle manner in which she held them and the small smile they brought to her lips reinforced this feeling.

"When I returned from Taketomijima, I found this." I handed Neko the note inviting me to meet Kimiko's parents. "One of my roommates explained how serious an invitation like this is."

"Yes. Serious," Neko agreed.

"I think the world of Kimiko, and I don't want to mislead her, but I have no intention of getting married," I told her. "I also don't want to cause her any problems with her family or anyone else in Fujinomiya."

Neko warmed our tea. She studied me over the rim of her cup and eventually said, "Would you feel comfortable with me talking to Kimiko about this situation, Waters-san?"

"Seriously!?" I hadn't expected such a gracious offer. "I'd really appreciate it, Katayama Sensei. I can't tell you how much."

"I will walk into town later and introduce myself." She handed the note back. "I will not mention the fact that you shared her letters."

I bowed. "*Arigato.*"

"Let us plan to talk in the cafeteria after dinner. It will be a little late for an office visit by then."

To pass the time, I met Sandy for a mid-afternoon run and worked out in the gym with Kudoh. I met Neko at our usual table after dinner and she greeted me in the usual manner. I was hoping we might share a Kirin or a Sapporo instead of tea, but Neko was nothing if not professional.

"How did it go?" I couldn't wait to ask.

"That is a special young woman you have befriended, Waters-san," she replied. "I am sure you know that."

"Very special."

"She is not in love with you, however. Well, not in the true sense of the word. She is attracted, to be sure, but there is little more to it than that."

"Okay." I was confused and said so.

"Kimiko's father is a janitor at the Toyota plant across the river. Just about everyone who is not a farmer in Fujinomiya works there. It is not the best paying job, steady, but with few prospects. Let me explain." I took this as an opportunity to fill her tea cup. "At the moment, her father works on the third shift, midnight to 8:00 in the morning. Competition just to advance to the first shift is fierce. Payoffs are a big part of advancement here in Japan, I am afraid. Quid pro quo you call it in the States."

"I see."

"The boss of the janitorial crew has a son. Kimiko described him as fat, ugly, and conceited. That is when she began to cry. You see, the boss's son needs a wife and he is willing to trade a position on the day shift for Kimiko's hand in marriage."

"You're kidding!"

Neko shook her head. "Kimiko's father has agreed."

"My roommates mentioned the fact that arranged marriages exist, but I never imagined it still existed in this day and age?" I couldn't believe my ears.

"Do not mistake the traditions in the Japanese countryside for those in America, Waters-san. They are worlds apart."

And then it dawned on me. "I was Kimiko's way out." Of course, I thought.

"Yes. You were her escape. You were the rich, well-educated American *gaijin* who would whisk her away to the States and a life far beyond the fate that awaits her here: stuck in the tiny village of Fujinomiya married to a man she despises, bearing his children, growing old and miserable, and knowing nothing else."

"Sorry."

"It is not an uncommon fate in many parts of Japan. Women are forced into marriages without love. They spend their lives as little more than indentured servants and watch their husbands work themselves into an early grave."

"Are you telling me that's all Kimiko has to look forward to, Katayama Sensei?" I asked. "There has to be something she can do."

"She does not strike me as the kind who will wait for that to happen, frankly." Neko smiled when she said this. "She may pack her things one day and move to Tokyo or Osaka. It would not surprise me."

"But what about her family? Wouldn't she be outcast?"

"That is the price she may have to pay. It is not easy. I know. But would I do it differently this time, myself, if I had the chance? I would not," Neko admitted. "I told Kimiko that you had misunderstood her that night at the sex hotel. I told her you could not marry her, despite liking her very much. I did not speak out of turn, I hope."

"No." I shook my head. "But I feel bad."

"Kimiko is a strong woman, Waters-san. She will survive." Neko paused, as if this was a statement that deserved a moment of silence, a tribute to Kimiko, but also a tribute, I thought, to all Japanese women searching for their rightful place in the world. It was, perhaps, a tribute to all women, everywhere.

My thoughts ran down the list of women who had touched my life since coming to Japan: Liliko, Neko, Sandy and Sherri, and Kimiko, even the owner of the private bathhouse in Tokyo and the petulant massage therapist who had nearly killed me with her strong hands. Even Kona. I realized it was not necessarily my obligation to change their world, but it was my obligation to respect the paths they had chosen. They had certainly done that for me. Quid pro quo as Neko had put it.

"Kimiko treasures your friendship. She told me that," Neko continued. "And she is hoping you will not mind if she attends your tennis tournament."

"I was hoping she would come," I said with a smile. "And you, as well. Will you be able to make it?"

"I may watch from a distance," she said politely.

"I understand." After a moment, I said, "Thank you for . . . you know . . ."

"For my contribution to healthy and evolving Japanese-American relationships?" she asked.

"Exactly."

"You are welcome. Thank you for trusting my judgment and counsel," she replied.

So, in the end, I was just a passport to freedom. Huh! A part of me was slightly disappointed. After all, I was a man and what man did not have a little ego in matters like this? But the bigger part of me was relieved. Now I wanted to just get through the next three weeks without any more romantic interludes. It did not sound very exciting, but I'd had enough excitement for one semester.

———

A Question of Loyalty

"A kite floats
At the place in the sky
Where it floated yesterday."
~ Buson Yosa

I knew it was too good to be true.

Other than my weekly teas with Neko, during which we discussed absolutely everything except our *yakuza* brethren in Tokyo, I had not given a thought in weeks to *Oyabun* Yamaguchi or our everlasting connection. Liliko occasionally interrupted my daily routine, but those thoughts were mostly sexual in nature and, therefore, did not qualify, I told myself, as *yakuza* based.

I had been fairly successful in not allowing the deaths of Ikeda and Kona to come between me and my life on campus. No one could ever hide completely from those extraordinary events, but I hadn't let them get in the way of my studies or the progress Kumayama Inc. continued to make on our impending tennis tournament. My arm was completely healed; even the scar had faded by now. Only the tattoo on my right thigh served as a reminder, but I no longer obsessed over it. Now it was more a work of art I glanced at periodically and enjoyed for what it was: a permanent part of me.

The note I found propped up on my pillow that afternoon made my heart skip a beat, and not in a positive way. "What in the hell?" I whispered.

I stared at the envelope and then actually looked around my tiny room as if the intruder who had left the note might still be lurking about. It was not a pleasant feeling knowing that someone had violated the privacy of my room. I did not have much to call my own, but the space beyond that door was one thing I looked at as sacrosanct. True, I hadn't felt quite so possessive when Sandy and Sherri were consummating their relationship on my bed; I was actually pleased in a guy sort of way. This invasion, on the other hand, didn't have that intimate feel to it. Quite the opposite.

The envelope was white and undistinguished, probably by intent. My name had been written across the face of it in Chinese characters. I wasn't very well versed in the look and feel of the letters, but this handwriting didn't strike me as belonging to Kimiko. Too bad.

I tore open the flap. A single sheet of similarly undistinguished white paper framed a dozen or so poorly written English words. They read:

> Mr. Kai Waters. Friend and brother. Please meet us at 3:00 this afternoon on the far side of the campus athletic field. Arigato.

It was signed: *Oyabun Yamaguchi*.

"Shit!" I said out loud. I shook my head and gazed at the ceiling. "What now?"

I looked at my watch and realized I had less than ten minutes to change my clothes and walk—unseen hopefully—to the southern most end of the campus and this unexpected rendezvous. I wanted to be on time. Not out of fear, but common courtesy. *Oyabun* Yamaguchi deserved that.

I pulled on a clean shirt, wasted ten seconds studying my reflection in a mirror the size of a dinner plate, and realized the nerve endings beneath the tattoo on my thigh were tingling.

I walked out into the common area of our dorm, and Moto hailed me.

"Ah, Waters-san. Can I ask for a moment of your time, please?"

Oh, no! Not now! Moto had his English language book opened in front of him and a look of complete and total consternation on his face. I had pledged him my assistance, and we had spent many hours working together already this semester, but his timing could not possibly have been worse.

I had no choice but to beg off. I said, "So sorry, Moto-san. I'm late for an appointment. Give me a half hour. We'll walk through the whole assignment as soon as I get back."

I expected him to say, "A 3:00 appointment on a Friday? With who? Everyone's gone for the weekend." But he didn't say anything of the kind. He shook his head as if his request had been unfounded and disgraceful and said, "When you get back then. If it's possible. *Domo arigato*, Waters-san."

At least he didn't say, "*If* you get back."

I jogged down the stairs, and then hurried across the well-manicured promenade that separated the school from the parking lot. It was a half-mile walk from there, but at least the athletic fields were empty. I saw a jogger headed toward the forest and someone studying next to the lake, but that was all.

I didn't see the limousine at first and for a brief, overly optimistic moment entertained the thought that whatever business the clan *Kumicho* had with me had seemed too unimportant to wait five extra minutes.

Then I saw a shadow materialize from behind a dense grove of blue spruce and recognized the compact and powerful figure of the Lone Ranger. "Damn," I hissed even as I raised my hand in greeting.

I considered jogging the last few yards but settled instead for a brisk walk. I called, "*Konbanwa*," even though it was still afternoon. Then I corrected myself and said, "*Konnichiwa*."

The Lone Ranger hadn't yet spoken a word in my presence, so I wasn't shocked when he didn't reciprocate my greeting. He did nod, though not with any degree of friendliness. Then he opened the limo's rear door and used an open hand to invite me inside. I didn't like the situation one bit, but I did exactly as I was told anyway. Just get it over with, Kai.

The space next to *Oyabun* Yamaguchi had apparently been reserved just for me because he patted the seat the way my Grandma Waters used to do when she was hailing her precious Pekingese. The dog's name was Malcolm, and he was no more rebellious than I was at that moment.

I tried to bow as I sat and said, "*Oyabun* Yamaguchi. Thank you for coming all this way." A complete and total lie that I dearly hoped did not show on my face. "How is the *Kumicho*?"

"The *Kumicho* has been better, Waters-san," he told me with a wholly mirthless expression. "And how is your shoulder? Your personal physician tells me you are healing nicely."

Dr. Hideki Iwakabe, my "personal physician," sat in the cross-facing seat next to my good friend Tonto. The doctor bowed, if only slightly. Tonto stared at me as if a wrong word, an adverse inflection, or an inappropriate gesture would be enough to trigger an attack of epic proportions. Not a look I normally reserved for friends and brethren, but then I wasn't one of the boss's bodyguards either.

"The doctor is correct," I said, glancing at Iwakabe. "Never have I been better cared for. I'm grateful."

"Excellent. Because he has one more test to perform before giving you his final seal of approval."

"What sort of test? Because I'm not sure it's necessary," I protested. "Everything's fine."

The doctor's medical bag looked more like a Wall Street briefcase; obviously he didn't make that many house calls. But the syringe he extracted from the case looked exactly like the needles our family doctor back home used when a blood sample was in order.

Dr. Iwakabe confirmed this when he said, "A simple blood test, Waters-san. If you would not mind rolling up your sleeve please?"

I hesitated. But my reluctance was more a matter of common sense than resistance. A blood test? What in the world for? "Is this related to my stab wound?" I had to ask.

"It is related to your place in the Yamaguchi clan, Waters-san," the *Oyabun* explained for my benefit. "It is related to my loyalty to you, and yours to me."

"Oh," I said meekly.

"Yes, loyalty. It is the one element that sets the animal kingdom off from the world of plants, would you not agree?" The *Kumicho* didn't wait for a response. He went on to say, "It is quite remarkable to see a black mamba snake fight to the death to protect a mate. Or what of the dolphin? He is as true to his family as a chimpanzee is to his. Wild dogs instinctively seek a leader to guide their pack. Penguins mate for life. Elephants will protect their young with such ferocity that lions on the hunt know better than to waste their energy."

The *Oyabun* did not seem as surprised as I was that I had unexpectedly rolled up the sleeve of my shirt. I was unconsciously making a fist with my right hand and exposing the veins of my right arm.

I was also listening rather intently as the *Kumicho* went on, saying, "Men seem more willing than any other mammal to kick loyalty aside in favor of advancement, money, power, whatever. Why is that, Waters-san? You are a man of the world. Help me to understand. Maybe we become victims of our own intellectual superiority. Is that possible?"

Oyabun Yamaguchi wasn't looking at me when he asked this question. He was peering out the window at the verdant forest and the great mountain filling the horizon. What a setup, I thought. And I naturally walked right into it, offering an observation from my vast empirical knowledge.

"I'm not sure I see that as advanced behavior, to be honest, *Oyabun*," I said carefully.

"No? Then you have your own view of loyalty. As an honorary member of the Yamaguchi clan and close friend of my only daughter, please share that view with me, Waters-san. I am very interested."

I felt the pin prick on my skin and watched like an uninvolved bystander as the tip of the needle sliced under my skin. I knew the *Oyabun* and his bodyguard were observing my reaction, looking for a grimace or a groan or a hint of discomfort. I hated to disappoint them. I had never been squeamish around needles, and I was not about to start now.

I had to admit, however, that my brain was running wild with speculation about the blood sample. What was this all about? Why this veil of secrecy? Every avenue I traveled down in trying to find the answers ended up with mind-numbing thoughts about hepatitis and scarlet fever and the Black Death, and they all had at their source the rusty and infected needles they must have used tattooing my right thigh. Wasn't it true that my thigh throbbed even as I sat there expecting to hear the good doctor say, "Sorry to inform you, Mr. Waters, but you've only got three days left. Make the most of them."

While the vial filled with my blood, I shared my view of loyalty, choosing my words carefully. I said, "Loyalty is about trust, and trust is a matter of predictability." I watched as *Oyabun* Yamaguchi relaxed in his seat, calm gray eyes settling on my face. A voice in the back of my head suggested very strongly that I say no more. Just leave it at that, Kai. Let them extrapolate. Unfortunately, it felt as if I had been led to a stream running fast and cool in the middle of a parched desert, and the urge to drink was more than I could bear. I kept talking.

"It's knowing that a man can be counted on to keep his word or do his part, not just once, but every single time. No questions. No hesitation. If a man says he'll be there, he is. Not nine out of ten times. Ten out of ten times. If a man gives his word, it's written in stone. You can count on him. He's predictable. In some circles, that's considered boring. Some people have this image in their heads that an unpredictable guy is mysterious and exciting. True, mystery and excitement have their place, but not when you're counting on someone. Not when you value trust. Not when you're counting on someone's loyalty."

"Very profound thinking, Waters-san. I am impressed with your insight." The *Oyabun* was a wiry man with a narrow, chiseled face and spectacular cheekbones. His face showed less age than most men in their sixties because his skin was stretched so tightly over the bones of his face.

His gray eyes were hidden beneath eyelids that formed inverted crescents that gave nothing away. The most I could read in his expression was a devout sense of irony.

He said, "And Neko Katayama assures me that the unfortunate situation with the woman named Kona will never be spoken about again." His eyes narrowed even further. "She says we can count on your predictability."

I said, "You can," and meant it. If ever I thought about that day again, it would be too soon. "Katayama Sensei also said that you would talk to . . ."

The *Kumicho* interrupted me, both with his voice and a raised hand. "I have spoken with Minister Ikeda. It is done."

I waited, expecting him to say more—like a hint of how that conversation may have gone, pro or con—but he didn't.

"Thank you," I said eventually because my otherwise vast vocabulary was failing me.

The *Kumicho* was watching me. He said, "And can I also count on your loyalty and commitment, Waters-san, the way I do Dr. Iwakabe's and . . ." He paused long enough to glance at Tonto, "and Mr. Muira? Without question and without hesitation?"

When I didn't immediately answer, the boss of the Yamaguchi clan said it again. "Can I?"

"Not if it means doing something illegal," was the way I answered. "Sorry."

"And if it has to do with my daughter? What then?"

This was a curve ball I hadn't expected. "Liliko? What about her? Has something happened? Is she okay?"

A growl rose up from the clenched jaw of Tonto, a.k.a. Mr. Muira, and the emphatic sound alone was enough to make me realize that I had committed some impropriety, though I couldn't imagine what the nature of it might have been. I asked a simple question. How inappropriate could that be?

Dr. Iwakabe helped me through my confusion. He said, "When talking to the head of a clan with nearly a thousand men at his disposal, it is never wise to answer a question with another question." He removed the needle from my arm, sealed the vial, and then taped cotton over the needle hole. "It gives the appearance of a man seeking the upper hand."

"I'm definitely not seeking the upper hand," I said honestly. "In fact, I'm not seeking anything at all. I apologize."

The *Kumicho* took the vial of blood from Dr. Iwakabe's hand and held it up between two fingers, an eye level view that made it quite clear that the vial had nothing to do with hepatitis or the Black Death. It had to do with his daughter.

Once again, our eyes met. And once again, he repeated, "Can I trust you when it comes to my daughter, Mr. Kai Waters? My Liliko?"

"Of course. Absolutely."

"Good." His fingers wrapped around the vial, and he was done talking.

The doctor took over. "Ms. Yamaguchi is pregnant, Mr. Waters," he said in his most clinical voice.

"Oh," I said miserably. "I see."

"She has admitted to a sexual liaison with you. Do you deny it?" he asked, clearly hoping I would not.

"No, I don't deny it."

"The blood test will prove whether or not the child is yours," he said without inflection. "If it is . . ."

With a sidelong glance, he turned the floor back to the *Oyabun*, who said, "If it is, you will do the right thing. The family will accept you. I will have it no other way."

He didn't explain "the right thing," but he must have seen the look on my face and anticipated my unspoken question: *Do you mean marry into the yakuza?*

The *Kumicho* expounded, saying, "If you run, we will take your finger.

If you run twice, we will take your balls. A third time and it will make no difference whether you have your finger or your balls."

He did not say this with malice, anger, or resentment. He said it with an objective calm that bordered on the mundane. Simple fact. The same rules would hold true for anyone in the clan.

"And if it's not," I said. "Not my child?"

"Then you will pay the price of freedom."

"And what is the price of freedom?"

The door on my side of the limo opened. "It was nice seeing you again, Waters-san. You will be hearing from us. May your semester go well."

"Wait a minute. What is the price of freedom?" I asked frantically.

Tonto was helping me from the car. The Lone Ranger had returned to his place behind the wheel. The limo's engine turned over. The door shut behind me. Tonto took my arm. He whispered, "The price of freedom is whatever the *Kumicho* decides it is. Hai?"

"*Hai*," I said. Yes.

"*Konnichiwa*," he said and climbed into the passenger side door of the front seat.

I stared at my own reflection in the mirrored windows as the limo pulled away. I watched the shiny beast start down the road to Fujinomiya and then on to Tokyo.

The fucking Mile High Club, I thought miserably. You couldn't just leave well enough alone, could you?

21

The Tournament

*"When a thing is placed
A shadow of autumn
Appears there."*
~ Kyoshi Takahama

I had a decision to make. I could fret about the results of the blood test and let it control my every waking hour—and probably most of my dreams at night—or I could do what I had come to Japan to do all along: live, learn, grow, change. I decided on the latter. I would deal with Liliko and her father in due course, knowing that when I told the *Oyabun* that he could trust me when it came to his daughter, I meant it.

With my Japanese language class and Professor Miura Narita's Culture class well in hand, I turned my attention to our tennis tournament. With luck, that would keep my mind at least partially occupied. The Mountain Lions of Kumayama Inc. began meeting on a daily basis, determined to put the final touches on an event that had the attention of the entire campus.

Ninety percent of the student body had signed up for the full $100.00. The money had already been earmarked for a scholarship fund in the school's name. We saw this as a good way to give back to the community and it was also a nice piece of PR in support of our advertisers.

Two days before the event, ten Suzuki motorcycles arrived from the company's Tokyo plant, beautiful machines polished to a high gloss. We arranged them in high traffic areas throughout campus and next to the athletic field. Come tournament day, all ten would be gathered together in a brash presentation next to the tennis courts. Suzuki models would be on hand to make them look even more spectacular and sales representatives would be there to answer questions.

The day before the event, we erected a huge white tent on the athletic field. Tables and chairs were arranged in anticipation of the post-tournament celebration. Banners celebrating the First Annual Fujinomiya Tennis Tournament were hung in strategic spots around campus and we had invited the town's mayor to be an honored guest at the tournament.

Trucks from Kirin arrived the morning of the tournament and delivered case after case of Kirin Supreme on ice. "Kirin Girls," as they were called, were recruited for the very important task of bartending. Six employees from the Ichiban Tempura restaurant in Fujinomiya delivered enough food for 150 people just before noon. They would begin serving a buffet-style meal once the tournament was completed. Gojo beverages were available at refreshment stands next to the grandstand.

All morning, friends and family of JIIS students arrived from Tokyo and elsewhere. When I saw the line of cars, I began to wonder if we had arranged for enough food and drink. Well, drink anyway.

My rusty tennis skills saw me through the first round of the tournament, a sloppy match against my bespectacled teammate, Kenzo Shinran, only to lose a better-contested set against one of Moto's Mori Kaisha colleagues. Well, tennis was never my forte. A huge crowd gathered for the grand finale match between my unassuming roommate, Yasuhiko Takeda, and the over-confident, trash-talking Frenchman, Pierre Trepanier. Pierre had thoroughly humiliated three opponents on his way to the final, and his arrogance on court made me want to thrash him even before the match started. If there was one person in the stands rooting for him, I couldn't find him.

The one surprising fact none of us knew about the gentle Takeda was his semi-professional tennis ranking back in his early twenties. So far, in three matches, he had played down to the level of his competition, smiling more than I had ever seen him and seeming to enjoy just being on the court. This changed in the finals. A raw determination emerged and the match was never close. Takeda, much to the delight of the audience, thoroughly crushed the fucking Frenchman: 6-1, 6-1.

I teased him later about allowing Pierre two games and he said, "I had no desire to completely humiliate our French guest, Waters-san. But I decided two games was a sufficient gift."

"I'll drink to that," I said with a wide smile.

And we did. The beer flowed freely for hours afterwards and Takeda's victory was toasted repeatedly. The food was superb and plentiful, and the Japanese proved once again that they knew how to celebrate.

As for the Kumayama Inc., we remained professional throughout the event. With the exception of Suzuki, who felt it necessary to match his company's representatives beer for beer, we went about our business of running the festivities the way a company with a bottom line profit of $63,000 should. I was proud of us.

The most embarrassing moment of the tournament was the drunken hug I had to endure from Professor Adrian Barrett.

"A wildly successful event, Mr. Waters. I compliment you. And giving your favorite teacher a chance to indulge himself free of charge? Now that might just be enough to earn your team an 'A+.'" Ha, ha, ha.

"Drink up, Professor," I said, wanting to say so much more, but holding my tongue for just one more night. "The beer is on us."

"Don't I know it!"

By 8:30 that night, our sponsors had packed up their motorcycles, their props, and most of their people and had headed back to Tokyo. The event officially ended half an hour later. Fortunately, Kirin had left behind four cases of ice-cold beer, and it was time for the Kumayama team to drink to their success.

"What do you say we clean up in the morning?" I suggested, a raised glass in my hand. No one objected. "Well done, Mountain Lions. Exceptionally well done."

We drank, we hugged, and we joined the party.

I fell into a conversation with a Suzuki representative who had stayed behind, as he put it, "For one more beer and a chance to thank the Kumayama Inc. for including us in their festivities."

"We couldn't have done it without you," I said. "You or my good friend and roommate, Kazushi Suzuki."

"You will soon be riding the latest Suzuki motorcycles back in the States, Waters-san. We will be number one there shortly. Perhaps you will go to work for us," he said blithely.

"I'd better learn to ride a motorcycle first," I said. I looked over his shoulder and saw Kimiko walking towards us. I shook the Suzuki rep's hand and excused myself.

"Konbanwa," I said to Kimiko. I reached out and took her hands in mine.

"Time for Kimiko to leave," she said.

"Can I walk you to your car?" I asked.

"Yes, please."

We took a deserted path away from the celebration, through the trees, and down the hill, in the direction of the parking lot.

"A beautiful night," I said in Japanese. I squeezed her hand.

"Yes, beautiful," she said.

We stopped in an isolated patch of grass next to a towering sycamore tree and faced each other. Kimiko threw her arms around my neck and I held her tightly. I felt the warmth of her tears on my cheek.

"Kai-san," she said. "I will miss you."

I whispered in her ear, "*Sumimasen. Anata wa totemo kirei demo watakashi wa ookii mondai.*" In the worst possible arrangement of Japanese words, I had tried to say, "Excuse me. You are totally beautiful, but I am a big problem."

This caused her to laugh, and I realized in that moment how much I was going to miss her. I kissed her cheek and touched her face one last time. I held the car door open as she slid behind the wheel and turned the key. Her sorrowful smile was imprinted on my soul, and I knew I would never forget it.

I watched the taillights of her car until they disappeared into the forested hills leading back to Fujinomiya. I could not foresee Kimiko's future. Would she allow Japanese society to dictate her path and guide her into a marriage beholden to a man she neither liked nor respected, or would she revolt against the archaic ways of the past and seek a new life, distanced from family and community the way Neko had? I didn't know. But I did not see Kimiko as the tool of a broken society. I saw her fighting for her rights as a woman and as a standard-bearer for a changing Japan.

I would probably never know her fate.

———

The Verdict

"Being awake
He says he is already asleep.
Autumn chilly night."
~ Buson Yosa

The owners of the Ichiban Tempura restaurant in Fujinomiya invited the members of Kumayama Inc. for one last company dinner in order to show their appreciation for our patronage throughout the semester and for our loyalty in hiring them to cater our tournament.

I wasn't eager to attend. The tournament had been a tremendous amount of work, and now it was over. I was excited to see the semester through. I could hardly have packed more into one six-month period if I had tried. But I was also not about to dishonor the restaurant, its owners, or Kimiko by staying home.

As it turned out, the only no-show for the event was Kimiko herself. I was disappointed and a little concerned. When I inquired as to her whereabouts, I was told that she was not working that night. That was all.

It was only later in the evening, when dessert was being served, that another of our servers and one of Kimiko's good friends, whispered a more detailed explanation in Kudoh's ear. I saw a look of delight fill out his face, and my concern evaporated.

"Hai," he said to her with a quick smile. *"Very good."*

And then he turned to me and said, "Well, well, well."

"Well, well, well? What does that mean?" I asked. "Speak up."

"Apparently, Kimiko-san has chosen a new career path. She is studying for the entrance exam to a language school in Ito. They train English-speaking interpreters and translators. And the breaking news? This is with her parents approval." Kudoh was beaming.

"Amazing."

"You want amazing? Guess who she's studying with? Our very own Katayama sensei."

Neko! I wasn't surprised. Not in the least. She had called Kimiko a special young woman. She had seen her potential. And knowing Neko as I did, she would never want to see that potential wasted. Good for her.

"This is great news, Kudoh-san," I said. "Just think of what the two of them can do together."

"You should be proud of yourself, Waters-san."

"Proud? Why?"

"Something happened that would never have happened had she not met you. I just have to believe that," Kudoh said.

"Well, I don't know about that. She was going to be a hard one to hold back no matter what. So whatever happened, I just hope it works out."

Kudoh and I clicked glasses, and he whispered a private toast. "Progress."

"Progress," I said, and we drank.

A few minutes later, I excused myself from the table and informed my fellow teammates that I was walking back to campus. "Are you alright?" Sandy asked.

"Better than alright," I told her with a smile. "A walk up the mountain just sounds good at the moment. See you later."

I stopped at the restaurant bathroom, stepped inside, and the door slammed behind me. I heard the latch lock. A split second later, Tonto and the Lone Ranger had me cornered.

"Waters-san," Tonto said. His expression wasn't as menacing as the

Lone Ranger's. He seemed more amused than angry. "Good evening."

"Jesus. You scared the hell out of me."

"As we intended," he assured me.

Something glistened in the dull light of the room, and I saw a knife materialize from the Lone Ranger's pocket. The blade settled six inches from my face.

"What the hell is this?" I demanded, though my voice was weaker than I had hoped.

"We have business to discuss."

"My blood test."

"Yes. It came back from the lab," Tonto said.

"And?"

"You don't remember what the *Oyabun* said?"

My heart jumped into my mouth, and I felt sick to my stomach. "'If you run, we will take your finger. If you run twice, we will take your balls. A third time and it will make no difference whether you have your finger or your balls.'" It was a direct quote. "Yeah, I remember."

"Good. Your finger."

"But I'm not running. I said he could count on my loyalty," I said almost desperately. "And I meant it."

"Good. Very good." His eyes narrowed. The knife twisted in the Lone Ranger's hand. "Because the blood test was negative."

"Negative?" I didn't get it for the longest time, and suddenly Tonto and the Lone Ranger could contain themselves no longer. They burst out laughing. "You mean . . .?"

"The baby is not yours, you crazy American. It is not yours," Tonto said, tears of laughter streaming down his cheeks. "We were just having some fun with you."

"You bastards. You scared the shit out of me."

"We were only playing, Waters-san." Tonto patted my cheek as if terror was a source of play I should try some time. "It was Liliko's old boyfriend back at college. They got together again just long enough to do it one more time, I guess. Bad luck for him. Good luck for you."

I still felt sick to my stomach. "Sure. Then why doesn't the Lone Ranger put his knife away? I'd feel so much better."

And then it dawned on me. I had made the mistake of asking the *Kumicho* if there were consequences even if the child was not mine, and his answer was that I would still have to pay the price of freedom. Those were his exact words. And the price of freedom was whatever the *Kumicho* decided it was; those were Tonto's words.

"Am I free to go or not?" I asked in a surprisingly strong voice. "Or is there still a price to pay?"

"None that we are aware of," Tonto said with a wry smile. I watched the knife disappear inside the Lone Ranger's coat. "And if there is, I imagine you have already paid it."

He unlocked the door. The Lone Ranger didn't even nod; he just walked out. Tonto was halfway out when he paused as if a last thought had just occurred to him.

"Oh, that is right," he said. "I have a message. The *Kumicho* said to tell you that your seat at the *basho* will be there any time you return. And he hopes you do so sometime in the not-too-distant future."

"I would be honored to join him again." I actually meant it, and that surprised me.

"We will be around," he said as the door swung shut.

"Don't know what I'd do without you," I replied.

I stared at the closed door for nearly ten seconds before letting myself out. The limousine was nowhere to be seen when I stepped out of the restaurant. A brisk wind swept down off the face of the great mountain, and the snow at the summit reflected the ivory hue of the moon. A ripple of clouds formed a halo high above it, and I thought of home for the first time in weeks. I was not homesick. No, I didn't imagine I would ever feel that again. But I did miss the people, and that was a good thing. I could do with some of my mom's home cooking and a round of golf with my dad. Whether they would recognize their prodigal son upon his return was another question.

I started up the road.

It was almost too quiet. I listened to the wind whispering through the thick branches of the surrounding pine and let my mind wander. It occurred to me that I hadn't dreamed about the dragon in weeks. I tried to find some significance in that. Maybe he and I had reached a truce of sorts. Maybe I was becoming the hunter. Maybe I was ready to take on the rest of my life and was just now beginning to realize it.

The Professor

"Cage of a leopard;
Not a water drop
Remains in the dark sky."
~ Kakio Tomizawa

The last week of the semester, the entire Kumayama Inc. team presented the results of our company's six-month enterprise to Professor
Barrett and the entire Organizational Behavior class. All four teams were
required to do so.

Each member of our team reviewed in concise, practiced terms his or
her contribution to the company. I introduced the presentation and, at the
end, summarized the financial picture, as I put it, "as of the close of business this morning."

Professor Adrian Barrett sat in the front row of the auditorium along
with the rest of the class and listened as intently as his hung-over state
would allow.

Each team went in order. The second presenters, Junrei Kuni—or
Pilgrimage Incorporated—had very ingeniously partnered with a Tokyo
travel agency and had ferried tourists to and from Mount Fuji every weekend. They had generated income both from the transportation side of the
arrangement and the personalized guided tours of the mountain. Their
net profit was $25,500, or 1,350,000 yen. Not bad. In fact, damn good.

Akindo Sha, the third company to present, had created and produced a 1985 color calendar featuring seasonal photographs of the great Mount Fuji and haikus of such famous Japanese poets as Basho Matsuo, Buson Yosa, and Hisajo Sugita. A working arrangement with Ito Publishing in Tokyo had produced orders from as far away as Australia, England, and the United States. Their net profit was $9,500.

Moto's Mori Kaisha and their two fledgling croissant shops—the one on campus and the street corner stand they had been permitted to operate in Fujinomiya—had actually sold 850 croissants at $1.00 each, or 200,000 yen. Less manufacturing costs and licensing fees to the tune of $670, the company had posted a net profit of $180. "Not overly impressive for six months on the job," was Professor Barrett's observation.

In Pierre's rambling dissertation in defense of the company, he noted that their revenues were growing week by week and that by the end of the year, they would have established storefront locations in Fujinomiya and Tokyo with expansion plans that included neighboring Odawara and Shimizu.

"Mr. Trepanier, was there something about this assignment that Mori Kaisha didn't understand?" Barrett's gaze traveled from the flailing Frenchman to one or two of his teammates and came to rest on Moto. "Mr. Moto? Yes? Correct me if I'm wrong, but I said the very first day of class that these very fine enterprises would be judged upon their performance over a six-month semester. Not a year, not seven months, not six months and one day. Six months. Your competitors seemed to have understood the concept of a six-month business model just fine. All showed a positive revenue stream and reasonable net profits."

Barrett stood up, staggered, and faced the students who made up his Organizational Behavior class. "While I might also congratulate Mori Kaisha on the $180 profit, which I think translates into about 45,000 yen, I doubt any reasonable Japanese, American, French, Canadian, or, for that matter, Eskimo businessman would deem that a success."

"I beg to differ, Professor Barrett," Pierre retorted.

Barrett's eyes widened. "If the Mori Kaisha team will please take their seats," he said thickly. "It's my favorite time of the semester. It's D-day. It's H-hour. This is when the rubber hits the road."

Barrett strode to the head of the auditorium with a gait that was both labored and stiff. He snared a piece of chalk and placed himself squarely in front of the chalkboard. He wrote four names on the board.

> Junrei Kunie Kuni—Pilgrimage Inc.
> Mori Kaisha—The Forest Company
> Kumayama Inc.—Mountain Lions
> Akindo Sha—The Merchant Corporation

"Kumayama's tennis tournament, and the associated advertising and sponsorship programs that supported it, produced a net profit of $63,000," said Barrett. "The majority of this profit, as I understand it, has been used to establish scholarship funds in the name of those sponsors. An admirable gesture, if I do say so. You showed initiative, creativity, and the kind of aggressive attitude that is the hallmark of successful companies everywhere," he added. Next to our company name, he wrote a large "A." Then he applauded, clapping three or four times and nodding his head approvingly. "Darn good work."

Next to Junrei Kuni, the transportation and tour company, he chalked a white "B." He said, "A good concept, simple, direct and effective, and a nice long-term model. Well thought out, Pilgrims."

"Akindo Sha," he said, scribbling a "C+" next to their name. "I thought you would never turn a dime of revenue much less a profit in just six months. You surprised me and, on top of that, the calendar turned out quite nice. You'll see it hanging on my wall next year."

"Mori Kaisha." He looked at the faces of Moto's team and seemed to find some pleasure in the dark expressions staring back at him. "A $1.00 product requiring a top flight manufacturing source, licensing agreements, and six months to make it a success is not a model for success in the real world of business. I can't imagine what you were thinking."

He placed an "F" next to the Mori Kaisha name, tossed aside his chalk, and walked out. The hush that fell over the auditorium was nothing short of funereal. It swept over fifty students, who seemed permanently glued to their seats. I glanced down the aisle at the nine-man team of Mori Kaisha and saw eight lifeless expressions. Pierre broke the silence when he slammed his briefcase shut, arose, and crashed noisily down the stairs, slamming the door behind him.

One student after another slipped out of their seats, most of them grateful for whatever passing grade they may have gotten, and silently moved towards the exit. The fallout from an "F" grade was lost on no one.

When the auditorium was nearly empty, Kudoh, Suzuki, Takeda, and I made our way across the room to our distraught, motionless roommate. Moto had not moved a muscle. He was slumped in his seat, a stack of books on his lap, his vacant eyes downcast.

Kudoh and Takeda did their best to console him, but he was inconsolable. I supposed that any other reaction would have surprised them. They rallied around him because it was good form, not because they expected Moto to dismiss his failure.

I wrapped an arm around his shoulder. "I'm sorry about this, Moto-san. You didn't deserve an 'F.'" I hoped the tone of my voice did not betray the ambivalence of my thoughts. I didn't honestly believe that the effort his group had put into the company warranted a failing grade, but the result was less than satisfactory. No one could deny that. I wanted to say, "It's not the end of the world," but for a man who lived his life based upon a code of honor, duty, and obligation, Moto had a hard road ahead of him.

"I have disgraced myself in the eyes of my family, my father-in-law who intervened for me at Sony, my boss who hired me and trusted my performance, my company, and my country." Moto struggled to his feet. "I have dishonored them and lost all face."

"Barrett's class had no relation to the real world, Moto-san. He chose teammates for you that you would never have chosen for yourself in the outside world," Suzuki suggested.

"Suzuki-san is right. Barrett's class had nothing to do with the actual business world. Your colleagues at Sony will see that in a second," I said, wondering if there was any truth in what I was saying.

"We are lucky the fucking class is over," Suzuki said. "Let us get a beer and forget it."

"Good idea," Kudoh agreed.

Suzuki relieved Moto of his books and Kudoh and I threw our arms around his shoulders. The five of us walked back to our dorm listening to Suzuki fill the silence with a rambling monologue about Professor Adrian Barrett's inadequacies as a teacher and a human being.

All I could do was nod in agreement.

Despite the crushing blow Moto had absorbed from our ill-fated Organizational Behavior class, the semester had proved successful for the majority of the Institute's student population. The graduation ceremony was scheduled for that afternoon and evening was meant to be a celebration, not a wake. I hoped Moto would see it as a chance to put the Fucking Frenchman, the Croissant Shoppe, and our drunken Stanford professor behind him.

The swell of energy and the anticipation on campus began early that afternoon as the Japanese businessmen, the six surviving foreign students, and even the faculty and staff shed their educational mindset in favor of celebration and thoughts of home. The attire of the afternoon was shorts and t-shirts. The grounds were alive with Frisbees, flag football, and a heavy dose of light chatter and unabridged laughter.

The Japanese contingent was already in deep discussion about the Sumo wrestling extravaganza that would follow the graduation festivities and launch a long night of partying, Japanese style. Talk of the Sumo Match of the Century—pitting the blue-eyed American monster, Kai Waters, against the great Japanese hope, Masato Kudoh—ran rampant. Our match had already received top billing, a dubious honor I was not taking quite as seriously as everyone else. Kudoh was carrying the hopes and aspirations of his countrymen on his shoulders. I was just looking to have a good time.

A telegram arrived for me that afternoon. Mom and Dad had written all the right things. *Wish we could be there to see you graduate. We're proud of our son, proud of you for just being yourself more than anything. We can't wait to see you. Love, Mom and Dad.*

Nice. They had always emphasized inner realization over external success and I found that grounding. I wish you were here, too, I thought.

I had great expectations for staying in touch with the special friends I had made this semester: Kudoh, Moto, Sandy, and Sherri. Would this resolve last? I hoped so. Even if the resolve waned, the experience would have lasting affects. I was sure of that.

I had finished the semester with three "A's" and an honor certificate. That was all well and good, a goal achieved. More important by far, however, was the deep respect I had come away with for the Japanese and their culture. A byproduct of this was an equally deep understanding of the Sisyphean-like mentality that pervaded their existence. While it was not futility in the classic sense, it was a constant struggle that pitted duty and obligation against initiative and the urge to break out of the norm. The commitment to honor that they espoused was a beautiful thing. I would try to make it a permanent part of my own day-to-day life.

It would not be right to say that I was a new person, but I had certainly evolved during the past six months and was grateful for all of the events that had made the experience one which would forever change the way I viewed the world. It had given me a better grasp on the subtleties of life. I would try to never again take for granted the people who crossed my path, whether it was for a day, a year, or a lifetime.

While I might not think of Takeda and Suzuki as great and lasting friends, they had shown me genuine kindness. They had allowed me into their world and accepted me as a man with goals and aspirations worthy of their respect. I could not have asked for more.

Kudoh and I had taken our relationship beyond that and a true friendship had emerged. The laughter we shared was the cornerstone of this friendship and the trust and confidence we shared bespoke a deep respect. It was hard to beat that!

Moto had simply won my heart. He was as generous a man as I had ever met. He cared for my well-being and I cared for his. The deep love he showed for his family was a priceless lesson in family intimacy.

I didn't know what I could learn from Ikeda's death, as senseless and devastating as it was. He had unknowingly taken a bullet for me. I was throwing a Frisbee around with my friends, and his family was grieving the death of a 23 year old kid without a cruel bone in his body. I had to live with that. I could spend the rest of my days blaming myself, but the circumstances that brought us to that fateful moment in the cafeteria were not of my making. Meeting Liliko was not something I regretted. I had not encouraged Kona to rob me, nor could I have ever imagined the incident would lead to a group called the *yakuza*.

I did not ask for protection from *Oyabun* Yamaguchi, but I was sure as hell glad Neko had shown up when she did. I would liked to have saved Kona from the cruel end fate had handed her. I would have liked to have made peace and helped her to return home again. There was a lesson to be learned there, but I was still groping to put words to it. Some things you cannot control. Some events leave you powerless. I may not have liked the feeling but, as with Ikeda's death, I would have to live with it.

The sadness I felt while packing my bags spoke volumes, I decided, about this six-month adventure. All things ended. Life was transitional and I knew that. When the transition caused an ache deep in your stomach, it suggested the passing of a good thing, a meaningful thing. We were scheduled for an 8:00 a.m. departure the following morning and a 90-minute bus trip back to Tokyo. I did not want to think about it yet. I wanted to be with my friends.

At 5:45, I walked with Kudoh, Sandy, and Sherri toward the bleachers next to the athletic fields. We found seats next to Kenzo Shinran, Suzuki,

Mitch, and Mavis. I looked for Moto, but he apparently hadn't arrived yet. I knew he was dreading the ceremony. It was disappointing that the "A" grades he had received in his English language class and Professor Narita's Japanese Culture class could not provide a balance to the disaster of Barrett's Organizational Behavior class. Well, I thought, how would you feel? When an answer did not come to me, I put it out of my mind and took in the surroundings. With Mount Fuji in the background, it was a fine setting for a graduation.

On stage, chairs had been arranged in a half moon for the faculty, and I saw Neko Katayama take a seat next to Professor Miura Narita. One chair remained unoccupied, and the one missing faculty member was Adrian Barrett. This was no surprise since something told me the ceremony meant even less to him than it did to Moto.

When the Dean stepped up to the microphone, he began by saying, "Stand up and give yourselves a hand. You deserve it."

I liked his approach of making the students the show. When we had finished applauding ourselves, the gnome of a man flashed a warm smile and said, "And let us not forget your sensei tachi."

I had to admit that I was clapping primarily for Neko. She had done what few other teachers had ever done for me. Part mentor, part confidante, she had also extended the hand of friendship and, in doing so, had made me a better student and a more complete person. Saving my life, well, that was another subject altogether, and one I would keep deep in my heart forever.

I had to give the Dean credit. He looked out at his audience and saw men and women far more interested in Sumo wrestling and celebration than words of wisdom, so he kept it short.

He did say one thing I hoped to remember. "Be courageous," he said. "Seek to explore that most original person you were created to be."

Courage and originality, yes, those were two characteristics that appealed to me. It was ironic because we were born with the instinct of fear. It was also ironic because the messages most often shoved down our throats by society were things like "fall in line," "be like everyone else," and "live according to the rule of the masses." No, I thought, fear may have come to us instinctually, but rising above the fear was the trademark of successful men and women. Stepping away from the norm led to invention and discovery. I believed it. In keeping with this belief, I reminded myself to write down the Dean's words in my notebook when I got back to my room and to underline the words courageous and original.

One by one, the Dean called out the names of each JIIS graduate. One by one, we made our way down to the stage, shook the Dean's hand and that of each teacher in turn, then received our diplomas. Neko gave me a warm hug instead of a handshake. It was odd how much this ceremony reminded me of other graduation ceremonies I had been a part of, going all the way back to grade school. It was partly a matter of successfully completing one stage of my life, I supposed, but it was even more about moving forward and facing the unknown. That was what we were facing here today, the next phase of our lives.

I cheered exceptionally loud when I finally saw Moto, as he solemnly accepted his diploma, in the hopes that my support would shake him loose from the disaster he was now living. The Japanese clapped, shouted and cheered every graduate with equal enthusiasm. All but Pierre, that is. Word of Mori Kaisha's "F" grade in Organizational Behavior had swept the campus like a winter storm, and blame had fallen directly on the Fucking Frenchman's shoulders, right or wrong.

I heard Mavis and several others clap politely, but the revelry bestowed upon the other men and women was not awarded Pierre. The Japanese did not lower themselves to jeering, but withholding their applause was not beneath them. I watched Pierre's reaction, or, more accurately, lack of reaction. He displayed aloofness, indifference, and maybe even a hint of enjoyment. Yes, it was there, that "fuck you" attitude I had first seen the day we were boarding our bus in Tokyo. It was sad and, for me, a steadfast reminder of exactly how I didn't want to conduct myself.

When all the diplomas had been distributed, we came to our feet.

Professor Narita assumed the microphone and led us in song, a Japanese folk tune called "Whispers of Mount Fuji" that Suzuki had often sung at the end of a long night of drinking. It was an emotional piece about our endless search for beauty and peace of mind. As I watched the tears flowing freely and unconsciously down the faces of my Japanese classmates, I felt a welling in my own eyes. What was it? Was it the illusiveness of the search? Was it the futility? Or was it the ephemeral nature of all things, the inevitability of change?

All I knew was that the song left no one with dry eyes, at least not among those I cared about. When the song ended, Kudoh turned and wrapped me in a huge bear hug that was part affection, part longing, and part ending.

"May our friendship weather the storm of time and distance," he said to me.

"It will," I said. "It will."

The song signaled an end to the graduation ceremony and we returned to our dorms thinking only of one last party and the art of Sumo. Of course, no Sumo competition would be complete without the requisite pre-competition toast, so my roommates and I gathered beforehand in our dorm's common area. In honor of Ikeda, we slipped the Motown tape I had given him that first day into the boom box and cranked up Aretha Franklin's version of "You Make Me Feel Like a Natural Woman." Suzuki filled five sake cups, we all shouted, "*Kanpai,*" and drank.

The sake had no sooner exploded in my stomach than Moto refilled our cups, raised his high, and said, "To my Fujinomiya roommates. I am sorry I brought disappointment to you after all the help you gave me. I owe you my apologies."

"To Moto-san, a man with a beautiful heart and a brilliant future," I said, touching his cup and drinking.

Ah, sake, I thought. It was a completely appropriate drink for celebration, song, and sorrow. Extremely versatile, sake was also a conversational key. In Japan, you could share a cup of sake with colleagues or business associates and discuss or debate that which otherwise might be considered hallowed ground and do so without fear of retribution. Sake set the stage for intimate conversation that had, at its heart, an unspoken expectation of confidentiality. It was quite a drink! I couldn't think of any symbolic ritual from back home that came with the same assurances. The unwritten rule in the States, as far as I could tell, was watch your back.

In Japan, sake served as a temporary escape from the constant pressures inherent in Japanese culture and exaggerated in the Japanese business community. Conformity and decorum ruled here. Individuality was more than discouraged; it was effectively stifled. In Japan, alcohol in general and sake in particular signaled a loosening of the collar, a momentary hiatus, even the turning of a blind eye to the inexorable and implacable tenets of the day-to-day business world.

With the heat of alcohol seeping into our veins, we turned our attention to battle.

Face

"The moon
Above snow-covered mountains
Dropped hailstones."
~ Sekitei Hara

A sumo match would not have been a sumo match without the mandatory uniforms.

Each man prepared himself in his own unique and very personal style. Kudoh did not need much extra padding to effect the sumo mode, so he pulled a pair of jockey shorts over his University of Tokyo sweatpants, proudly donned his Toyota company t-shirt, and improvised a pair of shoulder pads from an old chair cushion.

"You look like an aspiring champion," I told him, even though he looked more like a grinning teenager in a Halloween costume.

"Aspiring? Ah!" He flexed his muscles. "I am a champion, my blue-eyed American challenger."

I sensed a growing importance surrounding our sumo match and I told myself not to make light of the observation. As friendly as Kudoh and I were, and as drunk as we might be by the time our match concluded, this represented more to him and his Japanese cohorts than simple fun and games. Sumo was Japan's national sport. I had seen the country's fervor first hand at the *basho* in Tokyo, but I had also seen how much pride they took in the sport and how deep the nationalism ran.

So I understood that there was more than just pride involved in this sumo match. There was a tremendous amount of face to be won or lost, both for Kudoh and his fellow countrymen. I was not Japanese. I was a foreigner who had come to their country as a visitor and had done well for himself. That the blue-eyed monster might emerge victorious from a farcical sumo match was anything *but* farcical.

Sandy arrived at our dorm looking all the jock in her gym shorts and tank top. I could never get enough of that look. In her hands, she was holding a pair of dark nylon stockings that added an air of sensuality that was lost on no one.

"If you've come to model those for an appreciative male audience," I said among the hoots and whistles of my roommates, "you have come to the right place."

"These," she said in a most formal voice, "are for you."

There were more hoots and whistles. "Hush, you four, this is serious business," she admonished.

Sandy and I adjourned to the bathroom and when we emerged, the stockings had been converted into a classic Japanese ponytail dangling off the back of my head. I struck a sumo pose for the benefit of my roomies. Hoots and whistles turned to laughter.

"Ah, very appropriate," Suzuki said. "Now if you could just gain fifty pounds."

"*Mondai nai,*" I said. With Moto's help, I gathered together three pillows and a spare blanket. We strapped the pillows tightly around my waist, and then disguised my newly discovered girth with the blanket.

I waddled into the common area a true sumo warrior. "Introducing Waters-san. Undefeated sumo champion from Chicago, Illinois, USA," Moto announced.

"I'll drink to that," Sandy said, and once the laughter died down, we did just that.

Before we were too drunk to navigate the stairs, the Dorm Six brothers and one beautiful woman made their way to the campus grounds.

An improvised wrestling ring had been erected at the heart of the courtyard. Someone had absconded with a large mat from the workout room and had painted a large circle on it to indicate the *dohyo*.

"You have seen this in person, so you have a pretty good idea about the rules," Takeda said to me. "Toss someone outside the ring and you win. Simple. A true test of strength, agility, and maneuverability, all in one."

We had all the props: talcum powder, salt, and classical Japanese war songs. A dozen or so participants were introduced to a rowdy audience. The sumo outfits were outstanding, from leather thongs and skullcaps to waist-long ponytails and Pillsbury Doughboy stomachs.

The first match was announced. My roommate Takeda, naked except for the silk thong hiding his private parts, entered the ring against an inventive opponent who had enhanced his mid-section using water balloons. The match had not even begun and peels of laughter were echoing across campus.

They both played out the ceremonial pre-match ritual. They tossed salt over their shoulders to ward off evil spirits. They poured talcum into their palms and clapped their hands loudly, filling the air with clouds of white dust and receiving a cheer for their dramatic flare. They bowed formally to a referee who was dressed head-to-toe in a tie-dyed sheet. Then they bowed opponent-to-opponent. The referee blew his whistle, and the match commenced. The two men collided and water balloons burst in all directions. The audience roared. Ten seconds later, Takeda managed to toss his foe out of the ring, and the competition was well underway. Every match called for cold beer, peels of laughter, and the occasional exchange of a wager or two, all in good fun.

I glanced out the corner of my eye and saw Moto alternating shots of sake with tall cans of Sapporo. It may have been my imagination, but he seemed drunker and more oblivious than usual. I couldn't blame him. Tomorrow he would be back to reality. We all would. But for Moto, it would be a more complex re-entry. Tomorrow he would begin the process of amends, repairing the damage he felt he had inflicted upon himself, his family, and his company because he had chosen croissants over a tennis tournament or a calendar. If I knew Moto, he would find that diamond in the rough and turn it into a learning experience with a valuable upside. I hoped so, at any rate.

A drum roll shook me from my reverie. The announcer's voice crackled over the loudspeaker, first in Japanese, then in phonetically perfect, if heavily accented, English.

"Ladies and gentlemen, scholars and scatterbrains, wrestling aficionados and sumo neophytes. We have a first here at the Sumo International Classic, a match between two of the Institute's most fierce competitors and beautiful representatives. May I introduce Lady Sandy Hall, from sunny California, in the United States of America, and Lady Sherri Samstone, from the province of Quebec in faraway Canada." Quebec came out sounding like Key Bay, but no matter. There was a big round of applause.

The announcer did not need to exhort or prod his audience in any way. The cheering rose in spontaneous outbursts from a predominately male audience hungry to see two gorgeous women tossing each other about. In their tank tops and hip hugger shorts, no sumo wrestler had ever looked so good.

Sandy and Sherri followed the talcum and salt ritual with heightened gravity until Sandy sampled the salt with her tongue, grimaced at the taste, and washed it down with a shot of cold sake.

When the laughter died down, they bowed to the judge with extreme formality, turned, and faced each other with mock fierceness. Sherri's Indian war cry filled the air, and she charged. The two sumo-girls choreographed a playful match that was as sensual as it was fun, and they had everyone in the audience frolicking and cheering.

When it seemed certain the match would end in a draw, Sandy and Sherri clutched each other's arms, feigned a paired pirouette at the edge of the ring, and fell into the laps of some startled and extremely pleased

Japanese onlookers. They all screeched with pleasure. When the girls righted themselves, they toured the ring with raised arms and victorious grins.

Unexpectedly, Sherri struck a pose in the center of the ring, raised her tank top, and flashed her perfectly erect breasts for all to see. The Japanese signaled their absolute delight at the spontaneous gesture with the rowdiest cheer of the night and a standing ovation. It was a classic moment that would live on in the memories of the Class of 1984. I suspected it was also Sherri's rather unorthodox way of acknowledging the hospitality her fellow classmates had shown her and their immediate acceptance of her love affair with Sandy.

"It's going to be hard to top that," I said to Kudoh after the girls left the ring.

We had both been drinking for well over an hour, but that didn't stop Kudoh from toasting our upcoming match one more time. "We will thrill them with our speed, our strength, and our commitment to sumo."

I had no idea what he was talking about, but I held up my end of the toast anyway. "Speed, strength, sumo. *Banzai!*"

With sake running rampantly through my veins, my world spun. I heard the announcer hyping the Match of the Century and introducing me. "An American champion undefeated in his illustrious, if short career in sumo, please welcome Kai Waters, the Blue-eyed Monster."

Good, I thought as I jogged into the ring, my moniker has survived the semester intact. I circled the ring, high-fiving my fans and flashing the V-for-victory sign with arms extended. I threw in an Ali shuffle and nearly tripped over my own feet.

"And representing the island nation of Japan and the Land of the Rising Sun, from Nikko Prefecture and now residing in Tokyo, our very own Masato Kudoh," the announcer screeched.

This was a different kind of cheering. There was fervor infecting the raised voices, the bold and resonant tenor of nationalism. The raucous cheering came to a crescendo when Kudoh entered the ring performing two back flips. The pose he struck was part King Kong, part Samurai warrior. This, I decided, was going to be fun.

Kudoh was stout and hardy by Japanese standards and strong as a horse. I had been witness to that strength on many occasions in the gym and arm-wrestling in the dorm. But I was six inches taller, fifty pounds heavier, and in some of the best shape of my life. Bring it on, I thought.

Unfortunately, my world was increasingly out of focus as the courtyard shook from the combination of this deafening cacophony and the effects of the sake and beer combo I had been absorbing like a sponge for ninety minutes. I toured the ring, hoping to regain my composure, but the faces staring back at me merged in an unfocused blur of heads and out-of-control voices chanting, "Kudoh, Kudoh, Kudoh!"

I tossed salt over my shoulder, as did Kudoh. Well, if there were evil spirits lurking about, I had to believe they were rooting for the local hero. I couldn't blame them. A part of me was rooting for him, too.

I wished it were as simple as that. Like most everything else I had encountered in the Land of the Rising Sun, there were more than enough complications for any one man. I had no doubt that if I used every ounce of my strength and tapped into the athleticism of my high school and undergraduate years, I could overcome Kudoh's low center of gravity and powerful legs to maneuver him outside the ring. I loved to compete and I loved to win. I wasn't fanatical about it, but I wasn't going to deny it, either.

On the other hand, my six-month-cultural exchange had given me a new outlook on many things, among them a deeper understanding and appreciation of national pride and a growing respect for the monumentally powerful tool called "face," which the Japanese might define as "personal integrity." I thought of it as a man's or woman's personal power, the act of standing tall and accepting your responsibilities.

The beauty of face was the overriding need to grant it to your fellow man or woman. In the eyes of the Japanese, the maintenance and perpetuation of another's face was as important as the preservation and continuity of your own. Face didn't stop with the individual; that was clear. It sustained family, friends, and community. It touched work, religion, and politics. It had become, in many ways, part of the genetic imprint and nomenclature of this very secluded enclave.

What was my responsibility here? I had my own pride to think about, my own honor. I could hear my father urging me to stand up for America and my civic duty. There was history between our countries that had to be acknowledged. It didn't matter that I was a guest here. There was pride on the line.

In the big picture, one could argue, Kudoh represented Japan's industrial power and desire to establish itself as a worldwide juggernaut. I, on the other hand, carried the banner of U.S. economic clout and ingenuity. Japan had its face to defend. America had its pride.

In my mind's eye, I could see a victorious American flag staked out for all to see in the center of this makeshift sumo ring. But the mind did not always distinguish right from wrong, positive from negative, cause from effect. The heart was often a more effective barometer in these situations, and I decided to rely on my heart in this case.

We squared off. I looked across the mat at my friend and confidante. The serious, intent glint in his eye told me in no uncertain terms that this friendly match held far greater significance for him and his countrymen than mere celebration. So be it, I thought.

The referee sounded his whistle, and the match began. I had no idea that fifty people could manufacture such a wall of sound. Kudoh and I locked arms. Heads down and bodies bent, a flow of energy and strength resonated through his limbs as palpably as it did mine.

Why a flood of memories washed over me at that very moment, I had no idea. Perhaps Kudoh was squeezing them out of me with his immense strength. Perhaps one too many cups of sake ignited the flashbacks. In a matter of seconds, though I really had no solid concept of time, I saw the tattoo on Liliko's back, the Bengal tiger's claws reaching out to me in a moment of unparalleled pleasure. I saw Neko darting from the trees of the surrounding forest and saving me from my would-be assassin. I saw the silhouette of Kimiko's face and the delicate lines of her body as she hovered over me in the ocean room of the Happi Hoteru. I saw Moto's anguished expression after hearing about his failing grade in Professor Barrett's class. I saw the star-shaped sand of Taketomijima glittering in the sun. I traveled to the shrines and temples of Kyoto. I heard the voices of women: in the Tokyo bathhouse; over the intercom at the airport; that of my mother as she made her tearful farewell; and Sandy and Sherri, calling my name.

It was the last of these that penetrated my reverie and jolted me back to the reality of the sumo ring and the sweat rolling down my forehead. Sandy and Sherri were still shouting my name, and they may have been my only two supporters.

Well, two is better than none, I reminded myself, and the thought caused a surge of adrenaline and reminded me of the task at hand. I managed to grab a handful of Kudoh's makeshift thong with one hand and hooked an arm under his shoulder. With a deep-throated growl, I hoisted my friend off his feet. It was three steps to the edge of the ring and victory. I heard the crowd gasp, but they had no idea how far away those three steps were.

I felt Kudoh counteract my grip by wrapping a leg around my knee, but it was the sound of his voice that proved the best defense. As calmly as a man settling in for a stroll down a lonely beach, Kudoh whispered, *"Mondai nai,* Waters-san. *Mondai nai."*

I burst out laughing.

My grip loosened. Kudoh's feet were again on the ground. I had two choices. I could spin inward toward the ring and create another stalemate or I could hold my ground and let the chips fall where they might. It wasn't really a choice. I had already decided to hold my ground, and I already knew where the chips would fall. I knew Kudoh had the momentum as he planted his left foot and gripped the belt holding my pillows in place. He put a shoulder into my chest, leveraged the strength in his lower body, and spun me in one motion toward the ring's perimeter . . . and out.

Match over. Score one for Kudoh and his defense of Japanese honor. Score one for Kai, for securing his good friend's face.

The courtyard erupted. Cheers of ecstasy, triumphant shouting, and screeching whistles carried on the breeze and may have even echoed as far away as Tokyo, for all I knew. Kudoh's followers rushed onto the mat and hoisted their conquering hero onto their shoulders.

"Kudoh, Kudoh, Kudoh!" His name left an indelible mark on the JIIS campus, at least for one night.

I realized I was smiling as the first hints of a cool rain fell from the night sky. Sandy and Sherri, my two loyal supporters, hurried over to me. Sherri kissed my cheek and hugged me.

"You crazy man. What in the world are you smiling about?"

Sandy caught my eye. I would never forget the knowing expression on her face. "I know," she said, squeezing my arm. "You're quite a guy, Kai Waters."

They helped me to my feet. Sherri said, "And what the hell is that supposed to mean?"

"It means our blue-eyed monster isn't such a monster after all," responded Sandy.

"It means it's time to celebrate, ladies." I said, and wrapped my arms around their shoulders.

When Kudoh's adoring supporters finally relinquished him from his victory ride, he jogged over.

"Waters-san. My good friend! My learned guest!" A smile worthy of Mount Fuji broke across his face. He encircled me in a huge bear hug and lifted me off the ground. Then he shook my hand. "We gave them a good show, did we not?"

"That we did, Kudoh-san. Well fought, my friend."

Kudoh winked. "I will buy you a drink." He looked at Sandy and Sherri and added, "I will buy us all a drink."

"A champion with a fat wallet," Sandy said. "My kind of guy."

"Let's party," Sherri shouted.

As all good parties had over the last six months, this one migrated to Dorm Six. Suzuki surprised us with two cases of ice-cold Sapporo, several carafes of cold sake, and the all-important bottle of Ocean whiskey.

Motown music blared from the boom box, flashing cameras recorded the last night of the semester, and tears marking the event flowed freely.

Always eager to analyze and philosophize, I tried to put my feelings in perspective, but for better or worse, alcohol got the best of me. I settled for dancing and singing the night away. There was nothing like Motown to get the feet moving and everyone in the room knew the lyrics to the now famous cassette tapes I had presented as welcome gifts our first day on the campus.

Midnight seemed to be the witching hour for everyone. The migration back to our ordinary lives would begin for some of us as early as 8:00 a.m., when our bus arrived. The JIIS campus would be effectively deserted by noon, at least by the student population.

"Six months," Sandy said to me as she and Sherri made their way to the door. "It seems like yesterday you were helping me with my luggage."

I was fairly inebriated, but coherent enough to hear the lament in her voice.

"How did your search end up?" I asked.

She knew I was referring to our first run together that cool January day and her confession about trying to find the real Sandy.

"Ongoing," she replied. "But that's the way it's supposed to be, right, Kai? An ongoing process?"

"You didn't really expect to find all the answers, did you?" I managed to ask. "What fun would that be?"

"I don't like surprises."

I looked at her lover. "You sure about that?" I laughed.

"Some surprises are better than others," Sherri intoned.

I gave Sandy a brief nod and said, "Well, I like what I see."

"Thanks. You've been a real ally," Sandy said sincerely.

"And one helluva lover," Sherri blurted. "Oops!"

They staggered out of Dorm Six laughing as if the joke was on the rest of the world.

I reversed course, still fully garbed in my sumo outfit, and set my feet on a collision course with my bedroom. Concentrate, I thought. You'll make it.

Moto intercepted me.

"Waters-san." He was beyond drunk and staggered as he bowed.

"Moto-san. How are you, roomie?" We hugged. It wasn't a Kudoh-like bear hug; it was the strong embrace of brotherhood. Moto came away from the hug with a tear in his eye and sadness etched in the lines of his oval face. He bowed again, and the tear cut a damp trail down one cheek.

"Thank you for being a true friend, Waters-san," he said in broken English. Then he repeated the words in Japanese.

"You showed me genuine kindness, Moto-san," I replied, also in both languages and, for the first time in six months, unconcerned about the correctness of my Japanese. "I will wake you up before my bus leaves in the morning."

He didn't answer. "Sleep well, my friend," I said.

"A long life," he replied.

I struggled with the belt of my sumo outfit before giving up entirely and falling on my bunk, fully clothed and face down. Even at that, it was a fitful sleep, colored with images that were less like dreams than hazy snapshots without meaning.

I had at least demonstrated the good sense to set my alarm before the partying began and 5:00 a.m. arrived far sooner than my condition warranted.

"Damn." My head throbbed. My mouth tasted like stale cotton candy. The belt holding my sumo outfit in place had come free during the night and there were pillows scattered from one end of my bunk to the other. "Damn. I need to go on the wagon," I said to the empty bedroom.

I rolled to the side of the bunk, heard the melodic echo of rain pinging off my windowpane, and found the strength to stand up. I stretched, yawned, and realized all I really wanted to do was curl up on my bed again and hope our bus back to the city was late. That will never happen, I thought.

"Get some air. Maybe that'll help," I groaned. "Stand in the rain. Do something, anything."

I kicked aside the remains of my sumo outfit, put on a pair of gym shorts, and tied my robe around my waist. I swallowed three aspirin.

I walked out into the hall and into the common area. The silence was refreshing. I eased the door open and took the stairs down to the first floor. Outside, the scent of rain filled my nose and I sensed the smallest return to normalcy. I stepped out from under the eaves, felt the mist on my face, and took a dozen steps in the direction of the campus courtyard. I froze suddenly and felt a rush of nausea. Fear branched out from the pit of my stomach, and I gasped at the nearly impossible sight staring back at me. A man's body hung from the second story railing, a rope around his neck, and beads of rain streaming down his lifeless limbs.

"Oh, no." The words were hardly more than a whisper. And then I recognized Moto's ghostly face and cried, "Oh, God, no!"

I dropped to my feet and vomited. My body shook. I wiped rain from my face and realized it was mixed with hot, burning tears. I forced myself to my feet and stumbled across the grass to Moto's lifeless body. His head lolled to one side. His face was the color of cold ash. "Oh, my friend. What have you done?" It was a silly, meaningless question.

I held him around the waist with one hand and loosened the ligature around his neck with the other. I lowered him to the ground, cradling his head on my lap, and stroked his ice-cold brow. A welling of grief and anger burst out of me. I screamed at the top of my lungs, a savage cry of complete and total anguish.

"Moto-san." I wanted to scream again, this time in anger and frustration. I wanted to chastise and lecture. I wanted to tell him how sorry I was.

I wanted to tell him nothing in the world was worth this, not honor, not duty, not fucking obligation. I wanted to tell him how much I cared for him. I did none of these things. I just held him.

Behind me, I saw lights illuminating a half dozen windows. I heard a balcony door open and a voice call out: "Is everything alright?"

It was Kudoh. He must have heard my scream. I saw him look over the balcony railing; he must have seen the rope tied there.

"Waters-san?" I did not have the strength to answer. Then I heard the urgency and the uncertainty in his voice. "Waters-san! I am coming!"

Kudoh was the first to arrive, a flash of red coloring his face. He fell to his knees beside us. "This cannot be. Not Moto."

I could hardly talk. I was weeping like a child. "All because of a fucking failing grade in a . . ."

Kudoh silenced me with a gentle hand on my shoulder. "No, Waters-san. It was more than that. Much more."

He was right, and I knew it. But there was no time to say more. The courtyard was suddenly alive with people, all responding to the rapid spread of alarm and word of the tragedy that had beset the campus on this final day of our stay.

Takeda and Suzuki stood over us, paralyzed with anguish and fearful because they knew the pressures that had driven our roommate to this end.

Sandy, Sherri, Mavis, and Mitch held hands, dumbfounded and ripped apart at the utter waste. I heard Sandy mutter, "But he had so much to live for."

Neko, my sensei, friend, mentor, and counselor, stepped forward and put a hand on my shoulder. In her eyes, I saw an overwhelming sadness and just a hint of resignation.

I heard the sirens, but they meant nothing to me. There would be no heroics here this morning. The paramedics were just ahead of the police. They showed a respect for Moto that impressed me. Suicide was not new to them, the suicide of a Japanese businessman even less so. Their care and respect may have reflected their understanding of how common this event was.

The police demonstrated a thoroughness that almost struck me as morbid. They questioned the Dean, every teacher, and Moto's Japanese roommates.

I was impatient. What were they looking for? Foul play? Motive? A miracle? Moto was dead. All the questions in the world would not bring him back. All I could think about was the confused and mortified looks I imagined would be on his daughters' faces when they were told they would now have to go through life fatherless. I could hear seven-year-old Tomiko asking, "Why?"

Now that was a question worth asking.

———

The Weeping Bus

"Spring departs
Birds cry
All eyes are filled with tears."
~ Basho Matsuo

I had never before witnessed the death of a close friend in such a stark, personal fashion.

A college friend named Jesse Whitaker had died in a car accident after a night of hard drinking. He had slammed head first into a telephone pole, with four other friends onboard. Miraculously, all but Jesse survived. As heart wrenching and sad as it was, more than anything, I remembered taking solace in the fact that he had not taken anyone else with him. Maybe Jesse and I hadn't been all that close when all was said and done. I know I never felt as connected to him as I did Moto.

The depth of Moto's kindness set him apart from almost anyone else I had ever known. That he was genuine hardly described it. He held nothing back. It mattered not that I was a foreigner. That was rare for most human beings and essentially unheard of among the Japanese.

That he chose death, and death by hanging, seemed like such an immense contradiction in the face of that trusting, authentic kindness that I wondered if I would ever truly be able to reconcile it in my heart and soul. Taking your own life seemed to me an act of extreme cruelty. I could not imagine saddling my family and friends with such a lifelong burden.

On the other hand, I seriously doubted that Moto had seen this, given the pain and anguish he must have been feeling. How could he?

A cloak of utter confusion and chaos settled over the campus in the wake of Moto's suicide. The police cordoned off the area around the dorms, sealed Dorm Six with yellow tape, and treated the courtyard like a crime scene. They called it standard procedure. Paramedics photographed the body and carefully laid Moto, his blue suit soaked through with rain, on a gurney. Reporters arrived in a van from Fujinomiya with cameras and notepads, but by then, Moto had been zipped inside a body bag. All the while, a cool rain tried to wash the campus clean. I sat on the stairs outside the dorm in a state of mental paralysis, numb from my head to my feet. I watched the scene like a man lost in a foggy haze.

I sensed the hand on my shoulder even before I felt it. I was too numb to be startled. I turned my head into the rain, and the sight of Neko Katayama caused my eyes to burn.

"Kai." I was overwhelmed at the amount of sympathy and empathy contained in that one word. She crouched on the step next to me. She reached out for my hand and our fingers entwined. There was a wonderful kinship in the gesture. She said, "You have lost a good friend and I am sorry. And we have all lost a good human being."

She paused, as if a hand had gripped her throat. Her voice was a painful whisper when she continued. "It is difficult to imagine what his family will have to go through."

I nodded. "I'm devastated, you know, and almost too sad for words. But I'm also . . . I can't help it, but I'm also . . ."

I didn't finish the thought, so Neko finished it for me. "Angry? That he could do such a thing? That he could not see the damage he was doing to others? That he could not see the ripple effect of his actions?

"Yeah. I can't help it."

Neko said, "I am angry, too. I do not think you are supposed to control these feelings, Kai. You should know, however, that many people will look at his actions as honorable."

"The way of the defeated warrior, is that what you mean?" I shook my head. "The disgraced samurai?"

"Confucius once said, 'The superior man is modest in his speech but excels in his actions,'" Neko offered.

"I'm not sure Moto believed that," I replied.

"No," she admitted. She stood, rain falling in sheets around us. "But I do. And I think you do, too, Waters-san."

Then she bowed and turned away. I watched her disappear into the shadows, her words ringing in my ear.

I did not see the bus from Tokyo arrive. I was too numb to feel helpless, too adrift to question how the semester could have ended this way, and too disconnected to know why.

"Kai. We have to go." The voice belonged to Sandy. She put a hand on my arm and gave it a gentle tug. "The bus is here. We're loading our stuff. You have to get your bags."

"Okay. Thanks."

I didn't immediately move, though. "There's nothing we can do here, Kai," Sandy said. "They've already taken Moto away."

"Okay," I said again. I stood up and nodded. "I'll get my bags."

The police allowed me back in our dorm room long enough to change into my travel gear, lock my suitcases, and throw my backpack over my shoulder. I looked around Dorm Six one last time. Would every memory now be blackened by Moto's death? Would I ever be able to listen to Aretha Franklin again without picturing the ligature marks around Moto's neck or the death mask draining color from his face? Would every cup of sake from here on out recall his final toast or the sound of his vigorous laughter?

Did he have suicide on his mind when he wished me a long life, his last words to me? Should the tone of his voice have alerted me to his desperate state of mind? No, I told myself. That's asking too much of yourself. You're not to blame.

My other roommates were waiting for me in the courtyard. The rain coursed down with ever increasing vigor, and the clouds rolling off Mount Fuji took on an ominous blue-black hue. Midwestern clouds, I thought, remotely.

Takeda and Kudoh huddled beneath one umbrella, and Ikeda and Suzuki offered me a place beneath theirs. Kudoh shouldered my backpack, a last gesture of gentlemanly solidarity.

The five of us trudged toward the parking lot. There were no words. There was also no Pierre. He had decided to get his own transportation back to Tokyo. What could any of us say? The bus awaiting the five remaining foreign students looked exactly like the bus that had transported us here, and it made me wonder if anything else had really changed in six months. The previous day, I was sure of my new outlook and the change in perspective with which I would return home. Now, I was not convinced.

Hadn't forces developed and cultivated over thousands of years of Japanese history driven Moto to the brink? How did a man, in his short lifetime, fight the collective might of human development or the dictates of an entire society?

"One moment at a time," I heard a voice in the back of my mind say. "One step at a time, one conscious thought at a time."

Another voice, one even more urgent, said, "Don't forfeit everything you've learned over the last six months just because your friend chose a course of action you don't completely understand. Maybe this last lesson is the most powerful one of all: the freedom to choose."

Wasn't that what Moto had done? Hadn't he chosen death over what he saw as a life of shame?

I was surprised and pleased at the number of Japanese businessmen, unfazed by the rain, who had come down to say their farewells to the five of us. It was as if they did not want Moto's limp body to be the last thing we saw before we departed. I was strangely moved.

"I won't forget you guys," I said to my roommates as we drew up in front of the bus. I slid my suitcases into the luggage bay. Kudoh eased my backpack in next to it.

"Take care of yourself, Waters-san," Takeda said. We shook hands and he wiped a tear from his eyes.

Suzuki bowed. "I will look you up when I get to America. Keep the beer cold."

"Will do," I said.

I faced Kudoh. His eyes, like mine, were ringed in red. We shook hands and then hugged.

"Do not forget to write, Waters-san. I do not want to have to fly all the way to Chicago to track you down," he said with a weary smile.

"Good friends don't forget each other, Kudoh-san. It takes more than an ocean to do that."

"Okay then. Until next time." He hugged me again.

"Until next time, my friend."

I trudged onto the bus and stumbled down the aisle to the last row. It was a minute before 8:00. Sandy and Sherri were curled up in the seat opposite mine. They reminded me of two scared kittens giving each other comfort and strength.

"Hey," I said. "You guys all right?"

Sherri shrugged. Sandy managed a small smile. "Pretty shook up still. How about you?"

"Just glad I'm not making this trip back to the city alone," I told them truthfully.

Mitch and Mavis scrambled onto the bus thirty seconds later. Mavis hugged me. "I know what a good friend Moto was, Kai. I'm sorry."

"Damn, Kai. I wish I knew what to say." Mitch put a hand on my shoulder. "He seemed like such a great guy."

"He was," I assured him.

"Time to go," the bus driver called to us in English. "I do not mean to rush you."

Mavis and Mitch took the seat in front of Sandy and Sherri. "I'm ready to go home," Mavis said. "Hopefully, we can look back at these six months sometime soon and remember all the good moments. And there were lots of them."

"That's absolutely true. The good with the bad. The balance. It's always that way, isn't it?" Sandy conjectured. "I guess maybe Moto didn't see it that way."

I slumped in my seat. The bus was suddenly in motion. I looked back at the JIIS campus. I would try to remember it under a blue sky with Mount Fuji standing tall and statuesque in the background, lord of the forest. I would try to remember it the way Sandy and I had seen it during our first run together in January. I would try to remember the faces of my Japanese colleagues the day we arrived, filled with good cheer and optimism.

We left the parking lot. The Japanese businessmen scurried back to their dorms. I imagined that they couldn't make their getaway back to Tokyo or Osaka or wherever they had come from fast enough. I didn't blame them. They had come to the Institute with certain goals and well-stated mandates from their companies. Some had achieved them with flying colors; others would have a certain amount of explaining to do. But a suicide in their ranks would hopefully put it all in perspective.

Further along the road, framed by tall pines drenched in rain and shadow, I glimpsed the outline of a car parked on the shoulder. In the misty grays, the silhouette of a woman took shape. I sat up. I saw her midnight black hair soaked with rain and plastered to her fair cheeks. I saw her oval eyes squinting in the gloom.

I recognized the faded green of Kimiko's car a moment before I recognized her slender figure. She held a large cardboard sign in two hands. Painted in bright red across the face of the sign was a large heart, nothing else. The ink was slowly and irrevocably melting in the rain, staining the cardboard like tears, the same tears I could see melding with the rain on her cheeks.

I sat up further and put an open hand on the window, trying to reach out to her one last time, to secure a lasting memory, to hold onto a slice of the good that Sandy had spoken about earlier.

Kimiko's gentle smile struck a chord deep inside me. I saw all her strength and kindness in that one expression. I saw the ineffable contradictions that life tossed, piecemeal, in our paths and said, "Choose."

The pieces were all there. It was up to us to cast our lot, to gather the pieces up by whatever means, and to make them fit as best we could. Did that mean I had chosen poorly? Did it mean Moto had chosen poorly? No. We just do the best we can. Judgment would come from a higher source, I imagined, if judgment was appropriate.

My eyes locked with Kimiko's for one brief moment as the bus roared past. I was left with a heart weighted down by grief and uncertainty and realized I was not equipped to wage war against this type of sadness. I had no previous experience with it.

Kimiko was still holding her sign, but the heart had dissolved into a wash of soft pinks. She waved one last time. My hand was still on the glass as the bus swept around a corner, and she disappeared from sight. After a long moment, I turned away.

Outside, thunder cracked. Lightning speared the ground nearby and a flash of blue light illuminated the inside of the bus. I looked out at the small farm I had grown so accustomed to running by over the past six months and the tiny field now showing the first signs of lettuce, beans, and radishes. The farmer's dairy cow stood in the pasture, its dour eyes tracking our passage, oblivious to the rain. I saw his feathered friend, the cantankerous white duck, squawking and railing and flapping her clipped wings. But I saw something else, as well. Four baby ducks traipsed behind her in a line, full of vim and vigor, just like Mom.

It occurred to me that I had two choices. I was exhausted enough to sleep the entire way back to Tokyo. I had no doubt about that. I could rid myself of the image of Moto's body dangling from that rope and the icy touch of his skin as I rocked him in my arms. But the images would still be there when I awoke. Grief would still be waiting for me. I would still have to face the anger and confusion.

On the other hand, I would never travel this road again, and a part of me wanted these forested hillsides and these sculptured rice paddies implanted in my memory forever.

When the bus rumbled through the town of Fujinomiya, I took a snapshot in my mind of the Ichiban Tempura restaurant and replayed, in sound bites and flashbacks, a dozen amazing evenings spent there with my Kumayama teammates, savoring tempura, sipping sake, and bonding in true Japanese style.

The Happi Hoteru looked different in the light of day and less inviting, but the hour I had spent there in the arms of a remarkable Japanese woman was a movie that played in slow-motion details, frame-by-frame, as clearly as the night it happened. I could feel the emotion branching out even now through my fingertips, a river running at depths I would seek for the rest of my life. I could close my eyes and evoke the scents and sounds of that night as if the room and woman were an arm's length away.

As we left the town behind us, I watched the rainfall in glorious sheets across pines and poplars and marveled at the shades of gray and green that blinked from beneath the mist.

When I glanced back at my companions, I discovered Sherri and Sandy sound asleep, cuddled in each other's arms. Sandy's graceful hands were wrapped around Sherri's shoulders like a cloak and I realized that she was no longer wearing her wedding band. When had that happened? I took it as a good sign. The Sandy I now knew was more confident, but also more relaxed. She laughed more, yet there was less cynicism in her sense of humor. She was more energetic because she was spending less time trying to please everyone. I liked the woman she had become, but I loved the person. I could not predict where her relationship with Sherri would go. I imagined their time together as a bridge with a plethora of new relationships on the other side, but who could say?

Mitch and Mavis were a different story. When I glanced at her hand, still and peaceful in Mitch's lap, the ring on her finger seemed such a perfect fit that I could only look into their future with unfettered optimism. Their picture-book story was too fanciful and too serendipitous to expect anything less.

A clap of thunder returned my attention to the passing countryside, a canvas soaked in shades of impressionistic colors that ran past my eyes like an ever-evolving landscape painted by the Master Artist himself.

I caught a flash of black out of the corner of my eye and glanced out the back window. It looked more like a shadow in the distance than a moving vehicle, but the size and shape told me it was the Lone Ranger and Tonto in their ever-present limousine. I had to give them credit for keeping their distance. I was also glad they were there, but not because I felt threatened. That was long gone. This was about predictability, trust, and loyalty. *Oyabun* Yamaguchi, a man of his word, told me they would be there, and they were.

I settled back in my seat and let the questions come. Better now than later, though I was pretty sure I would never have answers that truly satisfied me. Shouldn't I have seen how desperate Moto had become? The signs must have been there; did I just miss them? What could I have said to make a difference? Could I have told him to think about his family, to quit his job if he thought it would lessen the burden? Could I have been more forceful in stating my case with Professor Adrian Barrett? Should I have taken my case to the Dean? Could I have beaten some sense into the fucking Frenchman? Were those really my responsibilities? And probably most perplexing of all: how could something so indefinable and abstract as "face" prove to be more powerful than life itself?

I knew the questions would haunt me every time I pictured Moto's lifeless body in my arms. They would probably haunt me even more when I pictured the Moto who was able to make me laugh until my sides hurt, who could sing every word of "In the Midnight Hour" by heart, and who seemed to have so much potential and so much to live for.

As the Tokyo skylight broke across the horizon, I heard Neko quoting her favorite sage. *"The superior man is modest in his speech but excels in his actions."*

Okay, then. That, at least, was something to hold on to.

The End

HAIKU

The Haiku is a Japanese poem or verse traditionally consisting of 17 syllables divided into three lines of 5, 7, and 5 syllables, and most often taking its theme from nature.

The wonderful poets noted in *Mondai Nai* include:

Basho Matsuo (1644 - 1694). He is known as the first great poet in the history of haiku.

Buson Yosa (1716 - 1783). He was an excellent painter and poet and succeeded in evoking clear images in his picturesque haikus filled with light.

Shiki Masaoka (1867 - 1902). The haiku innovation by Shiki created a great sensation in the whole of Japan and revived the languishing haiku world.

Kyoshi Takahama (1874 - 1959). Kyoshi's haikus are not limited to a fixed style. Among his haikus, several are splendid and virile, whereas others are subtle and delicate. Several give free rein to his imagination; others describe simply daily facts.

Sekitei Hara (1889 - 1951). He described the rigors of nature and succeeded in expressing its acute beauty, often sending shock waves through the haiku world.

Hisajo Sugita (1890 - 1946). One of the Taisho Hototogisu poets, she created a pseudo-perspective by combining the distant view and the foreground.

Suju Takano (1893 - 1976). An important characteristic of his haikus is the description of foreground. Often, his haikus contain only things right before the eyes.

Kakio Tomizawa (1902 - 1962). He was influenced by poems of the Symbolists. He introduced, in the Western way, the abstraction, the metaphor, and the analogy.

Ryu Yotsuya. One of Japan's current and most respected poets, he has explored many different versions of the ancient haiku.

———

ACKNOWLEDGEMENTS

To Shigeru Ikemoto, Kumayama Kudoh and Tsugume Mochizuki for sharing the beautiful country of Japan with me 20 plus years ago as a graduate student living in Fujinomiya. Your kindness and warm hearts have been with me every day since leaving the JIIS campus, which was quietly nestled up against the beautiful Mt. Fuji. If this book ever finds you, I would love to hear where your lives have taken you.

To Nick Zelinger, thank you for capturing the beauty of Mt. Fuji on the cover. Nick you are wonderful to work with and portray the beauty of the story through your art.

To Melanie Mulhall, you were a dream to work with throughout the editing process. Thank you.

To Mark Graham, thank you for all your guidance and most importantly for your kind friendship.

To Nobuko, thank you for your beautiful insight in helping accurately portray the delicate intricacies of the female Japanese characters in the book.

To Tomiko, your kindness and gracefulness helped capture the magic of the Japanese characters. Thank you.

To Wally Reams, *domo arigato* for previewing the book and sharing your expertise regarding the Japanese business world.

To Darlene King, Joanne Wyatt, Kevin Hurley and John Shors, thank you for previewing the book. Your feedback helped tremendously in the final design of the book.

To Hazel, thank you for your endless love and amazing Hurley Hugs.

To Emma, thank you for being my inspiration and providing me with the hope that the future will be spectacular. I love you.

To Carole, I am forever grateful for your love and faith in me.

To my entire family, I am blessed with your love . . . thank you.